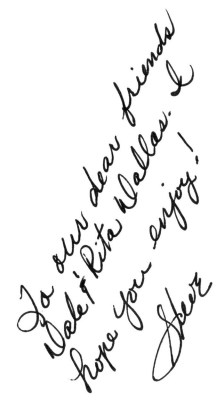

To our dear friends
Dale & Rita Dallas. I
hope you enjoy!

Steve

MW00778458

<u>Four Months, Three Weeks, Two Days</u>

This book is dedicated to my wife, Patricia, whose patience and encouragement kept me out of the bars and pool halls enough to complete this work. Her counsel and support were invaluable in finishing my first novel.

ACKNOWLEDGEMENTS

Sammye Goldston

Sammye is a dear and (near) life-long friend. She is also a retired English teacher. Sammye provided essential and constant input that kept me from making gross grammatical and content errors. Sammy's incessant requests (*nagging*) for more *feeeelings,* added character to the book that probably wouldn't be present without her help. I am forever grateful for her help and support.

Kaylea Burkhart

Kaylea read and critiqued the unedited manuscript after it was printed with the *Espresso Book Machine*. She was instrumental in the design of my cover and has continued to give valuable support – even after several revisions.

Dr. Kori Lewis

Dr. Lewis read the manuscript and was kind enough to check for any possible discrepancies relative to the medical situations critical to the story line of the book.

Brian Kelly

Brian is the family grammarian and has a remarkable eye for detail. His line editing saved me from the embarrassment of unseen grammatical errors that occur as a result of my *sleeping* in critical portions of the many English classes I attended in school.

Friends & Family

I gratefully acknowledge the many friends and family who have read the unedited manuscript and reinforced my hope that I might have create something fit to read.

CHAPTER ONE

Mark Stevens moved the year-old copy of *National Geographic* back and forth, adjusting, in a futile effort to keep the glare of the overhead lights from washing out the pictures and text on the slick pages of the magazine. He and the three other patients sat in the uneasy silence common among strangers in the waiting room of a doctor's office. His scheduled appointment was twenty minutes in the past. Mark was becoming rather irritated at this so-called *specialists'* inability to manage her schedule more efficiently.

Mark was 65 years old. He could count on one hand the times he'd needed to visit a doctor's office for anything other than his annual physicals, occasional flu, several broken bones and strains that occurred over his sports-active life. He was six feet three inches tall and weighed a trim 210 pounds. From all outward appearances, he seemed in perfect health. Vanity and an honest concern for physical fitness had dictated a fairly active regimen throughout his life. He had participated in most team, and individual sports since adolescence, and for the last five years or so, had played handball three times a week with a friend and co-worker twenty years his junior. The days he played well, leaving his friend defeated and exhausted, were some of the most delicious ego builders he'd ever enjoyed.

To be referred to a specialist seemed unusual at the least and had caused him some concerned moments as he waited the three days for his appointment. The additional waiting was not helping. He stared at the frosted-glass entrance to the office and in mirror-image read *"Keli Givens, M.D. Internal Medicine/Gastroenterology"*. Well, if nothing else, it's an impressive title, he thought.

Mark had contacted his family doctor complaining about a minor, recurring discomfort in his upper abdomen that was becoming more irritating and constant.

He had not decided to see the doctor until the discomfort become even more annoying when he was lying down and had recently spread to his back. It was beginning to interfere with his sleep.

Dr. Jim Morrison was a general practitioner who had looked after Mark's routine physical needs for nearly thirty years. Mark and Dr. Morrison were close friends and golfing buddies. If Mark had a health problem and Jim's examination indicated something out of the ordinary, he normally referred Mark to a specialist for further diagnosis and treatment.

After examining an x-ray of the symptomatic area, Dr. Morrison had called Mark to let him know the results.

"Mark, I got your x-ray back from the lab. The radiologist thinks there could be an abnormality around your pancreas. It may be nothing, but I'd like for you to save yourself some unnecessary anguish and have a specialist check it out.

"Did *you* see anything out of the ordinary," Mark asked.

"No, and I doubt if there *is* anything wrong. Given only the one x-ray, it would be unfair for me to try and make a judgment call. The area of concern in the x-ray was not pronounced enough for the radiologist to give any kind of a definite opinion; however, he thought you should have it checked out more thoroughly.

"Unless you have another doctor that you would prefer calling, I'll set up an appointment for you with Dr. Keli Givins. She's exceedingly talented at what she does and can provide you with a more definitive diagnosis than I'm set up to do here."

"Well, I don't have any other choice for a doctor, so go ahead and make the appointment. If you will, please ask your secretary to phone and let me know when I need to be there."

"OK, I'll do that. Ask Dr. Givens to keep me informed on her tests and diagnosis. Knowing you, you're going to become a hypochondriac once you get a look at the good doctor. You'll probably keep coming up with all sorts of new and unique symptoms just to get back in her exam room. *Lecher*! Anyway, good luck with it!"

"Right, you incompetent old *Chancre Mechanic*."

*   *   *

"Mr. Stevens?" A young woman in pale green hospital scrubs called out from the door leading to the exam rooms.

The nurse led Mark into a small room, equipped with an examining table, a small desk, x-ray backlighting boxes and medical cabinets with stainless steel trays containing instruments commonly used when examining patients. The attending nurse took his temperature and blood pressure, then asked routine questions about his weight, height, medical history and current complaint. Finished with her portion of the exam, the nurse smiled and said, "The doctor will be with you in a few minutes."

Mark sat on the table for another ten minutes reading medical certificates, all encased in identical, plain, wooden frames and scattered about the walls of the room.

Finally, a strikingly beautiful woman in a white medical smock opened the door. She had very dark brown hair pulled severely back from her face and wrapped in a large, tight bun behind her head. Although the hair was pulled straight back, small curls escaped around the temples. High cheekbones accented eyes with just a hint of a slant and rounded into almonds that were so green one would think she had to be wearing colored contacts. Her smock, open in front, exposed an equally fascinating figure, encased in a tailored business suit that somehow accented the entire woman without bringing undue attention to the long legs, the high breasts or the graceful neck. Her sensible working shoes, with inch-and-a-half heels, kept her from being taller than most of her male patients but still elevated her to about five feet eight inches. She appeared seriously young to Mark, but in actuality, she was probably in her mid to late thirties with a surprisingly naked ring finger, left hand.

Mark unconsciously adjusted his posture, and *sucked it in*. Even at 65, the tendency to do such nonsense was still intact when in the company of such a woman. He heard a clear, velvet voice saying, "Good morning, Mr. Stevens, I'm Dr. Givens – as she extended her hand in greeting. I apologize for my tardiness. Nothing ever seems to go on schedule around here."

Mark lied, "It's not a problem. I've scheduled the whole morning for the exam."

Dr. Givens then went directly to the x-ray-viewing screen where she placed an exposed x-ray film taken from the large manila envelope she carried with her. Although her beauty didn't disappear, it faded to the background as she magically became *Dr.* Keli Givens. She turned back to face Mark as the Internist/Gastroenterologist he had sought out for diagnosing a medical problem.

"Can you tell me what has been bothering you enough to bring you here?" She asked.

"Well, to tell the truth, Dr. Morrison thought I should see you. I've been having some discomfort along here," as he indicated with his hand an area along the lower edge of his right ribcage. "I wouldn't have bothered with it, but it's interfering with my sleep occasionally. It also hurts at about the same level on my back when I lie down. The pain isn't constant or severe, but the frequency of its presence seems to be increasing. And then, there's the x-ray that you know more about than I do."

"Dr. Morrison sent me this x-ray and asked that I examine you to find what may be causing your discomfort. The radiologist thought we should concentrate on the area around your pancreas, just to insure there is nothing wrong. I don't want you to become over reactive or frightened about this. There are several other tests you'll have to take before any positive conclusions can be made. It could, and probably will, turn out to be nothing at all. Let's hope so."

Dr. Givens pointed to the x-ray and with a pencil, and began tracing the different hues of gray on the film. The picture held no information for Mark, but to the doctor, it seemed to indicate something could be abnormal. She asked Mark to remove his shirt and lie down on the examination table. She then started to probe his abdominal area with her fingers, asking Mark continuously if any of her probing caused undue pain or discomfort. She also peered deeply into his eyes, looked closely at his skin and asked if he'd had any unexplained weight loss recently.

After probing and listening with the stethoscope for a few more minutes, Dr. Givens went to the small desk and started documenting her exam on the forms attached to a metal clipboard taken from the bin on the outside of the entry door. She then took a small pad of laboratory forms from the pocket of her smock and said, "Mr. Stevens, most of these tests are pretty standard, the urine, the blood, all that. I'm scheduling you for an ultrasound as soon as you leave here; hopefully, that will remove the cloud of doubt surrounding this one x-ray, and we won't have to go any further. If the ultrasound is as inconclusive as the x-ray, then we will probably do a CT scan to be as accurate as possible in determining what's causing your problem."

She then told him to check with her nurse for directions to the various labs and to see her appointment secretary to get an appointment for the same time the next day. There was some urgency in her instructions. "Do you have any questions I can help you with?"

"Doctor," Mark responded, "if the CT scan is the most definitive of the tests, couldn't I just do it first and eliminate the ultrasound? I realize it's more expensive, but I would rather eliminate a step in the diagnostic process, if I can, and get this all behind me. I *have* patience, but just not a lot of it."

"If you're not that concerned about the expense, I see no reason why we can't do that," she said. She shuffled through the lab request tickets she had filled out and dropped the request for the ultrasound into the wastebasket. She again took out the pad of prescription forms and wrote out the authorization for a *CT* scan and handed it to Mark.

The doctor offered her hand and smiled, "Mr. Stevens, it was a pleasure meeting you and I'll see you tomorrow, hopefully, with some decent news."

With the smile, the magic reversed itself, and the *Internist/Gastroenterologist* faded to the background, to leave a beautiful young woman, wearing a white smock, shaking his hand.

Mark mumbled his response and watched her leave – hurrying to attend other patients who were, by now, waiting as anxiously as Mark had been.

Mark, thoughtfully, started to put his shirt back on.

* * *

After the lab technician had drawn blood and asked Mark to "fill the specimen beaker at least to the halfway mark", he was directed to report to an imaging provider, located in the same building, for the CT scan. When he checked in for his scan, Mark was surprised to find that Dr. Givens had phoned radiology and asked that he be given priority. She wanted to have the results of the test ready for his appointment the next morning. The high priority became another flag in Mark's mind that underscored the possible seriousness of the situation.

Mark was escorted into a large room that contained an enormous piece of diagnostic equipment. There, as an integral part of the machine, was a movable table, upon which a patient could be placed and transported along the axis of a circle formed by the unusually large x-raying system.

Adjacent to the main room containing the *CT* or *CAT scan*, was a glassed-in control booth, with a powerful computer controlling the device. Inside, there were two technicians sitting at a large console, who, in turn, operated the computer.

The attending technician directed Mark to go into a small dressing room located in the corner of the larger room. "Mr. Stevens, if you will, please remove all your clothes and jewelry. You do not have to remove your underwear." He added, "You'll find a clean hospital gown hanging on the back of the door in the dressing room."

After doing as instructed, Mark reported back to the attendant who was preparing the machine for the upcoming test.

"Mr. Stevens," the attendant said, "We'll get started if you will lie down here on your back," as he patted the small transporting table that ran through the center of the machine. "Now comes the part that no one is particularly fond of. We have to insert an IV in order to introduce a liquid tracer into your bloodstream. With the tracer, the radiologist and your doctor will be better able to make a more accurate analysis of the x-rays."

Mark extended his left arm and the technician inserted a needle into a vein on the inside of his elbow.

"I'm starting a saline drip right now," the technician said. "We'll wait until just before we start the scan to inject the tracer." He then explained that the operating technicians in the control room would give step-by-step instructions over a PA speaker, located near the system. After asking Mark if he had any questions concerning the procedure, the technician left the room and in a few seconds, appeared behind the glass window of the control room where he picked up a microphone and asked, "Mr. Stevens, can you hear me clearly?"

Mark answered, "Yes!" from his supine position. A hidden microphone, located somewhere within the complexity of the machine, transmitted his response back to the attending technicians.

Communications established, the painless test began. After about twenty minutes of whirring, and following the instructions from the control room, the incremental movement of the table finally stopped. The table immediately returned Mark, smoothly, to its initial position.

Mark heard the technician's voice over the speaker, saying "Mr. Stevens, that's it! As soon as we can get that *nail* out of your arm, you can get dressed."

CHAPTER TWO

Art Fletcher was Mark's best friend and Mark had made a tentative appointment with him for lunch. *Tentative,* meaning that if his examination was completed in time, they would meet at one of their regular noontime haunts and rejoice in any good news or curse any bad news received during his visit to the doctor. Since Art had no other plans for lunch, he had agreed to be at the restaurant in any event. If Mark was unable to join him, he would have lunch alone and return to his office.

Mark was running about five minutes late, but knew he would be at the restaurant in plenty of time to enjoy a leisurely lunch with his friend. Since Art owned a small and profitable accounting firm, he enjoyed the option of returning late from lunch if he chose. The knowledge of Art's flexibility allowed Mark the freedom to be late, on occasion, for their regular lunches and still enjoy whatever time they had set aside for the meal/BS session. Still, he was in somewhat of a hurry to meet with Art and maybe unload some of the stress that had built up because of the exam. Mark also felt that today might be one of the times he would break his self-imposed rule of no-alcohol lunches. A drink (or five) might be appropriate today.

Art sat at a small table enjoying his usual Bud Light and waiting for the waitress to return with his food order when Mark entered the room. The permanent scowl etched in Art's face didn't change when he spotted Mark making his way toward him. In fact, the scowl seemed to deepen as Mark approached, as it always did when Art accepted the company of others. He thought of himself as a tough-guy and did his best to put on the face of a tough-guy during the initial phase of any meeting, social or otherwise. It didn't take a rocket scientist to see through the façade and after one realized it was, in fact, a façade, a sensitive and caring person of good humor was exposed underneath. The sensitive and caring person underneath kept the two friends, *friends*, for the past 11 years. They had growled and cursed each other as a matter of course over the entire length of their relationship but had been the first to the other's side when adversity or need might strike. They were comfortable with each other, and it was apparent to all who knew them.

Art stood a little bit over 5' 11" tall, but always told those who asked that he stood an even six feet. The little three-quarter inch lie became something Mark always enjoyed correcting during those minor infringements of the truth. In most of these instances, Mark could not resist throwing a small verbal dart, mentioning something about Art being "under-tall and over-fat". Art still looked like the linebacker he had been in college – thick, powerful and about 235 pounds. His close-cropped blond hair and "Paul Newman-blue" eyes accented a craggily-handsome, rounded face that rarely smiled. In fact, the face never seemed to smile, but when something struck him funny, his whole body would break into a smile somehow. The *body smile* was a characteristic Mark had never fully understood, but enjoyed it regularly during their give and take sessions of smart remarks and minor insults toward each other. He was dressed, as usual, in a sports coat, slacks, dress shirt and tie. And, as usual, his clothes never looked quite large enough for his bulk. The colors of the ensemble would change from day to day, but the ingredients – never. He wasn't fat – just big, rawboned and hard to fit.

The two friends shook hands, as always, and as Mark sat down, Art asked the inevitable: "Ok, asshole, how long have you got?" When Mark replied with only a half-hearted smile and a raised eyebrow, Art continued with, "Don't start that shit with me, man. I'm not buying it. So forget about it."

The waitress returned to the table and asked if Mark wanted his usual iced tea. He nodded in the affirmative and mumbled, "Yeah, that's fine!", but as she left the table, he said, "Wait, Barbara, I think I'll join my alcoholic friend here and have something a little more substantial. It's five o'clock somewhere! I think I'll have a 'Beefeater' Martini, with two olives; they'll count as the solid portion of my lunch."

Art looked at his friend and asked in a newly concerned tone, "Am I going to be late for work this afternoon?"

"I doubt it." Mark said, "I'm just stressed out about having to go to an Internist/Gastroenterologist because of something a Radiologist thinks he sees on an x-ray. All these *ists* are about to drive me crazy. I've been taking tests, being probed and all the other crap you get when you're invited to visit a *special* doctor who's supposed to be able to walk on water. I still don't know any more than I did when I visited with Jim."

"He didn't tell you anything?" Art asked

"The doctor is definitely not a *he*, and no, I guess she's saving that until tomorrow. I have another appointment with her at nine in the morning, and she's going to give me the results of the tests. She had me take a *CT* scan. If that's not definitive enough, I don't know what they'll ask for next. They'll probably want to take my pancreas out and look at it up close. Anyway, she told me *not to worry*. That was the only decent thing I heard all day. Like I can *not worry* about some gray spot on my pancreas until I visit with her in the morning."

Barbara returned with the martini Mark had ordered. Mark took the martini and gulped half of it. Art noticed the gulp, but said nothing and waited for his friend to continue.

"As far as the *not to worry* remark is concerned, that flew out the window when I found that she had placed me in a priority status with the CT people. She wanted to be sure to have the results back in time for my appointment in the morning. Hopefully, that will tell her if the shadows on the x-ray actually mean anything or if they are, in fact, just shadows of no consequence."

As confident and positive as Mark tried to be in his presentation of the day's events, Art could sense the uneasiness in his friend and in turn tried to accentuate the sparse positive aspects of the conversation between him and Dr. Givens. His attempts seemed rather shallow in his own mind, but, nonetheless, heartfelt and caring. Anxiety was building in him, just as it appeared to be building in Mark.

Mark had finished his first martini and raised the empty glass up above his head and called to Barbara, who stood at the waitress station across the room. She saw the upheld glass and in sign language asked if he wanted another martini. He nodded in the exaggerated way everyone does when "signing" across a room, then turned back to Art to extend their conversation. When she returned with the martini for Mark, she also brought the club sandwich Art had ordered earlier.

"Aren't you going to order anything to eat? I don't think those olives are going to carry you very far this afternoon. Jesus, I may as well stay here and get shit-faced with you. If we do that, it won't take super-doc two seconds to see what your problem is tomorrow. That is if she can stand close enough to you to do any examining – what with your bear-breath and all."

"Naw" Mark said, "I'm really not very hungry. I might take a quarter of your sandwich if you don't eat it all. I think I'll go back to the office and get on the Internet and see what I can find out about what's going on with me. If I remember correctly, pancreatic cancer is something you can't deal with very well and it seems as though that's what this is leading up to. I hate this morbid shit! Maybe I should just stay here and see how many of these martinis it will take to make me fall flat on my face."

"That's two! If you want me to, I'll stick around and count 'em for you. Then I'll drag your drunk ass home and give you the total in the morning," Art countered.

"I might take you up on that tomorrow – after I get the news."

"Well – if you're going back to the office, I think I will too. I have some work that should be done if I ever expect to be able to pick up another bar-tab. Look, why don't you do what you're going to do at the office and then come on over to the house for dinner. You can tell us what you found out and relax awhile before the big day tomorrow. I think Jean's cooking peanut butter and jelly sandwiches tonight. I know how you love her cooking."

"Let me give you a call at the office before you leave and I'll let you know if I'll be joining you. I can't wait to try out Jean's new recipe. I know how she likes to explore new and delightful culinary treasures. You're going to have to start beating her more, you know. I wonder why you haven't done it sooner. Is it because you're one of those wimp accountants and afraid she can whip *your* ass?"

Art had gone through the worst kind of hell with Mark and had proven to be the truest of friends. He was a friend that would not wilt when things got really bad. Art had sacrificed his own personal life as he steadfastly supported Mark in coping with the worst possible tragedy an adult can face – losing a child and a wife at the same time.

Marks' daughter, Sara, was killed instantly when a drunk hit their car from behind at a ridiculously high rate of speed. The impact of the two cars colliding was so violent that Karen and Sarah's car virtually exploded. The car was out of control and burning as it careened down a fifty-foot embankment with the two women trapped inside. Sarah was 34 years old and about to be married for the second time to a young man who adored her. Marks' wife, Karen, was less fortunate than Sarah and was not killed instantly, but remained in a coma, near death, for nearly two weeks before succumbing to the trauma.

As an only child, Mark had been left with no blood relatives. He was integrated into the Fletcher family and accepted as having always been there. In the beginning, he felt as though he might be imposing on their generous hospitality; but as time passed, he realized that there was no imposition, and he was, in fact, an extended member of the Fletcher clan. It probably saved his life – if not his life, certainly his sanity.

As a result of the accident, Mark had continued to work past the age that he and Karen had planned to retire. He was *Vice President of Engineering* for a moderate-sized equipment-fabricating firm that specialized in creating tools and equipment for customers needing products that were unavailable on the open market. Mark and his staff would analyze the particular needs of a customer and invent a tool or piece of equipment that would perform as the customer wanted.

It was the job of a lifetime for Mark. He had accepted a job with the company upon his discharge from the Marine Corps and never left. The company was genuinely supportive during the troubling times after the accident and made every effort to lighten his responsibilities until his life settled down again. There was no question that the principals of the company were devastated by Marks' personal losses, but they were also extremely pleased that he had postponed his retirement date.

Mark was a member of the Board of Directors and had been offered the Presidency during the last two searches when others had retired. Mark had refused in both instances – citing his love for engineering as outweighing his desire for more managerial duties. He was considered indispensable for the continued well-being of the company as a whole. Although his work was extremely satisfying, Mark found himself daydreaming a lot about what it would be like to just *head out* and do only things that were exciting and fun. Exciting and fun to a sixty-five year-old man meant different things than it did when he was a twenty-five year-old man; however, sailboats and fly-fishing came readily to mind.

Since Karen's death, he had kept putting off buying the boat of their dreams and sailing off to tropical paradises simply because he didn't actually want to go alone. It was a dream that he and Karen shared for more years than he cared to remember. It wouldn't be the same without her. Therein lay the main reason that he kept putting it off.

CHAPTER THREE

Leaving the bar, Mark paid particular attention to his driving after his unaccustomed martini lunch. He didn't actually feel impaired, but he realized that this wasn't a normal drive from a leisurely lunch. The stress of the visit to Dr. Givens, plus the two martinis had put him in a defensive mode. He tried to place particular emphasis on caution. The caution bore him well, and he arrived, safely, at his assigned parking space near the office in the standard 15-minute, uneventful drive he usually took.

Entering the office complex, he mumbled the usual office greetings to those he met en-route to his private office suite. When he arrived at his office, his secretary blatantly asked, "Well, are we going to lose you?"

"Probably, but not before I get to fire your sorry ass." he answered.

"You're not going to fire me" she replied instantly, "I'm the only reason you've been able to save your job as long as you have. Don't mess with me, sucker, or I'll quit right now and expose to the whole world what an incompetent shit you are."

"Matilda, one would think that, after 30 damn years, you'd show just a smidgen of respect for a man who has risked his reputation keeping you off the welfare rolls. I swear I'm going to call that damn secretary pool and tell them to send me up a *young* woman, with big tits and a speech impediment so I can get a little relief around here."

"Dream on, my elderly, fantasizing boss! Those babies with the big tits wouldn't take this job with twice the pay and half the hours. They all contribute to a monthly fund that supplements my meager salary just so I won't leave and expose one of them to all your ridiculous B.S."

Matilda was only the second secretary Mark had ever had with the company. She had sat outside his door for roughly 31 years, screening would-be guests, phone calls and efficiently doing all the things that made her virtually indispensable. She hated her name and Mark was the only person on the globe who was allowed to call her anything but "Mattie" or Mrs. Goldberg. Mark was only allowed to call her "Matilda" on rare instances without a vocal outburst that would make a seasoned sailor blush. She had wanted to retire for years, but had remained outside Mark's office door simply because she loved him and had vowed (only to herself) not to leave until he did. Mattie was not a bit reluctant to tell Mark that he needed to retire. She sometimes tried to lay guilt trips on him about how sick and tired she was and how she'd quit in a minute if she didn't have to stay and take care of his inherent male frailties.

Mattie was 68 years old and had been the quintessential secretary since she was a teenager. She was barely 5 feet tall and had the mouth of a crocodile – a 210-pound crocodile. She would snap, verbally, at any annoyance, with no mercy for her victim. Raised by confrontational Jewish parents, her verbal peccadilloes were honed razor sharp and accurate. Mattie had long since abandoned the religious aspects of her background; however, the Yiddish she injected into her verbal tirades served her well when English just didn't get the job done. She always dressed in dresses – constantly complaining that they were the only garments capable of sufficiently enclosing her bust and butt. Her dark hair had, with great subtlety, turned gray while sitting outside Mark's door. Her dark features were typical of her ethnicity and were always accented with her passion for diamonds that became larger in direct proportion to the success of her husband's business. To call Mattie Goldberg a secretary was like calling Michael Jordan a basketball player. Each, in their own way, had taken their chosen professions to a higher level. She, like Mark, had worked for only one company.

When Mattie went to work for the company, she was barely out of high school and was, essentially, on her honeymoon. She had moved to Memphis, from her native New York, to be with Maury, her husband, who had been drafted into the Navy near the end of the Korean War. They had postponed the so-called honeymoon until Maury finished boot camp and was assigned his first permanent duty station, the *Naval Schools Command, Memphis*; where he spent his entire enlistment, diluting credence to the recruiting phrase "Join the Navy! See the world!" After the Navy, Mattie's income supplemented the GI Bill that put Maury through college and launched his career as a highly successful retailer of quality men's clothing.

Mattie was the only person in the company with more tenure than Mark. She had been the secretary to a group of four junior engineers when Mark joined the company, and Mark became the fifth in her brood. The friendly banter between them soon became habit, and when Mark was promoted to senior engineer, requiring a personal secretary, he asked if she would consider being that secretary. She immediately said, "No". Saying that she was comfortable where she was and certainly didn't want to go through the stress of adjusting to a new job with little increase in salary or benefits.

Later, when his assigned secretary decided to quit work after becoming pregnant, Mark, again, asked for Mattie. This time, to Mark's delight, she agreed. She would later say that the substantial pay increase associated with the job actually had no bearing on her acceptance. She delighted in telling Mark and anyone else who asked, that the real reason she accepted was his complete ineptitude. He needed her as an anchor to avoid the constant embarrassment he was bound to face without her.

After the totally predictable exchange between the two friends, Mark entered his office, and uncharacteristically, quietly closed the door behind him. He sat at his desk, rather heavily, and moved the mouse on his computer to have it "wake up". As always, Mattie had started it for him and pulled up his agenda for the day and his scheduled appointments for the week. He had already cleared his calendar for the day, not knowing when he would be finished at the doctor's office.

Mark immediately opened his browser and *Googled* pancreatic cancer. He selected NCI from the various choices his search produced.

In the *symptoms* dialog, he was surprised to find that his discomfort was identical to those outlined. There were other symptoms listed that were not apparent in his case, but explained some of the questions asked by Dr. Givens earlier in the day. The "jaundice" mentioned was not evident as far as he could tell, nor had he experienced any noticeable weight loss. After seeing it listed on the symptoms list, he had noticed the color of his urine seemed a little darker than normal for the last couple of weeks or so. Mark thought this is not turning out to be as great a day as I'd hoped for. He continued to read through the symptoms list and was into the "diagnosis" portion of the information when there was a knock on his door.

"Yes, come in!" he said loudly enough to be heard through the door.

"OK!" Mattie said, "What went down at the doctor's office today? You still talk the talk, but you ain't walkin' the walk. I know you too well, so, don't start with pure B.S. Get down to the meat of it."

"Mattie, I honestly don't know a bit more about what's going on than I did yesterday." Mark said. "I took a bunch of tests, including a CAT scan, but we won't know anything for sure until tomorrow – maybe not even then. I have to admit that they are starting to get my attention. I have an appointment with her in the morning and we should get the results back from the lab along with the radiologists' report on the CAT scan. Hopefully, she will be able to tell me something definite once she gets that information."

"Did she say anything encouraging or give you any educated guess as to what she thought it might be?"

"She told me not to worry." Mark said, and then punctuated the statement with an exaggerated, loud and cynical "Ha!" "Then when I got to the CAT scan provider, I found out that she had called the appointment secretary and asked that they give me priority. I truly don't like it when I'm given priority in any sort of medical situation. It makes me nervous as hell. So, it looks like you'll be able to screw around all morning tomorrow just as you've been doing today."

"I'll show you screwing around, old son, as soon as *you* quit screwing around with the doctors and get your butt back to work. Someone is bound to find out that I've been running this department for years while you drew the high salary."

They both smiled at each other as Mattie walked toward the door to leave. "Do you want me to leave the door closed," she asked as she stood with her hand on the knob.

"Yeah, you might leave it closed for now," Mark said, and then added "I'm checking out some things on the Internet and I'd rather not be bothered with people seeing me and having an uncontrollable urge to casually drop in. Keep them away from me if it isn't something urgent. If you can, I'll see if I can get you some passes to the Bingo hall or a bowling alley somewhere."

"That won't be a problem, Hon. I'll just tell them you're having your usual gas problem, and they'll stay away for sure."

Finally, getting in the last word, she closed the door and returned to her desk. She found it difficult to end the conversation without knowing fully what was going on. She was more than a little concerned about a medical condition that needed a Gastroenterologist for diagnosis.

After Mattie left, Mark was drawn back to the NCI Webpages and, from the diagrams there, learned where the pancreas was located within his body, what it was supposed to do and the difficulty of access during surgery. He learned what might be expected during treatment and most importantly, the statistics associated with the success of any and all treatment. The last was an unusually short paragraph. There was a section on the pain associated with the disease – its severity and how it was managed. Finally, the other shoe fell when he read that the survivability of the disease was a mere two-percent and that survivors were almost always those patients who had somehow discovered the disease prior to the onset of symptoms, symptoms that rarely occurred unless the disease had already metastasized to other organs.

Mark had read all he cared to and leaned back in his chair with a fixed, unseeing stare at a point across the room where the wall met the ceiling. He found it impossible to take his mind off the two-percent survivability fact that he'd seen on the Internet. Even though he had not been diagnosed with anything, much less cancer of the pancreas, a sinking feeling engulfed his mind and body, and he visibly slumped in his chair as the mere possibility of living for only another three to six months eased from his subconscious into the conscious. Dread welled in him as he thought of the appointment with Dr. Givens in the morning.

With great effort and deliberateness, Mark swiveled his chair around and using his desk for support raised himself to a standing position and just stood, without knowing why he stood. He thrust his hands deeply into his pockets and started to walk with his head down, and shoulders slumped, slowly taking a couple of steps, then stopping, arching his head back till his eyes were vertical, then bowing his head again. He continued the aimless walk in a vague daydream. He had no conscious thought, but his mind was racing in a myriad of random thoughts that had no significant relevancy. He resisted the urge to think about what might be in store for him, if his suspicions were proven to be correct, at 9:00 o'clock in the morning.

He straightened himself and forced his meandering mind back into focus. He thought of the invitation Art had extended at lunch and decided that there was no way he could be decent company. He waited a few minutes to gain some sort of mental control before dialing his friend to decline dinner and friendly companionship.

"Hi, Ruth!" Mark responded to the familiar sounding voice that'd answered the phone in Art's office. "Was that lecher you work for put in jail for anything this afternoon?"

"No," she giggled back," recognizing Mark's voice, "He runs a pretty good cover here, and the feds haven't showed up yet; unless they're working undercover. I've often wondered where they got that term *Undercover*." Another giggle and she said, "I'll put you through to him, Mark."

"Thanks, Ruth." he said as the phone clicked a couple of times, and then started ringing Art's office.

"What's up?" Mark heard Art say.

"I just called to ask for a *rain-check* on dinner tonight. I wanted to let you know so you could call Jean before she got into her peanut butter and jelly stash. Can't have her chapped at me if I ever want to enjoy a home-cooked meal again. Maybe I can impose later in the week."

"Is this about the visit to the doctor today", Art asked, "or are you just trying to insult my wife's cooking?"

"Who could insult Jean's cooking?" Mark chuckled back into the phone. "Actually I think the two martinis I had for lunch had more to do with it than the doctor. I've been in a state of semi-sleep all afternoon. I'll grab a quick bite on the way home and then crash."

"Well, if you change your mind, we'll be home all evening." Art then added, "Look, man, I want a call as soon as you finish with the good doctor tomorrow."

"OK, *Mom*, I'll give you a call as soon as I find out anything. Give my love to Jean."

After the click on Art's end of the line, Mark held the phone away from his ear but was very slow to hang it up. What in the hell is wrong with me, he thought. This kind of bullshit can't be happening. I have to just settle down and not let my morbid imagination run away with me. I'm scared as hell over something that hasn't even been diagnosed."

Although it was only 3:15 in the afternoon, Mark shuffled the paper on his desk, signed a couple of authorizations for expenditures and heaved to his feet to leave. Work, even work that he enjoyed, was not in him this fine day.

He really didn't relish the thought of passing Mattie's desk on the way out of the office. Since there was no other way out, he steeled himself to run the verbal gauntlet to make his escape. As he passed Mattie's desk, she looked up from her keyboard, saw him leaving and went directly back to work without a word. Mark, on the other hand, couldn't leave without saying something to punctuate his early departure. Stopping next to her desk, he announced with extreme bravado, "Darlin', I've decided that it's time I did something for my-own-self. I just called *Rent-A-Hooker* and have two – count 'em – two, ladies of the night breathlessly waiting for me to show up at my humble home. Don't call me, I'm gonna be busy."

"I'm not even going to comment on that." Mattie said, keeping her hands on the keyboard and her eyes fixed on the monitor in front of her. Slowly turning her head, she donned her patented pained look that met his eyes and added, "I happen to know that your entire sex-life revolves around visiting with the librarian who allows you to check out 'R' rated books without a note from your parents. Get the hell out of here and call me when you finish with the doctor in the morning."

"Bitch!" he mumbled as he turned to walk away.

"Schmuck!" she responded, in perfect cadence.

CHAPTER FOUR

Mark left the office and walked rather slowly to his car, enjoying the sunshine on his shoulders. When he started the car, he suddenly felt a bit lost. "What in the hell does someone do at ten to four in the afternoon?" he thought out loud. He backed out of the parking space and went thru the unconscious motions of taking himself home, even if that wasn't exactly what he wanted to do. Although he was as alert as always in his driving, he was getting off the freeway near his house before he realized that he'd even been driving. When he woke up to the fact that he'd driven for twenty minutes without any conscious knowledge of the fact, he snapped back to attention and thought to himself, Spooky, man! Just absolutely spooky! I've got to do something about these *senior moments*.

Upon arriving at his house, he pulled the car into the garage, checked the pile of junk mail that had been pushed through his mail slot and dumped the entire lot in the trash can that stood by the entrance to his utility room and the interior of the house. He went directly to the refrigerator and reached for a beer. Then, changing his mind, grabbed a carton of orange juice, turned and got a glass from the cabinet and poured a full glass of the cold juice, replaced the carton in the refrigerator and headed for his recliner in the den.

Once comfortably seated, he took a long drink of the juice and aimed the remote at the TV across the room. God! He thought, it's still too early for the news, as a soap opera started struggling through unimaginable hardships, love triangles, rectangles and pentagons. He flipped the channel to ESPN and watched, with little interest, a taped basketball game between the Lakers and the Celtics. Anyway, it was better than the soap opera, even though he already knew who was going to win the game. After ten minutes of the game, he started to become restless and switched off the TV; opting for the paper he'd left lying in the caddie beside his chair. I honestly don't know what the hell to do at this time of day, he thought. It's too early to eat, get drunk or anything else I'd want to do tonight. I know one damn thing; I'm not sitting here all night like a cat hanging from a clothesline, worrying about what's going to happen tomorrow. With that decision out of the way, he drank down the last of the orange juice, got up and took the glass back to the kitchen and headed for his bathroom. I'll have one-hell-of-a *last meal* before I face the music tomorrow, as thick, juicy steaks started to invade his mind.

Mark undressed in the bedroom and after hanging his coat and trousers in the closet, dumped his shirt, socks and underwear in the clothes hamper. A cursory check of his face in the bathroom mirror exposed a bit of a 5 o'clock shadow, and reluctantly, he decided to shave before getting into the shower. After the decision, he made his weekly vow to grow a beard to eliminate one of the personal grooming tasks that he had always hated.

After the hated shave, he entered the shower --- turned on the hot water all the way and shuddered as the cold water hit him. The cold water gradually turned warm, then hot as he adjusted the cold water to keep from scalding himself. With the water comfortably adjusted, he extended his arms, and leaned on the front of the shower stall to let the warm water flow directly onto his bowed head. After several minutes spent enjoying the soothing effects of the shower, he washed his hair, relaxed for a few more moments as the water rinsed his hair and continued with his bath. Refreshed more than he expected, he dried himself, dried and combed his hair and walked, still naked, to his closet to select his clothes for the evening.

The Prime Rib was Mark's favorite steakhouse. It was an upscale restaurant and bar that posted a rather loose dress code that he'd never seen enforced to any extent; however, the clientele rarely abused the code and anyone inappropriately dressed would feel out of place. Mark didn't want to wear a tie, so he chose a lightweight turtleneck slipover shirt, slacks and a sports coat; just enough for comfort, he thought and still not be conspicuously underdressed. Lookin' good, he thought as he checked himself in the mirror – for an old fart.

It was still very early, only 5:45. Early or not he wanted to be out of the house and doing something. So, he called a cab and mixed a stiff scotch and soda that would carry him to the restaurant where he expected to have *several* more. Now I'm getting drunk during the week, he thought. I wonder what in the hell I'll do if the news is really bad tomorrow?

The honking horn of the cab pierced the racket being made by a motocross race being replayed on ESPN. Mark picked up his remote control, punched the off switch and left to meet the cab. He had made it a fairly strict rule, since Karen and Sarah had been hit by the drunk that he never drove his car when he was drinking or expected to be drinking. His monthly cab bill was nearly as much as his car expenses.

The cab driver knew Mark from his regular calls and greeted him as he opened the door to the cab. "Hey, Mr. Stevens!"

"Hi, Ernie!" Mark replied as he closed the door. "I guess I'm going to be running a few alleys tonight, so I thought I'd better leave the driving to you – again."

"I can hack it, my friend. I'll even tuck you in if I have to," He chuckled – as did Mark. "Where to?"

"Gonna check out *The Prime Rib* again and give all those tight-assed women that hang out in there one more chance to take advantage of my innocence. Funny – it doesn't happen as often as I would expect."

"Well, tonight may be the night." Ernie said as they both laughed at the fantasized scenario.

The friendly chatter continued the 20 minutes it took to get to the restaurant. Mark paid his fare and told Ernie to keep his cab in one piece until he called for a ride home.

"I work until four a.m. tonight, Mr. Stevens, if you need a ride after that, I think you might call an ambulance," he laughed. Mark patted the top of the cab and Ernie pulled back into traffic for his next fare.

The owner/maitre d' greeted Mark as he entered the restaurant. "Hi, Mark! This is a little early for you to be eating isn't it?"

"You have me confused with someone who's eating this early, my friend. I'm a'drankin'! I'm going to sit at the bar for a while before I try to eat that *Road-Kill du jour* you're so damned famous for. By the way, if you see any unattached women coming in here that aren't coyote ugly, tell them there's an easy mark – pun intended – at the bar."

"You're in luck! I just seated two of the finest specimens you will ever lust over. They appear to be too sophisticated to mess with a low-life like you, but you never know what whiskey will do to a woman's eyesight. Send them over *several* drinks before you make any kind of move. It will make you look much younger and better looking."

"Pig!"

"Go sit down before I call the nursing home supervisor and have you picked up before you have your dinner."

George put a friendly hand on Marks shoulder and escorted him to the darkened bar and told Mark to call him when he was ready to eat. George then went back to the entrance of the restaurant to meet his other guests.

Mark picked a barstool rather than sitting at one of the several tables situated in the bar area. He couldn't remember the new bartender's name, but when the new man approached, he asked, "What can I get you, Mr. Stevens?"

"I'll have a Johnny Walker Red and soda," Mark answered as he read the name "Ron" on the bartender's nametag.

Ron returned with the drink in a few moments and the two men engaged in small-talk before Ron walked back to the end of the bar and waited to be of service to the five or six other bar patrons.

Sipping his drink, Mark heard the most delightful female laugh he'd heard since Karen. It was a low, thoroughly-engaged laugh. The laugh was subtle, rather than boisterous and came from the genuine humor of some unrevealed occurrence at the table.

Mark fought the urge to turn and gaze at the source of this musical laughter. And, he did pretty well until it happened again and the urge got the best of him. He turned as inconspicuously as he could in the direction of this delicious sound and saw two ladies sitting at a table near the back of the bar area. They were both beautiful women of some maturity; early fifties, he guessed. At first glance, he couldn't tell which had the engaging laugh, so, he reasoned, I'll just have to stare at them until they laugh again. It didn't take long, since they were telling some story of great humor. Then she did it again – the low, sexy, uninhibited laugh that made anyone, within hearing want to join her.

From his vantage point at the bar, Mark could see that her short blondish hair was fixed for comfort and a style that complimented her oval face and lush lips. She was beautiful and full-grown. Even in the dimly lighted bar, Mark could see, in profile, that she had a lithe and athletic body sporting ample breasts and long legs. He forced himself back to the forward position and stared, instead, at the various liquor selections standing at the ready behind the bar. Mark fought the urge to turn and stare when something in their conversation prompted the laugh he found so appealing.

Mark was just finishing his drink when he heard a commotion coming from the table where his fantasies lay. The ladies had stood and were embracing in farewells – promising to get together again soon, etc. As he watched, Mark noticed that only one of the ladies was leaving, and the other (the one with the laugh) was telling her friend that she had another hour or so to kill and was staying to have another drink at the bar. Mark felt somewhat guilty with his eavesdropping, but not nearly guilty enough to stop.

After the farewell, *the laugh*, picked up her purse and headed directly toward Mark. There were several barstools vacant on either side of him, and he was surprised when she stopped and stood at the stool adjacent to his. He was more than a little surprised when she said, "Hi, I hope you will forgive me for being so forward, but may I join you for a drink? My friend had to leave and I hate sitting alone waiting for dinner. I hope your wife wouldn't mind my joining you."

Mark's mind went blank. He didn't actually know how to react to this sudden trip to *Fantasy Island*. "No," he said in a particularly awkward and embarrassed tone, "I am a widower, so I'm sure she wouldn't mind."

Goddamnit, he thought, that is the most uncool thing I could have ever said to anyone.

"I stand before you in my most vulnerable and out-of-character self. I watched you come in – saw no wedding ring and decided that I would take a terrible chance on embarrassing myself to death – or, I would have a drink and enjoy the company of an attractive man before leaving – if, by chance, you're not meeting anyone."

Mark gathered himself and waited a moment for his good fortune to sink in before he responded, "Of course you can join me. I can't think of a better way to enjoy an evening. I had been debating with myself about offering you and your friend a drink in order to improve my chances of meeting you."

"Well, if you aren't offended, I'm Carole Wilson, and I don't think we've met."

"I'm Mark Stevens, and I can't help it." He joined her in another laugh they both seemed to enjoy.

After Carole had ordered a glass of Chardonnay, the newly introduced couple began a casual conversation that lasted just long enough for Mark to think he'd known this incredible woman half his life. Based on his past history of being rather up-tight when visiting with women he'd just met, he thought it rather strange that he could become so comfortable in such a short period of time.

"Do you have dinner plans?" Mark asked.

"No, but I didn't necessarily join you to wrangle a dinner invitation. You just looked like someone I'd enjoy meeting. Taking into account that we're in a semi-safe social environment, I thought if we enjoyed each other's company, I might invite *you* to dinner – if not tonight, then at some other time."

"Wrangle away! I came here for the food, but I can think of no better way to make it a *dinner*, than to have you join me. If you say yes – you will have made my day."

"I guess that makes me a veteran *wrangler* – whatever that is," she said with her delicious laugh.

CHAPTER FIVE

Although Mark certainly didn't care why Carole had decided to make such a bold move to meet him, she seemed compelled to explain her out-of-character act of foolishness.

"My friend and I noticed you when you came in, and you immediately became the topic of our conversation. I guess you could hear the laughing and carrying-on coming from our table. We were laughing, not at you, of course, but about my friend's scheme as to how I could meet you. It was pretty bizarre, and I won't tell you how awful she had it planned, or the things she suggested that I do to gain your attention. Anyway, the wine dramatically reduced my inhibitions, and I decided to do exactly what I did. You will notice that I had my purse with me so I could make a quick exit in the event you thought I was crazy and wanted nothing to do with me. Had that happened, I would have slithered out the door with a very red face and a promise on my lips never to enter this place again. I truly hope you weren't offended by any of this."

"Offended?" Mark asked in mock astonishment. "I have never been more flattered in my life. You saved me the embarrassment of having to do something just as out of character. Your laughter at the table was something I just had to hear again. When I turned and saw you, I was even more convinced that I had to do something to meet you. I hadn't fully decided what I was going to do, but I knew you wouldn't be leaving without the opportunity to reject or accept some offer of a one-on-one conversation. Naturally, I fantasized about the conversation leading to you joining me for drinks, at a minimum, or dinner, as fulfillment of the fantasy."

There was the laugh again as she said, "My friend said you'd probably think I was a hooker if I came on with one of those old clichés like, 'Buy a girl a drink, big boy?' You'll notice that I asked her to leave before I pulled this stunt. The thought of doubling my embarrassment was too much for me to risk. Now I can't wait to call and tell her of my good fortune. I'm talking way too much. I'll stop before I bore you out the door."

"I'm enjoying it – big time," Mark replied, chuckling at her description of what had happened. "You know the reason for my single status; I can't believe you are not wallowing in marital bliss with some lucky rascal."

"We're single for the same reasons," she said. My husband was killed in an industrial accident three years ago."

"I'm very sorry to hear that. I have first-hand knowledge of what you went through. It's pretty awful."

"Now that you know, let's change the subject and not get somber on our first meeting. How do you spend your time," she asked.

"I'm a mechanical engineer and work for *Specialty Engineering & Design*, here in Memphis. You?"

"I gave it up a couple of years ago. The company I had worked for sold out to a larger firm and I decided to leave and maybe do some traveling. I haven't... but it seemed like a good plan at the time. I still do some consulting with a few of my former clients, but it's mostly done as favors to them and on a fairly infrequent schedule. I'm an architect, and specialize in interior design.

"I'm just about ready to retire myself." Mark replied. "I want to travel some before the grim reaper comes for me.

Maybe you have the same problem I do when it comes to traveling – who do you go with? I keep putting it off because it's only half the fun unless you can share it with someone. I want to buy a nice boat and go island-hopping for a while. I don't necessarily plan to be a boat bum for the rest of my life, but I'd love to do it as long as it was fun."

"Now I think you've been reading my mail and tapping my phone. I would have already bought a boat if I thought I could sail it by myself. You could stop talking right now knowing full well that you have my undivided attention as long as you want it, Captain." Carole's laugh, again, punctuated her emphasis on the word "Captain".

They had enjoyed their drink at the bar for nearly an hour when Mark asked Carole if she was about ready to go to the dining room for dinner, then added, "Give me a couple more drinks and I won't be able to walk to the dining room. Some impression that would make!"

"Any time you're ready," she said.

Mark motioned to Ron, the bartender, "Will you call George and let him know we're ready to go to the dining room as soon as a table is available. Please tell him there will be two of us." Mark asked for his tab then chatted easily with Carole until George entered the bar and told them their table was ready.

Making no reference to the fact that Mark would be eating with Carole, George politely escorted them to a nice table for four that was comfortably set for two. When they were seated, the wine steward was standing by to assist in selecting a wine if they chose to order wine.

"Do you enjoy champagne," Mark asked. "If you do, I can't think of a better reason to try some as a mini celebration."

"I enjoy it very much," She said, "but I don't drink it very often. I can't drink a whole bottle by myself and it ends up going flat. With your help, I'd love it."

After looking at the wine list for a few moments, Mark asked the wine steward to bring them a bottle of Dom Perignon.

"Any particular vintage?" the wine steward asked.

"No, thank you, my palate isn't sensitive enough to tell that much difference, I'm sorry to say." Then to Carole, "Do you have any preferences?" Carole rolled her eyes and quickly shook her head "no". When the wine steward left, Carole excused herself and asked Mark for directions to the Ladies Room. He watched, hypnotically, as she walked away. She was about 5'6" tall, he guessed, and perhaps 120 pounds – with a flat stomach and a slim waist. She wore nutmeg pleated dress slacks with Italian tailoring. The slacks stretched wonderfully tight across incredibly rounded buns, perched on long, straight legs that were tipped in brown leather heels of some height. She wore a collarless, over-the-hip, camel cashmere sweater – obviously expensive and in perfect taste. A beautiful, loose-fitting gold necklace, cut in a way to catch the light, sparkled with the movement of her walk. The ensemble didn't necessarily emphasize any particular aspect of her body, but it sure as hell did nothing to distract from it either. He was taken by the way she moved. She had the fluid walk of an athlete. No swishing or anything to attract attention, just a smooth, unhurried gait that covered distance in a very direct manner. How can she do that in heels? Mark asked himself.

Her return from the Ladies Room was even more enjoyable to watch. She kept the same unhurried gait. A smooth brown-leather clutch purse was swinging in her right hand, and her eyes stayed fixed on Mark the entire way. The realization that he was admiring her brought a slightly amused smile to her face and a distinct twinkle to her eyes. They were both enjoying the parade. Mark was, by now, completely enchanted.

Caught staring, Mark's face reddened as he fidgeted with his napkin. He stood as she arrived at the table, helped her with her chair and then reseated himself.

Before they could resume their conversation, the wine steward returned with their wine and started the ritual that Mark had always thought of as nonsense. However, he went through the drill with the steward and finally accepted the wine and watched as he filled both flutes with the effervescent, tawny liquid. It did look festive.

Mark asked the waiter to come back after they'd had a chance to look over the menu and relax some before they ordered.

Mark held his glass up for a toast and said, "Here's to your initiative – which has made me a truly happy man this evening." Then he added, "I hope to remain interesting enough to make it a regular occurrence."

"Regular will have to depend on you, I'm afraid. I only do bold hussy stuff once in a lifetime." She laughed again, easily, as she drank to the toast.

After ordering their dinner, Mark turned back to Carole and asked, "Now that you are a woman of leisure, how do you spend your time?"

"I've done a lot of the things I always wanted to do but never had the time or resources while tied to the grindstone. I've taken up golf and have become totally addicted to it. I've also gone to several cooking classes and learned to make some pretty neat dishes. I thought I'd just throw that in to see if you were paying attention." She laughed again and continued, "I have an aunt who lives here in Memphis whom I visit often. I try and help her enjoy some of the things she's missed out on earlier in life. I don't go for the Ladies Clubs and that sort of social disorder. I volunteer at the Salvation Army on a pretty regular basis. I've done a great deal of reading about sailing and honestly want to try it, but I haven't had the chance to do that yet. Vanity keeps me running and exercising. I keep pretty busy." After a short hesitation, she added, "And, of course, my main hobby is picking up attractive widowers in upscale bars."

They both laughed.

"OK, now it's my turn! Other than your work, how do you spend your time?"

"I'm also addicted to golf. I belong to a pretty nice club and hopefully, you'll join me one day soon for a round or two – or more. And please, even if you're way better than me, don't humiliate me too badly in front of my golfing friends. I'm such a wuss when it comes to humiliation. I also play handball regularly to try to stay in shape. I used to sail quite a lot on weekends, but an out-of-control powerboat sank my boat and I haven't replaced it yet. I also enjoy flying. I was a pilot in the Marine Corps and have continued to stay current since then. I don't own a plane, but I belong to a flying club that has several to choose from. I do enjoy my work, but I've just about had it with that. I find myself looking out the window more now than I did several years ago. I've delegated a lot of my actual engineering, and now I'm mostly stuck with the management of projects rather than the actual design of products. Naturally, the design function was what I enjoyed most during my career. It was always a big rush for me to see something go from an idea to a useful piece of equipment that functioned properly – and, knowing that I had designed, tested, refined and built myself. I will miss that, I'm sure."

During dinner, Mark was paying more attention to Carole than he was his meal. She was becoming even more beautiful the longer he was in her company. He studied her face, admiring the full-lipped mouth that, with little provocation, broke easily into a smile, exposing beautiful white and even teeth. He thought her eyes were blue, but on closer inspection, they looked more violet than blue, with little "crow's feet" fanning out toward the temples. Her face was not wrinkle-free; however, the few lines were from smiles and laughter rather than frowns. He couldn't guess her age. His only clue was her interest in him and, from that; he assumed she must be in her fifties at least. I don't care if she's thirty or seventy, as long as she allows me to hang around, Mark thought.

Because of the difference in the size of the portions, Carole finished her meal before Mark and sat back and studied his face as he finished eating. She guessed he was in his mid-to-late fifties. He had all his hair with only small streaks of gray disturbing the dark brown around the temples. From the way he was attacking his steak, he certainly did not have dentures. The face was a bit craggy, with a slightly bent nose. She assumed it had been modified in a sports accident or a well-directed punch during an altercation. The clear, brown eyes were set rather far apart with thick brows and long lashes, framed by the inevitable "crow's feet". He had a full mouth and smiled easily without showing his teeth to any degree until the smile turned to laughter and brought the even, white teeth into full view. He must have a great dental plan at work, she thought. She decided he was a very handsome man, in the rough. His personality was delightful, and they apparently shared several important interests. With that detached assessment, Mark became someone she would like to spend a lot more time with, the first such man she'd met since her husband had died.

Mark finished his steak, laid his napkin alongside the plate with a deep sigh and stated for the third or fourth time how wonderful the meal had been. He picked up his wineglass, swirled the remaining wine around the glass and asked, "Would you care for any dessert or an after-dinner drink... coffee?"

"I'd love a cup of coffee, thank you."

The busman was picking up the used dishes, and dinnerware and Mark asked him to tell Adam they would like some coffee. Within a couple of minutes after the busman left, Adam arrived with a carafe of coffee and filled the cups already waiting at the table. He asked the inevitable question, "Would you care for any dessert?"

"Thank you, but I don't think so." Mark replied as he reached for his wallet to retrieve a credit card. As Adam left with the card, both Mark and Carole became rather quiet, knowing that the evening was coming to an end long before they were ready. They sipped their hot coffee very deliberately.

"The evening has gone much too quickly for me." Mark said, "Is there anything else you'd care to do?"

"I can think of several things I'd like to do, however, given the hour, I think I'd better start home."

"Do you have your car?"

"No, I rode down here with my friend, Alice."

"I never drive if I've been drinking anything to speak of. I'd love for you to join me in my *Yellow Limousine.*"

"That's very nice of you." She said.

"Believe me – I couldn't have planned it any better."

Adam arrived with the check folder and discreetly placed it at Mark's elbow. He thanked them for choosing *The Prime Rib* and hoped they would return soon. Mark responded, "We enjoyed it very much. The food and service were excellent. Thanks for serving us and please, ask George to call me a cab, if you don't mind."

Mark added a generous tip to the check – signed it and placed the receipt and his credit card back in his wallet. He refilled the coffee cups from the carafe and said, "What a difference a beautiful woman makes in the total enjoyment of an evening. Even if you choose never to see me again, you have given me ammunition for great conversations with my golfing buddies that start with 'Man, you won't believe what happened to me last Tuesday.'"

Carole didn't give him the laugh he'd hoped for, but instead, a warm and beautiful smile as she reached and placed her hand over his and said, "Thank you! You have also given me the same ammunition when I visit with Alice in the morning. She'll be on the phone at daybreak, I'm sure."

As they finished their coffee, George approached their table and announced, "Mr. Stevens, your cab is here."

"Thanks George, the food and service were wonderful." Then, turning to Carole, he asked, "Do you have a wrap that I can collect before we leave?"

"No, I didn't think I would be out this late and came without a jacket."

"If you get chilly when we get outside, I'll lend you my coat." Then turning to George, he added: "OK buddy, that did it for us. We'll see you next time."

"Thanks for coming in. I'm glad you enjoyed."

Ernie's cab was waiting by the curb when they opened the door.

"Where to, Mr. Stevens," Ernie asked.

Mark looked to Carole for an answer. He was surprised when she gave an address fairly close to the downtown area of the city.

As Ernie drove, Carole moved closer to Mark and put her arm through the crook of his arm for the warmth. He asked if she would like his jacket to which she replied, "No I think you're warm enough for us both." Having said that, she snuggled closer, much to Mark's delight.

Silence engulfed the cab as the riders relaxed. There really was nothing to be said that could add to the feeling of well-being they were both enjoying. The warmth of the two bodies touching provided a contentment that said enough without their speaking. The trip seemed unusually short to Mark when Ernie stopped the cap and announced, "Here we are!"

Carole turned to Mark, "If you aren't too terribly tired, would you like to have a nightcap?"

"*Thank ye Jesus!*" Mark said as he threw his head and eyes skyward and spoke with his interpretation of a southern evangelical voice. He then asked Ernie how much the fare was, paid him, and asked if he could pick him up in an hour or so.

Ernie said, "No problem! Just give me a call when you're ready." Mark and Carole left the cab in front of what appeared to be a large brick warehouse with a striped canvas canopy leading from the street to a double doorway serving as the entrance to the building.

Carole said, "Home sweet home!" as she walked to the entrance and entered a code on a ten-key pad located on the wall next to the door. At the buzz, she opened the door to a rather small entry with two elevators.

She punched the "up" button on one of the elevators and as the door was opening, said, "This old building belonged to a client of mine who had planned to have it demolished. I begged him to reconsider and to sell it, by floors, for some upscale condominiums. He agreed to give it a try if I would design the interiors for him. I agreed to do the work if he would apply my fee to the purchase of one of the floors. So, to make a long story even longer, here I am. I made two condos out of my floor – live in one and lease the other. I just love it!

The elevator stopped on the fourth floor, and the door opened to a small, but elegant hallway with a door at each end. Carole led him to the door to their right, fumbled briefly for her key and then opened the door. She stood back and with the grand gesture of bowing and swinging her arm toward the room inside, said, "Welcome to my home!"

CHAPTER SIX

Mark entered a very large room, possibly 65 feet square. Interior walls did not section the room. Distinct living areas decorated to give the illusion of being separate rooms sectioned it. Tall folding screens of different colors and materials marked the corners of the several areas and camouflaged the load-bearing support columns, some of which were fake. Thick rugs covered the bare hardwood floors in each of the galleries with tasteful, comfortable furniture positioned to accommodate dining, living or lounging areas. The two outer walls of the room were made up of windows that reached from the high ceilings to the floor and were covered with a combination of plantation blinds and heavy draperies alternately covering two windows each. The only permanent interior wall that was visible was a half-wall enclosing the interior limits of the kitchen. It was remarkable that each area was decorated in a different color, with unique accessories, yet the colors never clashed with anything else in adjoining areas or even areas more distant. There was a set of double doors centered on the perimeter wall that he assumed led to the bedroom(s) and bath facilities. It was incredible.

"Amazing," Mark stammered.

"It's a bit different alright. I just let myself go, and did some things I was reluctant to do for anyone else. I had the floor space I needed, so, this is the end result of a year's shopping and decorating. I've had fun with it, and it's kept me busy."

"*Architectural Digest* would have a field day here."

"Let's go over near the bar, and I'll see if I can make good on my promise of a nightcap. I have a wonderful Napoleon Brandy that you might enjoy."

"That got my attention," he said, as they made their way to an area that contained a large wet bar, stools, a couch, two lounge chairs and a circular, freestanding, metal fireplace. Carole went behind the bar and retrieved two large snifters from the collection of glassware in a glass-doored cabinet. Under the bar she found the green, frosted bottle of brandy, sloshed a generous drink into each glass and slid one across the bar to Mark.

As Carole moved from behind the bar, Mark reached out and placed his hand on her waist. There was no resistance as he pulled her to him. He slid his other arm around her so his hands joined in the small of her back as Carole sat the brandy snifter back on the bar. Both arms around his neck, she arched herself backward to look into his face. She said nothing as she bent back toward him and slowly raised her lips to his. Mark felt as if an electric shock passed through him when her lips made first contact with his. Her lips were warm, very soft and open. Their tongues touched briefly, then again, much more pronounced. He felt the warmth of her thighs, stomach and breasts press eagerly against him as the intensity of their embrace grew. Seconds, or minutes, into the kiss her hands were on the back of his head, pulling him closer. Mark lowered his hands and felt the fullness of her as he pressed to be even closer. She abruptly pulled her head back and placed her hand on the front of his shoulder pushing him, gently, back and moved to release his arms from around her.

"When I offered a nightcap, I really meant a late night drink – not an article of bed clothing," she said in a very soft and sensual voice. "It's been too long, and I'm liking this much too much for a first meeting. I don't mean to seem like I'm teasing – because I'm not, I just don't want to be in such a big hurry with someone I met only six hours ago."

Mark turned and placed his elbows on the bar, but his eyes stayed on Carole. He said, "I'm truly sorry, but *you* will have to be the one with all the restraint. It's not disrespect, but an honest desire to hold you, kiss you and yes, take you to bed, more than any woman I've met since my wife died. I'll never force myself on you, but you can depend on me to try those things any time I'm with you in a suitable environment. A *no* will be taken as *no*! I have no desire to do anything that you wouldn't join me in, freely and without reservation."

"Being of the same generation" she said, "you know what a prisoner we all are to our upbringing. I don't want you to think that I hop into bed with every man I find attractive. And, I desperately hope that getting into my bed wasn't the only reason you spent, what I considered to be, a wonderful evening with me. Please humor me and let it grow a little before we play all our cards."

"I can't and won't argue with anything you've said. Let me say that getting in your pants was *definitely* not the only reason I spent the evening with you. I won't lie and say it never entered my mind, but whatever disappointment I may feel right now is also tempered with a great deal of respect. I'm glad you look before you leap, but you've got to realize, you are one beautiful and desirable woman. You bring out the *alpha* in those of us who still like to think of ourselves as men."

"If you're not too upset with me, why don't we finish our drink and visit a bit more? I love talking to you. I loved the other things too, but let's not go there tonight."

Mark picked up both snifters from the bar, handed one to Carole and followed her to the comfortable couch by the unlit fireplace. She kicked off her shoes and curled her feet under herself in one smooth motion before Mark could take his place beside her. Nothing was said, immediately, as they enjoyed the burn of the brandy.

Mark finally broke the silence by saying, "I have an appointment at nine in the morning that I really have to attend... so if I crash sitting here with you – throw me out before 8 a.m.

"Until you crash, may I dig deeper into your life – for my enjoyment? I want to know who you are, how you got to be *who* you are, and all the things that would probably take years to understand. That may be too personal, I don't know. I just know these are the things I want to know, and they are important to me. Tell me to back off if you need to, but I don't get this kind of opportunity often."

"There's not that much to know. I've had one job all my working lifetime, other than military service. I was married to a wonderful woman that I was religiously faithful to; one daughter who was killed at the same time as my wife."

Carole interrupted with "*Oh my God!*"

"I have no other relatives close enough to count. I'm getting older, of course, and this seems like a pretty rotten time to be alone in life. I've dated since my wife died, but really never wanted to spend much time with any of the women I've gone out with. Some were nice enough, but we just didn't cook. I've always looked, but never found, until now, anyone with whom I thought I'd enjoy spending real time. Now, I'm just hoping that you are everything you seem to be. You meet all the criteria: You're beautiful, of the same generation, talented and obviously not desperate to be taken in by some clown who doesn't fit a mold you may have established as a second for your husband. In six, no, seven hours now, you have made such an impression on me that you may be troubled by the future pursuit that is coming your way. Sorry, but that's the way you affect me. I'll leave you alone when you've had enough, but until you say so, I'm gonna be here."

"I've dated some, too," Carole replied, "with pretty much the same results. Friends seem to always have the perfect guy for me, who never is. The men who have made whatever effort it took to meet me on their own are usually married, and I don't go for that. So, I've stumbled around as an extra at the parties I've attended and find that I'm being paired with another extra who seems as uncomfortable with the situation as I am. I go to dinner with my girlfriends when their husbands are out of town. I'm also getting older without someone I care to grow old with. I'm not bored with my life, and I enjoy my own company, for the most part, but I often think it would be so much nicer to have someone I honestly care about to come home to."

"The longer I talk with you, the more I see the similarities in our lives." Mark replied, taking another sip of his brandy. "And if this is a representative sample of what one would expect of your company, I'd love to be a big part of your weekly schedule."

Carole launched another low, sexy chuckle and said, "I've already slipped one of my cards into your jacket pocket – you know, phone number, etc. I hope you use it often."

"Again, you have saved me from groveling. I hate groveling!" Mark said as he felt in his jacket pocket for the card. "Thank you!" he added.

Looking at his watch, Mark frowned at the time and finally said, "Well, it's getting late and if I enjoy another brandy, I'll be here forever as a lump on your couch. I'd better call Ernie and get my butt home while I can still manage."

"What makes you think I'd be real unhappy having you as a lump on my couch?"

They chuckled at that as Mark, laboriously, heaved himself off the couch and made his way to the telephone on the bar and called his cab. While still at the bar, Mark removed one of his business cards from his wallet, took a pen from his jacket pocket and wrote his home phone number on the back of the card.

He returned to the couch and handed Carole the card. "Here are all the numbers, just in case you need anything. I'll try and get back soon with a carrier pigeon if all else fails." Mark offered a hand to Carole and helped her to her feet from the couch.

"The cab will be here in a few minutes."

They made their way to the door with Carole's arm around Mark's waist and his arm around her shoulder. At the door, they turned to each other and found that the second kiss was just as delicious as the first. This time, Mark broke the embrace and opened the door.

"You're a hard woman to leave, Carole Wilson."

"Thank you, Mark! I had a wonderful time."

She released his hand as he stepped toward the elevator, watched from the doorway and waved as the elevator door was closing behind him.

Mark was euphoric as he made his way out of the building to find Ernie waiting by the curb.

42

"Seems like tonight was the night, Mr. Stevens," Ernie said, as he pulled smoothly back into traffic.

"Yeah, Ernie, tonight was the night!"

CHAPTER SEVEN

Although Mark could hear the alarm going off, it took quite some time for it to break through the deep sleep. The alcohol and the late hour had combined to make getting out of bed at 6:30 a.m. something that was not real high on his *To Do* list. He turned off the annoying alarm and rolled back over to snooze before getting up. That's when Dr. Givens' name popped into his clouded mind. He became instantly awake.

Gotta get ready for the good doctor to give me some good news for a change, he thought as he kicked off the covers and reluctantly slid his feet to the floor.

He had remembered to fill and set his timer-controlled coffee maker before he had gone to bed. Knowing the coffee was ready, Mark stumbled toward the kitchen, with some serious anticipation, for his morning jolt of caffeine. He retrieved a cup from the clean dishes in the dishwasher and filled it with the freshly brewed coffee. Leaning on the kitchen counter, he sipped the coffee for a couple of minutes, and then opened the refrigerator to complete his morning ritual with a glass of orange juice. The juice and half of his first cup of coffee partially washed away the stale taste lingering in his mouth. The cobwebs in his head began to clear. He thought he might make it.

He refilled his cup and headed back toward the bath for a shower and the inevitable, but dreaded, morning shave. Mumbling to himself, he completed his shave and entered the shower. The cold water hit him, immediately shocking his body into full wakefulness. Thankfully, the hot water arrived quickly and killed the chill. He didn't linger in the shower this morning, as he usually did, but immediately soaped himself, rinsed quickly, and was back in front of his sink in less than five minutes. After brushing his teeth, drying his hair and body he was ready to get dressed and be gone.

It was about 7:45 when he started the Buick, and he started computing the time it would take to drive to the doctor's office. After the little mental exercise, he decided that he had time to stop by the coffee shop and have some breakfast. "I might as well go in with a full stomach," he told himself.

After circling the medical center parking lot several times, searching for a parking space, Mark still opened the door to Dr. Givens office five minutes early. He checked in with the administrative nurse on duty at the time and took a seat, for the inevitable wait he'd learned to expect.

This time the wait didn't happen. The same nurse who greeted him the day before appeared in the doorway and asked him to follow her again. This time she didn't lead him to an examining room, but instead to Dr. Givens' private office, where she asked that he take a seat near the large, cluttered desk and said, "The doctor will be with you in a few moments."

The nurse and Dr. Givens both reached the doorway at the same time. Dr. Givens retreated to allow the nurse to leave and then closed the door behind her. She sat down at the desk and already had the look of "Dr." Givens etched into her still-beautiful face.

"Mr. Stevens," she said in a grim voice, "the radiologist sent me these x-rays yesterday afternoon along with his analysis of the scan. I've had time to study them myself and am very unhappy to say that I must agree with his dire projection. The results of the CT scan indicate that you have advanced pancreatic carcinoma, and it appears to have metastasized to the common bile duct and the stomach. I am so sorry to just blurt that out, but it's the only way I can make myself do it. Telling a patient news such as this is the very worst job I'm required to do. I always dread it above all others."

Mark could feel the blood draining from his face, and a sudden weakness permeated his body. He leaned forward in his chair, placed his elbows on his knees and lowered his head into the open palms of his hands. He could feel the clamminess of his face with his hands as well as the clamminess of his hands on his face. He sat there for several moments, rubbing his forehead, fighting the urge to vomit, unsure of his ability to respond, verbally, to the doctor's devastating announcement.

When he felt that he could speak with any degree of intelligence, he leaned back fully in the chair, crossed his legs, deliberately, his left ankle atop his right knee. After looking at the ceiling for a couple of seconds, he lowered his gaze back to the beautiful Dr. Givens.

In a husky voice barely above a whisper, Mark asked, "What now?"

"I can do a biopsy to verify, or decry, the results of the CT scan."

"When can you do that?" Mark asked in the same tone.

"I can do it at 1:00 o'clock this afternoon, if you'd like, and have the lab results back later in the afternoon or early in the morning."

Yes, I'd like to get it over with as soon as possible."

"You might want to get a second opinion. I can send these x-rays and your other lab results to any other doctor you choose or if you have no preference, I can suggest another gastro, outside our group. There are other respected internists located here in this complex that I can, perhaps, impose upon to see you before we do the biopsy."

"Do you think another opinion would be helpful in any way?" Mark asked.

"I always prefer not to stand totally alone in diagnoses of such gravity. I am rather confident with the diagnosis or I wouldn't be having this conversation with you, and two of the other doctors in our group have looked at the scanned x-rays as well. However, I always like to have someone else, who is qualified, verify or challenge my diagnosis if there is even the remotest possibility of my being wrong."

"If you do a biopsy this afternoon, will it prove one way or the other that I have or do not have cancer? Will the diagnosis be indisputable after the biopsy?"

"Yes, it will determine, without doubt, if there is malignancy." Dr. Givens replied.

"If that's the case, I think I will opt for the biopsy and not bother with a second opinion. Will you contact Dr. Morrison and let him know of your diagnosis? He asked that you keep him informed."

"Of course! Would you like to discuss what to expect if the biopsy proves my diagnosis to be correct?"

Mark thought a moment and said, "I've already researched the disease on the Internet and from what I read, there's no real chance of successful treatment after symptoms occur."

"I'm afraid that's true. There are several treatments that can be attempted, but, in most cases, the chances for satisfactory results are pretty dim. Even if you opt for treatment, I still advise you to get your affairs in order. The treatments available sometimes make the quality of life much less enjoyable than it would be if the disease is untreated and left to run its course, and, as you have discovered, there is really no effective treatment available. Treated or untreated, the disease is most often considered fatal within six months when it has spread to the extent it has in your case. If the diagnosis is confirmed with the biopsy this afternoon, I can refer you to an oncologist if you choose to treat the disease or at least get their opinion as to the chance of successful treatment. I am so sorry."

"I guess my next question is: How long before the pain becomes severe enough to require management and what methods are available to make it bearable?"

Dr. Givens thought a moment, and then said: "I can't tell you when the severe pain will begin. You should be able to continue a fairly normal lifestyle until the last month or so. At some point, you will need chemical relief from the pain. You'll be using everything from Tylenol to morphine before it's over. In the very latest stages of the disease, if morphine isn't sufficient relief, we can surgically sever nerves to bring the pain back under control. Obviously, such procedures are last-ditch efforts to keep you comfortable and the decision to endure such a procedure would be your option. Your use of narcotics will not be restricted; therefore, *you* will be the primary judge of 'how much and how often'. I will insure your access to the drugs as you decide you need them. Dependency is of no concern."

Mark did not interrupt, nor ask any questions. Dr. Givens continued, "I know this is unwelcome information, but I think you should know that you will undoubtedly experience severe jaundice at some point. There will be an increasing loss of appetite, to the point where you will find food almost intolerable in the final stages of the disease. Severe weight loss, as well as a loss of strength, will accompany the increased intolerance for food. We will be able to relieve some symptoms with endoscopy if you choose."

"Where will you do the biopsy? Do I need to do anything prior to reporting?" Mark asked.

"We'll do it in the Ambulatory Surgical Unit at Memorial Hospital. The procedure is done under general anesthesia so you will need someone to drive you home when we finish. You'll need to check in by 11:00 for the administrative work and prep. Have you eaten today?"

"Yes, I had breakfast about 7:30 this morning."

"I wish you hadn't, but maybe we can work around it all right. If I had been a little more foresighted and expected the biopsy, I would have asked you not to eat; but that's hindsight. Yesterday, I didn't think all this would be necessary." Dr. Givens said.

"Well, it's almost 10:00 o'clock now, so I guess I'd better get out of here and get ready to meet you at the hospital. Doctor, as bad as I hate hearing your diagnosis, I appreciate your candor in the matter. If the biopsy confirms the situation, as I assume it will, I guess there's no other choice but to accept the fact that shit happens in life and be done with it."

"After all my training, it's difficult for me to accept my helplessness in cases like yours and not be able to offer some hope of reprieve or have the ability to medically alter the outcome." She hesitated a moment then added: "I'll see you at 1:00 o'clock."

CHAPTER EIGHT

Mark was in a daze. After leaving the building, he couldn't remember where his car was and started wandering around the parking lot, confused. The recurring thought "three to six months" kept anything else from entering or remaining on his mind long enough to act. He felt like crying, but couldn't let himself. He felt like running, but didn't know where to run. He had to find his car. Think, damnit, think!

He forced himself back from near panic, took his bearings and finally remembered where he parked his car. Forcing his mind to remain focused; he made his way to the car, unlocked it and got in. He started shaking, badly. I hope I can drive, he thought, as he started the Buick. He didn't move for several long moments before he began maneuvering to leave the parking lot. His next conscious thought was pulling into his driveway and opening his garage door. Another trip of no memory, he thought. This ain't gonna get it.

Mark decided to call Art to ask if he would be able to take him to the hospital and home again. He hated the thought of trying to hide the truth from him until after the biopsy and decided to play it by ear. If he felt he had to, he'd tell him; but only if he must.

"Hi, Ruth," Mark spoke into the phone, "Could I speak to the resident lecher?"

"Sure, Mark, I think he's awake," Ruth answered with a chuckle.

After the clicks and a couple of rings, Mark heard Art's growl on the other end, "Hey man, did you get finished with the doctor already?"

"Not really, I'm sorry to say. I have a problem, of sorts, and need a favor if you're not covered up this afternoon."

"No, everything is pretty routine this afternoon, and I could skip it if necessary. What's up," Art asked.

"They're going to give me a goddamned biopsy at the hospital this afternoon. Because of the general anesthesia, they say I have to have someone with me to drive when it's over. I'm at home now, and if you can do it, I'll impose for a round-trip so I won't be afoot later. I know this is really short notice, but I have to be out there by 11:00 to check in. If it's going to be a problem, I can call a cab."

"It's not a problem. I'll be glad to. It's getting pretty late; so I guess I'd better get off the phone and head your way. I'll see you in about twenty minutes."

"OK! I really appreciate it," Mark replied, "I'll be ready."

At twenty minutes to eleven, Mark heard Art's car in the drive. He walked through the kitchen and utility room and punched the garage door opener to let Art know he knew that he was there. He then opened the door to his car and got his garage door opener and walked out to join Art.

"What's this all about; the biopsy and all," Art asked, even before Mark was all the way in the car.

"It's just the final part of the diagnosis. Nothing can be certain until they have a piece of meat to analyze. They have to go down my throat, or something to collect it. That's the reason for the general anesthesia."

"Didn't she give you some kind of a clue as to what they're looking for," Art asked again.

"They're looking for a malignancy in my pancreas."

"*Jesus Christ*," Art blurted, "Man, this is getting way too serious. I thought you might have an ulcer or something like that, but cancer never entered my mind. When will they know for sure?"

"She said she'd know something no later than first thing in the morning, maybe even this afternoon. I hope so."

Art was hurrying to try and make it to the hospital by the 11:00 o'clock check-in time. He was scowling more than usual when he finally broke the uneasy silence that had been with them for the last 10 minutes, "I think you're holding out on me, my friend."

"It ain't lookin' real good," Mark muttered, as much to himself as to Art. "I might have to deal with it."

They both fell silent, as Art turned into the hospital complex. "Why don't I just drop you off at the entrance and I'll go find a parking space and join you on the inside? If you wait for me, you'll probably be late checking in."

"OK! I'll be in the Ambulatory Surgical Unit," Mark said as he opened the car door.

Mark opened the door to the hospital's main entrance and started looking for signs that would tell him where he was going. When he found none, he approached the volunteer sitting at the Information Desk and asked where the ASU was located. He followed the directions he was given until he saw a large room with several rows of chairs neatly arranged for seating about twenty people. The sign over the door read "ASU Waiting". There was also a counter against the inner wall that had an administrative-type woman busily entering data on a PC. Another sign, on the counter, said, "Please sign in".

After filling out the required paperwork, Mark realized why he had been asked to report two hours early. He doubted if the surgical procedure would take as long as he handed the loaded clipboard back to the admin nurse.

After checking for correctness, she told him he'd just won a trip to surgery and then directed him to the prep area where he would be admitted and finalized for the biopsy.

The nurse assigned him a dressing room, and gave him pertinent instructions concerning the procedure and what he had to do to get ready

As he started to get undressed, Mark heard Art asking the nurse where they had him *stored*. Donna, his prep nurse, replied, "He's getting dressed right now, but you can see him in a couple of minutes."

When he finished with the undress/dress routine, Mark stuck his head out from the curtain and called to Donna, "I'm ready to be humiliated."

Art came over to the curtain, pulled it back and went in. Upon seeing Mark standing in the hospital gown and socks, he couldn't pass up the opportunity to mention, "Nice dress! You should have shaved your hairy legs though."

"Thanks, oh mighty fashion guru! There is a vast amount of reverse cleavage in the back of this thing," Mark replied, with some sarcasm, as he hoisted himself up onto the gurney.

A couple of seconds later, Donna re-entered the area with a roll-around tray, carrying all the paraphernalia necessary to prepare him for the operating room. She stuck an electronic thermometer in his ear, noted the reading on his chart, then put a BP cuff on his arm and took his blood pressure; again, noting the result on the chart. She listened to his heart and lungs with a stethoscope, chatting nonsensically all the while. Then, while holding his chart, she asked him his name, and after he responded, she asked if he knew what he was scheduled for. Noting that his responses matched the information on the chart, she hung a plastic container of saline solution on the hook attached to his gurney and after an almost painless injection of Novocain into the back of his hand, proceeded to insert the IV. Prep tasks completed, she pulled a warmed blanket up over him and said, "Mark, the anesthesiologist will be here in a few minutes to visit with you. After he's gone, I'll hit you with the *feel good* stuff."

"That's the only reason I agreed to this mess," he responded.

She left, returning in a few minutes with a plastic bag for his clothes, then suggested that he let Art keep any valuables he might have with him.

The silence in the room grew heavy. After several minutes of waiting for one or the other to say something, Art finally asked, "Do you know how long it will take them to finish?"

"She said the procedure itself wouldn't take long at all, but I'll be out for about an hour or so all together and kinda goofy for another couple of hours after that."

"How will I know when the anesthesia has all worn off – given your normal goofy behavior," Art asked in a monotone that lacked the intended humor.

As Mark laid waiting for an appropriate response to form in his unsettled mind, the curtain slid back, and a young man in green scrubs entered the area.

"Mr. Stevens? I'm Doctor Johnston," he said, as he extended his hand. "I will be administering the anesthesia this afternoon." He asked Mark questions concerning allergies, when he'd last eaten and if he'd ever undergone general anesthesia. After Mark had said "no" to his question concerning previous exposure to general anesthesia, Dr. Johnston asked if Mark had any questions about what to expect. After another "no" from Mark, the doctor smiled and said, "Then I guess I'll see you in the operating room in a few minutes."

As soon as the doctor left, Donna reappeared with a hypodermic syringe preloaded with a clear liquid. She picked up the surgical tubing of the IV and located a "Y" along its length and inserted the needle in the injection site. Seeing the needle enter the tubing, Mark yelled, "My *God*! Be a little easier with that, will you?"

Donna jumped, and gave him a look similar to one that Mattie would give him and said; "Any apprehension you may feel right now will be history in a few minutes. This is your treat for being a good boy; however, if I get one more smart-alec remark like that 'My God', I'll take it back."

Mark didn't know what she had given him, but he noticed that he was starting to feel warmer and much more relaxed after a few minutes.

Art asked, "Is it taking effect yet?"

"Yeah," Mark said in a drowsy voice. "It's a pretty fine trip."

Mark was enjoying the euphoria when a hospital aide entered the area and announced, "It's time to go." Then holding a chart, he asked, "Are you Mr. Mark Stevens?"

Mark answered, sleepily "I sure hope so. I'd hate to be doing all this for someone else."

With that, the aid said, "Great, let's get this show on the road."

He pulled the curtain back fully and started rolling the gurney toward the operating room. As he was leaving, the aid said to Art, "Sir, you can wait in the ASU waiting area until the procedure is over, if you like... the doctor will come out to visit with you after she's finished."

"Thank you," Art mumbled as he watched his friend being rolled down the hallway.

Inside the operating room, two nurses in green scrubs with surgical masks covering their mouths and noses greeted Mark. One of the nurses explained that they were going to transfer him from the roll-around gurney to the operating table. Positioning the gurney close and parallel to the operating table, the aid and the two nurses picked him up and made the transfer, welcoming all the help Mark could give them without exposing his backside in the process.

"Ahhhh, the lovely Dr. Givens," Mark slurred.

Although she was wearing a surgical mask, Mark could see that she was smiling as she said, "I see you're enjoying the sedative."

"Ummm!" He said, and then added, "I don't want you looking up my dress after Dr. "J" passes gas. You're supposed to start from the top end. Remember? And, by the way, if you visit with my friend that's driving me, please don't mention the full reason for the biopsy. I haven't told him what's going on, and I'd like to put it off for a while."

"I won't say anything. Now hush, and go to sleep," Dr. Givens said.

He awoke in a room very similar to the one in which he'd been prepped, oblivious to what had happened in the last hour and a half. A nurse whom he'd not seen before was saying "Mr. Stevens – Mr. Stevens? You can get dressed now."

He fought to focus his thoughts enough to do as the nurse instructed, and sat up on the gurney to see Art standing there with the plastic bag of clothes he'd left in the prepping area. Mark sat on the edge of the gurney for a minute or so and then reached for the bag that Art was holding. He emptied the entire contents of the bag onto the gurney beside him and sorted around in the pile of clothes until he found his underwear. The nurse pulled the curtain closed, and Mark lowered himself to the floor, leaning on the gurney as he put on his underwear before taking off the hospital gown. Still feeling somewhat woozy, he waited a minute or so before taking off the gown and continuing the routine of dressing. Art had to catch him once when he lost his balance while negotiating the legs of his trousers. Fully dressed and starting to feel a little bit more normal, he asked Art, "Did anyone tell you how things went in there?"

"Yeah, your Dr. Givens came out and visited with me for a few minutes. She said that everything went normally, and you shouldn't have any problems at all from the procedure. She also said she would call you as soon as they get the results back from the lab."

"Did she think she'd be able to get the results back today or will it be tomorrow before they find out anything?"

"No, she just said that she'd call you as soon as she had the results. *Jesus*, she's a good-looking woman. I think I'm starting to get some kind of sickness that requires her attention. I'll dream about that neat little exam that has her telling me 'Turn your head, and cough!' ".

"I thought you would," Mark said as he was putting his wallet and other things Art had handed him, back in his pockets. "She's obviously eaten up with beautiful."

"I'll go get the car and meet you at the front door," Art said - and left.

Mark leaned on the gurney for a few minutes until a young black man in street clothes approached, pushing a wheel chair. "Are you the one being discharged?" He asked.

"Yes," Mark replied and sat down in the offered chair to be transported – as per insurance regulations – to the outside of the hospital.

When they reached the door, Art was parked alongside the curb. The passenger door was open, as Art waited behind the wheel. Mark thanked the orderly and walked the several steps to the car – got in and closed the door.

After fastening his seat belt, Mark said, "Art, I really appreciate this. I know it's an imposition to take you away from your office for so long, but, I honestly didn't know what else to do."

"Forget it! You'd do the same for me, and I didn't mind a bit."

Again, the silence set in. Art finally asked, "Do you want to stop by the pharmacy and get your prescription filled?"

"Yeah, that might be a good idea. I don't really trust myself to drive back down here right now. God, I don't know how many of your bar-tabs I'm gonna have to pick up after today."

"Don't worry about it, you just keep picking them up until I tell you to quit."

They had stopped at the drugstore to fill Marks prescription, and were finishing the short drive to Mark's house, when Art asked: "What are you doing the rest of the afternoon?"

"I'm going to crash for awhile. I'm still a little woozy. I didn't get a whole lot of sleep last night, so between the drugs and the short night, a nap should improve my outlook on life."

"You lazy shit," Art answered, adding, "I'll make the offer for dinner one more time and if you say *no* this time, I know you're insulting Jean's cooking."

"That sounds like a good plan. Why don't you call me an hour or so before you're ready to eat? That way I can shake the cobwebs out of my head before I join you. I haven't seen the prettier side of your family in a while, so it will be a welcome relief from your ugly mug."

With the plans for the evening set, Mark went directly to his bedroom as soon as he was home, undressed down to his underwear and flopped down on the bed without turning the covers back. As he lay there, staring at the ceiling, he thought, I guess tonight is as good a time as any to tell them what's going on. I'm sure Art suspects more than I've volunteered anyway, so there's no sense in putting off the inevitable. I don't know how they're going to take it. Jesus – I don't know how I'm going to take it. With those dour thoughts filling his consciousness, he suddenly felt dead tired and drifted off into a restless sleep.

The incessant ringing of the telephone pulled him back from the protective envelope of sleep. After missing with his first grab for the telephone receiver and knocking it off the cradle onto the bedside table, he finally got his hand on it, pulled it to his ear and said "hello" while still half asleep.

He heard Art on the other end of the line saying, "You gonna sleep the rest of your life away?"

"I would if I could get assholes like you to quit calling me."

"Get your butt over here and we'll have a drink before dinner."

"OK! I'm going to take a quick shower, and I'll be right over."

After showering and getting dressed, Mark started the Buick and backed to his left to go directly to Art's house, then, halfway into the maneuver he decided to take a detour by way of the liquor store to get a bottle of wine for their meal. He pulled back into his driveway and reversed his course and headed toward the shopping center where he'd filled his prescription earlier. Johnny's Warehouse Liquor was located there and offered as good a wine selection as any store in town.

Halfway to the liquor store he realized his reason for the detour was dread of the upcoming meeting more than a need for dinner wine. Even after the realization, he shopped quite a bit longer for wine than he normally did. He splurged a little on the wine, justifying the $80.00 with, "I hear you can't take it with you."

When Mark arrived at the Fletcher home, the garage door was up. Art was at his workbench with a sack full of expended shotgun shell-cases, busily removing the spent primers in preparation for reloading. Art was an avid "Trap" and "Skeet" shooter and loved to complain (with tongue in cheek) about how dead clay pigeons still tasted like mud no matter how long you cooked them. He reloaded his shells both for economy and relaxation. He happily went through eight or ten boxes of shells on the weekends he spent at the range.

When Mark walked up to the garage, he yelled to Art, "Does yo' Momma know you're playing with gunpowder?"

"When you're badder than the gunpowder you're playing with, it doesn't make any difference, son."

Mark leaned on the workbench watching Art at his work/play. He turned, and they shook hands. Mark handed him the bottle of wine and said, "This is for Jean and me. I have a bottle of Muscatel in the trunk for you, but I'll wait a while before bringing it in so it won't smell up the house so bad."

CHAPTER NINE

When Mark and Art entered the house from the garage, Jean was in the kitchen preparing dinner. When she saw Mark, she dried her hands with a dish towel, smiled broadly and met Mark halfway to share a warm hug and kiss on their respective cheeks.

Jean was a tall woman and easily held Mark around the neck with only a slight up-tilt to her head. Her thick, dark, shoulder-length hair accented a rather long, beautiful face with near- perfect, unblemished, unwrinkled and tanned skin that belied her fifty years of living. Art had always commented about how the contrast of his light skin against her darker features complimented them as a couple.

She always complained about her weight and exercised regularly to counter a healthy appetite. In Marks view, she was overweight like Marilyn Monroe was overweight. "Voluptuous" was a much better description than overweight, and her *wasp-like* waist seemed to exaggerate the roundness of her full hips and bust. Long, straight legs elevated a delightful package to a full 5'10" that regularly caused male eyeballs to click sideways into the stops as she passed – much to her delight.

"Art," Jean asked, "why don't you and Mark get comfortable in the den while I finish up in here. And yes, cocktails would be in order."

Mark joined Art in the large and comfortably appointed den/family room located adjacent and open to the kitchen. The room was arranged so that one area was used for relaxing in front of the fireplace and large TV, and the other area containing a breakfast table and chairs used for informal dining and was tastefully preset for three.

A large, rounded bay window with a view of the wooded back yard formed a semi-circle around the table giving the illusion of patio dining. The placement of the couch and large recliners allowed equal opportunity to speak with others seated in the room, view the TV, or just enjoy the glow of the gas logs Art usually had burning in the fireplace. The bar with its four stools lay along the interior wall that sectioned off the formal dining room from the den.

Art met Mark en route to the seating area and handed him the drink he'd mixed without asking Mark about his preference. They continued to walk toward the large recliners where they both flopped down; saying, in unison, "Ahhh, that's better!"

"That's alright, honey, I'll mix my own." Jean whined from the kitchen.

"Oh shit! Art said as he heaved himself out of the recliner and headed back to the bar. "I'm cut off for a week!"

Art mixed Jean's drink and asked, "Honey, are you going to join us or should I bring it in there?

"I'll be finished in here in a couple of minutes; just sit it down and I'll join you when I can take a break."

"OK!" Art said as he rolled his eyes toward Mark feigning great exasperation with his wife.

Mark, in turn, spoke loudly enough for Jean to hear, "You'd better get your buns in here or you're going to miss out on hearing about the woman I met last night that is taking me away from you."

"I am on my ever-lovin' way, Darlin', and don't even think about starting without me."

Mark smiled while Art did his version of a smile and both shook their heads negatively toward each other upon hearing the obvious excitement in Jean's voice.

"Gossipmonger!" Art said half under his breath.

The audible sounds of dishes clanking together and falling on countertops came from the kitchen as Jean hurriedly put the finishing touches on what she was doing; anxiously anticipating the story from Mark about his new lady friend that she was totally unaware of.

She charged into the room wiping her hands on a dishtowel and wearing an ear-to-ear grin that measured her interest in a woman that, seemingly, had Mark's attention. The woman she had anxiously wished for since the tragedy of Karen's death. "OK, boy, no detail is insignificant. I want to hear it all." She said as she sat down on the edge of the couch, leaning forward with the body language often seen in puppies being teased with a doggie treat.

"Oh, there's actually not that much to tell." Mark teased as Art choked back a laugh that nearly blew a sip of his drink out his nose.

"Stop it or I'll slap you!"

"Well, this old *hide* made a run on me last night while I was waiting for dinner at *The Prime Rib*. She was obviously taken by my clean-cut good looks and rugged ways.

"I'm warning you. You're going to get punched and left with no dinner if you don't knock it off"

Mark couldn't help but laugh at her overt curiosity and decided to continue the story with some degree of accuracy. "Her name is Carole Wilson, and part of what I just said is true. She did make the first move on me, but – an old *hide* she ain't. She introduced herself, in a rather unique way, while I was wracking my brain trying to think up a really cool plan that would cause her to look upon me with great favor. She had more courage than I did and saved me further agony. We had a drink or two at the bar and then enjoyed a delightful dinner that seemed to pass in an instant. She had ridden to the restaurant with her girlfriend and agreed to share a cab with me for the return trip. We went to her apartment and had an after-dinner drink where we exchanged *cards* with promises of an early repeat of the evening. I'm completely taken by her, and I'm sure the two of you will love her as soon as you meet her. I can't wait!"

"I'm not going to accept that as, all there was to it. Details! Damnit! Details! Did you score?"

"*Jean!*" Art scolded, in a chastising tone.

She turned to Art and said with a frown, "Oh hush!" then back to Mark, continuing her questioning. "What does she look like? Does she still work? How old is she? Has she been married?"

"No, I didn't score. She's a *nice girl*, unlike some other women I know." Mark said, glaring at Jean in mock contempt. Then continued: "She has short, blondish hair; a terrific figure; perfect taste in clothing; great conversationalist and a widow for three years. She retired a couple of years ago as an architect – specializing in interior design. She still does occasional consulting projects for some of her former clients. Just guessing, I'd say she was in her mid-50s; however, the guess is not based on looks. The chronology of the events we visited about and her willingness to be seen with an old fart like me suggests that she would have to be somewhere in that age range."

"Why didn't you bring her with you this evening? God knows I could use a break in tolerating you two all by myself for so long."

"I want to be a little more secure in the relationship before I expose her to the seamier side of my personal life. You just don't spring friends like you on a girl you're really trying to impress as being *swave* and *deboner*." He said – emphasizing the mispronunciation of suave and debonair.

"Right," Jean said as she got up from the couch and then added, "Finish your drinks and I'll try and salvage the dinner I abandoned to hear about the intriguing Ms. Carole Wilson, whom I'm dying to meet."

The two men fell quiet when Jean left the room. They had been consciously avoiding discussing the events that had taken place earlier in the day. Art finally asked, in a voice low enough not to be heard by Jean, "Are you going to let us know about what's going on with the health, tonight?"

"Let's not screw up dinner talking about medical BS. Yes, I'll tell you both all I know after dinner and we can be done with it. OK?"

61

"I can live with that."

Jean was parading back and forth from the kitchen to the table near the bay window, carrying the food she'd prepared. "Jean, can I help you with anything?" Mark volunteered.

"No, I think I have everything under control for the time being. You might want to open the wine."

A few minutes later, Jean announced "OK, you guys! Call in the food tasters if you want, but you better get your butts in here if you want this. And please, no rude comments about the cook; she will be joining you and becomes vicious when criticized."

"Wow! You have to give me the name of your caterer. This looks wonderful!" Mark said as he filled his plate from the offered serving dishes.

"I can still spill this stuff in your lap, turkey!"

The meal progressed with the usual caustic chitchat enjoyed by the friends. The food was terrific and fully appreciated by the two men who lavished compliments on Jean's culinary expertise.

When the napkins were finally placed beside the plates with everyone complaining about eating too much – Art asked the inevitable: "Did you hear anything from Dr. Givens about the biopsy?"

Jean immediately asked in a startled voice, "*What biopsy?*"

"You haven't told her about this?

"No, I thought I'd leave that up to you. I knew you'd tell us both when you thought the time was right."

"Guys, the biopsy was just a formality, I'm afraid." Mark said in a low monotone. "But – to answer your question – no, I didn't get any additional information from the doctor this afternoon. I assume I'll get the final word in the morning." His voice began trailing off even more than before and with obvious difficulty in continuing, said, "I hate telling you this almost as bad as I hated hearing it – but, in the professional opinion of Dr. Keli Givens, et al, I have been blessed with advanced pancreatic cancer. In all probability, the biopsy results will confirm that fact in the morning."

A sudden, audible intake of air from both husband and wife was the only response for several seconds while the gravity of Mark's statement sunk in. *"Oh my God,"* Jean finally blurted out in total disbelief. "When did you find this out, Mark?"

"This morning, when I visited with my doctor to get the results of the CT scan. The radiologist and Dr. Givens were pretty much in complete agreement in their diagnoses. In lieu of a second opinion, I opted for the biopsy this afternoon. I don't expect a lot of good news from the results."

"If the biopsy confirms the diagnosis, what are the chances for successful treatment?" Art asked.

"I've been told to get my affairs in order. There is little or no chance for survival – with or without treatment. Typically, I have between three and six months to live." Mark said, dejectedly, to no one in particular as his glazed stare was fixed on some point outside the bay window. "I have to live really fast to stuff 20 years into six months," he added, with a hollow laugh.

Art was speechless hearing the terrible fate forecast for his surrogate brother. In an effort to compose himself, he got up slowly from the table and walked to the bar without really knowing why. At the bar, he took down three brandy snifters, sat them on the bar and stared at them as his hands gripped the edge of the bar waiting for his eyes to dry before attempting to fill the pregnant glassware. He was taking too much time with the glasses and began to feel uncomfortable about not rejoining Jean and Mark at the table.

Jean, too, was having considerable difficulty vocalizing her emotions. She got up from her chair – went around the table and stood behind Mark, placed both hands on the back of his neck and gently massaged his neck and shoulder. Then after several moments, she bent and placed her arms tightly around him with her face pressed firmly against his cheek and softly said – almost choking, "How can we help, my darling?"

Mark felt the warm tears from Jean's eyes share a common path down his face and hers as they dropped silently to his chest.

CHAPTER TEN

The confirming report from Dr. Givens hit him like a wrecking ball. Mark had never contested the fact that he would eventually die, but to medically establish the time it would happen was something he wasn't particularly prepared for. He had, on occasion, imagined the scenario, but had never dwelled upon it to any extent. Now is the time, he thought. I guess I'd better start getting my shit together and decide how I want to spend my last few months. Do I want to just lie down? Do I want to do all the life-threatening things that I've sometimes thought about doing – but didn't because they were, well, life threatening? Do I want to do something bizarre and out of character? *What*? *What*? God, I don't know. Should I travel all over the country and try each crackpot would-be cure or should I accept the fact that there is no cure and be done with it? God, I just don't know. Gotta think!

He knew there would be no more of his allotted time spent with the company. With that thought firmly fixed in his mind, he turned to the keyboard on his computer – pulled up his word processor and started his letter of resignation. His hunt-and-peck typing was not overly efficient, but he didn't want to have Mattie type it for him and learn of his decision through a dictation.

June 12, 2002

Mr. Robert Murphy
President, C.E.O.
Specialty Engineering & Design, Inc.
112 N. McLean Blvd.
Memphis, TN 38105

Dear Mr. Murphy:

It has been my pleasure to have served the Engineering Department of Specialty Engineering and Design, Inc. for the better part of thirty-four years. Aside from my Military Service, I have spent an entire working-lifetime with this company. I have no memory of regret. I hope my tenure lends credence to the sincerity of my comments. No man could be blessed with a more rewarding and satisfying career. My co-workers have been talented and dedicated to the growth and well-being of the company. The talents of management, engineering, and support staff have gained us tremendous respect throughout the industry and an enviable customer base that remains loyal and satisfied.

I have enjoyed participating in the evolution of Engineering Science from slide-rule calculations to the accuracy of powerful computers – from drafting tables, pencils and erasers, "T"-squares and triangles to computer-aided design programs that continue to leave me awe-struck. I'm sure the science will continue to evolve long after I've ceased to be a part of it.

Retirement, for some, is a time to look forward to. I, personally, have always looked forward to it with some dread and apprehension. How do I stop doing the things from which I gain such personal satisfaction? The time for me to find out is at hand, and with deep regret, I submit this letter as my decision to resign my position with the company and its board.

With further regret, the resignation will be effective immediately.

Reasons, perhaps, are unimportant, but age and declining health are at the forefront of my decision. I will remain at your service for any unfinished business I leave behind and will consult, at your pleasure, in assigning a replacement for my position.

Most sincerely,

Mark R. Stevens
Vice President, Engineering

Once satisfied with his letter, he reached for the telephone and dialed 1112, the direct line to Bob Murphy, the company President and CEO. He asked the secretary to connect him to the President if he didn't have anyone in his office at the moment.

"Yeah, Mark! What's up?"

"Bob, if you've got a minute, I need to come by and visit with you. It's pretty important."

"Sure, come on up. I'm free until after lunch. It's not about that *widget* that you're working on for Global is it?"

"No, it's a little bit more personal than that. I'll be right up."

"OK, see you in a minute."

Mark breathed a deep breath, held it for a bit, then heaved from his chair and headed for the door. As he passed Mattie's desk, he said, "Mattie, I'm going up to Bob's office for a few minutes. Hold my calls, please, and I'll catch them when I get back down. By the way, if you don't have any lunch plans, let's covey-up about noon, and I'll buy you a 'Kosher' ham sandwich. There are some things I need to go over with you and I don't know if I'll be around much this afternoon. While I'm visiting with Bob, will you contact the department heads and let them know I need to meet with them for a few minutes right after lunch – here in my office?"

"The sky is falling! The sky is falling! My tightwad boss is taking me to lunch." She drew the back of her hand to her forehead that she had pointed skyward and added: "Maury, pinch me. I'm having a nightmare and need to wake up. And yes, I'll contact the department heads. What's that all about?"

"Could you, perhaps, be just a little bit more dramatic?" he asked in the voice reserved for verbal bouts with Mattie. "I hate it when you are so damned blasé about everything I offer you."

He doubted if he'd gotten in the last word, but if she responded, he didn't hear her as he headed for the elevator that would take him the extra two floors to Bob's office-suite. Two floors that he usually accessed from the stairs; allowing him a brief opportunity to get his circulation going to relieve the tightness inherent to sitting at a desk most of the time. Not so, today! The tightness on this fine spring day was not a result of sitting at his desk.

Bob's secretary, Brenda, looked up from her work and said "Hi, Mr. Stevens, what brings you up to *high country*?" She was fairly new and hadn't gotten comfortable with calling the Vice President of Engineering (who was 30 years her senior) by his first name. "Mr. Murphy is *vacant* if you need to see him."

"Thanks, Brenda! He's expecting me."

Brenda pressed a button on the intercom and announced: "Mr. Stevens is here." To which the intercom responded, "Fine, tell him to come on in."

Bob Murphy was a physically small man of about 50 years old; with reddish-gray hair receding ever-farther back from his forehead. His black eyes seemed like they belonged in some other face and they shined like marbles over the half-lens reading glasses that seemed an integral part of his round, blustery, Irish face. A ready smile appeared when he saw Mark enter the room. He was impeccably dressed, as his *clotheshorse* personality dictated, without a wrinkle in a bankers-gray, Brooks Brother's suit. How can a man work all day in a suit without getting a wrinkle? Mark silently asked himself as he extended his hand in greeting?

"What's so personal, my friend," he asked while shaking Mark's hand. "You didn't knock-up one of the girls in the secretary pool, did you?" He let out a loud, good-natured laugh at his view of a "personal" scenario.

"No, it's not quite that bad, but it's pretty serious," he said as he took one of the comfortable chairs facing Bob's desk.

"I don't know any other way of starting this conversation, Bob, except to get right to the point."

He looked the CEO right in the eye, involuntarily hesitated as he took yet another deep breath and said, "Bob, I've been diagnosed with Pancreatic Cancer. I'll be leaving the Company immediately."

Bob Murphy slammed his hands to his desk and raised himself halfway out of his chair – almost shouting: "*Jesus Christ*, Mark!" Then after a rather long pause while shaking his head negatively, he continued with: "Rumor has it that you'd been seeing a doctor, but I had no idea it was something like this." He flopped, heavily, back into his chair and asked, "Are you absolutely sure? What's the prognosis? My God, man! Why didn't you let us know about this sooner? Maybe we could have helped you in some way."

"I just got the confirmation an hour ago, from my doctor. They've done all the tests, and a biopsy – it looks like the fudge is in the fan, as far as I'm concerned."

"Mark, I lost my father to pancreatic cancer, and I have to ask, did they catch it in time to give you any hope for successful treatment?"

"No, that's the really bad news. It's inoperable and seems to have spread pretty extensively. Not good!"

After letting the news sink in for a few long moments, Mark continued with, "Bob, I've written a letter of resignation to formalize my decision and give you something to present to the board."

"I don't know what to say. I'm devastated! I'm at your service if there's anything I can do to help. And, by the way, you're not resigning from the company. I'll put you on "Temporary Assignment" until this can be resolved. Do what you have to do and start this afternoon. I know the way you have your department set up and you can reassign your work and manage with a phone call a day for a couple of weeks until Mattie gets the others lined out."

"You don't need to do that, Bob. I'll get my workload spread out and submit my recommendations as who I think will be capable of taking over my job. There are several you might consider within the department. Of course, if you choose, you could search elsewhere for a replacement, but I'll put our guys up against any in the business." After a short pause with no response from Bob, Mark added, "You might want to call a special meeting of the Board and let everyone know that I've retired. I don't like it, but it needs to be done as soon as possible. I don't want to leave loose ends. I will appreciate your not going into a lot of detail as to why I'm leaving so suddenly. I hope the letter of resignation will take you off the hook."

"You're a special part of this company Mark and a major factor in our continued success. You know we don't abandon our people just when they need us the most. The "Temporary Assignment" still stands until this is resolved. I'll contact the board members and see when we can meet. They're all going to be very disappointed when I tell them of your *retirement*.

Mark handed Bob his letter and stood to leave. Bob stood with him and made his way around his desk. Because of his height, Bob felt a little awkward as he reached to put his arm around his friend's shoulder as he escorted him to the door, saying, "Look buddy, you do what you have to do, and please, if there is any way I can possibly help you get through this, all you have to do is let me know, and it's a done deal."

"Thanks Bob, I sincerely appreciate your offer. I would give anything if there was something anyone could do. Right now, I think I'm more afraid of having to tell Mattie what's going on than I am of the cancer." Mark chuckled a bit to himself and added, "*You* could tell her, if you genuinely want to help."

Bob feigned terror as he threw his hands up into in the universal "I give up!" position and said; "I offered to do anything *reasonable* to help you. I put that chore a little bit beyond reasonable."

They both chuckled at the description of *reasonable* as Mark continued while making his way to the door: "I'm taking her to lunch this afternoon and I guess I'll break the news to her then. Knowing her, she'll probably kill me on the spot, and all this will be moot. I've also set up a meeting with the department heads to inform them of my *retirement*. I won't be going into a lot of detail as to the reason, but they need to know I'm out, and the sooner the better."

Bob was still standing in the doorway as Mark nodded to Brenda and left. He was still unwrinkled, but had lost his "peacock" demeanor as he absorbed the sadness within him. Mark was a close friend, and he had little hope of seeing him recover. He turned, slowly, back into his office as the outer office door closed behind Mark.

The elevator came quickly. Too quickly, he thought as he dreaded the upcoming meeting with Mattie; and, too quickly, the doors reopened after the short two-flight trip. He found himself in front of Mattie's desk – all too quickly.

"Tell your boss that you've got PMS, or something, and you need to take your lunch break a little early. And no, we're not stopping by that little motel with the *full-flow* waterbeds and the hourly rental rates that you love so much. I am not your sex toy!"

Mattie donned her most-shocked, wide-eyed expression and said, "Is there *really* a little motel down there by the river that rents *full-flow* waterbeds by the hour… and maybe has XXX movies on the TV… and maybe has garages to hide your car in… and maybe it's on the west side of the street between those two *tittie-bars* that also *rent* their employees by the hour? I've never heard of such a thing!"

"You're new to Memphis, I see. You're going to have to get out more and enjoy some of our other cultural landmarks."

"OK, big spender, let's go. You better have a 'Visa' with you that isn't already maxed out. I was *born* to *do* lunch on someone else's money. By the way, your department heads will be in your office at one-thirty."

They continued the caustic chitchat throughout the elevator ride and on to the parking lot where they found Mark's green Buick. He opened the door for her and ignored the, "Ain't *this* some shit!" remark she made as she heaved her abundant body into the passenger seat of the car. He couldn't help but chuckle as he walked around to the driver's side and climbed in, thinking: Is she a piece of work, or what?

"Is seafood OK?" Mark asked as he was backing out of the parking space.

"I really don't care as long as it's expensive and presented in air-conditioned comfort." she replied.

"I was thinking of maybe a fish sandwich at McDonalds. That's pretty expensive for this *date,* and it *is* air-conditioned."

"You pull into a McDonalds, and I swear I'll tear my clothes half off and start screaming that I'm being abducted."

The idle banter continued during the drive to *Amos' Famous Fish Camp*; a locally popular restaurant specializing in

Cajun cuisine surrounded by a highly stylized and trendy *Fish-Camp* décor. The friendly, casual and comfortable atmosphere seemed like the best place to let Mattie know that their relationship was about to be altered by the most dramatic of circumstances – assuming of course, he didn't chicken-out on his announcement.

The parking lot was getting unusually full at Amos' even though it was only eleven thirty-five, and still early for the noontime crowd. Mark pulled up to the door of the restaurant and asked Mattie to go in ahead and sign up for a table, if they were full. He'd park the car and join her inside.

When Mark entered the restaurant, Mattie wasn't at the maître d's desk, so he went into the seating area and searched for her in the "no-smoking" section. When he finally spotted her, he wondered, How in the hell could that woman get a window table at this time of day? I won't ask how, but I *will* enjoy it.

Mattie was already devouring the menu as Mark approached the table; she looked up, briefly, as he pulled out a chair and said, "I'm going to have page two and maybe half of page three."

"Maybe I should call the Visa people before I let the waiter take our order." Mark mumbled in response.

The waiter brought water to the table and introduced himself as "Mark". Mattie rolled her eyes and mumbled: "*Oh God!*" The waiter asked if they were ready to order and would they care for a cocktail or anything from the bar.

Mark ordered a martini, dry, with two olives, without hesitation. Mattie looked up from her menu and gave Mark one of her "looks", and with a little bit of hesitancy, ordered a glass of "house" Chardonnay. Both Mark and Mattie asked to wait until the drinks arrived before ordering their food.

While waiting for the waiter to bring the drinks and take the food order, Mark asked Mattie about the several engineering schedules that were pending and what progress was being made. He asked if anyone was running behind enough to be concerned and other office nonsense that kept him away from the real reason for bringing her here in the first place.

Mattie responded with: "What the hell are you talking about? I put those schedule reports on your desk every morning. All that stuff I bring you isn't *junk mail,* you know. You might try reading some of it."

Before he could defend himself, the waiter brought their drinks and asked if they were ready to order.

Mark and Mattie ordered their lunch with Mark asking for another Martini – then adding, "I'd also like a glass of iced tea when you bring the meal. Hopefully, I'll still be able to recognize my food when it gets here." The waiter smiled and hurried back to the wait station to start the process of getting their lunch to them as quickly as possible so they would leave and make room for the growing line of customers, waiting at the entrance of the restaurant.

An awkward silence fell between them as they both looked out the window of the restaurant; watching the uninteresting flow of traffic on the busy street. Mark was about to break the silence when the waiter returned with his drink. Mark thanked him. Mattie rolled her eyes again before saying, "You don't have martinis for lunch, what's the occasion?"

"You're the occasion, my dear." and held the martini glass up to her as for a toast.

The silence fell again. Mark thought, *Jesus...* this isn't working out, as he turned again to the window. I don't have the guts to tell her. She knows something's wrong and I just don't have the guts to blurt it out. No openings! No appropriate time! Still, I've got to do it before we get back to the office. I hate to hurt her. God, I hate to hurt this woman. Where in the hell is our food? Oh God, I wish she'd light into me about something. Chew my ass! Anything! Just get that goddamned food out here so I'll have something to do other than look out this stupid window.

Although it was probably 70 degrees in the restaurant, Mark was starting to sweat, and he used the napkin in his lap to wipe his forehead and lips. Thankfully, the food came just in time, and he was off the hook for the rest of the meal. His sweating stopped.

The food was as good as they'd become accustomed to and the conversation turned to light comments about the food, its preparation and presentation. Mattie, inadvertently, made eye contact with a lady she knew from their travel club and smiled at her brightly as she made an exaggerated wave from halfway across the room. Then turning back to Mark she dropped the smile immediately, leaned forward over her plate to ensure confidentiality and said, "You have just seen the biggest Jewish bitch this side of New York City. I won't go into it, but trust me, they broke the mold."

"*You*? You, Matilda Goldberg, the quintessential Jewish bitch, can call that nice looking woman over there a Jewish bitch." Mark half raised in his chair as if to leave the table then added, "I have *really* got to meet this woman."

Mattie looked at Mark with one of "those" looks and Mark sat back down, laughing at Mattie's red face. The other woman was in a similar posture with her luncheon companion. Similar glances were also being exchanged. Funny! Mark would have loved to hear the conversation from the other table. It had to be a "classic".

The waiter had, with some discreetness, left the check folder on the edge of the table near Mark. "Have you about had it?" He asked Mattie as he picked up the check folder and opened it. He gasped loudly, and sheepishly looked at Mattie and asked, "Look, can I borrow about forty dollars till payday? I wasn't expecting *this* much fun."

Mattie balled up her napkin and drew back as if to throw it at Mark as he made the defensive gesture of putting both forearms in front of his face and ducking – laughing like the village idiot and screaming "OK! OK! I've got the Visa! I've got the Visa."

Mark placed his credit card in the folder with the check and told Mattie, "I'm parked a half block from here. Why don't you sign for this and give the waiter a twenty-per-cent tip and I'll pick you up at the door... just like the queen you are? Should I say 'Hi' to the other lady on my way out?"

Mattie picked up her knife this time. Mark chuckled his way toward the door, using an exaggerated *quickstep* the first few feet away from the table.

Well, I didn't spoil her lunch too badly, he thought. But I still chickened-out.

Mattie was waiting just outside the entrance of the restaurant as Mark drove up and opened the door for her without getting out of the car. She, again, heaved herself into the passenger seat and said, "Thanks for lunch, my friend," as she handed him his credit card and reached for her seat belt.

"You're welcome my friend. It was my pleasure." Then the silence set in again like a thick fog that could be felt within the confines of the Buick.

They drove the five or six miles back to the office in a strained silence. The sparse conversation was limited to comments about the food or the "Jewish bitch" and was mumbled almost incoherently with neither of them looking at the other.

Jesus, I've got to tell her, Mark thought as they prepared to turn into the office parking lot.

As he made the final turn, Mattie broke the silence with, "You're not going to tell me, are you?"

"Tell you what?"

"You know very well you didn't drag me out here just to feed me snapper, and then bring me straight back to the office. I'm not getting out of the car until you tell me what's going on with you. So, let's get with it, sport."

Mark pulled into his parking space, put the car in *Park*, unfastened his seat belt and deliberately folded his arms across the steering wheel and turned his head toward the driver's side window. He took about three deep breaths, and then turned slowly back toward Mattie. He was having trouble getting his breath now, and the sweat reappeared near his temples and on his forehead. He was looking at Mattie now, and saw the determined look on her face that meant she wasn't going anywhere until she was satisfied with some answer from him.

"Darlin'", he started with painful difficulty, "I'm leaving the company... tomorrow."

"That's bad, but it also means I can leave too, and I'm ready for that. You still haven't told me why, and I have to suppose it's something about the visits you've had with doctors for the past couple of weeks. Visits you haven't said a damn thing about since the first *specialist*"

Mark thought he was choking as he blurted out: "Mattie, I've got advanced pancreatic cancer. They've given me three to six months to live... with or without treatment."

Mark didn't see any change in expression on Mattie's face. She turned head forward and slowly unfastened her seat belt. She paused for a long couple of seconds then leaned her large body toward Mark as far as she could go; at which point she reached for him with both arms and pulled him toward her in an all-engulfing hug that only women of her stature can give. His head found her shoulder, and his arms joined in the awkward, loving embrace. She didn't say a word, nor did he.

After whatever time it took for them to meld their emotions, seconds or minutes, within the embrace, Mattie released her arms, placed both hands on his shoulders and pushed him and herself upright.

Mark looked into the saddest, driest eyes he had ever seen; knowing that he would never be able to erase the moment from his mind.

Mattie said, in a voice so soft and calm that it was almost surreal, "I won't be going back upstairs with you. I'm going home. Make any excuse you need to – or no excuse. I really don't care. I'll be at my desk in the morning."

Mark turned off the engine and watched Mattie open her door and leave. He got out on his side and stood to watch Mattie walk slowly toward the gray Mercedes 500 SEL Maury had given her for their 50th wedding anniversary. The distinctive, rolling, side-to-side gait, often seen in women of her size and age, accented the obvious trauma she'd received upon hearing Marks dreaded confession.

After watching Mattie until she entered her car, Mark made his way back toward the office, thinking, oh God I hurt her! I'd give an arm to take that back. She doesn't deserve it. What a day! *My God*, what a day!

*   *   *

Mattie fumbled in her purse until she found the keys to her car, opened it and sat down behind the wheel. She tried several times to get her key into the ignition and began screaming obscenities at the offending key and its would-be receptacle. She became increasingly agitated and violent with each unsuccessful try. Finally, her uncontrolled stabbing produced results and the key entered the hole, mostly by accident, and she started the car.

Still furious, she exploded in a fit of anger and hurled her purse into the passenger-side window with all her might; spilling the contents over the seats and floor mats, both front and rear.

With the car running and both hands locked firmly to the steering wheel, Mattie felt the first defocusing tear form – burning her eyes and blurring her vision. She didn't wipe it away and soon it grew until it fell through the heavy mascara lining her eyes and down through the other layers of make-up she routinely wore.

The first tear only opened the gates for more, and she sat, unmoving, until the front of her dress was noticeably wet. No conscious thoughts were with her, just the sadness, the anger, the helplessness – and the tears that flowed with increasing abundance – down through the brown streaks of mascara that had become an unattractive mask of despair. The sobs started slowly and at spaced intervals similar to labor, and then grew into great waves of heaving convulsions that couldn't be contained or stopped.

She rolled, slowly, from vertical to horizontal as she lost her grasp on the steering wheel. Even more than gravity, the weight of her anguish pulled her down across the front seat of the car as she buried her tear-soaked face into the folds of her arms. The sheer power of the large woman in her grief rocked the big Mercedes like an unwieldy, coffin-gray cradle.

*   *   *

Mark stood behind his desk; his hands thrust deep in his pockets, staring out the large corner window of his office. He was staring at Mattie's car in the parking lot below. God, what a day, he thought, as the knock on the door signaled the arrival of his department heads.

Two down, one to go, he thought as he opened the door.

CHAPTER ELEVEN

Mark left the parking lot not knowing, again, what to do in the middle of the day. For lack of a better plan, he pointed the car toward his house where he might be able to consider what to do for the short term and perhaps get a clue as to what he wanted to do for the last few months of his life. Carole came immediately to mind. Is it too selfish of me to want her in my life, knowing it will complicate the hell out of things if we become close? He asked himself. Hard choices – really hard choices!

By the time he made it to his driveway, the decision to call Carole had already been made. If she turned out to be no more than an occasional dinner date, then he would never have to let her know what was happening. However, if their relationship began to develop into something more serious, then more serious decisions would have to be made. He was somewhat embarrassed with himself for thinking only of his feelings and comfort instead of the serious psychological hardships Carole may face if they became too involved. All that didn't matter at the moment; he just knew he wanted to see her – not to whine about what was happening to him, but just to enjoy her company.

Mark went directly to the bedroom, after he entered the house and picked up Carole's card that he'd left lying on the dresser in his bedroom. He read the number on the card and without hesitation, dialed her home phone.

"Hello!"

"Hi... Carole? This is Mark Stevens. I don't know if you remember me or not, but I'm the guy that almost became the 'lump' on your couch the night before last."

"No – I don't think I remember you! She said. "You'll have to be more specific. There are guys threatening to become lumps on my couch all the time, and it's pretty difficult to keep up with all of you." Then, hesitating just long enough to let go the low, sexy laugh that Mark now felt she had a patented, continued with, "It's good to hear from you. I was starting to become a little worried that you might not have thought the other night was, uh, *fulfilling* enough to warrant another call."

"I wanted to call you yesterday, but I had a really full day and a pre-arranged evening with some friends. The friends have already chewed my butt for not inviting you to join us – but I didn't know at the time or I would have called. Which brings us to today – do you have anything *special* going on this afternoon? I gave notice at work today and have a beautiful afternoon that would be a shame to waste indoors. Would you like to join me for a beer and a walk down by the river?"

"You *quit*?"

"I damn sure did. And, it's about time. I'm just kinda new at spending beautiful June afternoons doing anything I want to. So, there's a little 'celebration' in me that makes it difficult to just sit around."

"Your sense of timing is awesome." She said. "I was just getting ready to call Alice to see if she wanted to do anything; for the same reasons you mentioned. That sounds wonderful to me."

"Maybe we can chunk some rocks in the river and sit under a bridge or something. I'll bring a bottle of wine just in case that may be more appealing than the beer. I'm going to take a quick shower and will be ready to leave here in about 30 minutes. Would that be OK for you?"

"Perfect! I'll see you in about an hour." She said, with obvious enthusiasm.

Mark was exhilarated. He suddenly felt all the excitement of courtship. There was vitality in him that had been absent since the early days with Karen. My God, he thought, as he rushed for the shower, you'd think I'd be too old for this kind of shit.

With his clothes strewn half on the bed and the other half tossed in the general direction of the clothes hamper, he felt his face as a matter of habit and decided he'd better shave, just to be on the safe side. I swear I'm going to ask Carole what she thinks about beards, he thought, as he started shaking a can of shaving cream.

He rushed, headlong, into the task of cleaning up and was shaved, showered, dried and nude in front of his closet in less than 20 minutes. Selecting a pair of fresh khakis and a knit golf shirt, threw them on the bed with the clothes he'd just taken off and grabbed underwear and socks – with the speed of a man leaving the bedroom of a married woman whose husband was knocking at the door. Dressed, he made his final trip to the closet and slipped on a pair of loafers and headed for his car – stuffing change, wallet, handkerchief and money clip into his pockets as he went.

He punched the garage door opener to free the Buick, and jumped in with a sense of urgency – wondering, *why*? Perhaps it was the newness of Carole – an attempt to feel the freshness of a new relationship and enjoy all the pleasures of learning about someone that appealed to him so much – so quickly. It made no difference. He liked the way he felt and unconsciously committed to enjoy all this new and wonderful experience had to offer – come what may.

Making a quick stop by the liquor store, he selected a bottle of wine and was out the door in less than five minutes - headed for the freeway on-ramp. Driving much faster than he normally did, he arrived at Carole's apartment about ten minutes short of the allotted hour, thinking, if she's ready, maybe she's looking forward to this afternoon as much as I am.

Looking at the mailboxes embedded into the wall of the entryway, he found *Wilson* and punched the button next to the built-in speaker above the mailbox. Almost immediately, Carole answered, "Yes?" To which Mark responded, "I'm here representing Jehovah's Witnesses and would like to visit with you about... well, you know."

"Do you have videos?"

"No, but I was hoping we could make a few."

"Will we have witnesses?"

"You know, I could be freezing down here while you fantasize about videos."

"It's nearly 80 degrees out – but come on up anyway," Carole said with "the laugh".

When he left the elevator on Carole's floor, she was standing at the entrance to her apartment – posed as provocatively as she could by standing on one leg with the other leg bent at the knee so the foot could rest flat on the door casing. She had one hand on her hip, and the other stretched to the far casing. Her head was lowered slightly with the look of a drugged-up, open-mouthed Ralph Lauren model – dressed, essentially, as Mark was – in khakis, knit shirt and loafers.

"Are you truly a witness for Jehovah?" she breathed, heavily, as Mark approached.

"Well, to tell the truth, his name was Jehovah Ortowski and I went with him to a Notary, once."

When Mark got to the door, she relaxed the pose, and they hugged warmly as she kissed him on the cheek, saying excitedly, "I'm so glad you called. I was about to go stir crazy trapped in this apartment."

"And I am just as glad I caught you before you called Alice. It's a perfect day, and the river should be beautiful. We should have three or four hours before we lose the sun. Let's make it fun."

"You've got it! Do I need to bring anything or are we just going to *wing* it'?"

"No, I don't think you'll need anything. I've got the wine in the car, and if we get hungry, we should be able to find some *grease* burgers or dogs somewhere on the riverfront. It's our day – we'll do as we choose."

"I am so ready!" she said as she closed the door behind her and reached for Mark's hand.

With Carole's help, Mark found his way to the Interstate and made the short drive to the huge lattice-covered bridge that joined Tennessee and Arkansas across the *Big Muddy*. Taking the last exit before entering the bridge itself, he slowly drove alongside the mammoth concrete abutment supporting the east end of the bridge. After a few moments, they arrived at a small park that was sheltered by the bridge and offering several tables, portable toilets and two rows of marked asphalt parking spaces. He parked the Buick, and they both just stared at the expanse of the Mississippi spread out before them in a panorama of boats, barges and rolling, muddy water that faded out of sight in both directions.

"I'm always fascinated by it," He said as he removed his seat belt and opened the car door.

"I hate to say this, but this is my virgin view of the river from down here – and I agree, it is fascinating."

Mark started around the car to open Carole's door, but she had it opened on her own and was stepping out by the time he got to her. He extended his hand to help her and they walked hand in hand to the shade of the bridge, listening to the strange mixture of sounds and silence that permeated the area. The liquid sound of the river was almost imperceptible, and it was strange that so much power and movement could remain a whisper – interrupted by the steady thump and creak of the traffic crossing the bridge above. The river traffic, too, had its own sound, and combined, they all contributed to the serenity of the place. The sharp contrast between the shade of the bridge, and the sunshine extending from it, made it somewhat difficult to decide where they should position themselves to enjoy these marvels of engineering and nature.

After what seemed like an unusually long period of silence from the two visitors, Carole finally asked with mock sincerity, "Are there any trolls?"

"You never know. Maybe you should stay real close to me – just in case."

They walked slowly along the asphalt pathway that followed the bank of the river; enjoying the sunshine and light conversation. And, as promised, they "chunked" rocks into the muddy waters as they made their way – trying, unsuccessfully, to hit various floating targets that rushed by in the strong current. Each made unflattering comments to the other when the cast stone landed far from its intended point of impact. "Wow! How embarrassing would this be if Mary Magdalene or some other 'ho' needed to be stoned… and they had a whole *multitude* of folks like us?" Mark commented to her giggling.

After walking for about 15 minutes, Mark asked, "Why don't we go back toward the car, and I'll open the wine so I can keep my blood/alcohol level within acceptable limits?"

"You're the tour guide," She said, "and you haven't disappointed me so far."

After their 30-minute walk in the sunshine, the cool shade of the bridge was a welcome relief from the heat of the afternoon. Mark had retrieved the wine, the glasses and a corkscrew from the car, and they had taken a seat at one of the several concrete bench-tables scattered about under the bridge. As he poured wine into the plastic "glasses", Carole asked, "What made you decide to quit your job so suddenly… or was it sudden?"

"Oh, I haven't quit entirely. I'll be consulting with them for a month or so until they have a replacement. I won't be doing the daily office routine, but I'll be in phone contact to put out any fires that need my attention, and if necessary, I'll show up. It's been in the *planning* stage for some time now, and I don't think there was a great deal of surprise when I presented my letter of resignation. I hate leaving, and they hate my leaving, but it's time – and I don't want to put it off until I can't have any fun. In other words, I met you and retirement now seems like something I can enjoy."

"Thank you!" she said.

"I don't mean to sound like I'm placing demands on you for making my retirement enjoyable. You have just brought to light the fact that I can still have fun with a woman, and that was an incredible gift. It gave me the little push I needed to go ahead and bail out."

They enjoyed their wine and watched the sun descending over the water while making idle chitchat – enjoying themselves. Mark asked, "Are you getting hungry? We could search out some wild burgers if you'd like?"

"Why don't we start back toward my apartment before the poor people having to work for a living make their break and I'll fix a snack there? I'll go one step further – if you don't have other plans, I'll let you decide if I learned anything from those cooking classes I told you about the other night. We're back to where we started – dinner on me".

"Well – I am pretty busy this evening. I have to watch *Gilligan's Island* about six. It would have to be a pretty special dinner for me to miss that."

Carole slapped/shoved him on the shoulder several times, feigning anger at his remark and said, "I understand that the *better* brands of rat poisons are nearly tasteless. Nearly as *tasteless* as some people I know!" She then tickled him, aggressively, in the ribs as they both laughed out loud at the nonsense. He stood and pulled her up from the bench. With his arms wrapped tightly around her waist, he twirled her around several times, to their mutual delight. When he stopped twirling and let her feet back to the ground, they kissed lightly on the mouth and suddenly the laughter was put aside and they became more serious. Mark put the half-empty wine bottle, and the plastic "glasses" in the nearby trash barrel, then placed his arm around Carole's shoulder as they walked slowly toward the car – each quietly enjoying the closeness of the moment. It had been a delightful afternoon and the evening promised to be equally enjoyable.

Back on the Interstate, headed for Carole's apartment, they were pleasantly surprised at the ease of passage in what was supposed to be "rush-hour" traffic. Mark asked Carole if they needed to stop for anything before reaching the apartment.

"No, I think I have everything we need. I've had plenty of time to stash *goodies* designed to trap unsuspecting males; assuming I could ever be successful in luring one to my lair. You seem to be about as *unsuspecting* as they come." She laughed, and Mark punctuated the laugh with a brief tickle to her ribs, in response to her smart-alec remark.

CHAPTER TWELVE

"Why don't you fix us a drink and I'll see what I can find in the fridge that hasn't turned green," Carole said as they entered the apartment.

"I can do that," Mark responded. "Is everything behind the bar?"

"I think so," she said, and then added, "There's wine back there too, if you'd prefer that."

"Scotch seems like the Christian thing to do at this time of day. What can I get you?"

"I'll have the same – with soda, please."

Mark made his way to the bar – took down two glasses and scrounged around the unfamiliar storage cabinets until he found the scotch, soda and finally the ice in the icemaker – built-in under the bar. Without measuring, he poured two *serious* drinks and carried them back to the kitchen area where Carole was busily preparing fruit, cheese and bread for the promised snack. He sat one drink on the countertop near

Carole and sipped from the other as he asked, "Is there anything I can do to help?"

"No, I'm about finished. Just make yourself comfortable and I'll be with you in a minute."

Mark sat his drink next to Carole's and wrapped his arms around her from behind and said, "This seems pretty comfortable right here," as he pulled her close, enjoying fully the feel of her body pressed next to his.

"I have a *knife!*" she said.

"You can use it to make me stop – or, you can use it to take advantage of me. Either way, I'd never argue with a woman carrying a *knife,*" he said as he felt her wiggle deliciously in his arms. "Besides, that's not a knife – it's a cheese cutter, and I think I'm tough enough to have you take a few thin slices off of me before I'd willingly let go of you."

Carole looked back over her shoulder and smiled at Mark. Then turned back to her work and shook her head negatively, chuckling at his remark.

He unlocked his hands from around her waist and moved them to the roundness of her hips, feeling the smooth contour of the flare from waist to hip and pulled her even closer. There was no resistance, and the firm contact of her body was becoming less friendly and more erotic. Carole was showing less and less interest in the condiment tray on the counter and apparently a much greater interest in Mark's state of arousal that was becoming more and more apparent as they stood in an upright *spoon* position. She turned to face Mark without releasing the close body contact and reached high with her arms to engulf his neck – pulling him to her as she leaned back, bracing herself on the counter.

The kiss was different from the brief exchange of two nights ago. He felt an eagerness and sense of urgency that was not present during their first meeting as her hands moved to the sides of his face pulling him deeper into the warmth of her mouth. The kiss was long, and her hands became more agitated as they moved from his face to his hips to pull him closer as the heat between them became an integral part of the moment. She released the kiss abruptly and for a second, Mark thought, *déjà vu* – until he looked into the half-closed eyes that were surrounded by a feverish flush to her face. She gasped for breath – twice, then hungrily searched for his mouth with a determined ferocity that took him by surprise.

The passion was not lost on Mark as his hands sought out the softness of her breasts and the firmness of the *buns-of-steel* that had so intrigued him in the beginning. Carole had pulled the tails of the golf shirt out of his trousers and was eagerly exploring the bare skin of his chest and back as they kissed. In order to maintain the intimate closeness while her hands were occupied elsewhere, she had raised her left leg and curled it around the back of Marks thighs – sporadically *spurring* him with her heel in cadence with an involuntary thrusting of her hips.

Mark, reluctantly, removed his arms from around her and in one quick, continuous movement pulled his shirt over his head and dropped it to the floor. Almost in the same movement, he raised Carole's shirt up over her breasts, exposing the skin of her torso and the lacy insignificance of a *Victoria's Secret* bra. When his arms were once again in place around her, he pulled her to him and felt the first exciting touch of her bare skin against his.

Still wrapped in each other's arms and still trying to maintain as much contact of lips and body as possible, Carole pushed herself (and Mark) away from the counter and started pulling him, wordlessly out of the kitchen toward the hallway leading to the double doors and the bedroom. Halfway to the doors, she stopped and in the same manner as Mark, removed her shirt. It too fell to the floor. After two more steps with Mark trying unsuccessfully to negotiate the hooks of her bra, Carole stopped again and in one deft manipulation, magically unfastened the offending hooks in the back of the garment. Then, with a simple shrug of her shoulders it too fell to the floor. At the most inappropriate of moments, Mark thought, well, we can always find our way back to the kitchen.

He couldn't contain himself when he first glimpsed the milky whiteness of her untanned breasts, and as the pulling and shuffling continued toward the bedroom, he lowered his head and kissed the taunt nipple exposed through his hands that had cupped the breast into a perfect cone. The vocal response from Carole indicated that she had noticed the attention – and the nipple, in return, rose to the occasion.

Somewhere between the kitchen and the double doors, Mark had discarded his loafers, adding to the clothing trail that led back to the kitchen. Upon opening the door to the bedroom suite, Carole pulled her feet off the floor by hanging onto Mark's neck. She then kicked her shoes in different directions to let them fall where they may. As soon as her feet were back on the floor she started fumbling with Mark's belt. She was having a difficult time in getting the job done, not unlike the problem Mark had faced with the bra. Mark released his arms from around her and quickly unfastened the belt, the button and the zipper on his trousers. Carole's hands slid down the smoothness of his skin and under the elastic of his boxers and began the slow descent of his trousers and underwear down and over the prominent bulge so desperate to be set free.

With her hands, she measured the entire length of his legs, following the khakis until she was kneeling. Her hands cupped his ankle and allowed him to step from the trousers without entanglement. Still kneeling, she placed her hands behind him on his upper thighs and pulled him forward as the side of her face fit evenly and snuggly on the upper portions of his muscular legs. He felt the softness of her hair and the warmth of her face next to him and stood quivering in anticipation as she slowly moved upward delivering warm kisses as she pressed herself to him. Without hesitation or inhibition, she engulfed him with her mouth and held him for several exquisite moments before continuing her trek back to his upper body.

Mark reached and pulled her back to standing and immediately started the same undressing scenario. She stood immobile with closed eyes as he slowly unfastened the beltless slacks. He knelt before her and was devouring the sight of each inch of her as the soft khakis were stripped away; first the delicate lace of the high-cut bikini panties and then the silkiness of her legs. Once the slacks were removed, she stood before him in only the most delicate of laces. As deliberate and calm as he tried to be, his hands shook, noticeably, as he reached to place the palms of his hands on her hips and then slid them down to caress the silkiness of her legs as the panties followed on the backs of his hands.

Once the panties were removed, Mark, still kneeling, sat back on his heels, dropped his arms to his side and uttered the first words spoken since they'd left the kitchen. "May I just stare at you for a moment? You are incredibly beautiful, and this is what I want to see each time I close my eyes and you are not within my reach."

She gently cupped his head in her hands and softly replied, "Do as you will."

He stared, in awe, for the several moments it took for him to be satisfied that the sight of her was indelibly frozen in his mind. Once satisfied, he reached for her again and instinctively mimicked Carole's trail of kisses until he was once again standing in a warm frontal embrace.

Once naked and aware of what was about to happen, the soon-to-be lovers relaxed somewhat. The driving urgency of the kitchen gave way to the more disciplined actions of an adult couple preparing to engage in an exercise that was expected to bring them each immense pleasure – anticipation and restraint now became an integral and important part of that pleasure.

Carole walked around the king-size bed and while staring openly at a nude and fully aroused Mark, pulled the bedcovers back. Standing on opposite sides of the bed, they both placed a knee on its edge, and as if choreographed, tumbled, one to the right, the other to the left, in perfect synchronization. They met in a full embrace near the center of the big bed.

Locked in another deep and wonderful kiss, their hands explored the other's body with the tactile dexterity of the blind. Reaching, pulling, caressing until the kiss finally broke and Mark started exploring with his mouth the wondrous places he'd found with his hands. He rolled over on top of her, and she wrapped her legs around his waist as he kissed first her breasts, then her stomach and finally the sensitive folds of her inner thighs at the junction of inner thigh and abdomen. He was surprised at her strength as she writhed beneath him. Even with all the weight of his upper body lying heavily on her hips, she tossed him about with apparent ease; unintelligible mumblings and moans escaped her open mouth as she rolled her head side to side. He placed his mouth full on the lips of her soul and entered with his tongue. The involuntary quiver he felt lasted a long ten seconds as she thrust toward him and a whimper of relief was heard as she momentarily relaxed and slumped back to the sheets.

With another burst of urgency, Carole reached for Mark's shoulders and pulled him upward with all her might. She was now the aggressor and was furiously positioning him for further intimacy. As soon as her lips could reach his, she attacked his mouth and forced her hand between their melded bodies, groping, successfully, for his penis. He transferred weight from Carole to his elbows and forearms and allowed her to guide him toward the center of her hips that were eagerly tilted up and forward in acute anticipation.

Poised at the entrance of her being, Mark slowly began the transfer of weight again, and as he entered her, concentrated with all his might on the incredible warmth that engulfed him. Inch by delicious inch, the gentle resistance gave way to ready acceptance until they were again pressed into a tight mold of sensuality. At first, there was little movement as they adjusted to each other – enjoying fully, the intensity of the moment. With slow, deliberate tenderness, Mark withdrew partially and with equal enjoyment returned to full penetration, repeatedly, with increasing frequency. Each of Mark's thrusts was met enthusiastically by opposing thrusts from Carole as they kissed feverishly and sporadically. With her knees up and widely spread, Carole's heels had once again found their way to the back of Mark's thighs; giving added leverage to the pounding she was encouraging. The first of several intense climaxes hit her almost by surprise as she arched fully to maintain contact, shuddered uncontrollably, relaxed and immediately repeated herself until Mark, unable to resist the inevitable any longer, was forced to join in the ultimate human pleasure.

They fell, totally expended, on and beside each other. Slowly coming back to reality, Mark noticed that Carole was quietly sobbing with her face turned away from him. He was startled and asked with great concern, "Are you all right?" as he gathered her in his arms and cradled her head with his hand.

"Yes... it had just been so long, and I was afraid that I might not work anymore. Give me a minute to get myself together, please. I'm sorry!"

Mark rolled to his back, pulling Carole with him. Her head snuggled on his chest as the sexual tension subsided and gave way to a feeling of deep, deep contentment.

CHAPTER THIRTEEN

Untangling from the entwined arms and legs without waking Carole was a bit of a chore, but Mark was able to get the job done with just minor adjustments, sighs and facial contortions from the offended bedmate. His clothes were in perfect reverse order as he made his way back to the kitchen and he was fully dressed as he started looking for the coffee filters and coffee in the unfamiliar surroundings of Carole's kitchen. He found both in the cabinet above the coffee maker and began the brewing ritual that would provide his accustomed caffeine jolt. After watching the pot until he heard the familiar gurgle, he searched for juice glasses – found them and poured two full glasses of orange juice that he found in the refrigerator.

He debated with himself as to whether or not he should wake Carole. He decided to carry the orange juice back to the bedroom, and if she was awake – give it to her and say goodbye. If she was still asleep, he would leave a note explaining the early exit.

When he opened the bedroom door, he could see that Carole was still sound asleep with the pillow he had just left, wrapped tightly in her arms. Smiling at the sight of her, he gently closed the door and carried the juice glass back to the refrigerator. He found a note pad and pen by the phone in the kitchen and wrote, "OK, so you saved my life... what else can you do? I had to be in the office early this morning. Coffee is in the pot! Will call later!"

On his way back to the bedroom, he snatched a flower from the vase of fresh flowers sitting on the table near the entry of the apartment – wiped the water off the stem with his handkerchief and carried the note and the flower back to the sleeping Carole. He took care to be as unobtrusive as possible as he laid the flower and the note where he should still be sleeping. He hesitated a moment, then bent and gave her a soft kiss on the lips. She smiled in her sleep, but still did not wake up.

He went back to the kitchen and stood by the counter, sipping the hot coffee and thinking, I am in *trouble!* Why does something so wonderful happen to me just when I'm unable to take advantage of it? I really don't know how to handle this. After spending the better part of seven years looking for someone I found interesting enough to spend real time with – she pops up when I have no time left. If I had an ounce of character, I'd tell her the situation right now and get it over with – let her make the decision as to whether or not to trash my sorry ass now or let the relationship run its course. Selfishness – that's what it is! I want, so badly, to feel the closeness again that I don't have the guts to take a chance on her acceptance of the situation. I couldn't blame her if she just walked away to avoid the consequences of losing someone for a second time in her life; assuming I've evaluated her interest correctly. My God! I just don't know what to do. It's pretty awful to discover, at 65, that you're a coward. I guess I haven't completely accepted the fact that I've had it. Where's the fear? Where's the feeling of hopelessness that should be in me by now? I know it's happening, but I can't get a grip on everything being over within a few months. I know one damn thing – cancer will not decide when I leave. It will definitely be a factor in my decision as when to go, but, by God, it will be my decision. I will not die of cancer!" Anger was building in him – not leaving room for fear and he decided that he'd rather be mad than scared – if given a choice.

With the troubling thoughts still racing around in his head, he rinsed the coffee cup and placed it in the dishwasher before heading for the door to leave. More uncharted waters lay ahead for him this fine morning as he tried to reorganize his thoughts to include the meeting with Mattie and how to arrange his affairs so that he might exit this earth with some acceptable degree of order.

After going home to clean up and get dressed for the office, Mark pulled into his parking space at five minutes till nine. He gathered the paperwork he'd brought and thought how ironic it was that it was still uncompleted after two years.

His attorney had suggested that he make some sort of arrangements for his estate should he become involved with a run-away *Peterbilt* or some other catastrophe that would leave him sort of dead. After promising to have the legal instruments back in his lawyer's office *in a few days*, Mark had procrastinated way too long and would have forgotten about them completely if his lawyer hadn't kept asking, "When are you going to get that estate stuff back in to me?" To which Mark would always reply – "I'll get right on it." Well, he thought, I'm finally getting *right on it*.

Mark saw Mattie at her desk as he left the elevator and asked, "How are you feeling this morning? I hated to hit you with all that bad news yesterday, but I knew you'd kill me if you heard it from someone else."

"I had some trouble turning off the tears last night, but I think I'll be alright." She paused for a couple of seconds, and then added, "Actually, I feel like I'm going to vomit every time I think about it."

"I know that feeling pretty well myself, so let's not think about it. Deal?"

"OK, deal," she said as her eyes started to glisten with unwanted tears. She regained her composure quickly and added, "When can I quit? I've about had it too."

"Well, of course, that's up to you, but it would be nice if you'd put it off for a month or so to get the new guy squared away. *You* can't be replaced – but you should select someone to sit at your desk and give them a few clues as to what goes on."

"No, I won't leave until all that's done. It won't be a labor of love."

"I know you won't leave before everything is in order. Just another reason I love you. Anyway, can you get someone up here today to take the calls? I'd like to have most of the day with you to take care of some personal things that need immediate attention."

Mark entered his office and placed all his paperwork on the conference table. He then sat at his desk and started rummaging through the short pile of documents and correspondence needing his attention.

He fought to maintain focus as he waited for Mattie and after about thirty minutes of initialing and signing papers, she opened the door and said she was ready to begin.

Mark got up from his desk and met Mattie by the conference table and said, "Mattie, before we start this mess, I have to ask if you are willing to be the 'Trustee' to my estate. I really don't have anyone else, so I'm in sort of a bind. I know it's an imposition, but you've been taking care of me for half my life and I hope you will do me this one last favor."

"Mark, I will be glad to do anything I possibly can to help you. I told you that earlier and I meant it, sincerely. Just let me know what you need done and then, please, forget about it. It will be taken care of – just as you choose to have it done."

Mark opened the envelope containing the papers from his attorney and said, "I've had this stuff for over two years but haven't filled it out because I didn't really know who would be handling it for me. There's an 'Advance Directive for Health Care'; a worksheet for my 'Will'; a 'Trust Agreement' for a 'Living Trust' and a 'Durable General Power of Attorney'. I also have my last Tax Statement and a current Financial Statement that will pretty much tell the tale of everything I have of value... personal items excepted. I've never been one to 'count my marbles' and I'm always pretty surprised when I see that I've amassed a small fortune without really being conscious of it. When the insurance is added to the total it will become even more substantial."

He slid the Financial and Tax Statements over to Mattie and as she glanced at the documents, exclaimed, "Mark, you're worth over ten and a half million dollars."

"I know!" he said. "And there lies the problem. What the hell do I do with it? I've never been a 'Scrooge', but then again, I've never been a spendthrift either. It's just sort of piled up – especially since Karen died. The company has a million-dollar life insurance policy as one of my benefits and I have also kept paying on my personal insurance policy of another half-million. I sure wish Karen and Sarah were still around to enjoy the spoils of my labor."

"Have you thought about what you want to do with it?"

"Yes, but not too seriously until the last couple of days. I thought I'd leave Art & Jean's kids a hundred thousand each, when they graduate from college or as an assistance to finish college if something should happen to Art. I think Art Jr. is a sophomore now and Nancy is a freshman. I can't keep up with them – maybe Nancy is a sophomore and Art Jr. is a junior. Don't know why I'd forget that. Anyway – I want you and Maury to take whatever you want and then, if there's enough left over, I'd like to have a foundation of some sort set up to help talented kids, without resources, be able to attain a decent education. You know, help them in high school or college if financial problems are keeping them from reaching their potential. If the foundation is more than you'd like to deal with, then I'll ask Dr. Givens if she'd be interested in placing the rest of the money in some research program that has potential for the treatment of pancreatic cancer. Maybe it would help speed up the time when she won't have to announce such dire consequences to others facing the same situation as me."

"As much as I appreciate the thought – Maury and I have done pretty well ourselves, financially. We're in about the same boat as you're in, regarding beneficiaries, I doubt if we'd be taking any of your money. Maury plans to sell the stores and retire as soon as I get things taken care of here. I do like the idea of a foundation for the kids, but I also would like to see some of it go to cancer research. It would be a difficult decision to select a favorite."

"I trust your good judgment. Do as you see fit. It's money that you can use or play with – your choice. You, Art and Jean are the only family I have, so I don't put a whole lot of restrictions on what's left after I check out. I'm glad you and Maury don't actually need the money, but you're welcome to it unless something really special comes up – really fast."

"Well, I wish something really special would come up really fast if it would make things more enjoyable for you."

"Funny you should mention that! Something really special has already entered my life – special to me anyway. You'll see the irony in this – I met a beautiful and interesting woman the other night, and I think I'm falling in love with her. Things like that don't happen to me and here I am with another problem ladled atop the cancer. I haven't told her what's going down – out of a selfish desire to hold on to her for just a little while. Help me with this – am I being cruel or is it just selfishness? She seems to care for me too, and I don't know where to stop it. I don't want her to be hurt by all this – and yet, I keep putting it off because I enjoy her company so much. She's bothering me more now than the cancer is."

"Oh Mark, it's not you that's being cruel – it's life itself. I have prayed you'd find someone to join your life for so long, and now – *life* manifests the definition of cruelty. I can't tell you when you tell her, but we both know you must – and sooner would be better than later if you think her feelings for you match your feelings for her. The longer you wait after you've discovered she's in love with you – if she falls in love with you – the closer you come to cruelty, and I don't think there's a cruel bone in your body. *And* – before I say another word – no matter what happens, don't even *think* about leaving town or breaking this off before I meet her. She has to be special. If she will be badly hurt when she finds out the truth, maybe I can help at some point in time."

"Oh, you'll meet her all right. I can't wait to show her off to you. You'll see the problem once you meet her. She's incredible!"

"Talk about paradoxical feelings – I'm so happy that you've met her and so sad that you meet her now; instead of five years ago while you still had the time to enjoy her. It just ain't fair!"

Mark stayed lost in thought for a few moments and then said, "I'll deal with it – it's just hard." After a few more moments of silent thought, he continued, "Well, I guess we'd better get on with the chore at hand. I'm leaving these documents with you to *fill in the blanks*. I think you know all the information that's called for. There's no need to mention the foundation or the research projects. Those items will be your decision once I'm out of here. Just fill in your name and my name where appropriate and I'll sign them. Art's kids' names are Nancy Louise Fletcher and Arthur James Fletcher, Jr. We'll have to get a couple of witnesses up here... and a notary for the signatures. When that's all done, I'll send them over to the attorney for filing. I guess you should make copies, after we've signed, for your records. We should make a copy of that *medical thing* for Dr. Givens and a copy of it for me to carry around just in case I unexpectedly end up in a foreign hospital or something."

"I doubt if I will, but, if I need you, will you stay pretty close to your cell phone?"

"Yeah, I'll keep an ear out for you. Darlin', I know this is a strain on you, but I really don't know of any other way to get it done. I want you to know how much I appreciate your help. You are truly wonderful. If you don't have any 'company business' for me, I'm going to go plan some *fun things* to do for the rest of my life."

"Get out of here before I start bawling."

CHAPTER FORTEEN

On the fourth ring, Carole's answering machine responded with, "Hi, this is Carole at 555-6712. Please leave a message."

"Hi, this is Mark, and I need to talk to you about a super-plan I've got cooking, and I ..."

Before he could finish the message to the machine, Carole picked up the phone and said, "Hi, I was drying my hair and didn't hear the ring. What's up?"

"What's your schedule for the next ten days or so? I've been drooling over the *Yacht Trader* magazine for the past hour or so, and I have an almost uncontrollable urge to buy a boat. Would you like to fly down to Ft. Lauderdale/Miami and help me pick one out? You can be my interior design consultant; so I don't buy something that looks more like the inside of a trailer than the inside of a yacht."

"When would you like to leave? I have a couple of things I was supposed to do, but I think I can either get them done early or postpone them until we get back—if we ever come back."

"I'll check and see when a plane is available and call you back. If you'd like, we could wait a couple of days, or take off tomorrow if we have wings."

Carole was quiet for a few seconds and then said, "If it won't interfere with your plans too much, could we wait until the day after tomorrow? That will give me time to get things settled so I won't be in a big rush to get back."

"That will be great. I'll call the airport, and if a plane is available, I'll schedule it for a 9 o'clock departure on Friday. I'll call you back in a few minutes."

"OK! Bye."

"Bye." Mark said, and without hanging up the phone, dialed the airport to check the schedule log for the flying club's airplanes.

The desk clerk said that there were no planes available for the entire period of Friday through the following week and weekend, but the T-210 only had two local hours scheduled on Sunday. "You may be able to negotiate with Mr. John Rollins to reschedule," he said.

"Fine, I'll check with John and see if he'll agree. Go ahead and block out the 11 days from 0900 Friday till 1730 a week from Monday. If he can't change his plans, I'll call you back. If I can hustle him out of the two hours, I'll ask him to call and cancel."

"OK, Mr. Stevens, you're all set," the clerk said.

Mark went to his desk and rummaged through the drawers until he found the flying club's roster – found John Rollins phone number and dialed.

"John, this is Mark Stevens," Mark said, identifying himself.

"Hi, Mark! What's up?"

"Well – I wanted to *big-deal* you a bit on the *Centurion* this weekend. You have a couple of hours scheduled on Sunday, and I was trying to reserve the plane for a short vacation to Florida. Is there any way you could reschedule or select one of the other planes for Sunday so I won't have to come all the way back from Florida to let you have your two hours?"

"*Florida*? Why don't you just take me with you?

"John, I'd be glad to, but you'd get down there among all those bikinis, and I'd never get you back on the plane. I just can't take a chance like that; knowing that your wife would shoot us both."

"Yeah, I hadn't thought of that, and you're probably right. Nah – I don't have a problem with rescheduling. All I was going to do was practice instrument procedures with a short trip to Little Rock and back. I'll see if there's another plane available – and if there isn't, it's not a problem. I'll give the desk a call and cancel out."

"I really appreciate it, John. If you ever need a similar favor, let me know. I'll take some pictures of the bikinis and let you have them, in a plain, brown wrapper, when I get back. Take care and I'll talk to you later."

"OK, Mark! Have a safe trip. Bye!"

With the phone still in hand – Mark redialed Carole's number and when she answered, said, "It's a done deal. I have the plane scheduled for 9:00 A.M. Friday, but if that's too early, we can leave anytime you choose."

"No, that's not too early for me. How long will it take us to get down there?"

"It will be about five hours flying time... total. I thought we'd stop in Gainesville for fuel, lunch and a potty-break. We should get in there about noon-thirty or so. We can take our time and still be in Ft. Lauderdale in time to freshen-up and start searching for all that fine seafood I'm looking forward to."

"Great!" Carole said. "This sounds like so much fun. I've never flown in a small plane before. Will you let me drive or fly – or whatever they call it?"

"You can fly as much as you like. I'll just get in the back seat and sleep while you take us down there."

"*Right!*"

"If you don't mind, I'd like to invite my friends, Art and Jean Fletcher, to join us. I doubt if they can go on such short notice, but they're fun, and I think you'd enjoy them... if they're able to swing it."

"No, I don't mind at all. We can make a party out of it."

"I'll get on the horn and make some reservations on the beach – get a car, etc. You start packing those *itty-bitty* bikinis you've got stashed away somewhere, and we'll be all set up for some serious boat shopping and beachcombing. "

"What a lovely surprise," she said. "I can't wait!" After a short pause, she asked, "Am I going to be blessed with your noble-pilot presence this fine day?"

"Oh yes! You've got this old boy hooked. Unless you run me off, I'm gonna be hanging around every day. I've got some errands to do this afternoon, but I thought we could go to dinner later; if you don't have other plans."

"In other words – you don't trust me to try the cooking bit again. Is that it?"

"I have *never* been more impressed with someone's *cooking* than I was last night. You seem to have a knack for it." He chuckled. "I just didn't want you slaving over a hot stove all evening when there are better uses for all that energy."

"Good answer – hot shot! Why don't you try and come by about six and we'll have a drink before we leave."

"Great answer – hotter shot! I'll see you then. Enjoy your afternoon. Bye!"

"Bye, 'Sky King'!"

Feeling as though he'd been on the phone for hours – Mark finally hung up the phone and went directly to his computer to check the Internet for lodging in Ft. Lauderdale. Once the computer was up and running, he found there was a wide choice of hotels directly on the beach in Ft. Lauderdale. He chose the Doubletree Oceanfront Hotel and jotted down the number to call later – after he'd talked to Art about joining them for the trip.

He felt like he was running the risk of getting a *cauliflower ear* when he picked up the phone again to call Art.

"Hi Ruth, is my friend too hung over to talk this fine day?

"I don't think so, Mark. He only spilled one cup of coffee when he came in this morning, and that's a pretty decent sign. He's on the phone right now, but I don't think he'll be... Wait, he just got off. I'll connect you."

"Thanks Ruth!"

"Whazzup?" Art growled after picking up the phone.

"This is pretty short notice, but Carole and I are flying to Ft. Lauderdale Friday morning and would like you and Jean to join us if you can get away. I've got the *Centurion* booked for the trip, and there's plenty of room."

101

"What the hell are you going to Ft. Lauderdale for?" Art asked – surprised.

"I can't be wasting any more time, buddy. I'm going to buy a boat and lust after Carole in her bikini – play some golf and sunburn my ass off."

"So you're finally going to get that boat I've been hearing about forever? I'm glad! Let me talk to Jean, and if she's for it – I'll try and get things squared away enough here to make my escape. How long are you planning to stay?"

"I don't have to get the plane back until a week from Monday, but we can come back on Sunday if you feel you need to be back in the office. I'll wait until you talk to Jean before I make hotel reservations. I checked on the Internet, and the Doubletree on the beach is where I decided to stay – if that's all right with you."

"Now you've got me excited about it. It sounds like a perfect way to spend a week. I'll get back to you in a few minutes. And yes, the Doubletree sounds great."

"Art, if you can go, I will appreciate no mention of this cancer thing. I haven't told Carole about it, and I'd rather not do it right now. Let's keep it a fun trip."

Art was quiet a moment and then said, "Yeah, I can understand. I'll tell Jean to try and keep her mouth shut about it as well. Keeping her quiet will be a first."

"Great! Put the *hard sell* on her and we'll have some fun for a change. I'll wait for your call."

Mark, too, was getting a bit excited about the trip. The expectation of a week on the beach with Carole flooded the morbid thoughts of the cancer out of his mind and in his excitement, forgot about everything but the fun. He looked forward to shopping for the boats he'd earmarked in his *trader* magazine. He wondered how long he would have to wait to take possession if there were any specific modifications necessary to fit his ultimate plan for the boat. Not many gasoline engines on the size boats I'll be looking at, he thought. I'm going to have to be pretty careful in making out my *must do* list to be sure it's complete. With that thought, some of the reality of his condition forced its way back into his consciousness, and he didn't like it.

As he sat thinking about the specific equipment or modifications he would want, the telephone rang and brought him out of his reverie.

"Hello!"

"Well, it looks like you're going to have no less than half this family joining you on the trip." Art grumbled into the phone. "Jean said she would leave tonight if you wanted to and if I couldn't get away – she'd tell me about it when she got back. I guess I'd better get my ducks in a row. The way you two turkeys carry on in front of me conjures up powerful thoughts of what would happen if you were alone together for a week on the beach in Florida."

"Yeah, you got that right! You'd better not chance it."

"We'd love to join you. Jean is more excited than I am and dying to meet Carole. She thinks there's *shopping* in Ft. Lauderdale, or something like that – and will have another female to assist. *God* – I'd love to get that excited about *anything*. She's promised, under the threat of being maimed, that she won't mention anything about the *problem*." After a short pause, he added, "It's not a big problem, but if you don't mind, coming back on Sunday it would be better for me."

"Good, I'll call Carole back and let her know the good news. We should have everything taken care of by Sunday, so coming home a day early shouldn't be of any consequence. I think it would be best if I picked you and Jean up at home. That way we only have the one car to leave at the airport while we're gone. If you don't have a problem with that, I'll be by about eight. Bring your sticks – I have to have some way of paying for this trip and you happen to be the *mullet*."

"You shouldn't have said that my friend, it's going to cost you big bucks. I'll see you at eight on Friday. Bye!"

"Bye, Art!"

Feeling like a telemarketer – Mark dialed the toll-free number of the Doubletree in Ft. Lauderdale and reserved two oceanfront suites – adjoining if possible. He also asked the desk clerk if he had the telephone numbers of any car rental agencies. The clerk gave him the national reservations numbers of three rental agencies and after ending the one phone call – started another to rent a car for their stay. Hertz assured him there would be a car available when he got there and after deciding on a mid-size Chevrolet, changed his mind immediately and asked if there were any convertibles available. He finally decided on a Pontiac convertible – just for the fun of it, and hung up with the trip fully planned.

Just as he was getting up from his desk, the phone rang - and while mumbling "Damned phones!" picked up and said, "Hello, this is Mark," with some irritation in his voice.

"Mark," Mattie's voice said over the phone, "Bob Murphy asked if you could drop by the office tomorrow about 10:00 A.M. He wants to visit with you about your replacement. He said they'd narrowed the list down to two and would like your input before making the final choice."

"Yes, I'll be glad to. In fact, I was about to call you and see if I could visit with him tomorrow about that. I guess it's true that the great minds think alike."

"How would you know?" Mattie responded with dripping sarcasm, and then she added, "I've got to cut that out. I'm sorry... habit!"

"If you ever 'cut it out', I'll haunt you from the grave. Do you need me for anything today?"

"No, I don't think so. Mr. Murphy has asked to route everything needing your direct attention straight to him until they get a replacement up here – so, that's what I've been doing, and he's keeping up pretty well. He may want to talk to you about some of the projects when he sees you tomorrow. Do you have any idea who they're going to bring in for your job?"

"I made a few recommendations, but I don't actually know who they might be considering. The people I recommended were all pretty well qualified, and I guess it will boil down to personalities and tenure – unless, of course, they decide to bring in someone from outside the company. I hope they don't do that."

"I don't think they will." Mattie responded. I think I'll wait until they make a choice before I start getting serious about who is going to relieve me. I've got a couple of girls in mind, but I definitely want the new guy's input before dragging anyone up here for serious interviews."

"Mattie, I will be leaving town for about 10 days on Friday. I'm finally going to buy that boat you've been hearing about for fifteen years. Carole, the lady I told you about yesterday, and I will be flying down to Ft. Lauderdale to make a selection from a list of boats I want to look at. Art and Jean have decided to join us, so I think we'll have a terrific time. As soon as we have a boat in hand, I'd like for you and Maury to come down for a trip. You both need a vacation as badly as I do."

"I don't know if my fat ass would fit on a boat or not, but it's something to think about. I've always wanted to do that."

"Don't think too much – just be prepared to do it. I'll see you tomorrow, and if you need me before then – I'll have my cell phone at the ready."

"Are you still feeling OK?"

"Yes, I feel fine. No more talk about that – please. Bye Darlin'."

"Bye, I'll see you tomorrow."

CHAPTER FIFTEEN

The anticipation of the upcoming trip had built up, in all the travelers for the two days since Mark had planned the trip. The excitement was evident as Mark said, "OK – is everyone buckled up? Let's get this show on the road."

It had taken a bit more time than expected to pre-flight the plane, get the luggage loaded, and the car stored in the hangar than they had expected. It was a quarter to ten when Mark pushed the throttle to the firewall and felt the surge of the big 300-horsepower Continental come growling to life. After hurtling down the runway for about 2500 feet, the trim Mark had applied during preflight, lifted the plane smoothly off the runway to a chorus of *All right!* coming from the passengers. Carole said, in a very solemn whine, "I have to go to the bathroom."

Mark responded, "Will someone in the back choke her for me until I'm not so busy?"

When the wheels were up, and the people on the ground started to *look like ants,* the radio squawked, *Centurion Three Zulu Charlie, left turn is approved – contact departure on*

124.15. Have a safe trip. Mark in turn, responded with, *"Roger, Memphis - thank you,"* and then, manipulated the dials on the radio to comply with their instructions. The radio chatter continued back and forth for about the first 15 minutes of the flight as they exited the "Class B" airspace and climbed to their cruising altitude of 7,500 feet.

The *Centurion* was equipped with a Satellite Ground Positioning System; allowing Mark to fly direct to Gainesville as opposed to using the "Victor Airways" that connected the various navigational aids along the route.

After adjusting his mixture, trim, prop and radios, he announced to his guests, "Folks, God forbid something should happen to me on the way, but – if for any reason, you have to get help, tune this (as he pointed to his communications radio) to 121.5 and this (pointing to the *transponder*) to 770.0. After you have the frequencies entered – scream in a highly frenzied voice, *Mayday*, several times over the microphone. Someone will answer and tell you what to do. Remember one of the basic principles of flying – taking off is optional, but landing is definitely mandatory. So... ask for help and someone will be there to give it." He then pointed to the GPS display and showed them how to read the longitude and latitude of their position when control asked for it. And, finally, he pointed out the emergency frequencies that were printed on small placards mounted on the dash under each instrument.

"If 'Jay Cee' is calling me home – I really hope He waits until the return trip. I don't want to miss out on this week." Mark chuckled as the flying became routine. "And, by the way, we're VFR today, so everyone kind of keep a lookout for other aircraft. Radar is following us, but it's always a good idea to stay alert."

Art and Jean had flown with Mark before and were not as fascinated by private aircraft flight as Carole. Carole kept up a constant barrage of comments on the view, the feel of the plane as it encountered the mild turbulence associated with lifting off, the exchange between Mark and the traffic controllers on the radio and the complete newness of the experience that she found so exciting. Seeing her complete enjoyment, Mark was relieved of the usual boredom of in-route flying and found himself immersed in the excitement Carole was feeling. Just wonderful, he thought.

"Well, lady, you wanted to fly – here's your chance." Mark said as he turned to Carole.

"Oh God," she said. "I don't know if I'm ready for this or not."

"Piece of cake," Mark responded as he explained and demonstrated the effects of moving the control devices back and forth to induce roll, pitch and yaw to the plane. "Keep your eyes on the horizon and mostly just apply pressure on the controls rather than moving them a lot. You'll love it."

With some apprehension, Carole took the half-wheel of the control yoke in her hands, placed her feet on the rudder pedals and said, "Forget about that going to sleep crap – and if I scream – I want to see *immediate* and *positive* response from *you*, 'Sky King'."

Jean was enjoying the scenario from the back seat and tried to encourage Carole with, "You've got to remember Carole, if our turkey pilot is able to handle this thing, it should be a snap for you."

"Did you hear something from *coach*? I didn't think they let those people visit with us up here in *first class*. I'm going to compose a *strongly* worded letter to management if this continues."

"Smart ass," Jean said, as she sharply pushed the back of Mark's head several times to emphasize her remark.

Art, on the other hand, was already dozing in the back seat and paying little attention to the prattle going on around him. He had taken his usual dose of Dramamine to combat the mild airsickness he was susceptible to, and the drowsiness was not unwelcome. He would enjoy the flight in his own way and leave the other "B.S." to those who chose to stay awake.

"Try some turns," Mark said to Carole as she was sitting rigidly, holding the controls and obviously uncomfortable in moving anything.

"Turn the wheel to the right a bit and apply a little right rudder. When you get about a 10-degree bank, bring the wheel back to center and apply a little backpressure to keep the nose on the horizon." After she had made the maneuver, Mark continued with, "See how easy? Now, do the same things to the left to get us back on course."

The flying lesson continued for about 30 minutes. Carole had enjoyed about as much of the flying as she wanted and asked that Mark resume control of the plane. Mark, in turn, switched on the autopilot and relaxed with the others for the remainder of the trip to Gainesville.

The constant drone of the engine tended to lull everyone into a semi-trance as the passengers stared out the windows, making occasional comments about something on the ground and the rare occasions when other aircraft were spotted along the route. Mark struggled to maintain focus and was glad when they approached Gainesville so he had something to do rather than listen to the engine and scan his instruments.

After making radio contact with the appropriate controlling entities in Gainesville, he was approved for a left-downwind approach to Gainesville Regional Airport – Runway 6. As he made his final left turn over the middle-marker, he said to his passengers, "This is the part that always just scares the shit out of me." He then feigned terror at the controls and was immediately pummeled by Carole and Jean alike; one on his arm and the other on the back of his head that was exposed above the seatback.

"No respect! I get no respect!" He mumbled as he went back to the business of landing the plane.

The big single sat down smoothly; even with the 10-knot crosswind. Mark cut power and switched to the ground control frequency as soon as his speed allowed safe ground maneuvering of the aircraft. After informing "ground" of his intentions, he immediately received instructions to exit the active runway at intersection "A1" and proceed to the General Aviation area of the airport. Once parked, as directed by an employee of the Fixed Base Operator, he asked that they refuel the plane and further direct them to the "Ptomaine Palace" where visitors might eat upon landing in Gainesville America.

As planned, it was a short stop in Gainesville. After andwiches of choice and visits to the "necessary rooms", they were back in the air in less than an hour.

The flight became routine again, with very little sustained conversation. Mark thought of the "Trivial Pursuit" game that was a permanent part of the plane's internal inventory and asked Jean if she would try and dig it out from behind the seat. When it was found, she asked, "How are we going to roll dice and all the other things this game requires?"

"We'll just take turns answering the questions without the dice roll. Let everyone select which category they want to try, and if they correctly answer the question – give them a 'pie slice'. When someone gets a complete set of 'slices' – they win. I'll sit out if you'd rather I not play – knowing that I'll undoubtedly be the winner."

"I think we all may have a slim chance of beating your dumb ass – unless there's a category called the 'Joys of Bestiality' or some other off-the-wall nonsense that you've probably been exposed to."

Jean's comment was greeted with boisterous approval from Art and Carole. She continued with, "What legitimate category would you like to humiliate yourself with first, Mr. Know-it-all?"

"I think I'll take 'Literature'. If I can get that one out of the way, then there will be no stopping me."

"OK – for bragging rights for the rest of the trip and a green pie slice – What does the 'QB' stand for in the Leon Uris novel, *QB-VII?*"

Mark thought for a few moments and finally said, "Look if you can't come up with something a little more challenging than that – I probably shouldn't play. It may be better if you saved that question for someone else, so they can show off a bit."

"He doesn't know!" Jean screeched, joyfully.

"I *know*! I just refuse to reduce myself to answering such infantile questions."

Jean gouged Art with her elbow and enthusiastically repeated, "He doesn't know the answer. OK dummy – five more seconds and I pass the question on to Carole." She then started counting, dramatically, backward from five.

When she reached "two", Mark shouted out "Quarterback!"

"See – I told you he didn't know." Then continued with, "Carole, will you please humiliate him just a little more by telling us the *correct* answer?"

Carole, in turn, said, "Yes, I'll be happy to. I really enjoyed the book, and the 'QB' stands for 'Queen's Bench'."

Carole and Jean both were jumping around in their seats like they'd just won a prize on "Let's Make a Deal" while

Mark was mumbling – "I actually knew the answer. I just didn't want to show off this early in the game."

"Give the lady her green pie slice! Carole, what category would you like for your very own question?"

The game made quick work of the remaining two hours of the trip from Gainesville to Ft. Lauderdale, with appropriate 'boos' and 'cheers' for correct or incorrect answers.

When Mark contacted *Miami Approach Control,* no clear winner had been established, and the game was reluctantly put away with vows of continuation on the way home.

Reminding everyone to be alert for other aircraft, Mark went about the serious business of navigating the congested "Class-C" airspace surrounding the Ft. Lauderdale International Airport. When the aircraft's position was positively established by *Approach,* altitude and heading instructions were given and followed, precisely, by Mark until he was told to contact the Ft. Lauderdale tower when the airport was in sight.

Carole was fascinated by the myriad tasks Mark was accomplishing during the approach. He seemed to be twisting knobs, answering questions, making maneuvers, asking questions – all at the same time, while some disembodied voice uttered staccato commands over the radio in some unintelligible tongue.

Marks responses were equally unintelligible, to her, and sounded like a recording of what the "voice" had just said. Whatever the language – it seemed to serve them well and the plane touched down smoothly on Runway 9R – Ft. Lauderdale, Florida. Well – she hoped it was Ft. Lauderdale, Florida .

After informing the flight-line attendant of his intentions and specific instructions concerning the plane, Mark suggested that he go find the rental car and bring it directly back to the plane; thus, eliminating the necessity of hauling the heavy luggage all over the airport. The passengers could stay in or by the plane as they chose – or if anyone needed to "freshen-up", they could go to the lounge area of the terminal and meet back at the plane when finished.

Mark had been gone for about twenty minutes before he came driving up to the plane in a beautiful, white Pontiac convertible. The top on the car had already been lowered, and the ear-to-ear grin Mark had plastered on his face made it obvious that he was enjoying the sunshine – and the convertible.

"I asked for a 1965 Lincoln convertible, but this was the closest they could get. It's a bit smaller than the Lincoln, but maybe it'll do."

Art had unloaded the plane and had their luggage ready to be transferred to the car. After putting the golf clubs and a couple of smaller suitcases in the trunk, it became obvious that there was going to be a problem with space. Mark offered to have a cab deliver the bulk of the gear to the hotel, but Carole and Jean were laughing about their plight and finally came up with a workable solution. "Everyone, except poor ol' Mark gets to ride on or under a suitcase. Their choice! Forget the taxi crap and let's get this party started," Jean declared.

It was a decidedly happy foursome that departed the Ft. Lauderdale International airport; stacked in a convertible and way too boisterous for ladies and gentlemen of their seniority.

CHAPTER SIXTEEN

Mark had seen their hotel from the air and had little trouble driving there on the ground after the rental-car attendant had given him elementary instructions and a small map of the area. Upon their arrival at the Doubletree Oceanfront Hotel, the bellmen waiting at the curb were obviously amused by the four *fully grown* men and women handing out luggage that they had been sitting on or carrying in their laps. They were standing in the open top car, laughing and making outlandish comments to each other concerning the uncomfortable ride from the airport. The bellmen asked, in thought and universally, "Are they drunk or just intoxicated by the joy of finally arriving at their destination?" In any event – they were having fun and appeared harmless enough.

After picking up the key-cards from the front desk in the beautifully appointed hotel lobby, Mark and the others were escorted to their adjoining suites on the eleventh floor; Mark turned to the bellman and asked, "Are we next to *them?*" – then without waiting for an answer, turned back to Carole with an anguished look on his face and explained, "He always has gas so bad that I doubt if the filtering system can protect us fully," indicating Art, with a sideward nod of his head.

Art in return said, "Yeah and when he snores, it sounds like a runaway *Poulan* chain saw with a defective muffler." He then turned to the bellman and added, "I know we're going to enjoy *our* rooms up here, but would it be too much trouble to, perhaps, find a more remote location for our friend here. The other guests on this floor will appreciate it."

Carole looked at Art with a shocked look on her face, placed her hand to her breast and said with considerable indignance, "What do you mean? I *assumed* this was to be my room alone. I'm a *nice* girl, and if this is some elaborate scheme to get me to relax my morals – forget about it." Then, turning to the bellman, she asked, "Where are your mangers? *I* will be sleeping with the sheep."

"*Au, contraire, ma Chérie!* I've made arrangements to share a basement room with one of the janitors," Mark said, then immediately added, "There wasn't enough room for my belongings down there. I hoped I could leave them up here. Of course I'll be leaving as soon as they're put away. I wouldn't want Art and Jean to think that we were, uhhh – *you know.*"

To the pained looks of Art and Jean, Carole raised her nose until it was pointing nearly skyward and said, royally, "I just wanted to be able to *face* everyone in the morning without them thinking, well – *you know.*"

Caught in the middle of the friendly banter, the bellman laughed as he opened the draperies and sliding glass doors leading to the balcony and said, "Folks, if you'd like to enjoy the view for a few minutes, I'll get the luggage sorted and put away."

Both couples had entered the one room together and they all went immediately to the balcony to "Oooo" and "Ahhh" at the fantastic panorama of ocean, surf and sand – glistening in the sun, eleven floors below them. In a firm, commanding voice, Art told the girls, "*No spitting!*" Mark returned to the doorway with the bellman to make sure the luggage was properly sorted and sent to the right room.

After giving a generous tip to the bellman, Mark returned to the balcony, and handed out plastic *key-cards* to everyone and then said, "OK, we're here! Does anyone have any preferences concerning plans for the evening – and if you do, the plans had better include *seafood* if I'm expected to be a part of them."

Both Jean and Carole spoke up almost as one and whined, "I wanted *barbeque*!" The spontaneity of the simultaneous statement brought peals of laughter from each of the women and *killer* stares from the men. Mark addressed them both and said, "I want you to look down and see how high up we are before you consider making anymore cracks like that – *ladies*."

After a brief pause, he added, "It's been four or five years since I've been down here, but I imagine *The Down Under* is still in operation, and it was a wonderful place to eat back then," Mark said. Then he added, "Their food was as good as I've ever eaten and I think it's only about four or five miles from here; so it's not a big deal, travel-wise. There are several places fairly close by that cater to the beach and boat crowd where we could have some drinks, dance and people-watch later – if everyone agrees. Whatever! We're on vacation, and no one has to get up real early in the morning – do they?"

Jean answered with, "I don't expect to see a *morning* all the time we're here. I expect my days to begin around noonish and end *well* after dark."

Art then asked, "Is there a dress code for this place?"

"It's pretty *upscale*, but this is Ft. Lauderdale and I think a decent sports shirt and slacks or khakis will be fine. I don't remember seeing a lot of people in coats or ties the last time I was here. You could wear that green polyester leisure suit you're so fond of – if you want to make a fashion statement."

"I think you're right. That suit fits in with just about any 'decent' crowd. I've noticed lots of people admiring it nearly every time I've worn it."

"Good, I'll try and get reservations," Mark said. "If, for some reason, we can't get in, there are many, many places up and down the beach where we can eat; all of which have enough liquor in stock to keep up with Art and his problem. I don't think we'll go hungry or thirsty."

Art replied, angrily, "Look, smartass, I know I have a drinking problem – but she's my *wife* and I won't allow any more rude comments about her. So – knock it off!"

Jean began pounding Art on his shoulder as Carole dramatically rolled her eyes at Mark and said, *"My God!* Let's freshen up and get this party moving. Did he put our luggage in here or the other room?"

"It's in here. These are much nicer rooms than the others."

Art said, "Come on, Jean, let's go next door and see if we have to complain to management about inadequate facilities. We'll see you guys in about an hour. If you're ready before we are – give us a call and we'll speed things up. I'm afraid to leave Jean in a bathroom with a full inventory of makeup. We could miss the whole evening."

When Art and Jean left for their quarters, Mark asked Carole, "You or me – first in the shower?"

"Why don't you go first and I'll know how much time I have before we're supposed to leave. I'll unpack and hang up our clothes while you shower. Would you like me to fix a drink? I think there's a liquor stash in the courtesy bar over there."

"You read my mind. I'll hurry."

The hour they'd planned on turned into an hour and twenty minutes when they rediscovered the fact that showers can also be used as adult playgrounds. When Mark finally called Art's room and found that they were about ready, he flashed the telephone and dialed the desk to ask for a cab to pick them up in ten minutes.

Mildly surprised, Carole asked, "You're not going to drive the convertible?

"No, I'd rather not. If things go as planned – I'll be in no condition to drive later. You're welcome to chauffeur us around in the convertible if you like."

"I doubt if I'll be in any condition to drive either. Yours is a better plan."

"Tomorrow night, I'll get a limo with a 'moon roof'. I'd have done it tonight had I thought about it earlier. Another one of those damned 'senior moments'!"

When Jean and Art met them in the hallway outside the rooms, Art asked, "Were you able to get reservations?

"No! I didn't even try. We can go down there, and if they can't seat us right away, we can wait in the bar or on the deck. If it looks like the wait is going to be too long – we can find someplace else very easily. Let's go – I have a cab waiting for us downstairs."

The elevator ride was mostly filled with the girls complementing each other on how lovely the other looked. When it got a little *gushy* for the men – they started the same dialog in voices as high and effeminate as possible. Art said, "I *really* like the way you've done your hair this evening."

"To which Mark replied, "Ooooo, thank you! Yes, I've found this new product that really gives me the freedom to be *me* for a change. You might want to try it – it's called 'Brylcream'."

"Ooooo! I will!" Art replied as the car stopped at the lobby.

As they left the elevator, Jean asked Carole, in a low seething voice, "Did you ever have an almost uncontrollable urge to just slap the shit out of someone?"

"As a matter of fact ..." Carole replied without finishing her sentence, but with clenched teeth and squinted eyes – glared at the men who were chuckling good-naturedly, back and forth, at each other.

*   *   *

The ride to the restaurant was relatively uneventful; with quiet comments on the beauty of the city, the perfect weather and the excitement associated with the upcoming week's loose, enjoyable schedule. A schedule that was eagerly anticipated by good, compatible friends.

Arriving at the restaurant, they were immediately taken by the beauty of the structure, nestled along the intracoastal waterway with its private dock for those wishing to tie-up their boats and have dinner. It was like an entrance into a Ft. Lauderdale *Chamber of Commerce* brochure; glass everywhere to take advantage of the spectacular view of the waterway and the parked or passing boats.

Carole grabbed Mark's arm as they stepped from the cab and said, "I wanna live here... not just in Ft. Lauderdale, but right *here*."

"OK!" Mark said. "I'll see what I can do about building a loft apartment above the place. I can just imagine how cool it will be to go downstairs for breakfast every morning in a robe and no makeup."

"It was just a thought; however, the comment about 'no makeup' made it a passing thought."

After speaking with the maître d', Mark and the others made their way through the sea of white tablecloths in the spacious dining area and found the door leading to the similarly appointed, canvas-covered deck. They found the bar easily enough and ordered drinks before wandering to the docks around the perimeter of the deck where several beautiful boats were tied up.

Mark and Carole went directly to the only sailboat that was present and stared at it while sipping their drinks and making comments about how well maintained it was. Mark guessed it to be a 36-footer and made of wood; telling him immediately that the boat was far from being new, but refurbished to new condition. The teak deck, with its white caulking, was polished to a high sheen and was spotless. The long wooden bowsprit, mast, and boom were equally spotless with deep coats of marine varnish acting as a barrier against the harshness of the nautical elements. All the boat's gear was stowed with great care. The white nylon mooring lines and sheets were all neatly coiled and ready for the next upcoming journey. The jib was furled, and the main was lowered and covered with a blue sheath, adding to the neatness of the vessel. It looked seaworthy, and someone loved this boat. The overall condition of the craft made it obvious that countless hours had been spent in getting it to its present pristine condition. Although he hadn't a clue as to who it might be, Mark already liked the owner of the boat, and hoped he had done the work himself, rather than having it done by others.

A feeling of melancholy washed over Mark as he stared at the boat. He wanted a boat like this and wished he'd spent quality time working with his hands, bringing a boat such as this one back to life. The harsh realization of the fact that he no longer had the time to start such a project was the first of such thoughts to inject a feeling of deep regret in his mind. It's much too beautiful for my purposes, he thought. I couldn't do what I have to do with a boat like this.

Art and Jean had been looking at the several cabin cruisers rimming the dock area, but joined Mark and Carole as they admired the wooden sailboat. Mark was glad when they joined them and was relieved when Art spoke and brought him back from his reverie.

"*My God*! Somebody has really been busy with this baby. It's beautiful!"

"I know," Mark replied. "*Somewhere*, there's a stack of used sandpaper you can't throw a rock over. This guy has done a remarkable job and invested an awful lot of time and money. Whoever he is – I admire his effort." Then audiblizing his previous thoughts, he added, "I hope he did the work himself and didn't have it done professionally. Can you imagine the pride he must feel – completing a project like this? It shoulda been me!"

They kept admiring the boat, until a waiter in a starched, white, cutaway-jacket approached them and said, "Mr. Stevens, your table is ready, sir."

* * *

Dinner was marvelous. The good conversation was enhanced by several bottles of wine – bringing about deep, philosophical rhetoric that made perfect sense during the meal, but would be somewhat less remarkable when thought back on in the morning.

Art and Mark wanted to play golf early, but the women decided they'd rather sleep late, have brunch at any given time and then go into a shopping frenzy. The men were to be called as pack-mules when the frenzy was over.

Dancing and people-watching slowly became something to do later in the week as the long day, the food, and the wine mellowed the group into occasional yawns, and quick glances at watches.

Carole finally said, "I move we call it a day. All in favor indicate by saying aye." Three *ayes* were heard like an echo around the table – accompanied by sighs of mild relief.

CHAPTER SEVENTEEN

The phone on the bedside table rang at exactly 6:00 a.m. After the untangling process from interlocking arms and legs, Mark finally got the phone off the hook. "Get your lazy ass out of bed and load up all your money. Our tee time is in an hour and a half," Art's voice boomed from the receiver.

"What will I need money for if you're bringing yours? I wish you were a lot richer, and I had time to play more golf. I'd never have to worry again – *mullet*! Give me a half hour and I'll meet you in the coffee shop downstairs."

"OK! Do you want me to order you any breakfast?"

"Yeah, whatever you're having. I don't want to faint from malnutrition while I'm whipping your ass."

"*Right*! I'll see you in a few minutes."

Mark saw one sleepy eye open under Carole's tangled mass of hair, and he leaned over and kissed her lightly on the lips as he got out of bed and hurried for the shower. He watched for a moment as a contented smile grew on her lips and the eye closed again as she wriggled back into her comfort zone.

On the way to the shower, he chuckled to himself and thought, I've got to get my priorities straightened out. I'm crawling out of bed with *her* – to go play golf with *Art*? What's *wrong* with this picture?

After a quick shower, and an even quicker shave, Mark was dressed and ready to leave in 25 minutes. On his way out, he sat on the bed next to Carole and caressed her shoulder enough to wake her again and said, "You've got my cell phone number – so when you and Jean are ready to covey up with us again, give me a call and we'll make our plans." With that said, he lightly kissed her again as she mumbled her understanding.

When Mark arrived in the Coffee Shop of the hotel, the waitress was placing the food orders in front of Art. "I guess I planned that just right." Mark said as he sat down in the booth across from Art.

"Yeah, you're pretty strong at that. I told her to wait until you're here before she brings the check. Eat fast – I'm in the mood to play some Florida golf."

"After we finish with the golf – I'd like to go by a couple of the marinas and look at some boats I had checked in my magazine. I doubt if the girls will want us back real early anyway. I'd rather do some screening before we bring them down and make the final decision on which boat, etc. I wouldn't want them bored looking at boats – especially when they're never bored with the Ft. Lauderdale shopping."

"Sounds like a plan to me. Do you know where the marinas are located, or are you just going to drive up and down the beach and spot them randomly?"

"I've got the addresses and the map. I doubt if we have too much trouble finding them."

The two men force-fed themselves as quickly as possible and hurried to the valet station to ask for the convertible. When it arrived, Mark asked the valet if he knew where the golf course they were to be playing was located – in an effort to avoid trying to plan a route with the small map he was using. The valet knew exactly where it was and gave relatively simple directions. They would make their tee-time easily – with enough time to spare for warm-up on the practice tee. Life was good!

Mark's club professional had made arrangements for them to play at several private courses each of the days they were to be in the area. All they had to do was call for tee-times and show up. The ability to play the other private golf clubs was one of the really enjoyable benefits of being a member and Mark took full advantage of it whenever he was traveling.

The course was beautiful and the weather perfect. They were finished in three and a half hours, unhurried and without waiting for a single shot.

The bets were small, as always, but collected by the winner with great drama – with just as much bitching by the loser. The game had been close all the way and Mark was particularly dramatic and demonstrative in folding the dollar bill Art had given him and placing it into his money clip. An equal amount of fanfare was used in deliberately counting and pocketing the additional two dollars in small change Art had unceremoniously tossed onto the table in mock disgust. The small change made the winnings as inconvenient as possible for the winner, with pennies and nickels being the predominant denominations given in payment. Both men carried large quantities of the inconvenient change in their golf bags – just in case they lost and had to pay up.

Bragging rights established, they loaded up and started for the marinas. "What, exactly, are you looking for?" Art asked as they were driving away.

"I want a *sloop*, roughly 40 feet long that needs work but is still seaworthy... with a full inventory of sails. I don't really care how old the boat is, but I think I'd like something about 10 years old. I'd love for the boat to already be equipped with an autopilot and modern navigational equipment, but that's not particularly important, since I can get that installed quickly. If it's not rigged for 'one-man operation', then I'll have that done before I take delivery."

"Is that going to be hard to find?"

"No, I don't think so. I've got several boats on my lists that seem to be about what I'm looking for. They vary in size from 38 feet to 50 feet in length and, from the ads, look to be about right. I just have to look at them up close. I imagine that the marinas will have others that they would like to show me as well – so we'll just have to see what catches my eye. I hope you don't mind running around with me while I do this."

"No, I don't mind at all. In fact, I'm pretty excited about the whole thing. I might see something I can't live without either. Jean and I have visited about buying a boat too; although I don't think we'd be interested in a sailboat. I don't know enough about them to get any real use out of one."

"Maybe you'll become addicted to sailing when we all get together on mine. It's really pretty wonderful – I think."

*   *   *

The first marina they chose to visit was huge. Rows and rows of floating slips containing hundreds of sailboats, powerboats and other vessels that could be called *ships* with little argument. The dealer's office and showroom was equally large with several new boats sitting on keel-blocks and trailers. The air-conditioned comfort of the showroom was a much more acceptable buying environment than the heat and humidity of the open docks.

When Mark and Art entered the building they stood near the door for a full minute, gaping at the beautiful new boats before they were pounced upon by one of several sales people lounging around waiting for the next victim to walk in and lust after the boat of their dreams.

"Good afternoon, gentlemen, may I help you?" He then extended his hand and introduced himself as Don Lopez as he handed Mark his business card.

Mark, in turn, took his hand and said, "I hope so. I'm Mark Stevens, and this is my financial advisor, Art Fletcher. I've got to admit that he advised me not to come in here."

Don smiled as he shook their hands and said, "That's probably good advice. I'm glad you didn't take it."

Mark smiled back and said, "I've got a list of several boats, tied up here, that are for sale. I hope you can show them to us. Some are for sale *by owner*, but I assume the owners have left the keys with you just in case someone like me happens to drop by."

"In most cases, we have access to the boats. Let me see the list, and I'll see what I can do. If you like, you can go look at them from the dock. Then, if you're interested in going aboard for a closer look, come back, and I'll get the keys, or we can call the owner to come show it. Let me get the slip numbers for the boats you want to look at, and I'll give you directions."

"Great!" Mark said as he handed him the list.

The salesman left them and was gone about five minutes. When he returned, he had a small map of the marina and had circled the slips containing the boats on Mark's list. "If you don't find anything you like from your list – I have quite a few more boats for sale that you may want to look at before you leave. We probably have the largest selection of new *and* used boats in town. I'll be glad to help – but I won't *hover* while you look around. Enjoy yourself and I'll visit with you when you're finished."

The first two boats they looked at were not as advertised and Mark quickly scratched them off his list. The third boat was not bad, and he placed a checkmark beside it on the map. There was no one aboard, so they just looked at it from the dock. It was one of the smaller boats on the list, and they decided to go check out the others before going back for the salesman and a closer inspection.

They spent nearly an hour walking up and down the different finger docks looking at the six boats on Mark's list. There were only two that he wanted to go aboard, so they started back toward the showroom to see if Don, the salesman, could gain access for a more thorough inspection.

After returning to the slips with Don, Mark found that he *liked* the boats he'd gone aboard, but he wasn't real excited about either of them. After explaining to Don what he was looking for, the salesman said, "I have a boat, that's about to go on the market up in the boatyard that you really ought to take a look at before you go. The owner is having the hull cleaned for painting right now, but we can still go aboard and look it over. The boat is in excellent condition, but it hasn't been used much and needs cleaning and some general maintenance – but other than that it's a great boat."

"You have my attention!" Mark said, "Let's go check it out."

On the way to the boatyard, Don kept up a running commentary, describing the boat to Mark. "I don't know if you've ever had any experience with a cement hull before, but they're very sturdy and strong. Some people hesitate to look at them just because of the stigma attached to a boat made of cement, but they are just as structurally sound as any other material. This one is a '45-footer' with diesel power for maneuvering, two 150kw generators and six batteries, lots of electronics and a full sail inventory. It also has a custom-made shade cover that you can use while you're at anchor. I don't know what condition the sails are in, but you can check them out before you make a decision about buying. It's twelve years old, but there's no real damage to the boat. A little paint and maybe some re-upholstery work and you have a great boat for just about any type sailing you care to do – including, of course, ocean sailing. It's set up for cruising, and I doubt if you'd want to do a whole lot of racing with it."

As the trio approached the boat, Mark could see that the cleaning process had been almost completed. There were some bare spots on the hull where the paint had been rubbed away, but there were no apparent patches visible that would indicate any serious hull damage. He immediately liked the lines of the boat and was starting to get excited about going aboard. He hoped the excitement wasn't too obvious to Don. An excited boat-buyer is not necessarily a prudent boat-buyer.

Although Don was still maintaining his running commentary, Mark had mostly tuned him out as he started a tactile and visual inspection of the exposed hull. Running his hands over the smooth surface of the cement, it seemed *fair* and he could see no cracks that would indicate stress of any kind. It looked terrific, and he was becoming more excited than he wanted to be. He was thinking, I've got to remember, this is a poker game. Get the face, man – get the face!

There was a portable ladder leaning alongside the boat and after about fifteen minutes of hull inspection, Mark started up the ladder – with Art following and Don guarding their escape from the ground. He told them to look around, and he would be aboard in a few minutes; as soon as he checked with the maintenance people to find out how much longer the cleaning process would take.

Once on deck, Mark could see that the boat had not been as well maintained as you would think a boat of this size and expense should have been. The varnish on most of the woodwork was bleached by the sun and was either missing in spots or peeling. The covers over the jib and mainsail were very dirty but seemed intact with very little wear. He unfastened a few of the clips holding the cover on the mainsail, and tried to see if the sail was worn or chaffed. From what he could see – it looked fine, just unused. He knew he could have all the sails taken to a sail maker for inspection prior to heading out on an extended trip – so that was of little concern right now. The rigging was old, and he would have it all replaced if he decided to buy the boat. The stainless steel winches and cleats looked in decent shape, and all they would need is polish to look like new. He opened the hatch to the forward sail locker and saw that there was several more sails stowed below – including a brightly colored spinnaker. There was very little corrosion around the mast and boom fittings. The boat would be safe, he thought.

Finished with the cursory inspection topside, he called to Don when he found the cabin entry locked, and asked if he had the key so they could look inside. When Don tossed the key up to him, he entered the main saloon of the boat and was greeted with the smell of a boat that had been closed for a long time. It was not an overpowering smell, but it was unpleasant. The furnishings looked dusty and unused, but did not seem to be frayed or otherwise damaged. Other than that – the compartment was beautiful – with rich mahogany woodwork and cabinetry. There was a navigation table in one corner with myriad instruments mounted into a console behind and alongside the table. Chart stowage filled the space between the bottom of the tabletop and the deck. The galley area was compact and well designed. It included a refrigerator, propane stove, sink, microwave and conventional ovens. It seemed to have everything necessary for extended cruising.

The rest of the boat was essentially the same – with beautiful woodwork (that needed polishing) and ample space to accommodate six or more sailors in relative comfort. Mark was fighting an urge to buy the boat on the spot, but steeled himself to check out the others on his list before making any serious decisions.

Don had not come aboard and was still visiting with the maintenance workers when Mark and Art returned to the ground. "Don," Mark said, "have the owners definitely decided to sell this boat?"

"Yes, that's why they're trying to clean it up a bit. They don't use it, so they've decided to get rid of it. Are you interested?"

"Yes, it's about what I'm looking for. What are they asking for it?"

"I don't think they've set a price yet. I'll ask, and I'm sure it will be reasonable – reasonable for this size boat anyway."

"Ask them what they'll take for it *as is* and I'll check back with you tomorrow. I have several more boats that I want to look at, but I'm definitely interested in this one if they choose to sell."

* * *

The search for more marinas/boats continued, but Mark no longer had the urgency he'd had before seeing the cement boat. He still wanted to look – but now, everything would be a comparison to his first choice. That choice would be hard to beat. He might be able to find *newer and prettier*, but he doubted if he'd find anything that was as well suited to his criteria.

They did find two more boats that he really liked, but the 50-footer now seemed too large, and the 40-footer he really liked was too new and well maintained. However, he wanted to bring Carole and Jean down to look at the three choices just so they could be involved in the buying process. Mark also knew that his mind was made up, for the most part, on which boat he was going to rename "Carole's Wet Dream or something to that effect. The name "Carole" would certainly be included in the final choice of names.

Mark and Art had just started the convertible, to leave the last marina of the day, when Mark's cell phone rang. "Hello!"

"Are you guys at sea, or what?" Jean's voice asked from the receiver.

"We thought about it, but didn't have any clean underwear – so, we were going to try and sneak back to the hotel before we left. Now that we've been caught, I guess we'd better come on back and join you guys. Did you have fun today?"

"Oh, yes – and how you ended up with someone as cool as Carole is a mystery I'll never be able to solve. Get your butts back here and *pamper* us. We're on vacation."

"We're on our way. We'll see you in about thirty minutes. Bye!"

CHAPTER EIGHTEEN

The day had gone perfectly for everyone. Jean and Carole had immediately become close friends, and although the shopping experience had not reaped a bountiful booty, they had enjoyed themselves immensely – finding counsel in the other's taste and honest criticism or approval when asked.

The evening had gone just as well as the day. They'd had a wonderful dinner, the luxury of the limo ride and the ongoing banter that was so enjoyed by the entire group. Now lying comfortably in bed with the lights out, Jean rolled toward Art and put her arm over his shoulder in prelude to conversation. "Honey, I'm worried about Mark and Carole."

"In what way?" He asked as he rolled toward her and propped his head onto his hand supported by his elbow so that he could speak to her directly.

Jean, in turn, rolled onto her back and stared at the darkened ceiling and continued with, "Well, Carole and I talked quite a bit this afternoon when we were shopping, and I think she's fallen in love with the big coot. It's going to cause both of them a great deal of trouble when he tells her what's going on."

"Yeah, I've thought of that too. I know he thinks the world of her already and it's going to be a bitch to let her know about the cancer. I can imagine what he's going through trying to make the decision – whether to tell or not to tell. It's going to be painful for them both. If he doesn't tell her, he will have to get her out of his life – now. If she's in love with him, as you say, then it will cut her to pieces, and I know Mark would die before he'd hurt her. It's a miserable choice in either direction."

"Have you asked him what he plans to do?"

"We talked about it, briefly, on the golf course this morning, but I think he wanted to avoid the subject. He didn't offer any insight as to what he planned to do. I think he'll probably wait until we get back to Memphis to tell her – if he decides to tell her. I know his decision will depend on how he thinks she feels about him. If he thinks she loves him, I know he'll tell her. If she just enjoys his company and wants to hang out with him, then he might not and will just enjoy her company until he becomes too sick. When that happens, I think he'll just make an excuse for leaving town – and leave."

"Oh, *God*! I've waited so long for him to find someone to share his life and now that it seems he's found her, this happens – and they're both screwed. They seem perfect for each other. You can tell by just being around them that they're having more fun than people their age should have. I just can't get enough of it. I've only known her for two days, and already, I love her to death. I hope we can continue to be friends after this is all over. *God*, I hate putting it that way. To know Mark has very few months to live is something I can't quite get ready for. I find myself already missing him, and it hasn't even happened yet. Every time I get close to him, I want to hug him, and every time I leave him, I want to cry. *Goddamnit*!"

"I know what you mean. I don't think he's fully accepted the facts himself. He surely doesn't seem to be dwelling on it in any way, but I know it's never out of his mind. I hope I'm around when it finally hits him. I might be able to help him cope. There's a breakdown coming, and it's like the old feeling of waiting for the other shoe to fall. I can't get it out of my mind, and I can only imagine what it must be like for him. The fact that he won't be in our lives for the expected number of years just breaks my heart. I already miss him too."

After several moments of silent meditation, Jean continued, "I won't meddle in his life, but I sure hope he makes the right decision about Carole. I wish I *knew* what the right decision was. I feel certain she will need help in any case. I will do what it takes to give her that help if she'll let me. I know Mark would want me to. You know... it only happens a few times in a lifetime, being close friends – and two of those times are in the next room. It's pretty remarkable the way I feel that I've known Carole half my life after such a short time. I'll have to make myself behave so I don't come apart like a cheap toy. That would be an intolerable disservice to them both. I can only pray for the strength to get it done."

Art thought for a few moments on his wife's comments, and then said, "It's horrible trying to act like everything is *normal*. I can't talk to him about it for fear of Carole hearing prematurely and causing more problems than any of us can solve. Maybe I'll have a chance to visit with him when we're shopping for the boat tomorrow – if he hasn't already decided which boat he's going to buy. Do you and Carole want to abuse your 'Visas' again while we finish up? If he has decided on a couple of final choices, then we can come pick you up to look them over before making a decision. That would give you a chance to talk more with Carole and I could have the opportunity to see what his thoughts are on the subject of telling her about his problem – with no guarantees of him telling me anything. He's pretty closed mouthed when it comes to this sort of thing. He always has been."

"She's pretty excited about seeing the boats, but maybe I can talk her into going with me again. It will give me a chance to better evaluate *my* thoughts about how she feels about him; although I don't think I'm wrong.

Sometime during the conversation, Art had thrown his leg across his wife and had been idly massaging her abdomen and breasts with his free hand. The seriousness of the conversation failed to inhibit the sexual stimulation building, in both husband and wife, and they were soon paying less and less attention to the problems of Mark and Carole and more and more attention to the immediate set of circumstances they found themselves in.

Jean had been wiggling closer to him under his hand and had snuggled her head provocatively onto his chest and was kissing him each time it was his turn to respond to a statement she had made. Art, in turn, had become thoroughly aroused by the intimate contact and whispered softly in his wife's ear, "Now that you have me *totally* awake and there seems to be nothing more to say about our friends – do you have any suggestions as to what we might do to pass the time?"

Jean snuggled even closer and moved her hand to the elastic of the pajama bottoms Art was wearing – reached inside and after the briefest of searches, grasped him firmly and said, "You can use it – or lose it, my darling."

CHAPTER NINETEEN

Mark woke up in a heavy sweat, feeling like he'd been harpooned. He was doubled up and fighting, unsuccessfully, to stifle the moan that escaped his clenched teeth. Fear engulfed him as he struggled out of bed and headed for the door to the bathroom. He turned on the light and sat heavily on the toilet to catch his breath and thinking, my God, is this just the beginning? He hoped the pain would subside enough to rejoin Carole before she woke up and found him missing. "*Jesus* – what am I going to tell her if I have to call an ambulance – or a doctor? I didn't expect this. Not this soon anyway," he mumbled through clenched teeth.

The pain gradually started to subside, and become bearable. He straightened himself – leaning heavily on the bathroom sink counter. His hair and body were wet with cold sweat. The pain and the sweat seemed to be in tandem. As the level of pain went down, the sweat followed. He wanted to shower before he went back to bed, but didn't want to wake Carole. What would he tell her? "I'll think of something", he mumbled under his breath, and stepped into the tub, welcoming the soothing effect of the warm water cascading down his back.

The pain was gone by the time he finished his shower; however, the echo of its intensity was still with him – a stark reminder of how bad things would become.

Mark quietly slipped back into bed, hoping not to wake Carole. Not to be. She was sleeping on her stomach and when he slid between the sheets beside her, she rose sleepily to her elbows and asked, quizzically, "Did you just take a shower?"

"Yeah, I was having trouble sleeping with the sheets sticking to me. You worked me pretty hard tonight, you insatiable wench."

"I never heard you yell *uncle*," she said as she moved closer to snuggle.

Mark cradled her head on his chest and in a very few moments, heard the slow rhythmic breathing of her deep sleep once again.

Mark loved the feel of her sleeping next to him. This simple pleasure usually brought the quick and blissful slumber of a contented man, but not tonight. His eyes were wide in the darkness as he thought how terrible tonight's episode would have been if he'd been driving – or even worse – if he'd been flying. He understood, now, how intense and crippling the pain would be, and he worried that he might be putting the others in harm's way. He could not continue as if nothing was wrong, yet, he didn't want to ruin the vacation if this was only a one-time occurrence. I wonder if I should call Dr. Givens and ask if I should see a doctor down here? Maybe I could find out if I am going to be safe while driving or flying for now. I just don't know what to do, he thought. I know I can't handle any prolonged episodes like tonight without chemical help. I just *thought* I was tough.

The self-debate lasted for an hour before he decided to try and wait until he was back in Memphis to take any serious action – unless he was harpooned again. In that case, he knew he would have to come clean with everyone, meaning Carole. If it happened again, he couldn't take a chance on flying and would have to call the FBO to see if he could hire a pilot to fly them home.

He also knew that he had to buy his boat tomorrow. No more dilly-dallying around. It would take some time for them to outfit the boat the way he wanted it and he wanted it ready when he needed it. The *need* had made itself evident tonight.

*　　*　　*

At breakfast the next morning, Mark sat rather silent as the women were trying out different plans for their day. Jean was trying to get Carole to do one more day of shopping, but Carole was waiting to see if she was invited to see the boats before committing.

Mark finally spoke up and said, "I don't think it will take a great deal of time to look at the three boats I'm interested in. Why don't we all go down and look at them so Carole and Jean can see what we're talking about. Maybe they can help finalize the choice. All three boats are really suitable. I have a favorite, but I won't say which until we've seen them all and I get your input. After that, I will try and make a deal with the owner(s) while the rest of you go play. Jean has her cell phone and I can call you when I'm finished. That way you won't have to stand around like totems and wait on me doing paperwork."

Carole spoke up right away, "I'm dying to see the boats. I'm also dying to do more shopping; so – Marks plan sounds ideal to me. If Art doesn't want to be dragged around looking at women's stuff, we can park him down on the beach somewhere so he can drink beer and lust after the honeys in, *or mostly in,* their bikinis."

"Naturally, I'd hate to leave the two of you to shop alone," Art said, "but I guess I could be forced to sit on the beach – drink beer – look at those poor children without funds to adequately clothe themselves. I'll check with you first, honey, but there might be a couple of them we could adopt. I've always wanted to be a humanitarian."

After Jean finished beating Art on the shoulder, she said, "Seems like we've planned another day in paradise. If everyone is finished, why don't we get started? Carole, do you have to go back to the room for anything?"

"No, I've got my camera and everything else I need. I'm ready to go."

                              *   *   *

They decided to go to the most distant marina first and
then work their way back to be closer to the hotel. Mark had
planned it that way because the cement boat was the last one
he wanted to show the women and it was only a couple of miles
away.

They stopped at the marina office to get the key to the
boat and asked the salesman if it was OK to just go aboard and
look around for a while to let the ladies see what they'd been
looking at. If he wanted to join them it was fine – but not
necessary.

It was the 50-footer and the girls were immediately
taken by its size and the room afforded by such a large boat.
Mark on the other hand became more and more critical of the
boat – saying that it would be more difficult to handle without
a crew and would take quite a bit of work before it would be
ready to sail. The sail inventory was not in good shape and
would have to be redone. There was quite a lot of corrosion on
the aluminum mast and boom and the shrouds were frayed.
The woodwork was in about the same shape as that on the
cement boat and would need a lot of sanding and varnishing
before it would look presentable. However, below decks, the
boat was beautiful – with abundant room for comfortable
sailing. If his plans had included a long-term relationship with
the boat – he would probably have been more serious about
buying it. He knew the boat he wanted and this was just an
exercise in letting the women become involved.

The visit to the second marina was essentially the same
as the first – the ladies liked the boat, but were not as
enthused about it as the larger 50-footer. Mark did the same
with the 38-footer as he did the 50-footer – put it down –
emphasizing the lesser aspects of the boat and ignoring the
finer. The newness and good maintenance of the second boat
was well received and they, like Mark, liked the boat, but it
just didn't quite get the job done.

When they were back in the convertible – driving to the
marina where the cement boat was located – Mark started the
same commentary Don had given him the day before. When he
told Jean and Carole that it was made of cement, they thought

he was joking and cracked wise about, "Using it for sea-snipe hunting" and "If you buy a cement boat – I want to sell you a cement bridge you can sail it under." They were laughing and carrying on about the absurdity of a boat made of cement. "Going down to the sea in ships – *ships made of recycled sidewalks.*"

Mark turned to Art and said, "God, I hope there's a *slave trader* tied up down here. I know we'd have to pay him to take them, but I think it might be worth it."

Once at the marina, Don just gave them the keys and told them to take their time inspecting the boat. He said he'd talked to the owner and he had given him a price. If they were still interested, he'd go over the details when they were finished looking.

Walking toward the boat – and seeing it out of the water – the women were again impressed by the size of the vessel. It did look a lot bigger sitting on the keel blocks with the large fixed keel in full view. The women were not too interested in the inspection of the hull and wanted to go right aboard.

They looked at the vertical ladder and Jean immediately turned to Carole to complain, "These guys have this all planned so they can look up our dresses while we're climbing this thing."

"Watch this," Carole said, and walked directly to the ladder – climbed the first three rungs and then called to Mark, "Honey would you come over here for a second?"

When Mark joined her at the foot of the ladder, she pushed herself backward while still holding the rails and forced the back of her dress over Marks head and through her legs. She then lowered herself down until she was sitting on his shoulders. "Up please!" she said to the wails of laughter coming from Art and Jean.

Mark struggled blindly to the top of the ladder with Carole riding comfortably on his shoulders as if she were having the time of her life. She stepped gingerly onto the gunwales then called down to Jean and said, "See how easy?"

Mark exaggerated the display of his exhaustion and clung tightly to the ladder – complaining about the lack of respect he was getting as a potential boat captain. He was trying to make light of what should have been a simple task for him – carrying 115 pounds up a ten-foot ladder. He was, in fact, exhausted and didn't know why. Had he not rested, he would not have been able to climb aboard the boat without help. It was starting!

Once on board, Mark continued his sales pitch as the women made a cursory tour of the topside area and then plunged into the lower deck spaces to inspect the living quarters – especially the galley and head facilities. With Mark still running his mouth, Carole finally said, "Look, I know this is the boat you like. Why don't you just go talk to the man and get it over with. I love the boat and with just a little soap and water, I can have everything down here looking lovely – or do you call it *shipshape.* You'll have to take care of everything on top. I don't know anything about that stuff." She tiptoed and kissed him lightly on the mouth and continued with, "You've got your boat – now be *happy.*"

"Was it that obvious that this was the one I wanted," Mark asked.

"Mark Stevens, you can be read like a *Dick and Jane* primer," she said with her patented laugh.

After another thirty minutes of looking in drawers, cupboards and other storage spaces, Carole and Jean were satisfied that the boat was habitable if it could be aired out and dipped in *Febreze.*

Mark said, "OK, ladies, you've done your duty – boat-wise. I'll go find Don and get this deal settled and you can get started on your shopping spree. Art, don't let them drop you off in front of one of those retirement condos for Jewish widows. Be selective, and make a note of the location in case we both need to go back and check it out. I'm going to spend a little time here on the boat to make a list of things I want done before I take delivery."

CHAPTER TWENTY

So many things in his life had changed in the past two weeks that he was becoming overwhelmed by it all: The pressure of not being open with Carole – the realization that he only had a very short time to live. The desire to actually have his boat to sail the way he'd always dreamed of sailing it – to work it – to bring it to life and maintain it as something he loved. He longed to see Karen – her hair sun-bleached and her skin tan from the sun of the Caribbean. And now, he wanted to have Carole enjoy the freedom of sailing to wonderful peaceful places where memories could be made for old-age reveries. The stark reality of his situation screamed to him – saying, "None of this will ever happen. You're screwed, man."

Alone on the boat he started to reminisce about his life and how he could have changed it to make the present more bearable. He couldn't think of any real changes he would have made. He'd loved and provided for his wife and daughter until circumstance took them away. He'd worked hard in a rewarding career that he fully enjoyed. He'd done the best he could to maintain his personal relationships without intentionally hurting anyone. It didn't make sense. He'd done everything right – according to convention, and still he'd been dealt some pretty heavy blows that seemed hard to explain. Then it dawned on him – there are no explanations.

I did nothing particularly wrong, nor did Karen and Sara – it just happened and here I am asking myself how I could change anything. I couldn't – obviously – just as I can't change the circumstances of my life today. Maybe I should be somewhat thankful that I am aware of how much time I have left – barring accidents – and make the most of it. I'm fortunate in that I can afford to do just about anything I choose to do. That's a lot better off than thousands of others facing the same circumstances. Strange that I don't fear the dying part as much as I do the effect it will have on those that I care about and those that care about me. I don't want them to see me deteriorate to nothing while they stand idly by in their helplessness. What a shame to finally have my boat and having to use it for this instead of what it was made for. Now, I envy those of religious conviction. At least they believe they have something to look forward to. I hate a hypocrite too much to try and fake it in the eleventh hour and become a hypocrite myself. No, that's not me. I just don't know what to do in these uncharted waters. I guess I'll just do the best I can and see where it takes me. Maybe I should even keep a diary and make it available to others in this situation. Maybe they could make better choices after reading it – if I screw it up. Maybe after enough diaries are read – we could all die perfectly.

Still feeling somewhat melancholy, Mark removed the notes from the notebook and went back down below to see if he'd secured everything. After closing some cabinets and putting away some of the owner's things that had been disturbed, he locked the boat again and climbed down the ladder to go find Don and close the deal if the selling price was reasonable.

When he arrived back at the showroom, Don was waiting on another customer. Mark stood around a bit, casually looking at the boats in the showroom until Don broke away from his customer and came over to ask Mark if he would like a cup of coffee and that he would be finished in a very few minutes. Mark went to the coffee pot, poured a cup of coffee and sat down in the waiting area.

He had been waiting about five minutes when Don, again, came over to him and apologized for the wait – then asked Mark, "Well, are you still interested in the boat?"

"Yes, I'd like to talk to you about it."

"Great! Why don't we go down to my office and I'll go over the details with you. I thought you'd like it. It's a heck-of-a-boat."

On the way to the office, Don kept the conversation going by telling Mark, "The owners have already contracted to have the hull painted – so that's one less thing you'll have to worry about. However, they set the price of the boat 'AS IS" other than the painting already contracted. I assume they'd do more with a corresponding increase in cost."

They were entering Don's office, and as Mark was being seated, he asked, "What did they say they wanted for it?"

"He said he was *firm* at $120,000, and did not care to take any counteroffers. Since it's my job, I advised him that he could spend another $10,000 on the boat, and it would sell for $180,000 with very little trouble. With that bit of free advice locked safely in his memory banks, he said that he would consider my advice, if you didn't want the boat. For right now, he just wanted to avoid the hassle, and sell it without a whole lot of fixing up prior to putting it on the market. He no longer wants to be a boat owner and the sooner he can be removed from that category, the better."

"I'd guessed that the boat would be somewhere in that price range. Naturally, I'd hoped that it would be a little less – but that's the way it goes. You won't take him a counteroffer?"

"No, I can't do that. He was pretty firm when he told me that as well."

"OK, I'm going to give you a list of things I want done on the boat. If you think you can have all of it done in two to three weeks – I'll take the boat. It's a pretty long list, so I'd like for you to consider your answer before you commit; because I'm going to be pretty hard to deal with if you can't produce."

"Let me see the list."

Don took the list and studied it carefully. After several minutes of looking and thinking about it, he said, "I can't give you an answer without checking out the availability of the things you've asked for. If the sails need extensive repair – I can't speak for the sail shop. I don't think the GPS will be any problem at all or the sanding and varnishing of the woodwork. I've got to ask – why would you want the diesels replaced? They're in very good shape with unusually low hours. They are somewhat safer than gasoline as well. I don't think we'll have any trouble finding a gas engine, but it will be pretty expensive to change everything out. It will also reduce the resale value if you ever decide to sell the boat."

"Don, I'm a pretty fair hand with gasoline engines and I don't know a damned thing about diesel. I know it's going to be expensive, but I'd rather have the gas. It's a personal thing with me."

"If that's what you want – I'll see what I can do. Are you going to be in town for another day or so? If so, I'll get the sails to the sail shop and check on the availability of an engine. If the other vendors can assure me they can get the work done within your time frame, then I'll commit to the other things on the list that we'll be taking care of here in the yard. After I've gathered the information, I'll call you and let you know what I've found out. I really don't think the sails will need anything done to them. They haven't been used that much. It's the engine and generators that I'm concerned about. I really wish you'd reconsider that part of the deal."

"No, I want the gas." Then after a short pause, he continued, "Well, get the information you need and give me a call as soon as you have it. I want the boat – and for some pretty serious personal reasons, I need it to be ready to sail in a maximum of three weeks. I hope we can make a deal."

"OK, Mr. Stevens, I'll get right on it. I'll give you a call later today or in the morning at the latest, and if it looks like everything is going to work out, I'll give you an estimate on the additional work you've requested. Do you want us to work out the financing, or will you do that yourself."

"I'll take care of the financing. I just want you to do what you can to be able to have the boat in the water and ready to sail within three weeks maximum. If it can be done sooner – I will appreciate it. I'll be looking forward to your call."

With the negotiations out of the way – Mark stood and handed Don his business card, saying, "I'll have the cell phone with me all the time, so use that number and call me as soon as you have the information you need."

"I hope to have the information before the day is out, if not, no later than tomorrow morning. I think you've just bought a boat, Mr. Stevens, and I know you're gonna love it."

"I hope so, Don. By the way, I still have the key to the boat. Do you mind if I go back out there for a little while and look it over more carefully? There may be a few more things I'd like done. If so, I'll do them myself, and they won't affect the time schedule. I'll drop the key off on my way out."

"Help yourself and stay as long as you like. I've got to get busy if I want to get you some answers by this evening."

Mark walked slowly back to the boat, climbed aboard and sat in the cockpit. Here I sit, he thought, where I've worked my whole life to be, only to find I'm here for a different purpose than I ever imagined. I expected to have several years to enjoy sailing to the places I've charted in my mind for years. Maybe I should have bought a boat that was ready to sail today instead of burning three weeks waiting on this one. I just wanted to have some of *me* in the boat. I want it to be mine, rigged as I want it and not as someone else had it planned. I just don't have the time. I don't know if anyone ever has the time – now that I think of it. You just think you do until you learn something different. It would probably be best if I just took off and left Carole and the others. Sail until my time is up and do what I have to do without their involvement. I think I'm too selfish for that. I want them to enjoy some of it with me – at least until I'm unable to be an active part of the adventure. I can't just sail off without any explanations to anyone. No, I want to share the fun with someone I care about. Maybe Carole will go – even after she finds out the truth. I hope so.

After about 30 minutes of depressing thought – Mark shook off the despondency and took out his cell phone and called Jean's number. After a couple of rings, Jean picked up without saying hello and said, "My God! Are you going to spend forever on that boat?"

"I was just calling to ask if you would bring my clothes down here. I'm ready to go."

"Well – not before you feed us again. Are you about ready for us to come back and get you? I told Art that we'd pick you up first and then come by for him – so he could lust after the bikini babies a little longer. Maybe we can have a drink or something while we're next to the beach."

"I breathlessly await your appearance. I'll be next to the showroom. You didn't spend your children's inheritance did you?

"No, but I'm damn sure making a dent in it. We'll see you in about 20 minutes. Bye!"

Mark hung up the phone and climbed back down the ladder. On the ground, he looked back up at the boat and thought, I'd always pictured this day as being one of the most wonderful of my life. Where's the wonder?

CHAPTER TWENTY-ONE

"Do you want to drive?" Jean asked as Mark approached the convertible.

"No, I'd much prefer to sit in the back and be chauffeured around by two beautiful women."

"*Right,*" Jean spouted back.

"That way I'll have plenty of chances to wave at the poor, less-fortunate types that will envy my approach to life as we cruise down the boulevard to recapture my friend and bikini scout."

"I have a plastic bag we can put over his head if you'd like," Jean said, as she turned to Carole, pretending confidentiality. "That way, if we see any of those cute guys from the restaurant they won't think we've *settled* for something less than we are capable of."

"Please drive," Mark answered back "and I will appreciate a little more adulation from the two of you, if you don't mind. I am, quite possibly, the newest *captain*, of a *major* sailing vessel." Then, after a short pause, he added, "I also have a decent memory and once we are at sea – there may be hell-to-pay if proper respect isn't afforded the Captain when he is ashore."

Carole rose to her knees and spun around to face Mark and squealed excitedly, "You bought the boat?"

"I think so. I made a list of things I wanted done, and if they can assure me they can get them done on time – it's a done deal."

Carole lunged over the back of the front seat and threw her arms around Mark and started kissing him all over his face in her excitement. "It's the most beautiful boat in the world, and I am so happy for you I can hardly stand it! When will you be able to use it?"

"I told them I had to have the boat within three weeks maximum. Don is to call me tonight or in the morning to let me know if they can commit to my schedule. If they can – we're in business; if not, then we have more boat shopping to do. I hope I'm not being overly optimistic, but I honestly think they can have it ready by then. Anyway – I feel like a boat owner, and I love the feeling. Are *you* ready to go?"

"The only thing that could keep me from going would be the lack of an invitation. And, if that were the case, I'd *whine* until you asked me – even if it was just to shut me up. I hate whining, but I'm extremely adept at it if I have to be."

"Believe me, you won't have to whine. I hope we can all enjoy it. It was made for fun, and I think this crew could maximize those capabilities. I feel as excited as when I got my first bicycle, and I'm afraid to start talking about it for fear of not being able to stop. Pour a bucket of water over my head if I get too carried away."

*   *   *

Driving down North Atlantic Boulevard, six eyes were searching for the beachfront café Art had designated as his base of operation. They passed the *Café Capri* and saw Art sitting under an umbrella in the open-air portion of the restaurant. He dutifully watched the bikini babies as they paraded past – drinking beer and looking as though he'd found paradise.

Parking was impossible near the restaurant, so they circled the block and found a parking lot just off the beach, but still within easy walking distance of Art's lookout station.

Art had not seen them drive by and luckily had not heard the caustic comments of his bride as she evaluated his situation under her breath, to no one in particular, but to everyone within earshot. No one within earshot was confused about her words of endearment. Art might have a little trouble explaining his look of total contentment while watching the parade.

The sidewalk split the outdoor portion of the restaurant, and as the trio approached the constellation of tables and umbrellas, Carole rushed ahead of the others and excitedly announced to Art – "He bought the boat."

Jean, on the other hand, held back slightly and stood with her hands on her hips with a painful look of disgust etching her face. After a few moments of staring at her contented husband, she said, *"Darling,"* with dripping sarcasm, "please wipe your face. The drooling is starting to become encrusted and is *exceptionally* unbecoming."

Art just looked up at her with a satisfied smile that, in itself, told Jean and the world, that *Bud Light* had played a particularly active role in his afternoon at the beach. Without erasing the smile and ignoring the sarcasm, Art turned to Mark and asked, "Did you have to *bend over*, or anything like that during the deal making process?"

To which Mark replied, "No, not really. Don tried to kiss me, but I told him to wait until after he was sure he could get the boat ready on time. I should hear from him later this afternoon, or in the morning, to find out if the modifications I asked for could be completed by the time I got back down here. If they can do that, we've got some sailing to do."

"Great! I think you made a smart decision. I thought it was the best of all the boats we looked at, and I'm sure you'll be happy with it."

As the newcomers were seating themselves in the waiting chairs positioned around the table, Jean leaned forward and lightly kissed Art on the cheek and said, "I hope they have at least three cold beers left. I want to check out what you've been looking at all afternoon and see what's put that Cheshire-cat smile on your ugly mug."

The descending sun had brought the shade of the restaurant over their table. The friends sipped the frosty glasses of beer and watched the exodus of sun worshipers as they left the beach. It was a *people-watchers* paradise. The quartet kept a running dialogue with comments that generally concerned the attire of those leaving the beach or just walking the sidewalk. The ladies were commenting, in mock disbelief, on the brevity of the bikinis worn by the girls and the *Speedos* worn by the male bodybuilders. It was good-natured finger pointing with several of the comments declaring, "*My God*, if I had a body like that, I'd wear it too." And, "If I caught Art in something like that, I'd take pictures – and then kill him."

The sun had dipped even further toward the horizon, and the beach crowd had just about disappeared. A majority of the customers in the *Café Capri* were dressed in cover-ups and shorts – reflecting the casual atmosphere of most beachfront dining in the area.

Mark spoke to the others to get their views on plans for the evening, "Do you think we should go back to the hotel and get cleaned up, or would you rather just have dinner here and make an early night out of it?"

Art was ready for anything and mumbled to anyone listening, "Party, party!"

To which Jean replied, "I think the *Beaver Patrol* has about had it. Why don't we just order something here and head on back before my *darling* Art faints on us?"

Again, the mumbled "Party, party!" from Art.

Carole said, "I could not be happier with any decision you guys make. Early night – late night, I'll enjoy either."

Mark then said, "OK, let's see if I can capture a waiter and get some menus."

They all ordered burgers, to break the seafood regimen they'd found themselves in since arriving in Ft. Lauderdale. The mood was festive and three out of the four were enjoying making a lot of unflattering comments about a mentally unarmed Art. He, of course, made a few unflattering responses as he tried, unsuccessfully, to defend himself. He was a good-natured drunk.

Mark was somewhat disappointed that Don had not called, but let the disappointment slide, hoping the anxiety was not affecting the others.

Art was obviously unaffected by his anxiety, so when the burgers and fries were finally finished and the three sober members of the party had tired of staring at a nodding Art, Jean said, "A man can only stand so many bikinis and *Bud* in one afternoon. I think we'd better try and get him to the car."

Art reached the convertible, with assistance from the others, still mumbling "Party, party!" and was sound asleep before they left the parking lot to return to the hotel.

CHAPTER TWENTY-TWO

Mark had not slept well. The painful episode of the night before still lingered in his mind. He was acutely aware that the pain could occur again. He tossed and turned most of the night. The discomfort he'd become accustomed to was not the reason for the sleeplessness. It was the dread of a recurrence of the staggering pain from his last (only) attack that made him intensely aware of any subtle changes occurring throughout the course of the night. If Carole had not been sleeping so comfortably beside him, he would have gotten up hours ago. Instead, he waited, fretfully, for the dawn to escape the confines of the bed he would normally find difficult to leave.

Finally, light was filtering in through the east window of the bedroom as the sun was struggling to climb the horizon. The dawn caused Carole to become somewhat restless in her sleep as she snuggled next to him and stretched to try and prolong the unconscious joy of sleep. It didn't work and soon she was fully awake, yet reluctant to leave the comfort of the bed. She placed her arm over Marks chest and pulled her bent leg over and up to his waist as she snuggled even closer in the curl of his arm, mumbling a sleepy good morning.

"How would you like to have breakfast in bed'?" Mark asked.

"I'd settle for a cup of coffee right now, but if you can keep me chained here until about ten – the breakfast would be wonderful. I'll be *blimped-out* if I eat every time you offer."

"Why don't we throw on some shorts," Mark said, "and we'll have our coffee down on the beach. Between the coffee and wading in the ocean – one of them should jolt us back to life on this fine day. We can come back up here a little later and see if Art lived. I can't wait to watch him suffering this morning. Maybe we can sing to him, or something to help him along. *Ninety Nine Bottles of Beer on the Wall* should be an appropriate wake-me-up."

"Let's do it", she replied, and bounded across him, out of his arms, out of bed and on a beeline for the bathroom.

Mark dressed in the bedroom and was slipping on his sneakers when Carole reappeared, wearing snug khaki shorts that terminated an inch or two above mid-thigh and a floppy sweatshirt with *Guess* emblazoned across the chest. The floppy shirt seemed to accent her long, smooth legs and rounded buns enough to make Mark stare some.

"Dallas Cowboys Cheerleader," he blurted out.

"What?" Carole asked, quizzically.

"The sign said *Guess* – and that was my guess."

"You are a born smartass, Mr. Stevens, but that little remark didn't cost you any points at all," she said, smiling at his obvious approval of her clothing and the nonsense.

They had left the room and walked a few feet down the hallway, when Mark said, "Wait! I'd better take my phone with me, just in case Don calls. It's probably too early, but I'm really anxious to hear from him." He then returned to the room, picked up his phone and rejoined Carole.

*   *   *

Mark and Carole picked up large Styrofoam cups; and filled them with steaming coffee from a huge container located on a service table in the lobby. They walked slowly to the water's edge behind the hotel. The beach was pristine and nearly deserted in the early morning, with the soothing sounds of a nearly calm Atlantic washing quietly ashore. Seagulls squawked their disapproval at the intrusion as they dove gracefully to the sand or water to pluck morsels of debris from their respective resting places, screeching loudly when one beat another to a mutually attractive target. Sandpipers raced along in front of their path, pecking quickly at insects and small shells as they ran, helter-skelter, at the water's edge. There was a slight early-morning chill in the air that made the sweatshirts they wore welcome attire. They walked, mostly in silence, breathing the fresh, salt air and sipping coffee from the steaming cups. It was good. There was no real need for conversation, other than the comments from each that vocalized just how good it really was, as they walked barefoot in the cool morning sand and surf with his arm around her shoulders and hers around his waist.

In the silence of the walk, Mark thought, If I had any guts, now would be as good a time as any to tell her what's going on. He tried to start speaking, but the words just wouldn't come out. He was enjoying himself too much seeing Carole immersed in the vacation. It was too big a chance to take right now; he rationalized.

The cell phone in the pocket of his shorts interrupted his dreary thoughts. "Hello," Mark said, glancing at his watch.

"Mr. Stevens, this is Don from the marina. I hope I'm not calling too early, but I thought you'd like to know that you've just bought a boat, if you're still interested."

Mark had dropped his shoes and handed his coffee to Carole as he answered the phone. He was squeezing her shoulders excitedly as he said, "Yes, I'm still seriously interested. Will all the things on my list be finished on time?"

"Yes, the sail maker checked out the sail inventory, and they are just what you'd ordered – the three jibs, main and spinnaker; all in excellent shape with no repairs needed. The engine and generator that I was concerned about are in stock and the electronics can be installed today if you say *go*. Our men can take care of the other things you wanted."

"Well, I'm saying *go*, right now. I'll be down about mid-morning to sign the papers and reach deep into my pockets for the finalizing funds. I'm very happy that you called with the good news. I'll see you later this morning."

"It's my pleasure, Mr. Stevens. I knew you wanted the boat, and I'm sure it will be everything you expected. I look forward to seeing you in a couple of hours. Bye."

"Goodbye, Don and thanks."

Mark engulfed Carole with his arms, lifted her off her feet and began to twirl her around as she squealed in delight; spilling coffee in a wide circle on the sand as she spun. Mark kept repeating, "We *got* it! We *got* it!" over and over again.

Mark stopped the spinning and let Carole's feet touch down and then went serious while his arms were still around her, holding her close. "Do you think you could get your personal things squared away enough to do some extended sailing within the next couple of weeks? You are my very first choice as a mate, both in the nautical sense *and* the social."

"If I *can't*, then things will just have to stay in disorder until the sailing is done. I can't wait."

Then Carole became more serious as she placed her arms around Mark and put her ear to his chest. After a few moments of silence, she said, "I may be saying this a bit premature, but I really want you to know how happy you have made me since we met. It's been such a short time, and yet I feel like you've always been with me. You feel as comfortable as an old shoe, and no matter what happens later, you have made me feel *alive* for the first time in a very *long* time. I appreciate it and thank you. If you should choose never to see me again after we get back, I will still be able to look back at the time we've spent together as being some of my most delicious memories."

Mark said nothing, but was somewhat amazed to hear Carole verbalizing *his* thoughts. He held her for a moment then kissed her softly on the lips. Still holding on and enjoying the tenderness of the moment, he said, softly, "Let's go back and tell my hung-over buddy the good news."

They walked slowly at first, but the excitement was too much for Carole and she started dragging Mark along by the hand – rushing, pulling, laughing – trying to get this slug-of-a-man moving. It was good, really good.

*   *   *

"This is my *only* warning," Art growled from inside the suite. "I will shoot through the door if you bang on it one more time – *whoever* you are, go *immediately* from this place."

"Oh *wow*," Mark whispered to Carole as he held back the laugh trying to erupt. "It's even better than I'd hoped for," as he banged even louder on the door of Art's room and yelled, "Get your sorry ass out of bed and get ready to apologize to us all, for your unacceptable behavior last night. I'm sure Jean has already trashed you, but you still have us to deal with."

"I'm warning you, man, I *am* armed."

"Not *mentally*! Now open this goddamned door. I want to see if you've abused my friend – your long-suffering wife."

As Mark was shouting his last comment, Jean opened the door, rolled her eyes majestically toward Art and motioned them into the room. Art was still lying in bed, on his back, with a pillow pressed across his face and head. Low, muffled moans escaped through the feathers of the pillow.

Mark turned to Carole and asked, as seriously as he could, "What is that stuff they say at AA – 'One Day at a Time'?"

Mark delighted in going over to the bed and violently shaking it, yelling, "Get up, you lazy shit! You've got to take care of these young lovelies while I go finalize my boat purchase."

"Call Dr. Kevorkian," came the muffled response from Art. "I need his services, now."

Mark turned to Jean, who was sitting sprawled in one of the casual chairs in the room and asked, "If I can get this boat deal settled by this evening, would you mind if we cut our stay a day short and head back home tomorrow? I've got some things I need to get taken care of in Memphis, and I want to get started on them so I can be ready when the boat is ready."

"No, I don't think it will be a problem at all – if Art lives. He's got a business to run – supposedly – and I'm sure he can make some excuse as to why we were kicked out of Florida a day or so early."

"Well, it's only a 'speed bump'. I want you to start planning a couple of weeks' vacation, real soon, to check out the boat on the high seas. Carole has already agreed to be my *Mate* and I can't imagine a better crew than the two of you. I'm in a hurry to *pop a chute* and swim in the Caribbean. You've *got* to talk 'Dumb-Ass' into going with us. I'll even make payroll for him while he's gone if I have to."

Carole was smiling at the exchange between Mark and Jean, but started to become a little anxious when the intensity of the plea became something more than a simple request. She thought, "My God, what's this all about?" however, it was a passing thought, and she said nothing.

"Ladies," Mark said, "I hate to lay this on you, but I've got to get down to the marina before someone else grabs our boat. Can you take care of the blob while I'm gone? Keep your cell phone on and I'll get with you as soon as the paperwork is taken care of. We can make our last night in Ft. Lauderdale a memorable one. While I'm gone, would one of you call a limo service for our transportation tonight and have them here at 7:30 sharp. I think this is the night I might pull an *Art*. We'll find out if he's as tough as he thinks he is – party-wise."

CHAPTER TWENTY-THREE

Mark parked the convertible at ten minutes past nine and was met at the door of the marina showroom by Don. "I was just going down to the yard," he said, "to see how the work is coming along on your boat. Would you like to go with me now or wait until the paper trail is established?"

"Why don't we go ahead and finalize the deal; unless you have something in particular you need to visit about with your *hands*."

"No, nothing in particular. I know the cleaning is finished, and they're getting ready to mask and paint. They were going to paint the boat it's original white, but if you'd rather have a different color, it's not too late to change it."

"If it's no more trouble, I think I'd rather have the hull a navy blue or black; however, if it's going to push the envelope of my schedule, I don't want to change anything."

"I don't think it will make a bit of difference. I'll call the yard from my office and see if there will be any problems in changing the color."

The paperwork didn't take long. Mark wrote a check for half the amount of the boat and modifications, and then gave Don the telephone number of his bank – to verify his credibility. The final payment was to be made when the boat was accepted and delivered. Mark also offered a $500-per-day bonus to the marina as incentive to get the boat ready early. The bonus would max out at seven days.

When the paperwork was finished, they walked to the boatyard for Marks final inspection before returning to Memphis. He asked that Don call the owner and have him remove all personal items from the boat before the work on the topside areas began. Then after a quick visit with the workers, to check if the color change would alter the work progress or schedule, Mark told Don he was ready to leave the men to their jobs.

Walking back toward the showroom, Mark said, "Don, I will need to hire a Captain to take me to Nassau once I take delivery. I will fly him back home after I'm satisfied that I can handle the boat safely. If you know someone who is dependable and qualified, I will appreciate your getting in contact with him and see if he's available, for a week or so, after the boat is ready. If we can work out a deal, I'll want him to check out the chart inventory, etc., to make sure we've got everything we need to sail the Caribbean area with no problems. I think we have to have software for the GPS, as well. I'll give you another check for $500.00 as an escrow account for the boat. If you need more, just let me know, and I'll add to it as necessary."

"We have a fairly extensive list of Charter Captains, and I know several of them personally. It won't be a problem finding someone. I'll check around and let you know a couple of suitable candidates that you can contact."

"Great! You have my numbers in Memphis; so if you're having any problems that I can help with – give me a call and we'll take care of it. Thanks a lot, Don. It's been a pleasure doing business with you."

"The pleasure has been mine, Mr. Stevens. I'll see you in a couple of weeks."

Mark was back in the convertible and on his cell phone at five minutes 'til ten, calling the hotel. When Art finally answered the phone, Mark asked, "Are you going to live?"

"No! I'm just getting cleaned up and dressed so Jean can get a discount with the mortician. The women have abandoned me and should be in the coffee shop planning how to spend my estate."

"Art," Mark asked, "do you think it would break anyone's heart if we headed back to Memphis early this afternoon? I know I had mentioned doing another night here, but I've got a bunch of things to get settled at home before I can take delivery on the boat and I'd like to get started on them as soon as possible. Don has assured me that it will be ready within three weeks maximum, and I've offered bonuses for them to get it ready sooner. I could, conceivably, take possession within *two* weeks, and if that's the case, I really need to hurry. I don't need to tell you how critical time has become to me."

"I understand, Mark, and speaking for myself, I've enjoyed about as much of Ft. Lauderdale I can stand at one time. Jean will understand the reason for the rush and I know she'll go along with anything you choose to do. You know more about what Carole would think of leaving early than I do. I'm about to join them, so I can ask. I don't think they will have a problem with it; if not, we can start packing while we're waiting on you to get back."

"Great! I'll call the airport and ask them to get the plane fueled and ready. We can be back in Memphis by dark, and you can die in your own bed. I'll see you in about forty-five minutes."

*   *   *

When Mark opened the door to the hotel room, he was somewhat surprised to see their luggage spread out on the bed and Carole busily packing their clothes.

"So," Carole said, "now that you've had your way with me for a few days, you're bored and ready to move on to more challenging projects?"

Mark didn't answer, directly, but instead walked over and pulled her into his arms and said, "We both know it's quite the opposite of your smartass evaluation. I know I have an awful lot to do in Memphis before we can get underway and I assume you have just about as much to do as me. I don't want to put off coming back down here because of some nonsense I've left undone at home. If you were serious about coming with me, I don't want to waste a single minute once the boat is available."

She looked up at him for a moment, then put her arms around him and said, "I know – and I'm just as excited about it as you are. Art said that you sounded like you were dancing on air when he talked to you a while ago. I knew it would be awful to sit around down here loafing while there were things to do at home. I'm having the time of my life, but if it will speed things up, I'm ready to head back and make ready for the real reason we made this trip. I might even be able to lure you back into my arms a couple of times while we're in Memphis if you aren't *too* awfully busy."

"I sure as hell won't be too busy for that," he said as he broke the embrace. Continuing, he said, "Wow, you're real handy at this packing. If I'd known you were this close to being finished, I'd have gone by the coffee shop for another half hour or so."

"I always take care of a pilot who is about to fly me 1,100 miles in a small plane."

"Why don't I call a cab and have it deliver our luggage to the airport? That way we can *comfortably* drive to a restaurant, of your choice, for one last lunch in magnificent Ft. Lauderdale. Maybe that will partially make up for the early departure."

"You'd make a better salesman than engineer. See how easily you sold me on that program?"

Mark helped finish the packing, called to make sure Jean and Art were ready and then called the front desk for a bellman and a cab. He then called Reliance Aviation to alert them that their luggage was en route and asked that they store it in a secure place until they arrived.

Everyone agreed to have their last lunch at the same place they'd had their first dinner – *The Down Under*. As expected, the food and service were superior, with champagne toasting the success of the shortened vacation. Mark, reluctantly, had his 7-Up in a champagne flute to fake his participation in the celebration.

Once at the airport, Mark was becoming more and more anxious while filing his flight plan, loading the airplane and

159

doing his pre-flight. The underlying fear of another attack while flying had forced itself into his consciousness and he became less and less sure of the wisdom in his decision to attempt the flight home. He kept reassuring himself that he felt fine, but the reassurance seemed rather shallow when he remembered the severity of the attack from the day before yesterday. It was way too late for any serious modifications to their plans, he thought, and at a quarter past one, Mark keyed his microphone and announced, *"Ft. Lauderdale Ground, this is Centurion 473 Zulu Charlie at Reliance Aviation. We're ready to taxi, with Information Lima."*

The flight was uneventful. The travelers resumed the *Trivial Pursuit* game and the time passed quickly, however, Mark felt like a heavy load had been removed from his shoulders when the plane finally touched down in Memphis. He had been as tight as a fiddle string the entire flight, fiddling with his instruments, making unnecessary calls to the various flight centers along the route and just generally doing "busy" work to make the tension bearable.

All three passengers noticed the difference in Marks behavior. Art and Jean shared more information about Mark than Carole did, and therefore didn't mention the difference. Carole, on the other hand, had commented, "Mark, you seem as nervous as a long-tailed cat in a room full of rocking chairs. Don't even suggest that this flight isn't going normally."

To which he responded, "No, everything is going well. I'm just a little anxious to get this part of the trip out of the way. You guys have had your champagne, and now I'm ready to get mine."

Once on the ground, with the car loaded, Mark delivered Art and Jean to their home. Jean invited Mark and Carole to join them for a drink and a *Pot Luck* dinner, having no clue as to what food might be available after the trip. Carole begged off, and asked for a *rain check*, saying she suddenly felt like she'd been through the wringer and asked if Mark would mind taking her directly home for a warm bath and the comfort of her own bed. Mark, too, was feeling the effects of the long day and was glad when Carole declined Jean's invitation. Jean didn't haggle over the invitation and seemed somewhat relieved that she didn't have to entertain guests for the rest of the evening.

After fond farewells of hugs, kisses, handshakes and promises of almost immediate group reunions, Mark and Carole found themselves alone in the Buick. A quietness settled around them as Carole snuggled close to Mark for the twenty-minute trip to her condo.

When they arrived, Carole asked, "If you aren't in too big a hurry to get rid of me, why don't you come up for a drink and I'll try the snack-thing again? You look worn out. Maybe I could dip you in the Jacuzzi or something like that."

"I'd love to." Mark said, and then proceeded to unload her luggage for the trip upstairs.

Once in the apartment, Mark carried the luggage to the bedroom and Carole went to the bar to mix drinks. "I'm going to open a bottle of wine." Carole said, "Would you like to join me or would you rather have something else?"

I think I'll have the scotch for right now, maybe a glass of wine later. I need immediate relief."

When the drinks were poured, and Mark had joined Carole in the den area, she asked, "Can I fill the Jacuzzi?"

"No, I don't think I can handle that tonight. I'd crash in a heartbeat, and I honestly need to get to my house before I do that. If I had my office clothes here, I wouldn't even hesitate to take you up on your offer, but I know what will happen, and I'd better use common sense for a change. As a matter of fact, I think I'll skip the snack and just relax a few minutes and then head for the house. Waking up without you beside me is not going to be something I'm looking forward to, but maybe I can fight it for one night. Then again – you could come with me."

"I'm like you – I love waking up with you there, but I'd better stay here tonight. We're going to have to work out better sleeping arrangements in the very near future. I'm not liking this a lot."

"Nor am I," he said.

CHAPTER TWENTY-FOUR

When Mark arrived at his house, he found that he hardly had the strength to get his luggage inside. A fearful fatigue had settled around him and he went directly to his bedroom, carrying nothing but his shaving kit. He already missed Carole's company and felt a little bit lost without her, even in his own bedroom. He stood in the middle of the room; waiting for some expected response from his body. Finally, he made his way to the bathroom and brushed his teeth in preparation for bed.

Mark's body had had it, but his mind wouldn't shut down enough to grant the sleep he knew he needed. Lying in the darkened bedroom, he tried to schedule the next day's activities. A call to Dr. Givens was his first priority. He had to know if the painful attack he'd experienced earlier in the week would be a part of his regular existence. If so, he had to get prepared. For the first time since learning of the disease, fear raised its ugly head. Dying was one thing – living day to day with the pain of his first attack presented a problem he didn't know if he could survive for any extended period of time – drugs or no drugs.

The anxiety associated with the disease soon gave way to the dilemma he faced in telling Carole about his condition. There were only two choices: to tell or not to tell. If he told her, she could (and probably should) leave him to his own fate and avoid the commitment of staying with a dying man. Just the thought of spending his last few months without her made him physically ill. If he chose not to tell her, then he didn't think he could live with himself, leeching the pleasure of having her with him in a totally dishonest relationship. Continued silence, on his part, would be cruel and being cruel to Carole was totally unacceptable. He knew that he'd already waited too long, and guilt gnawed at his mind. The decision came as if a switch had been turned on. He chose what he thought to be the less destructive of two hugely undesirable choices.

I can't put this off past tomorrow. I have to know what is going to happen after the fact, he thought. This is driving me crazy, and it's grossly unfair for me to let it go unresolved any longer.

With his decision made, he drifted off into a fretful sleep - laced with dread for the upcoming day.

*   *   *

He awoke early, still restless, but resolute in his decision to end the charade with Carole.

After his shave and shower, Mark dressed for the office and in so doing, realized how little he had missed wearing a tie for the past week. He looked forward to the *tees* and shorts of the boat crowd.

Still too early to call Carole or Dr. Givens, he thought, so I might as well have breakfast on the way to the office. I can make all my calls from there.

It was only a quarter to six and time seemed to be crawling, adding to the anxiety.

He bought a paper at the restaurant and tried to catch up on the world's problems while he ate breakfast. After killing as much time as he could, he arrived at his office parking space at five minutes past seven, just as the maintenance foreman was unlocking the doors for the day.

Mark felt that Dr. Givens would be making hospital rounds about now, and he wanted to contact her answering service before her office opened. Maybe they could contact her to see when she might be available for another consultation. He had not seen her since she had given him the news about the disease.

At his desk, he searched his wallet for her card and dialed the "Emergency" number that was listed along with her regular office telephone number.

The answering service said that they would deliver his message.

Mattie had put the week's telephone messages on his desk. While he was waiting for her to show up for work, he shuffled through the pink copies to see if there were any messages of importance. He found that Dr. Givens had called earlier in the week and asked that he call her when he returned from vacation. There was also a call from his friend, Dr. Morrison. It was a call that he hated to return.

It was still too early to start returning phone calls and other messages, so Mark decided to get the coffee pot going in the break room before Mattie and the others arrived for work. On his way to the break room, the phone on Mattie's desk started ringing, and he stopped to answer the call.

It was Dr. Givens.

"Good morning, Mr. Stevens," he heard her say when he answered. "My service just delivered your message, and I thought I'd return your call while I'm changing hospitals. How was your vacation?"

"It was fine," Mark replied. "Of course it wasn't long enough, but I'll be taking off again in a couple of weeks. What I'd called about was to ask if I might be able to drop by and see you sometime today. I need to visit with you a little bit more about pain management. I had a pretty severe attack while I was in Florida, and I'm afraid it really got my attention."

"I don't know how full my schedule is today, but I'm sure I can find some time for you. I'll call the office as soon as they open and see when I can fit you in. I'll have them give you a call back to let you know what time to be there. Are you going to be at this number for a couple of hours?"

"Yes, I'll stay here until I hear from your secretary. I really appreciate your taking the time to see me on such short notice," Mark answered.

"I've been expecting your call and I hope I can help. I'll see you later in the day. Bye!"

"Good bye," Mark said, hanging up the phone.

He continued his trip to the break room, turning on lights as he went. After filling both coffee pots with water and coffee, he started back to his office and arrived just in time to see Mattie putting her purse in her desk drawer – getting ready for the day. As always, she was fifteen minutes early.

"Welcome back, stranger," she beamed when she saw Mark.

"Hi, good lookin'," he replied. "Did you miss me?"

"Naw – the mailroom guy had to tell me you were gone," she said as she hurried over to give him a hug. After the hug and a quick kiss on the cheek, she added, "I didn't expect you until Monday. Did they run you out of Florida or did you miss me too much to stay?"

"Well, let's say I missed you too much to stay. I'd finished up the boat deal and needed to get back here to make an attempt to get things squared away enough to leave again – for good."

"I can't wait to hear about the boat," she said. "When do you take delivery?"

"As soon as they can get it ready. I gave them three weeks, but they may get it finished within two. Carole took a bunch of pictures, and I'll show them to you as soon as they're developed. I'm going to really have to hump it to be ready if they call early. How close are we to having my affairs in order?"

Mattie's face darkened when he mentioned his "affairs", then answered glumly, "I think all the paperwork is ready for you to look over. It nearly breaks my heart every time I have to work on it, but it's pretty much done."

"Thank you, Mattie," he said as he placed his arm around her shoulder and escorted her back to her desk.

"Let me have it and I'll look it over now, before things get too hectic around here. Do you know if Bob has made any decision about my replacement?"

"I think he has. He's waiting on you to get back before he makes any announcements. He asked that you get in touch with him when you were back in the office."

"I'll call him when I finish with this stuff," he said, entering his office. He called back to Mattie as he was closing the door, "I've got the coffee on in the break room. If you're having a cup, would you bring me one on your way back?"

"Wow! You sure went domestic while you were gone. Making *coffee*? What will the other V.Ps think if they hear about this?"

Mark smiled at her, and then closed the door. Once seated at his desk, he took the thick ream of paper out of the manila file folder Mattie had given him and started the gloomy task signing away his estate. She had prepared three "originals" of all documents and had yellow markers sticking out the sides where his signature was needed. As expected, everything appeared to be in perfect order. He signed his name in all the appropriate places then called Mattie and asked that she find a Notary and someone to witness the signing of the documents.

In order to put the "Carole problem" behind him or at least get it out of the forefront of his consciousness, he picked up the phone and dialed her number.

"Hello," she said.

"Well, did you sleep alright without my snoring?"

"I nearly fell off the bed, once, trying to get my buns next to you. Other than that – no real problems."

"Yeah, I did the same thing. Look, since you never cook for me, why don't you come to my humble house this evening and I'll try to burn a couple of steaks for dinner. You may never want to cook again."

"Man, you are so slick. How could anyone turn down such an offer? I'd love to! What time?"

"I should be finished up here well before five, so, pick your time. Come early and stay late – or forever, your choice."

"I'll be there as soon as I can, after five. I'm hustling, trying to get things in order for a sailing trip I've been invited on, but I'll stop before dinner. I'll see you around six or so, if that's good?"

"Perfect," he said, "I'll see you then. Bye!"

Committed, he hung up the phone and immediately picked it up again to call Bob Murphy to see when he would be available to meet.

After welcoming him back, Bob said that he could meet with him immediately if he wanted to. He had no other pressing appointments and wanted his input on the replacement the board had chosen for "Vice President of Engineering".

Mark was still dreading the phone call to Dr. Morrison and decided he would wait until after his meeting with Bob before making the call. Mark hated putting off unpleasant tasks and was surprised at doing so now. Give yourself a break, he thought.

Passing Mattie's desk, he said, "Mattie, I'm going up to Bob's office for a short meeting about the replacement. I'm expecting a phone call from my doctor's office and they're supposed to tell me when I can get in to see her today. If they call while I'm with Bob, just ask them when I need to be there, and I'll show up. It they want me there real soon, call upstairs, and I'll leave immediately."

"OK," Mattie replied. "Is there anything else I need to do?"

"I don't think so. I'll see you in a little while."

*   *   *

When Mark arrived at the Executive Suite, Bob's secretary, Brenda, greeted him and said, "Mr. Stevens – Mr. Murphy is expecting you. You can go on in."

"Thanks, Brenda," he said and then went directly into Bob's office.

After socializing for several minutes, Mark asked, "Well, have you decided who will be our newest V.P.?"

"I think so," Bob said, "but I wanted to visit with you before we made any firm commitments. We have decided to promote from within, as you suggested, and have narrowed it down to two of the senior engineers on your list. Both are extremely well qualified and could do us a great job I believe."

Bob then pulled two file folders out of his *hold* basket and pushed them across the desk to Mark. Without speaking,

Mark took the folders and thumbed through the personnel files of Paula McIntire and John Martin.

Mark knew the selectees well. Both were qualified, and he really didn't want to make a choice, but commented to Bob, "Either of them will make you a good hand, Bob. The only thing that would put Paula in a little better position is that she has a *minor* in accounting that could prove useful on occasion. Other than that, they're pretty equal. They're well informed, personable and dedicated to the company. I think Paula has a year or so seniority on John. It's a hard choice."

"I know," Bob said, "but I think you're right about Paula. We were leaning toward her as our first choice. I just hope John isn't offended by being passed over and starts looking for another job."

"I don't think he will. He enjoys his work too much, and I am not real sure he'd take the job if it were offered. In any case, I'll start getting my personal things out of the office and should have it cleared out over the weekend. I'll be in town for another two or three weeks and can be here pretty regularly to help with the transition. Mattie will stay until things are running smoothly, but I think she's about had it, work-wise."

"Mark, is there anything we can do to help *you?*"

"I wish there was, Bob, but I can't think of a thing."

With that, Mark shook hands with his friend and started back to his own office.

As he was leaving, Brenda said, "Mr. Stevens, I'm very sorry to see you leave the company. We'll all miss you."

"Thank you, Brenda. I really appreciate it."

*   *   *

Dr. Givens had asked that Mark be at her office at 1:00pm. He had arrived on time and was escorted directly to her office instead of one of the examining rooms.

She stood and greeted Mark as he came in, offered him a chair and started cleaning up the remnants of a salad she had eaten at her desk.

"Just once, I'd like to have lunch in a restaurant like normal people," she said, with a chuckle as she threw the plastic container into her desk-side wastebasket.

"I sometimes have the same feeling," Mark replied as he sat in the chair where he'd received his death sentence.

"Mr. Stevens, I assume you have digested the seriousness of your condition. Have you made any decisions about whether or not you want to try and treat the disease?"

"Straight up, Doctor, do you think it would do me any good?"

"It could prolong your life to some extent, but ultimately I don't think there's much chance for success. If you like, I will be happy to arrange an appointment with an oncologist before you make a final decision."

"No, from my research, I've found that the only thing treatment will do is make me sick for the rest of the time I have left and I don't want that. I did want to ask you about the attack that I had and what I might expect in the immediate future. Is this a normal progression or was it unusual. The severity of it makes me worry about whether I'm safe to be driving or any other thing that requires my full attention. I was a nervous wreck flying back from Florida. I don't know what would have happened if I'd had a similar episode during the flight."

"I'm sorry I can't give you an answer as to whether or not your attack was *normal* or not. It happens to some and not to others. Later, the pain will become intense and rather constant. You will need medication to tolerate it. Sometimes, if these attacks occur, you can just lean forward, in a sitting position, to get some relief. If that doesn't work, then you'll have to start taking medications in increasing dosages, depending on the level needed to get relief. I'm going to give you a prescription today for *Lortab*. You can take it for pain as long as it's effective and then we can go to another level when we need to. It may impair your motor responses to some degree, but not severely. You should be able to function normally, in most instances."

"Should I call you at specific intervals, or do I just fly by the seat of my pants? I just bought a sailboat and plan to go sailing for a while until I get too sick to do it. I'll be here for another two or three weeks, but if I'm not here in Memphis, will I have any trouble getting medicines as I need them?"

"Yes, you'll have to have a local doctor write prescriptions for narcotics. If you'll let me know where you'll be, I'll have someone for you to contact. Have you noticed any more symptoms up while you were gone?"

"No, not really, just that one attack. My appetite is still good, and I haven't had any noticeable weight loss. I don't think there are any signs of jaundice, but my urine does seem to be getting a little bit darker since I've been paying attention to it."

"Well, I'd like for you to come in again before you leave and we'll do more blood work and check the urine again. Have fun while you can, Mr. Stevens. Things are going to be pretty rough... and sooner than you expect."

"Thanks, Doctor, I will. Now, I'll get out of your hair and let you attend to the *sick* folks' in your waiting room."

"I'll be here when you need me. By the way, I had a long visit with Dr. Morrison. He's taking the news worse than you did, I think. You need to give him a call. He's quite worried about you."

"Yes, he's next on my phone list. I honestly hate making the call. We've been friends for a long time."

*   *   *

Back in his car, Mark picked up his cell phone and dialed his office. When Mattie answered, he said "Mattie, I don't think I'll come back to the office today. I'll be cleaning out my personal things over the weekend for the new V.P., so if you have anything that needs my attention, just leave it on my desk, and I'll take care of it. If you will, have a courier take one copy of the estate papers over to my attorney's office so we can get that out of the way. He may have some changes to make, but I doubt it."

"How did things go at the doctor's office," Mattie asked?

"Pretty much like I'd expected. No real good news to report."

"*Oy vey,*" Mattie replied. "I wish there was something I could do to help."

"You help by just being there, Mattie. I'll talk to you later. Bye!"

Without putting down the phone, he dialed Jim Morrison's office. When Jim came on the line, he offered his condolences and apologized, with fervor, for not being able to detect the disease earlier.

"C'mon, Jim, you can't diagnose without symptoms, and there were none. Let's just put that behind us and try to play some golf on Sunday. We can talk about it then, if you'd like."

"Do you feel like it?"

"Sure – I'm not dead yet, and I want to get as much of your money as I can before I check out. I'll get us a tee-time and let you know when to show up."

"That sounds great. I have to get back to work, buddy. I'll see you Sunday."

"Bye, Jim," Mark said, and hung up the phone.

CHAPTER TWENTY-FIVE

Since their week in Florida, Mark knew Carole had fallen in love with him – just as he had fallen deeply in love with her. Depression and guilt consumed him for encouraging rather than discouraging the relationship. How could I do that? He thought. How could I let this go on knowing it could, possibly, turn out like this? It was against his nature to knowingly hurt someone – especially someone he cared so strongly about. I guess I should have thought of the consequences two weeks ago. I didn't – and here I stand, paying a terrible price for my lack of insight.

He went to the bar and mixed a strong scotch and soda; hoping the alcohol would provide the courage needed to tell Carole the truth. After drinking the highball in two gulps, he didn't feel any better – so, he mixed another. He would have mixed the third had the doorbell not rung.

Post time, he thought. He really wanted to run, but where?

Mark opened the door to a beaming Carole – who bounded into his arms, exclaiming her fascination about whatever radar he used to read her thoughts. A steak, after a week of seafood, was exactly what she wanted. There he was, right on cue, providing another unexpected delight.

She kissed him – deeply at first, and then, with a more relaxed embrace and several playful *pecks* on his lips. They made their way out of the entrance to his home and into the den/bar area. "If you continue to spoil me, you know I'm going to end up more rotten than I already am."

"I'll spoil you for the rest of my life – if you'll let me," he mumbled. The depression had filtered through the excitement he'd felt when she was in his arms. Oh God, I wish I hadn't said that, he thought – immediately after having said it.

It was Carole's first visit to Mark's home, and she was looking about trying to see and make comments on the general décor and specific items of memorabilia, pictures and trophies Mark had scattered around the bar and den.

"You had help, didn't you? This house is too well done for a man to do by himself – unless, of course, you're one of the more *gifted* men-types that I've seen sprinkled about my line of work."

"It's pretty much the way my wife left it – with some small additions from the golf course or work. It's comfortable, and I see no reason to change things when I can walk it in the dark."

"Nothing needs to be changed – it's perfect." She said, still admiring the adjoining rooms from the doorway of the den.

"Would you like a drink?" Mark asked.

"Of course! After living with you for a week, it's become habit to drink like a fish."

"Spoken like a true sailor!" He chuckled.

Mark poured the drink and refreshed his own, then escorted her to the wood and glass French doors leading to the covered patio and barbecue area adjacent to the pool.

The patio was extremely comfortable – with the constant, gurgling sound of a pump-driven fountain/waterfall enhancing the serenity of the pool.

"The pool is just too beautiful!" Carole said as she seated herself in one of the thick-cushioned patio chairs.

"Taking care if it is a pain in the ass, but it's worth it for the most part. Would you like a swim before we start getting ready for dinner?"

"I didn't bring a suit."

"I have *fantasized* about this moment – *and*, I built a unusually tall fence just in case it ever came to pass."

"Maybe later—in the moonlight, so you won't make rude comments about any cellulite I have groomed so carefully over the past few years."

"*Me* – me make rude comments??? You have me confused with some other undesirable from your sordid past. I'm *shocked;* absolutely *shocked,* that you would think of me with such low esteem."

"Oooo! Did I hurt his 'ittle bitty feewings', she asked in soothing baby talk – followed with the delicious laugh Mark still found intriguing.

"You will have to remember that I'm a white American male, and I've been put down so much I have become psychologically fragile."

"I couldn't hurt you with a *board*," she responded – still laughing.

Mark could see that Carole was enjoying herself. The relaxed demeanor and easy conversation between them had become routine and natural. Today – Mark was finding it more and more difficult to maintain his end of the free-flowing dialog. It was a welcome relief to see the need to refresh drinks and allow a brief reprieve as he escaped back into the house for refills.

Once inside, he leaned heavily on the bar and hesitated in blending the drinks. He was desperately trying to escape the inescapable. Hoping he could keep his wits together until after they had eaten – he refilled the glasses and resolutely walked back to the patio. He chose not to bring the drink ingredients to the patio with him in order to have an excuse for getting away again if he needed it.

When he returned to the patio, he remained standing after handing Carole her drink and asked, "When do you think you'll be ready to eat? I've got steaks big enough to feed a small third-world country and it might take a little time to get them out here. I have them tied up in the utility room."

"I'm not starving. If the growling stomach is not bothering you, I think we could wait until after we finish our drinks. Is there anything I can do to help? I *have* had lessons, you know."

"No! I've already *cooked* the salad and the potatoes are baking as we speak. The bread goes in when the steaks go on. I'm good at this shit, lady! You may be able to help keep the steer quiet while I'm cutting off what we want to eat. I like *really* fresh steaks."

He sat his drink on the small table separating their chairs then said, "I'll go ahead and start the grill. Ten minutes before you fall into a diabetic coma or something, I'll provide the medical heroics necessary to bring you back to life. Spoon-fed – by Dr. Do-little!"

Mark busied himself with the grill, reluctant to return to Carole and his half of the "stimulating" conversation. Even though it was a gas grill, Mark was taking as much time as he could – cleaning the grate and going back inside the house for cooking spray to help keep the steaks from sticking in the intense heat.

When he was finally ready to light the fire, he called to Carole, "You might want to come over here and see how I can rub two sticks together and make fire... very similar to the way primitive folks used to do it."

"How?" she asked immediately.

"How primitive – or how fire?"

"How *fire*! Motor mouth with forked tongue!"

"By rubbing two sticks together until fire appears. I was a scout."

"Mark Stevens – you are so full of it."

"OK, but you still might want to see this so you can show-off sometime. It's pretty impressive!"

"This had better be good enough to warrant my leaving the comfort of this chair," she said, in the most menacing tone she could muster while on the verge of laughing.

"See these two sticks," he asked as she approached the grill?

"Those are *matches*!" She screeched, and burst out laughing at the same time.

"Matches are sticks," he said in his most serious voice while closely examining the matches in mock fascination.

She slapped him, playfully, on his chest as his arms went around her. He pulled her close in a spontaneous burst of affection so strong he nearly choked. Carole was giggling at the nonsense, but Mark could hardly breathe as her head pressed to his chest. He was thankful she couldn't see his face. He held her until he felt he could allow her to look without giving away the anguish he felt welling within.

Once he released her, they kissed lightly. He then turned quickly – and as promised, rubbed the two sticks together to create fire.

When he'd finished with the grill, Mark went back inside and gathered the placemats and dinnerware for the outside table. "We can't tune the air-conditioner well enough to beat this," he said, motioning with his hand the sweeping expanse of the backyard and pool. "This is just too nice to leave."

"It just now dawned on me what you're trying to do! You're trying to make me feel guilty because I've never done any of this for you. I *tried*, if you will remember, but *something* came *up* and I didn't get it done. Well, you can forget about it! I'm going to sit here and enjoy this to the fullest, without the slightest hint of guilt."

"Oh, *God*, I hate being found out this early in the evening. All my well-thought-out plans – down the toilet. OK, darlin', it's about time to put the heat to the meat," he said as he finished with the table.

Mark then went back into the house and reappeared in a few minutes wearing an outlandishly tall chef's hat and a cooking apron with a cartoon character painted on the front declaring, *I am so hot*! He walked to where Carole was sitting and uncovered two beautiful New York-cut steaks and grandly presented them for her approval.

With a disdainful look befitting a Queen Victoria, Carole motioned the steaks away with a haughty flip of a limp wrist, saying, "*Please* – you know I eat nothing but fillets."

"These are not for eating – they're for the black eyes you're about to receive, my dear." Mark said, threateningly, as she balled up into a defensive fetal position in the chair, feigning terror and laughing maniacally at his threat.

"*OK, OK* – I'll *suffer*! No, Darling, they're beautiful, and I can't wait." she said as the laughter subsided.

With a protesting sizzle and a puff of white smoke, the steaks were placed on the preheated grill to sear. Mark checked his watch for cooking reference, then turned to Carole and said, "Honey, I forgot to bring out the wine. I left a nice Merlot and Cab Sav sitting on the bar. If you'll bring either, or both, out here, I'll open them and let them breathe while the steaks are cooking. The corkscrew is lying on the bar too – I think. If not, it's in the drawer by the sink."

"Finally – I get to do *something!*" She said as she got up from the chair and started walking toward the house.

When the steaks were done, Mark put them on a clean plate and headed for the kitchen, asking Carole to come with him so they could fill their plates inside, where the rest of the meal and the condiments were waiting. She followed and with little fanfare, Mark took the frozen salad plates from the freezer – the salad from the refrigerator and the bread from the oven. After putting the toppings on their potatoes and filling the salad plates, they returned to the patio table and poured the wine.

When they were seated, and Carole had stopped repeating how delicious everything looked, Mark held his wine glass toward her in a toast.

"Sl'ainte!" He said.

"*Slawn-cheh*," she asked, repeating the pronunciation. "It's a beautiful word – but I'm afraid I've never heard it before. What does it mean?"

"I hope it means what the table-tent said at an Irish restaurant I went to once. It's supposed to be a toast in ancient Gaelic, meaning *To your health*. Even if I'm wrong about the meaning of the word – *my* intent for the toast is definitely, 'To your health and well-being'. Thank you for being with me tonight. You sweeten my life."

In a rare moment of seriousness, Carole simply murmured, "Thank you! I love you for that." Her eyes were lowered to her plate instead of being on Mark as she spoke, unconsciously emphasizing the sincerity of the simple statement.

The prime beef Mark had ordered was good – really good and Carole attacked it like a field-hand who hadn't eaten in a while. Mark, uncharacteristically, was having trouble eating anything and picked at his food – becoming more melancholy the longer he tried. He was having no problem with the wine, however, and was into his second glass before

Carole had hardly tasted hers.

Carole's idle chatter diminished rapidly, without the accustomed input from Mark. She found herself becoming uncomfortable with the increasingly mumbled responses coming from his side of the table.

The food before her had suddenly become very bland and uninteresting as Carole tried to read the meaning behind Mark's sudden glum behavior. In as bright a voice as she could muster, she said – half jokingly, "Don't tell me that this evening was all set up to tell me that age-old cliché – 'Can't we be just friends'?'"

When Mark didn't answer, Carole spoke again – this time in a more serious tone, requiring a response from Mark, "Well – is that the case?"

"No!" Mark replied, "I'm afraid it's something that I haven't told you about myself that you have to know. In fact, I should have told you the day after we met or at least had the decency not to call you again after our first evening together."

"*What*, for God's sake," She asked. "I'm confident you're not gay or married – so what could be so bad?"

"Before I alienate you forever – may I give you the reason for this late confession?"

"Yes, of course, but I'm getting extremely bad vibes about this conversation and it's not that enjoyable."

"First – I didn't know myself until the day after we met. Secondly – I don't think I had fully accepted the facts when I called you the next time. After that – the trip to Florida – it was gross selfishness, and I apologize from the bottom of my heart.

My falling in love with you was a natural response to your being all the things I've ever admired or wanted in a woman. No man could ask for more. You've said you love me; the selfishness kept me from discouraging that love. I wanted it badly. I'm not ashamed to admit it.

"Carole, do you remember when I said I had a very important meeting the day after we met?"

"Yes," she said

"That meeting was with my doctor. I learned that I have terminal pancreatic cancer. I'm done in three to six months. I'm so very sorry!"

Carole let out a sound that was like a person being

violently struck in the stomach. In absolute shock, she staggered to her feet – overturning her chair and spilling the wine on the table.

Mark stood quickly too, upsetting his chair in the process. He rushed to Carole's side and tried to hold her in his arms.

She was having trouble exhaling, as comprehension of the statement sunk in. Choking, tearless sobs violently contracted the muscles of her stomach. She clutched her abdomen with her right hand and reached out with her left for support from the table.

"I don't know if I can take this, Mark," she said, between contractions. "I just don't know if I can take it."

Mark tried to hold her again, but she turned away, still trying to absorb the complexity of his revelation.

"I knew it was too good to be true. I *knew* it, but I never imagined this. I *couldn't* have imagined this."

"I should have told you the day I quit my job," Mark said, quietly. "You would have had options then. I really wanted to tell you, but I couldn't make myself. I was still trying to digest the situation, and I don't think I honestly believed it all. It had to be happening to someone else."

"Well, what about you?" she asked. "How have you been able to deal with this as if nothing were different?"

"I'm scared, confused, indecisive, and mad as hell. I don't know what to do. If I'd met you six months ago the news would have been just as damaging, I guess, but I wouldn't have this unconscionable guilt. Now, I don't know what I'm doing. I have dreaded telling you this a lot more than I've dreaded the disease. I didn't know what to do. I'm just so sorry it has to be this way. I don't know what to do."

Mark then collapsed into one of the chairs still standing by the table and buried his face in his hands. He kept mumbling, "I don't know what to do," in dismal agony.

Carole looked at Mark and could see the torment. The sobs stopped, and she knelt in front of him, encased his face and hands with her own, and said, "Like it or not, it looks as if we have to find out what to do together. I find now, that if it happens to you, it happens to me. I no longer have another choice."

CHAPTER TWENTY-SIX

Carole released her hands from Mark's face and silently stood beside him with a comforting hand on his shoulder. She was still digesting his grim confession and found it difficult to speak.

When Mark hadn't spoken for several moments, Carole asked, "When do you start treatment?"

Mark hesitated a few more moments and then said, gloomily, "I don't think I'll be taking any treatments. From what I have read and from what my doctor tells me, there's no real chance of success. The available treatments will most likely make me sicker than the disease. It doesn't seem worth it."

"Oh, Mark! Please don't give up on it. The thought of you doing nothing to fight this is appalling. Even if it would give us just a few more months, the treatments would seem worth it."

In a dejected monotone, Mark said, "If I thought treatment would give me a few more months of quality life, I'd do it in a minute. The facts indicate that the quality wouldn't be there. Just being alive isn't *living*. If I can't *live*, then I don't value being *alive* – just to breathe the air that a *living* person might use.

"Won't you do *anything*?"

"Dr. Givens thinks I should have three or four months before things really get bad. I plan to stuff *years* of living into those months. That was the reason for the rush to get the boat ready. I'm glad I found out about the cancer in time to sail the Caribbean – for a little while at least. Without knowing, I could have put it off until it was too late. Finding out has definitely given me the motivation to get it done. I have to do it. I'll do other things if time permits."

"May I help," Carole asked. She was crying again – silently, as she stood beside him.

"Nothing could please me more than you joining me in trying to enjoy a lifetime of fun in the next few months," he said. Then, after a brief pause, added, "Carole, I love you and I know it's going to be painful for you when I start going downhill. I don't know if I'm willing watch you watching me become less and less able to function. You have to tell me now if you'll be willing to let me go when I think the time is right. I refuse to become totally infirm, and this goddamned disease will not dictate when I leave this earth. I've already made that decision. It won't be changed."

"I've never been faced with anything like this, so I can only speculate on how I will be able to handle it. But, I *will* handle it. I doubt if we will totally agree on when the time is right, but when you decide without question that you've had all you care to stand, I won't interfere. I'll never be comfortable with it, but your wishes will be carried out. I feel that if the roles were reversed, I'd want the same."

"My only real complaint, at this moment, is that I didn't meet you three years ago."

"Mark, I don't know your financial situation, nor do I care; but, due to the nature of *Punitive Damages* after my husband's accident, we don't have to worry about enjoying ourselves anywhere on the globe. So please, don't let affordability be a factor in anything we choose to do. I don't like to flaunt it, but I'm a *rich bitch* and if we can think it, then we can do it."

"You continue to amaze me. It's no wonder I love you more every minute I'm near you. Fortunately, there will be no financial restrictions on what we do. To think that you would make such an offer just digs right into my heart.   I can't tell you how much I appreciate it."

"OK! It's time to get serious. Do you like my house or your house? Unless you have serious objections, from now on any roof over your head will be over my head – and that includes tonight. Do you have an extra toothbrush?"

*   *   *

For the first time since he and Carole had been sleeping together, there had been no attempt at making love before sleeping. They had gone to bed and simply held on to each other for most of the waking period without a great deal of talk from either. Mark would have comments form in his head, but before he could utter them, they would go away. Nothing seemed appropriate as far as conversation was concerned. The easy banter they had always enjoyed just wasn't there. The impact of his confession had left Carole virtually speechless and instead of talking, she seemed to try and get inside him, physically, by continuous adjustments of her body that placed her closer and closer to Mark. If he moved slightly, she mirrored the movement to maintain the closeness. Seemingly, afraid he'd get away if physical contact were momentarily lost.

As he lay there in the dark, Mark sensed the change in their relationship. He knew he would have to commit to serious dialogue concerning their continued romantic involvement. They would both have to learn to live with the fact that he was dying and still have the fun that had marked each day since they'd been together. Carole was not the only one guilty of the change. Mark had also found himself clinging to Carole much tighter than before and without the wisecracks.

*   *   *

Mark awoke from a restless sleep at 5:20 a.m. He felt like he needed more sleep, but he knew it would be useless to lie in bed trying to catch another forty winks. His mind was already racing, trying to prioritize the extensive list of "to-do" items that would be necessary to complete before he could head back to Florida and pick up the boat.

Carole was still asleep and pressed close to his side. As he edged toward the side of the bed to get up, she moved with him – trying to maintain the physical contact. When she no longer touched him, she raised her head and looked sleepy and confused by his absence. He pulled the covers back up over her shoulders and quietly said, "Go back to sleep. I'm just going to get the coffee going. Be lazy. Join me when you run out of sleep."

She mumbled, "Okay," and was back asleep as soon as her head touched the pillow.

Mark put on a terrycloth robe, found another and placed it on the foot of the bed for Carole. Then, as quietly as he could, he left the room to start the coffee.

While waiting on the coffee to brew, he rummaged around the cluttered desk in his office and found a yellow legal pad to jot down the things he needed to do and when he planned to do them. With pad and coffee in hand, he went out onto the patio and started the dismal task of finalizing his plans to leave Memphis for good. Mark had outlined nearly a full page of tasks he felt needed his attention before he could leave Memphis. He knew he would have to spend some time at his office. Even though he was officially retired, he felt obligated to assist the new V.P. while he was still in town – assuming the new V.P. would welcome any assistance from him.

He had completed his second cup of coffee and finished the list of things he knew he needed to get done, when Carole walked out onto the patio. She still looked sleepy, but was smiling and appeared fully rested. The cup of coffee she carried was sloshing out of the cup as she walked, paying more attention to Mark than the coffee.

"You're retired now," she said as she came closer, "and you don't have to get up with the chickens anymore."

"I know, but it's a strong habit. I'll get over it. Just give me a little time." Then, after a brief pause, he asked, "Do you have anything planned for the day, or would you like to follow me around to make sure I don't screw something up?"

"If we only have a couple of weeks to get things in order, I'd better get my buns moving and be ready when you are. I hate loose ends, and if I don't get started, there will be a bunch of them to deal with later."

Carole caught herself and felt guilty about using the term *later* to describe her loose ends.

Mark saw the expression of regret in her eyes and immediately said, "Carole, don't *ever* feel as though you have to walk on eggshells before saying something to me that might relate to the limited time I have left. We're both aware of it now, and there's nothing *taboo* about it. I hope we can learn to live with that knowledge without it spoiling our ability to have a good time. We've got to squeeze a bunch of living into a pretty short amount of time, and it would be a shame to worry about stepping on toes by referring to what will occur after our time is up. Either of us could be hit by a bus before day's end, and the tippy-toeing would have all been for nothing."

"I'm sorry," she said. "I'm just not used to the cold, hard facts yet, and I really don't know how to deal with it. Give me a couple of days and I hope I can put it far enough in the background to resume the unrestricted pleasure of your company."

"I was just jotting down a few of the more obvious things I have to do before we head back to Florida. I'm sure there will be *loose ends*, as you called them, but I would like to get as much done as I can to relieve the strain on Mattie. I'm sure she's better at all this stuff than I am, but I hate to leave things unfinished."

"When can I meet Mattie? She sounds like someone I can't live without knowing."

"What would be a good night to take them to dinner? I'm anxious to show you off. She's on my case, big time, to meet you. I'm sure she'll tell you that you're too good for me, but then, I know that too."

"You really should be in *sales*, you know—with a line like that. Any evening will be fine with me. I refuse to be busy after 5 o'clock from now on. The sooner we meet the better. By the way, I want to show you off too. If you don't have lunch plans, would you like to join Alice and me? She'll haunt me from the grave if I don't bring you around real soon. I've already given her a brief report on our trip to Florida, and she's *screaming* for details. The *witch* is brazenly taking credit for our meeting and will probably throw herself at you as soon as she's within range. Just remember, there are some things I don't share."

"Awww! You never let me have any fun." Then, after the pummeling he immediately received from Carole, added, "Yes, I'd love to meet her and thank her for whatever input she had in getting us started. I'll be on the phone here at the house for most of the morning, so just give me a call as to when and where and I'll be there."

"Good! I have to go back to my place to change and make a few calls myself. I'll get back to you in a couple of hours. Now, if you don't mind, I'd like to take a shower and get things started. Care to join me?"

"I'd better not. We'd be late for lunch."

Carole got up, gave him a quick kiss on the lips and disappeared into the house.

CHAPTER TWENTY-SEVEN

Carole was showered and gone in thirty minutes. Mark was left with his list, and a cold cup of coffee. He decided to make the best of it and went back to his desk to retrieve a cordless phone and his personal phone book. Back on the patio, he dialed his club to set a tee-time for his planned meeting with Jim Morrison. He knew their round of golf would not be the usual dog-eat-dog match they always enjoyed, but a more somber encounter that would inevitably lead to a serious discussion about his health. Maybe Jim could enlighten him as to what he might expect in the following few months. Although he didn't necessarily look forward to the conversation, he felt that it would provide him with valuable information. Information that could help him cope with the cancer's more serious symptoms as they developed.

Mark was busily making calls as he went down the list. He'd just hung up from his Real Estate Broker when the phone rang. It was Carole.

"Hi," she said. "Alice suggested we return to the scene of the crime for lunch. Could you stand going back to *The Prime Rib?*"

"Sounds good to me. If I'm going to be in the hot seat, I might as well do it in a familiar environment. What time?"

"Can you be there around noon?"

"No sweat. I'm looking forward to it. You've been out of my sight too long already."

"Good answer, sport. I'll see you at noon. By the way, I didn't tell her about our problem. So it doesn't have to come up unless you choose to."

"Thank you. I appreciate that."

*   *   *

There was a short line of lunch patrons waiting at the maître d' station when Mark entered the restaurant. George was just beginning to take a couple to their table when he saw Mark, and as he was leaving said, "Mark, your party is waiting in the bar. I already have your name on the list for seating. Let me know when you're ready."

"Thanks, George. We'll see you in a few minutes."

Mark was starting to feel a little uncomfortable about the imminent meeting of Alice. He wanted to make a good first impression and questions of being overdressed or underdressed clouded his mind as he approached the entrance to the bar. He instinctively looked to the booth where he'd first seen the two of them. His instincts proved correct. Carole stood and waved when she saw him. She remained standing until Mark got to the table and gave him a quick kiss on the lips. After the kiss, she turned back toward Alice and said, "Strange as it may appear, this is what the fuss is all about. Alice, meet Mark Stevens" – then continued with, "Mark, this is my dear friend Alice Preston."

Alice extended her hand, and as Mark shook it, said, "What a pleasure to finally meet you. Carole has told me so much about you that I feel like we're already friends."

"Oh, my God, I hope she didn't tell you *everything.*"

Carole spoke up. "See, I told you. She's already flirting. You *will* remember what I told you about that nonsense."

"It happens to me so infrequently that I just don't recognize it anymore. I *do* appreciate it when it happens. Especially when I have someone around who recognizes flirtation, when observed, and can point it out to me so I'll be able to enjoy the experience."

Alice was, essentially, a mirror image of Carole with dark hair and eyes. They weighed within two pounds of each other and appeared to be of identical height. Mark still didn't know or care about Carole's age, but he guessed she and Alice had gotten their drivers licenses in the same year. Neither would have a problem finding something to wear from the other's wardrobe. The only thing that really set them apart, other than hair and eye color, was the 10mm wedding band Alice wore and the large emerald-cut diamond that sparkled above it. Her face was used to laughing. Mark liked her immediately.

The waitress approached as Mark and Carole were taking their seats and asked if Mark would like something to drink.

Mark turned to Carole and asked, "Do you want to sit here in the bar for a while, or would you rather go on into the dining room?"

"I'm starting to get a bit hungry, so, unless you'd like to have a drink in here, why don't we get a table and place our orders. We can sit and visit as much as we want in the dining room."

"That's fine with me," he said. Turning to the waitress, Mark said, "We'll be going in to lunch, would you mind sending our tab to us in the other room?"

"That will be fine Mr. Stevens... enjoy your lunch."

Mark, Carole and Alice slid from the booth and made their way toward the maître d' station to let George know they were ready to be seated. The line had disappeared, and George beamed as he watched them approach. He grabbed three menus from the side of his podium and met them a few feet short of his station and extended his hand to Mark.

"Good afternoon, Mr. Stevens. I think your table is ready."

"Rather formal today, aren't we?"

"I'm vainly trying to indicate to the ladies that you might command a little respect in here, but I see that it's hopeless."

"George, meet Carole Wilson and Alice Preston. They will be as regular as I am. Be sure and let them know before they order spoiled food if I'm not around."

"Ladies, it's a pleasure to have you join us. If you'd like, I'll seat you way in the back so no one will notice you're having lunch with such a lout."

George seated them in one of the prime tables that was out of the more traveled routes used by the waiters. A waiter, that Mark did not know, was waiting with poised pen to take drink or lunch orders – dependent upon the wishes of the trio. The ladies opted for refills for their chilled white wine, and Mark asked for a house Merlot while each guest examined the menus placed before them.

The drinks arrived at the table rather quickly, not allowing time for a great deal of interaction between Mark and the two ladies. Once the food orders were given, Alice initiated revealing dialogue relative to the first meeting of Mark and Carole.

"I had given her some really foolproof lines," she said, "that were sure to get your attention. I had suggested that she approach you and simply say, 'If you're not meeting someone – you just got lucky.' The other scenario was: 'May I join you for a quick drink? I hate sitting alone in a bar like this. My boyfriend just dumped me because I demanded too much sex. I just don't know what to do now. May I treat you to dinner?' She wouldn't take my advice, and, of course, I was flabbergasted when she called the next morning and said you had enjoyed a wonderful dinner and nightcap. As she tells it – neither of you scored on that first try." Alice was laughing with a laugh that rivaled Carole's as she revealed her version of their first meeting.

Carole interjected with, "You bitch! If I had done the things you wanted me to do, he'd probably have called the manager and had me removed for *soliciting*. I think my plan worked to perfection, so maybe you can take a lesson or two from a stay-at-home widow."

Mark was laughing along with the two women as they described the conversation immediately prior to the execution of the plan. He finally intervened with, "I don't care how she got here, I'm just glad she did. Had she not approached me, I would have done *something* to get an introduction, even if it meant tripping over myself and falling into your table. I was not going to let her get out of here without having the opportunity to reject me as an asshole, or accept me as a decent dinner partner. I still can't imagine how I was picked as someone worth all the effort. I'm *really* glad it happened."

Alice said, "Mark, you looked like a *stud puppy* when you made your appearance in the room. We silently checked you out, and the result was too much for a couple of old gals to resist."

"If you two are examples of 'old gals', then I need to spread the word that there *is* life after maturity – in my case, anyway."

Lunch was served, and the easy dialogue between the three continued – with Mark giving a loving description of the boat he'd just bought on their trip to Florida and what their plans were in the immediate future. Alice was fascinated by the turn of events that took her friend from a *stay-at-home-widow* to a gutsy sea-going woman of expeditionary fervor. She assumed, correctly, that Mark had a lot to do with the changes in attitude – and she was very happy to see those remarkable changes.

Lunch had lasted nearly two hours when Mark revealed his appointment with his real estate agent at three o'clock. "Do you both have your cars with you, or do I need to chauffeur either of you around before my meeting?"

"We're both mobile this time," Carole said, then continued with, "I have to pick up some things at the supermarket on my way home."

"Does the stop at the supermarket involve dinner ingredients?"

"It does, and I expect you to stay out of the kitchen during the preparation. I remember what happened last time I tried to cook for you. *Lecher!*"

"Oh, *that*," Mark replied, with a big smile splitting his face.

Alice caught the undertone in Carole's voice and said, "You forgot to tell me about that," then after a brief pause, "perhaps later?"

Carole feigned disgust at the remark and suggested, "You can use your vivid, and somewhat warped, imagination my dear, and I doubt if there will be anything left to tell. I refuse to go deeper into the subject." The frown she wore morphed into a warm smile as she grabbed Mark's arm in preparation to leave the restaurant.

*   *   *

After the meeting with Marty Westmorland, Mark collected his overnight *necessities*, plus a change of clothes, and fought 5 o'clock traffic all the way to Carole's condo.

Once inside, he found Carole busily preparing a *mystery* dinner that smelled wonderful, but was to remain a secret until it was presented. She told Mark to park his butt in the den and mix a drink until she could join him.

Mark did as he was told, and once he had his drink in hand, grabbed the remote for the TV and started watching the local news. After about 15 minutes of *gloom and doom* from the news broadcast, Carole joined him and – as she placed the back of her hand to her forehead – said, in a whine, "This crap of cooking over a hot stove is not all it's cracked up to be. If I had the *strength*, I'd mix a drink and join you."

"Your attempt at subtlety is remarkably effective. What would you like and I'll see if I can pull myself off this couch to get it for you."

Carole smiled and said, "No, I'll get it. I was just checking to see if you *would* pull yourself off the couch. You done good, m'boy."

Once seated beside Mark, Carole asked, "Well, what did you think of my friend, Alice, this afternoon?"

"She seems like she would be a lot of fun to be around. She does have a talent for innuendo, but it seems to enhance her personality. How long have you been friends?"

"About seven or eight years. When we first met, she was a bartender at a club my husband and I went to pretty regularly. We usually made it a point to sit at the bar for a while before going in to dinner. We enjoyed the lively chatter she always provided – and from those encounters, we became friends. The friendship evolved from her being just our friendly bartender to social encounters outside the bar. When she met her present (third) husband, Ryan, we both endured and encouraged the courtship. Afterward, we joined them regularly outside the club. When my husband was killed, she was, unexpectedly, the first by my side to offer support and was there when I really needed someone. During that time, we became very close and continue to meet pretty often for lunch, shopping and other *girly-stuff*. Ryan is the Vice President of Marketing for a big clothing manufacturer and has since, made her a woman of leisure. She's good at it. His job requires quite a lot of travel, and when she doesn't join him, the frequency of our meetings increase – sometimes, a bit too frequently for comfort on my part."

"What do you mean?"

"Well, since she no longer works, she has a lot more free time than I choose to have. I still love her, but she likes to party more than I do and I don't usually join her with other friends for the after-dark scene. I joined her a few times, but the crowd was a little wild for me. Most of the parties tend to be with friends she knew while bartending. I don't condemn her choices, but then I don't really care about participating. We have a very close relationship, and I wouldn't change it for the world. It's just that some of our social activities are somewhat separate."

"I hope we can see more of her. She seems like she could add a bunch to any gathering. Not to change the subject too far to the left, but – what is it that smells so good coming from that kitchen?"

"Why don't I go find out? I've already got things set up on the table, so we'll give it a try in a very few minutes. Hopefully, you'll discover my cooking classes were not a waste of time and money."

After Mark had washed up from the grime of the day, Carole called from the dining area, "It's *soup!*"

Mark entered the room to see Carole lighting two tall candles over a beautifully appointed table set for two – with perfectly browned Cornish game hens, wild rice and fresh steamed asparagus tips filling the two bone-china dinner plates. A chilled, fresh garden salad anointed with chunky bleu-cheese dressing heaped atop the greens was placed next to the dinner plates. Sitting on the floor, next to the corner of the table, a small wrought-iron stand held a silver ice bucket, with an open bottle of Chardonnay within easy reach.

"Wow," Mark said. "I feel a little bit humbled by my outdoor cooking spree the other night. I can tell the cooking classes were neither a waste of time nor money. *Dwarf* chickens – what won't they think of next?"

"Sit down and eat – the back of your neck is turning a little bit red."

"Yes, ma'am."

After the dinner was enjoyed – the table cleared, and the utensils were washed and returned to storage, Carole said, "I'm going to go take a shower and expect my dessert in the bedroom. If you'd like, you can pour us a brandy and join me?"

"I'll be glad to, but don't expect too much after a meal like that. All I seem to want to do right now is loosen my belt. Thank you for a beautiful dinner. I'm really impressed; however, I had no doubts about anything you do being less than perfect. Maybe I'll deflate by the time we meet with Mattie and Maury tomorrow."

CHAPTER TWENTY-EIGHT

"What am I to expect?" Carole asked as they were pulling out of the drive.

"I don't know what to expect. You never know with Mattie. I know that you'll love her twenty minutes into the meeting. She's brassy as hell. She will never go out of her way to impress you with any of her rather bizarre opinions, but you will never have any doubts as to what her opinions are. You take them or leave them. For the most part, they coincide with mine, but the *degree* is generally the part that causes the *exchange* between us. We've been at battle stations for over thirty years, and I wouldn't trade a minute of it. She'd die for me, and I would do the same for her."

"What about her husband? Does he generally get into the fray or does he just let her do her thing?"

"Maury is the ideal Jewish husband, I guess—if there is such a thing. He has been very successful in business and seems to think the world revolves around Mattie. I don't know him as well as I should, but every time we've been together, he's played the part of the doting husband – catering to her every whim. He doesn't seem to be a *henpecked* husband. He just seems to want to do things that make Mattie happy. He's a master tailor, but you'd never believe it when you look at him. You'll think his clothes were bought at the Salvation Army – but that's Maury. You'll like him, but he won't be doing a lot of talking this evening. Maury just sort of lets Mattie do her thing and enjoys the benefits of what she stirs up."

"I'm nervous about meeting her. If she doesn't approve of me, it will break my heart."

"Believe me, she'll approve. Before the evening is over, she'll be questioning whether or not I'll be acceptable for *you*. Anyway, the *argument* will be fun, and there will be no malice in her view of my acceptability. You'll probably think we're going to kill each other, but it's only a façade. I wouldn't know how to take her any other way. Please don't be uncomfortable. Just roll with the flow."

"Whatever you say."

*　　　*　　　*

Mark and Carole pulled into the parking lot of *Junior's* at ten minutes to eight, a little early for their reservations, but still close enough to be seated on time. Mark had never eaten here, but had heard wonderful reviews about the food and service. He thought Mattie probably had a discount coupon for dinner or she wouldn't have chosen the place for a first meeting with Carole. Whatever the case, it looked nice, and he expected everything to be as enjoyable as advertised.

When they entered the restaurant, Mark asked the maître d' if Mr. and Mrs. Goldberg had already been seated.

"Are you Mr. Stevens?"

Mark answered, "Yes."

"They've just been seated and are expecting you."

Mark said, "Thank you," and he and Carole followed him to the dining room.

Mattie was reading the menu as if it were gospel and didn't notice Mark and Carole approaching the table until the maître d' pulled a chair out for Carole.

Maury and Mattie both stood up when they arrived at the table. Mattie reached for Mark and gave him one of her all-encompassing hugs. When the hugging was over, she

195

immediately turned to Carole, with an undisguised look of evaluation. Just before the *look* became embarrassing, she said, "*My God!* How could a *shiksa* with your looks be seen in public with this *goy?*"

Mark was shaking hands with Maury, but turned to Mattie and said, "Look, lady, any bullshit that you put out about me tonight had better be approved before you tell it. So watch yourself. I might have a few things I can counterattack with."

"Don't you wish?"

Mark made introductions, and Maury and Mattie greeted Carole with warmth and welcome.

Carole just smiled a lot when Mattie and Mark went through their pre-dinner dialogue. It seemed as if she and Maury were bystanders to a ritual that had been rehearsed over and over again through the years. It was fun to watch and listen as the two friends stabbed each other verbally. No one was hurt, and finally Mattie turned to Carole and asked, "Where have you been *hiding*? I knew you were out there somewhere, but I didn't know if he had enough *bloodhound* in him to find you. He's even been halfway decent to me since he met you. I'll be in your debt forever."

Carole responded with, "Mattie, so far, you've been my only rival. Maury must have a very large gun or I wouldn't have stood a chance."

"Maury, listen to this woman. How could he *not* love her?"

Maury, true to character, just smiled at the interaction and shook his head negatively in an attempt to remove himself from the social turmoil in which he found himself.

Waiters came. Food and wine were ordered and served. The friends visited amicably with a majority of the questions being directed toward Carole. Mattie was enchanted with Carole's rendition of the way she and Mark had met, and kept interrupting the story for more detail.

Carole mentioned that she'd brought some of the pictures taken on the Florida trip. Mattie nearly knocked Maury out of his chair as she pushed him and said to Carole, "Honey – move over here so you can direct us through the trip. I'm dying to see what all the fuss is about over a boat."

Mark and Maury might as well have been on Mars for the next twenty minutes as the two women giggled and pointed and made rude comments about the subjects in the pictures. It was easy to see – they were already friends and becoming closer and closer as the evening went along.

The meal and conversation had lasted for nearly two hours. Both were fully enjoyed by the foursome. Finally, Mattie looked toward Carole and said, "I know my nose is shiny – what about yours?"

"Let's go check it out," Carole said, as she pushed back her chair to stand.

After the real reason for their trip to the restroom was taken care of, the two women were sitting in front of the well-lighted mirror re-applying their makeup when Mattie stopped and turned to Carole.

"I know Mark has told you about his health problem. Can we talk about it?"

"Yes, he told me. I'm having a hard time comprehending the full impact of it all."

"Do you think you can still have any kind of relationship with him, now that you know it won't last as long as one would expect?"

"Mattie, I don't have a choice. I love him beyond words, and I could no more walk out on him now than I can sprout wings and fly. I hate the situation. He hates the situation. We're just stuck with it, and dealing with it is a new experience for us both every day. The real test will come later. When the disease becomes more symptomatic, I pray for the strength to do my part. I feel bitter, cheated and utterly heartbroken, but, by God, I'll be here until one of us is gone. I *will* it to be the best time of my life."

"I thought this damn mascara was supposed to be waterproof. Anyway – he's been the brother I've never had, and I cannot tell you how sad it makes me, knowing I'm going to lose him way too soon. Since Karen and Sara's death, he's been a robot. Then, when you came along, he became human again. It's ironic that his humanity brought with it the frailties associated with the species. I can't describe Mark in English, but in Yiddish, he's a *Mensch*."

"What a lovely description. I have very little knowledge of Yiddish, but, fortunately, I am aware of *Mensch* and it fits him perfectly.

After a short pause, Carole continued with, "I was married before. I lost my husband to an accident and didn't have to go through the pain of seeing *him* in pain – unable to help. I don't know how I'll be able to bear seeing Mark deteriorate from the beautiful man we both love, to a disease-ravaged shell. One of my biggest battles will be fighting the urge to feel pity for that shell. He couldn't stand that, and will probably run me off before it gets to that point."

"I only wish that you could have met sooner and enjoyed the time you deserve together. You are the answer to my prayers. I want you to know that, and I am here for you whenever you need me. He loves you – I love you. That's the way it works."

"Thank you, Mattie. I'm sure I'll have to call on you before this is all over, but until then, I'm going to do everything within my power to make a fun-filled lifetime out of the few months we have together. Like you, I wish we'd met sooner. It would have been wonderful."

"You've eliminated any doubts I may have had about you. Bless you for it. Now, we'd better get back to the table before they start rumors about us."

*   *   *

"My God, did you have to use the blow-dryers to get out of there?" Mark asked as the women were being seated.

Without missing a beat, Mattie responded with, "Don't start with the crap, smart-ass. There are two of us now, and your mental armor isn't quite up to the task of being an adequate defense."

Carole stifled a giggle and nearly sprayed a sip of wine through her nose. *Most* unladylike, she thought.

Mark caught Maury looking at his watch and sensed his urge to call it a night.

Checking his own watch, Mark said, "Well, we've done about as much damage as we can do here. Would you like to continue the evening with some dancing or other bizarre social activity?"

Maury responded by looking at his watch again and saying, "Unlike others at the table – I still have a business to run, so we'd better opt out this time."

Mattie added, "Anymore, when I dance, it causes seismic fluctuations over at Memphis State. It drives the geology students crazy."

"I'm not stupid enough to comment on *that*," Mark chuckled.

"*Maury* – beat him up."

Maury, in a rare attempt at humor, stretched his 5'6"/155-pound frame out of his chair and said, "I think I'll just drag his ass outside before I do it. No sense in messing up the dining room when we're leaving anyway."

Mark recoiled in mock fear as Carole cracked up. Mattie, on the other hand, simply said, "Thank you," with a queenly air and a flip of her wrist.

While the valets were bringing their cars around, Carole asked Mark, "Do you really want to go dancing?"

"Now why would I want to do that? You've already agreed to go home with me."

Carole pummeled Mark on one arm while Mattie beat him on the other. Maury was checking his watch again and wishing the valet would bare-a-hand.

The cars came and as the women spread hugs all around, Mark and Maury shook hands and said goodnight. It had been a wonderful evening.

Once in the car, Carole snuggled close to Mark and kept murmuring about how much she enjoyed Mattie and Maury, the dinner, and the night in general. Mark, in response to her babbling, stuck his index finger to his tongue – moistened it – then touched the moistened finger to Carole's blouse. While the quizzical expression was still on her face, he explained his action by saying, "I'd better get you home, and out of those wet clothes."

It was a pleasant ride home.

CHAPTER TWENTY-NINE

Eighteen days after their return to Memphis, Don Lopez called and said the boat was ready to go in the water. All modifications had been completed as per their agreement and Mark could take delivery as soon as he was able to get back to Ft. Lauderdale.

"That's wonderful, Don. I was beginning to wonder if the deadline could be met. Now that I've got a boat, were you able to locate a qualified charter captain that would give me a shake-down cruise to the Bahamas? I might want him to sail with us for a couple of weeks before it's all over. I don't want to take off alone unless I'm comfortable in handling the boat."

"Yes, I've talked to several that would do you a good job. As a matter of fact, I just visited with an excellent captain about your request. He normally works an eighty-footer that we just placed in our yard for overhaul. He's still employed by the owner, but I think he might be able to get away for a couple of weeks to help you out. I know he won't have anything to do with his boat for a month or so. He's very experienced and has sailed all over the world."

"He sounds ideal. If you'll give me his phone number, I'll see if he'd be willing to go *slumming* for a couple of weeks on a miniscule forty-five footer?"

"I'd be glad to. His name is Sean Jacobson."

After giving Mark the number, Don continued with, "I don't know if you'd be interested in having a cook on-board or not, but Sean's wife, Maria, usually sails with him, on the eighty-footer, as the chef. I can personally vouch for her cooking and can guarantee you won't lose any weight with her around."

"Don, you read my mind. I'd love to have them both. I need someone to show me around the galley as much as topside – probably more. I'm looking forward to talking to them and hope I can get it done today. If we can work out a deal, I want them to go aboard as soon as possible to see what will be needed to outfit the boat for extended cruising."

"He seemed interested, and I'm sure you'll be more than happy with their service. When do you expect to come back to Ft. Lauderdale?"

"We'll be driving down, this time, and will leave tomorrow or the next day. I expect the trip to take two days if we push it. I'm very anxious to see the boat and get it underway."

"You'll love it, Mr. Stevens. I wish it were mine. It turned out beautifully."

"Thanks, Don. I'll see you in a few days. By the way, if Sean chooses not to join us, will you line me up with another skipper and have him give me a call? I'll talk to you later."

"If, for some reason, Sean doesn't accept the job, I'll have someone else standing by. Have a safe trip."

*　　　*　　　*

Mark was ecstatic. For the first time in recent memory, he felt anticipation equal to the time when he received his driver's license. Tension had been building in him for the past few days – worrying if the deadline he'd set for the boat would be met. The relief was immediate, and he couldn't wait to tell Carole the good news. He called her cell phone and got an automated response asking for a message. He left a voice message asking that she call him when she got a chance. He then sat impatiently for another ten minutes before giving in to the urge to call Sean Jacobson.

Don had given him Sean's cell phone number along with his home number. He decided to take a chance with the cell phone first and dialed the number. He was rewarded with, "Hello, this is Sean," on the second ring.

"Mr. Jacobson, my name is Mark Stevens, and I was given your name by Don Lopez at *Safe Harbor Marina*. He recommended that I call you concerning a shake-down cruise on a boat I just bought from the marina."

Sean spoke back with, "Yes, Don said you were looking for someone to go cruising with you for a while. I won't be available for any extended length of time, but I might be interested in something that would take less than a month."

"Hopefully you will be able to get me checked out and safe in a couple of weeks. I have had quite a bit of experience with inland day-sailing, but nothing in something as large as the boat I have now. It's a forty-five-foot sloop, and we want to do some extended sailing in the Caribbean for the next few months."

"When would you like to start?"

"We'll be leaving Memphis for Ft. Lauderdale either tomorrow or the next day. It should take us a couple of days for the drive, but we will be ready to go as soon as possible after we arrive. The boat has just been refurbished, and Don assures me that it's in excellent shape."

"Yes, I'd be interested in sailing with you for a couple of weeks."

"Don also tells me that your wife usually sails with you as chef. Do you think she would consent to coming along?"

"I'm sure she would."

"Man, you have made my day. I have already told Don to give you free access to the boat if you accepted the job. I'm sure you will want to check it out before finalizing the deal. It's still out of the water so you can do a full inspection on the hull before it's launched. If you're still interested in taking the job after you've looked at the boat, please outfit it with anything you think we need. I don't really know what the previous owner left aboard, but feel free to shop for anything that will make our trip safe and comfortable. You're on the payroll as of today, Cap'n Jacobson, unless I hear from you stating otherwise."

"How many will be sailing with us?"

"There will be just the two of us, plus you and your wife, for now."

"I'll get right on it, Mr. Stevens. I look forward to meeting you. Have a safe trip coming down. By the way, do you have an assault rifle?"

"No, will I need one?"

"I always suggest that one be on board. You can never tell what you will run into down here with the drug trafficking and all. I have one that I could take for the shake-down cruise, but you may want to buy one for yourself after I leave. I have not, personally, had any encounters with the bad guys, but several of my friends in the business, have. As we used to say in the *Boy Scouts*, 'Be prepared!'."

"I'll see what I can do. If I can't find one here, maybe I can get one when I get to Florida. In any case, I'll see you in three or four days. Will I need to forward you any funds for the outfitting? If so, let me know, and I'll get it done. If not, just hang on to the receipts and I'll reimburse you as soon as I get there."

"I don't think my *MasterCard* will max out before you get here. I'm sure the boat will be ready when you are."

"Good-bye, Sean."

"Bye, Mr. Stevens."

Mark didn't put the phone down, but instead dialed Don Lopez's number at the marina. When Don finally came on line, he said, "Don, this is Mark Stevens again. I just talked to Sean Jacobson, and he has agreed to take us a'sailin'. He will be by to look at the boat and outfit it for us. He'll also be available to give you a hand in putting it in the water. If you have any slips available, I'd like to rent one for the boat. One more favor and I'll leave you alone – I need a name painted on the boat. Will you call a sign painter and have him paint *Cruzin' Carole, Ft. Lauderdale* across the stern and on the life rings. Since the boat is navy blue, I think gold paint would look really good. Perhaps a bit gaudy, but good gaudy."

Don laughed and said, "Maybe I could get him to do it on black velvet first and just paste it on the stern."

Mark laughed with him but didn't say anything.

Don continued with, "It won't be a problem. I'll have him do it before we put it in the water."

"Don, it's been a pleasure doing business with you. You're a good hand, and I appreciate all you've done for me. I'll see you in three or four days."

"Thank you. I'm looking forward to seeing you when you look at this beautiful boat for the first time since it's been redone. Bye, Mr. Stevens."

Mark was still holding the phone as Carole walked in the door.

CHAPTER THIRTY

"You're grinning like the cat that just ate a canary," Carole said as she came into the den area where Mark still held the phone in his hand.

"Are you ready to get your sea legs? Don just called, and the boat is ready."

"*Oh, my God!*"

"Add to that, my due-diligence work, and I have a captain and chef hired for our maiden voyage to the Bahamas. What's the earliest you'll be ready to get this show on the road?"

"I'm still working with a couple of clients that need a replacement for me, now that I'm going away. I'd hoped to have it all done by now, but it's those *loose ends* I'd mentioned before. It doesn't look like I'm going to have it all cleared up for three or four days at the earliest."

"I knew you were a little pressed for time, but I was hoping it could have been taken care of by the time the boat was ready. Looks like we'll have to go to *Plan Bravo*."

"And what would that be?"

"It's a long drive down there, and it might be better if you fly. We can pack all your gear in the car, and I can drive it down with me. Then, you can take the silver wings, and we'll be in Ft. Lauderdale about the same time. You'll be able to take care of the *loose ends* and avoid a long, boring drive."

"Mark Stevens, are you trying to get rid of me?" Carole pouted.

"You know better than that. I just think I need to be there as quickly as possible to take care of all the paperwork at the marina. I want to make sure the boat is outfitted as I want it. You won't miss out on a thing – other than the drive."

"I *swear* I'll call and have Don chain that boat to a pier until I get there."

Mark stood and pulled Carole into his arms. She was still pouting, but finally said, "I just want to be with you."

"I know – as I want to be with you." He then added, "When I drive, I usually have a lot of gas – so you probably wouldn't enjoy the ride that much."

She pounded him softly on the chest with both hands before replacing her hands with her head and engulfing him with her arms – silently holding on. She finally said, "I know *Plan Bravo* is good. I'm just selfish enough not to want to spend a day away from you."

"Have you got your bikinis ironed and ready to go?"

"I still have a few things I need to pack, but, for the most part, I have everything in a pretty neat pile. When did you want to leave?"

"I told Don that we'd be leaving tomorrow or the next day – depending on your schedule."

"I think I can get everything that needs to go in the car packed this afternoon. That way I'll have some extra time in getting my clients happy. Happy or unhappy, I will be in Ft. Lauderdale the same day you get there. If the ends are still loose, it will have to be their problem."

Mark released her and said, "Good, let's get packing."

*   *   *

Mark and Carole worked hard for the rest of the afternoon getting everything packed and stuffed into the Buick. When the car was just about over- weight, Carole said, "I know

I have twice the things you have for the trip, but I also want you to know that this is the least amount of *necessities* that I've ever packed – if I thought I'd be gone for more than three days."

"I knew I should have gotten the 50-footer."

"Probably so – you haven't seen the makeup and other *personal things* that will be with me on the plane."

"Perhaps I can get a small dinghy to drag behind us – similar to a landlubber pulling a trailer."

"Would that be *Plan 'C'*?"

"Whatever! Anyway, you've worked a retired person way too hard this afternoon. Why don't we get scrubbed up a little bit and we go get an early supper? Maybe I can recharge before morning."

"I think that is a wonderful idea. I'm way too tired to try and prepare anything worthwhile here. We can make it an early night, and I can bring you back here to get you prepared for the drive. In other words, screw your brains out so you won't be inclined to pick up any *hippy* hitch-hikers you might encounter along the way."

"You are *so* thoughtful. I'll race you to the shower."

"What if it's a tie?"

"We'll think of something."

Carole bolted for the double doors leading to the bed/bath area with Mark in hot pursuit. They were giggling like schoolgirls as they were undressing and throwing clothes at each other. Carole would try and take off her shorts and Mark would pull them back up as he was trying to get out of his pants with one hand. Carole pushed him while he was on one leg and he crashed to the floor – pulling her down with him. They wrestled on the floor, still taking off clothing until they were nude – then the wrestling stopped as they embraced and kissed deeply. The passion was abated when Mark leaned back from the embrace and flatly stated, "My God, you smell terrible. Don't you ever clean up?"

Carole jumped from the floor and started banging on Mark as he tried to defend himself and stand at the same time. When they were both standing, he picked her up in his arms and carried her to the shower – turned on the water and pulled her in with him. The soaping was fun, and they were both *very* clean when the shower was over.

*   *   *

Leo's Bar-B-Que was quick and delicious. The conversation at dinner revolved around the adventure that lay before them. They were both excited, and a feeling of urgency was building as they fantasized grand visions of tropical sailing. The meal went by quickly, and they hurried, for no apparent reason, back to Carole's condominium.

Once inside, Mark asked, "Would you like a nightcap? I think I'll have a brandy to unwind."

"Why don't you bring them into the bedroom and I'll try and make good on my earlier promise concerning the hitch-hikers."

"You smooth-talkin' devil."

Mark poured the brandy and carried the two snifters into the bedroom just as Carole was finishing turning down the bed. Mark sat one of the snifters on the nightstand by where Carole was standing. She didn't take the drink immediately but instead started unbuttoning her blouse. Mark sipped his drink as he watched her and then slowly backed across the room to one of the large easy-chairs arranged in the corner of the room. With her blouse unbuttoned, Carole, wordlessly, took a sip of the brandy – picked up the TV remote and dialed in one of the many cable music channels available. A slow and sensual jazz tune emerged from the speakers. She started to sway with the music and resumed removing her blouse – all the while looking at Mark who was obviously enjoying the spectacle of her undressing. Doing her version of a dancer in a *titty bar*, she slithered over in front of the chair Mark was sitting in and asked, in a deep, slutty voice, "Would you like a lap-dance, sailor?"

Still slowly sipping his brandy, Mark responded with, "I knew I should have installed that damned brass pole in here."

Carole reached down and removed the snifter from Mark's hand – sat the glass on the adjoining table and grabbed both his hands – pulling him to his feet. When he was standing, she continued the sensual dance. Her knees were spread wide as she caressed his body with hers. Still swaying with the music, she started to slowly undress him. When he would try and help – with anything – she would remove his

208

hands and continue with the slow, sensual undressing, caressing and general erotic behavior. Nothing was spoken, and when the undressing was complete, Carole maneuvered Mark to the bed. Locked in his embrace, they rotated onto the sheets as eager lovers.

Carole changed her mind about *screwing his brains out*, and opted to make love. She touched and tasted his body as he in turn touched and tasted hers. They both took advantage of having free and totally uninhibited access to the other. The lovemaking was slow, long-lasting, and incredibly enjoyable. Both were saturated with the intimacy, and afterward, sleep was deep – immediate, for both.

CHAPTER THIRTY-ONE

The thousand-mile-plus trip to Ft. Lauderdale was as boring as expected. Mark had driven over seven hundred miles the first day without seeing even *one* hippy hitch-hiker. Having nothing to keep his mind off it, the discomfort in his side was with him for most of the trip. The pain was not intense, but still nagged him to some extent when he had nothing to distract his mind from the dread of things to come.

Mark arrived in Ft. Lauderdale about noon on the second day and drove directly to the marina. His curiosity concerning the boat was almost overwhelming as he searched the showroom area for Don. He found him in his office and hated the social amenities necessary prior to the direct question, "So where's the boat?"

Don smiled and said, "I think it should be in the water by now. Sean was supervising the launch, and I think he should have it in your slip by now. Let's go see."

"Great, I'm dying to see it. I feel like a kid just getting his first car.

"Well, I think you're going to love it. It looks like a new boat. The crew did a really terrific job on it. I think it is especially good given the time frame you set up for them."

They walked the quarter-mile down the piers and finger piers to the slip Don had assigned Mark, and as the boat came into view, Mark quickened his pace in anticipation – leaving Don a few steps behind.

Mark stopped at the head of the slip and just stared at the beautiful boat before him. The new paint and the fresh varnish on all the woodwork glistened in the bright sunlight. The fittings and winches had all been freshly polished, and there appeared to be small prisms, reflecting sunlight, scattered about the weather deck. The canvas cover protecting the mainsail was color coordinated with the deep-blue of the hull and presented a slash of color emphasizing the stark white of the cabin, deck and gunwales. Mark was thinking, if I didn't own this boat, I would buy it right now – and damn the cost. The first sight of his dream-boat was actually causing him to hyperventilate. He was embarrassed by it.

There were two men and a woman securing bright white mooring lines to cleats mounted on both sides of the slip. They had placed white foam fenders in strategic positions around the hull for impact protection and were positioning a small gangplank in an opening they had made in the lifelines.

When the taller of the two men saw Don and his guest standing at the head of the slip, he waved and said, "Well, we know it floats."

Don, in turn, said, "Sean, I'd like for you to meet the boat's new owner. This is Mr. Mark Stevens, from Memphis, America."

Sean finished tying off the brow and walked to the head of the slip. He was a tall man, roughly Mark's height, with sun-bleached blond hair and an incredible tan. He was on the heavy side, with a protruding stomach, but quite muscular. It was difficult to judge his age, accurately, but Mark guessed he was in his late 40s or early 50s. He was wearing jeans, t-shirt and boat shoes. A yachting cap covered the top of the blond hair that fell down the sides – covering his ears and most of his neck. His blue eyes sparkled from inside the deeply wrinkled crow's-feet that seemed to be the result of his sun-swept lifestyle. As he approached Mark and Don, he exuded the aura of a happy man that loved what he was doing.

When he was within arms-length of Mark and Don, he extended his hand to Mark and said, "Damn, that's a fine boat. I'm Sean Jacobson and I've been looking forward to meeting you, Mr. Stevens."

Mark replied as he shook his hand, "I can't tell you how happy I am that you were able to sail with us, Captain. I'm sure I'll need a lot of help, but it's a long-term dream that seems to be coming true. I'm glad you like the boat. It's my first glance at it since all the hard work was done and I am absolutely tickled to death with the way it looks. Have you had an opportunity to take her out yet?"

"No, we just brought it over here from the yard. We've been getting everything you'd asked for taken care of and actually haven't had any time to give it a shake-down. Would you like to do it now?"

"I'd love to, but I've got so much stuff in the car to bring aboard before we move, I don't think we could get it all done today. I think Don may have a few things we need to get settled as well. I do want to go aboard and see if things are as beautiful below deck as they are topside."

"I'll let Maria give you that tour. She's been doing her thing while I do mine. It does look pretty good down below. I think you'll be comfortable." He then turned and called to the woman that was still adjusting lines and other things around the boat, and said, "Honey, come over and meet Mr. Stevens. He just got into town and wants to see the inside of the boat."

Maria stood by the brow she had just adjusted, and watched as the men approached her. She was as dark as Sean was fair, and dressed, essentially, as Sean was: jeans, t-shirt and deck shoes. She wasn't wearing a hat and her dark hair cascaded nearly to her shoulder blades. She seemed quite a bit younger than Sean – maybe thirty or so. Maria was rather thin in stature, but one couldn't help notice she was generously endowed, breast-wise, and the t-shirt she was wearing, strained to contain the ample bounty. She smiled with straight, white teeth as they approached and extended her hand when they were at arm's-length. Mark took the offered hand and said, "Mrs. Jacobson, thank you for joining us. I'm looking forward to your company, and the wonderful food, I've been told, you prepare as a matter of course."

Maria spoke with the slight accent of a Latina who had lived in the United States for a long time. "Mr. Stevens – it's so nice to meet you, and, by the way, my name is Maria. Mrs. Jacobson is Sean's mother." Then she added, with a happy laugh, "I probably wouldn't know to answer if someone called me Mrs. Jacobson."

The three men followed Maria onto the main deck and then aft to the cockpit. Mark admired the cleanliness of the boat in general – as well as the new mooring lines, main halyard and sheets – all neatly stowed and out of the way. He hated to go below with just a cursory inspection of the topside spaces, but Maria had already disappeared into the boat's interior and he, reluctantly, followed. He wasn't sorry he did. The musty smell of the boat's interior had been replaced with the fresh aroma of wax, soap and water. Whereas before, the boat had seemed neglected, it now had a life about it. All signs of neglect were gone – no clutter, no dust – just the polished beauty of mahogany and the finely upholstered appointments of the saloon.

Maria was telling Mark the previous owners had left the china and cooking utensils on board. She decided to wait until Mark arrived to see if everything was suitable, or if the service should be replaced or augmented. Maria then told Mark that she had taken the liberty of buying new bedding throughout, but had kept receipts for returning the items if they weren't happy with the color or quality.

Maria said, "I've bought and stored essential foodstuff, but I'll need input from you as to what your   eating preferences are. Towels and other items will also have to be brought on board. In other words, there is still a bit of shopping to do."

"There will be a *professional* shopper joining us tomorrow," Mark said, "and she will be delighted to help you with all that stuff. I am no help at all in that department. I'm sure the two of you will have more fun than the law should allow."

Mark was thrilled with the boat. He went back topside and joined Don and Sean, who were sitting in the cockpit arguing the prospects of Miami and Florida State football. He started to inject his opinion, but hesitated when he realized Memphis State might not be up to the task of meeting his optimistic forecast of their chances to win the national title.

Once back in the sunlight, Mark asked Don, "Do you think I can take care of all the paperwork needed to take possession this afternoon?"

"Mr. Stevens, if I may paraphrase *Leftie,* just a little bit: *If you've got the money, then I've got the time.*"

"How long do you think it will take to get everything taken care of?"

"No more than thirty minutes or so. It's mostly a few signatures and the inevitable exchange of legal tender."

"Great!" Mark then turned to Sean and said, "Captain, I know you just got the boat tied up, but do you think you could bring it around to the guest dock so I can unload an overstuffed Buick without having to make two-hundred trips back and forth to the slip? This sounds childlike, but I want to sleep on this boat tonight."

"No problem at all. I'll be waiting for you when you and Don finish your business."

"Since it's time to pay the fiddler, I'd like for you to tally up the expenses you've incurred and I'll take care of that while I'm in a check-writing mood."

Sean said, "I think Maria has everything logged and ready for your approval."

"I'll see you in a half-hour or so," then he added, "What a day this has been."

CHAPTER THIRTY-TWO

The almost imperceptible movement of the boat and the soft lapping of the water against the hull quickly lulled Mark into a deep, restful sleep. He awoke early; feeling more relaxed than he had in years. Maria had installed a coffee pot in the galley and after a very few minutes of scrounging through the cabinets he found coffee and filters. While the coffee was brewing, he hurried to the *head* for an abbreviated shave and shower, anxious to go topside and watch the sun come up while he drank his coffee.

He broke out into the fresh morning air to see vapor hovering over the calm waters of the marina and the bright orange of the morning sun peeking over the horizon. The wind was calm – the sky, cloudless. Screeching seagulls soared – then dove to pluck bits of food from the water's surface. The effortless aerobatics of the gulls presented a natural air show that seemed to demand his attention. A sense of peace fell over him as he sipped the steaming coffee and blankly stared at the wonder about him. If there is no after-life, he thought, it will be awful to miss mornings like this.

Mark had given Sean and Maria the day off. Carole would be arriving at one-thirty in the afternoon, and there would be no time for the much anticipated shake-down cruise.

It was way too early to look for a tag agency to get the boat title changed to his name and get it registered. So, he decided to find a restaurant – have a leisurely breakfast and read the newspaper. Killing time was not easy, and he wanted the morning to speed by. One-thirty seemed an eternity away.

*   *   *

The IHOP served its purpose with a good breakfast and a thick *Miami Herald* newspaper. Mark finished the paper and his chores but still arrived at the *Ft. Lauderdale International Airport* at twelve forty-five. He reasoned that he could wait at the gate as easily as anywhere else.

Carole stood out among the mass of people in the aisle for arriving passengers. She wore chic designer jeans and a white t-shirt. Her *Prada* handbag matched the smooth, black, high-heeled boots she wore. She had no carry-on luggage. It had only been three days since he'd seen her, but at first sight – she took Mark's breath away.

Mark pretended not to see her and donned the quizzical look of someone searching a crowd. Carole hurried up to him as he craned his neck above her – seemingly absorbed in crowd-searching. She placed her hands on her hips and with a deep scowl on her face, cleared her throat – loudly.

Mark finally looked down at her and said, "Excuse me ma'am, do I know you?"

Carole replied, through clenched teeth, "I hope you've found a good dentist since you've been down here. If you don't give me a hug real quick, you're gonna need one."

Mark swooped, and grabbed her in a bear hug – pulled her off her feet and twirled her full-circle before letting her back to the ground. They exchanged a warm welcoming kiss.

Mark finally broke their embrace and said, "I just *thought* I remembered how good you look. I see that I was a wee bit short with my mental picture. You are such pleasure to my eyes."

"I'll bet I didn't sleep two hours last night. I've been ready since five o'clock for a nine-fifteen flight. It's been a long day, but seeing you has made it all worth it."

"Wait until you see the boat. It's beautiful. You won't believe the differences from when you saw it last. I wish now that you'd have driven down with me so we could have seen it for the first time together.

Carole was beaming as she said, "Let's hurry and get my luggage. I can't wait to see it. Have you taken it out yet?

"No, I haven't had time. Even if I'd had the time, I would have waited for you before taking it anywhere. It's only fair."

*   *   *

"*Oh, my God!* It's beautiful," Carole squealed when she saw the boat.

"You've got to go look at the name on the stern before you go aboard. It's a surprise."

Carole walked down the slip until she could see the name *Cruzin' Carole* emblazoned across the back and said, "Oh Mark, thank you so much. I love it. *Gold* paint???"

"It's the red-neck coming out in me. Ah cain't hep it."

"It's the thought that counts," Carole replied as she hugged Mark and gave him a light kiss on the lips. She was chuckling to herself and shaking her head, mumbling, "*Gold paint!*" as they crossed the narrow brow onto the deck of the boat.

Carole was immediately impressed with the cleanliness of the topside area – repeating herself several times about the shine of the stainless-steel winches, fittings and wheel. When she could wait no longer, she dove into the interior – anxious to inspect the living quarters below.

Mark could hear her squeal from his cockpit vantage point. He followed, and enjoyed the excitement in Carole as she tore around the saloon and galley area – peering into cupboards and other storage spaces with obvious delight. She marveled at the efficient arrangement of cabinets and seating in such a restricted area. Every inch of bulkhead, deck, and overhead was considered in the design for maximum utility. Calling on her own experience, as an architect/interior design specialist, she understood the difficulty in planning such compact efficiency into a limited volume of inner space. "My complements," she said aloud to the unknown and absent designer.

As Carole disappeared into the living quarters to continue her inspection of the boat, Mark said, "It's obvious you're more interested in exploring than you are in my company. I think I'll mix a drink and go topside until you're curiosity is satisfied."

"Okay!" he heard her yell from the owner's berthing area.

There was a small bar near the control station with four decanters fitted into their mahogany cubicles with highball glasses similarly stored beneath. Mark selected the decanter marked *Scotch*, and poured a couple of fingers of the amber liquid into one of the glasses. Happily, he found ice in the freezer section of the refrigerator, but hadn't a clue about where to look for his customary club soda mix. What the hell, he thought, I'm tough enough to sip it on the rocks, as he made his way topside.

With nothing to do, Mark walked off the boat to the shaded area of the pier and sat on one of the many benches lining the slips. He took out his cell phone and dialed Sean's number. Sean answered on the third ring and Mark said, "Captain, I hate to bother you on a day off, but do you think we will be able to take the boat out early tomorrow morning? Sensible thinking is the only thing that keeps me from untying it right now."

Sean answered, "Go ahead and give it a whirl. If you're not back by tomorrow morning, I'll call out the Coast Guard to look for you."

"No, I think I'll wait on you and Maria before I have to buy another couple of boats that I'd probably crash into. My sailing partner is here, and I'd hate to destroy my *macho* image by looking inept at something. If we can get the rest of the shopping done for our trip by the day after tomorrow, I'd like to get out to the *blue* water and test our sea legs. That is, if you think we'll be ready to go by then."

"We should be ready. I think Maria has gathered most of the provisions we'll need. You'll just have to personalize it by getting things you would like to bring along."

"I didn't bring any fishing gear with me. I was hoping you could join me while the girls are shopping, and clue me in on what to buy for salt-water fishing. The only gear I had was for inland lakes and streams, and I don't think it would hold up under the strain of the giants I plan to catch in the next few months."

"That's a fantasy of mine: Shopping for fishing equipment with someone else's money. We'll make a list tomorrow – while we're out."

"Good! We're really looking forward to the day."

"We'll see you about seven in the morning – if that's not too early."

"That will be fine, Sean. Bye!"

Mark saw Carole's blond head pop up from the saloon like a jack-in-the-box. "Over here," he called from the dock.

Carole joined him and was beside herself with delight about the transformation of the boat. She crashed, heavily, into Mark's lap.

"I unpacked my suitcases, so you're stuck with me."

"It was my plan all along," he said. "I've just talked to Sean, and they'll be here at seven in the morning to get this show on the road. Are you up to it?"

"I wish we could go *tonight*."

"We have to *christen* the boat before we leave. It would be bad luck to leave on an unchristened boat."

"Does that mean you expect to have your way with me this evening, sir?"

"I expect."

"The things I have to go through for a damned boat ride. You *animal!*"

"Had you rather *not?*"

"Well – I certainly don't want the boat to be unlucky," Carole said as she engulfed him in her arms and nuzzled his neck. She then whispered in his ear, "I guess I can do *my* part to ward off the *haints*." Carole continued in a pitiful tone, "I'll take my place with all the other women that have had to suffer the cruel whelms of a lascivious Captain."

Mark rolled his eyes at her facetious bullshit and said, "*Right!* Good thinking, woman," in his version of a stern *Captainish* voice.

CHAPTER THIRTY-THREE

Mark awoke early – full of energy and anticipation. He tried to ease out of bed without waking Carole, but as soon as he moved, she came alive and said, in a sleepy, contented voice, "This will be the luckiest boat in the Caribbean after *that* christening."

Mark replied, "I'm sorry I had to *lie* to you, but the boat will have to be *christened* regularly, to keep the good luck intact. I'll have to check my book on *christening*, but I think we worked out a couple of extra days good luck from last night. You are a fantastic *christener*."

"Thank you, sir. Better safe than sorry is my motto – when it comes to *christening*."

"Stretch, and feel good for a few minutes while I get some coffee made. Sean and Maria won't be here for another hour or so."

"Good! That will give me time to clean up some. I'd love some coffee, though – as soon as it's ready."

"You got it."

*   *   *

Mark and Carole were sitting in the cockpit of the boat when they spotted Sean and Maria meandering down the pier – bumping each other with their hips, laughing and carrying on like a couple of teenagers. When they saw Mark and Carole watching them, they stopped the fooling-around and walked directly to the boat with smiles on both their faces that forfeited their more serious approach.

"Good morning," Sean called out when he was within earshot of the boat.

"And a good morning it is," Mark called back.

"We're a little bit early, but I see you're up, and about anyway, so I guess it doesn't make much difference."

"Not at all – I've been ready for this morning for over twenty years. Sean – Maria, I'd like for you to meet Ms. Carole Wilson. She's my partner in crime for this adventure."

After social amenities were exchanged all around, Sean said, "Mr. Stevens, if you're ready to get underway, we'll get things ready to cast off. If you haven't had breakfast, Maria will expose herself as one of the mighty fine shipboard chefs sailing the Caribbean."

"We are definitely ready to get underway, and no – we haven't had breakfast, but it's not that important."

"It's all important," Sean said. "We want to make this the most enjoyable trip of your life. Good trips start with good breakfasts."

"You're the Captain."

Sean started removing the cover off the mainsail and boom and said, "Mr. Stevens…

Mark interrupted and said "Captain, for my part, please don't be so formal. Let's just keep it on a first-name basis, if you don't mind. I'll call you *Captain*, just because I like the term, but if that's not comfortable – then I'll call you Sean or whatever you prefer, but this is a *friendly* cruise and I'd like for it to start and end that way."

"Thanks, Mark. I prefer it that way myself. Anyway, *Mark*, what we're going to do is use our sails to get us out of here. After we've hoisted the main, I'll untie the boat and hop

221

back aboard. Once aboard, I'll push the boom out to gather wind and it will move the boat backward. You'll steer as we're backing down, and when we've cleared the slip, you'll turn the wheel hard to starboard. As we come about, I'll adjust the main sheets to fill the sails, and we'll simply sail this baby out into the wild blue waters of the Atlantic. No sweat! So, if you'll take the helm, I'll throw off the lines, and we'll see what your new boat will do."

"You want me to take the helm?"

"Didn't you say you wanted to learn to sail your boat?"

"Well, yes – but isn't this a little early to try that? Shouldn't we start the engine?"

"It's never too early to start, and *no* – this is a sailboat. Engines are for emergency use or generating electricity for your comfort. Sails are what propel a sailboat."

Maria listened to the conversation between the two men and chuckled as she mounted the steps leading to the lower deck and the galley. Carole was torn between watching the boat get underway or watching Maria prepare breakfast in the less-than-spacious galley area. Maria's task won out, and she followed with some regret. Topside stuff was for the guys, and she felt that anything she could learn from Maria would pay for the missed opportunity to see the boat get underway. This would not be the last opportunity for observing topside seamanship.

"I think I can hack it," Mark said to Sean, "but don't be far away if I start to screw up."

"Where could I go? There's no way I could be more than thirty-five or forty feet away. You've sailed before – nothing changes other than the size of the vessel. You're gonna love it."

"As the *Cable Guy* says: *let's git 'er done!*"

*   *   *

They cleared the breakwater with no problems. Sean was right; there wasn't much difference in sailing the forty-five footer than sailing the twenty-one footer he'd sailed in Memphis. It didn't take any time at all to adjust to steering with a wheel rather than a tiller. The wind was a perfect nine/twelve knots, and the boat responded as though it was a thoroughbred – exercising on a new track.

As they entered the ocean (proper), the wave height increased to about two feet – not rough, but high enough to let them know they were no longer inside the breakwater and protected from the harshness of open water. For Mark, it was the thrill of a lifetime. He was embarrassed as he thought: *Jesus Christ* – I'm getting a hard-on. I haven't had that happen since I was doing night carrier-landings in the Marine Corps. Wait'll Carole hears about this. I'm sure it will be a riveting conversation.

Sean had unfurled the jib sail and was feeding the sheets (line) back through the fairways toward the cockpit and to the jib winches. Once in position, he tightened the rope (sheet) and the sail filled – stopping the maddening flapping noise of a luffing sail. There was an instant response from the boat. The increased speed was thrilling to Mark. With the exception of the splashing water on the hull, there was silence. The silent power of the wind pulled them along at a crisp five knots.

Carole topped the steps from the saloon and stopped, momentarily, to breathe the fresh, salt air and scan the landscape that was receding in the background. "This is just the way I have imagined it would be," she said as she sat on the windward side of the cockpit next to Mark – who was getting up and down from the seat to make periodic adjustments to the helm – keeping the sails full.

"I really hope you are getting the same rush out of this as I am."

"I have probably dreamed of this as long as you have – and here we are. It's wonderful. There's more: Maria has just prepared the most fantastic breakfast you've ever seen – all the while rolling around on a boat at sea. I don't know if I'll ever be able to do that."

"All this *seafaring* shit does work up an appetite. What's she got?"

"Eggs Benedict without the Canadian bacon. She's smothered the hollandaise sauce with crab meat. I think it's going to be 'to-die-for'."

"Too bad we don't have Champagne to go along with it."

"How *common* would that be?" Carole asked. She continued with, "Chef Maria has been chilling the wine since she started cooking. She's thought of everything. I think *it* may be ready when *we* are ready – and *I* am *ready*."

Maria stuck her head out of the saloon and said, "Mark, Carole, it's *soup*. You might want to get it while it's hot."

Mark yelled at Sean, who was digging into the sail locker on the forecastle – to let him know breakfast was ready.

Sean, in turn, yelled back, Maria, and I will eat after you've finished. Enjoy your first meal at sea by yourselves."

Mark started to protest, but Carole gouged him softly in the ribs and shook her head no. She then rose from her seat to go below.

Mark yelled again to Sean, "You've got the helm, Captain," and proceeded to join Carole and Maria below decks.

Maria had set the table for two but had not placed food on the plates. When Mark and Carole were seated, she presented her meal of Eggs Benedict, freshly steamed asparagus, and several types of fruit slices.

"Maria, this is wonderful. We didn't expect such a feast on our first outing."

"Thank you. I wanted it to be pretty special today. I hope you enjoy. I only prepared two eggs each, but there are plenty more if two doesn't quite get it done."

Mark and Carole both attacked their food like they hadn't eaten in days. Halfway through their first bites, they heard the pop of the Champagne cork. Maria filled the tall plastic flutes sitting next to their plates, explaining the plastic flutes were probably best for serving at sea.

The breakfast was delicious and well received by both Mark and Carole, but Mark was anxious to get back topside to hone his sailing skills.

Sean was in the cockpit, doing as Mark had done earlier. Sitting and standing as necessary to keep the boat steady on a broad reach – port tack.

"Go below and get your breakfast. No wonder you are, shall we say, *substantial* – with food like that on a regular basis."

"You can go ahead and say *fat*," Sean said, laughing at the comment. I told you – she's a *hand* in the kitchen."

"You can say that again."

"I'll be back shortly. I've taken out the spinnaker so we can have a drill on its rigging and operation. I think you'll enjoy it. Whoever the sail maker was, he made himself proud with yours. It's gonna be beautiful when it pops."

"Eat fast!"

Carole came out of the saloon and said, "Maria kicked me out of the kitchen, so, I guess you're going to have to put up with me."

"If you're going to be up here, you'll have to earn your keep. You now have the helm."

"I don't know anything about driving a boat."

"Well, you have to learn. It's going to be just you and me after our skipper and cook leave us in a week or so.

Mark pointed out two pieces of yarn that were sewn into the luff of the mainsail and jib. "If you keep the *tell-tales* lying smoothly and horizontally along the main part of the sail – you've got it right. Experiment and see what it takes to make all that happen. There are no other boats in sight, and we're ten miles from the nearest shore. It's a perfect time to play."

"I really want to do this, so don't yell at me if I screw up."

"There's no yelling allowed, unless there's an emergency. Get after it. There are two ways of keeping the tell-tales right: one is with your heading and the other is with the adjustment of the sail. Since we have no obstacles in our way, let's just start with maintaining a particular heading that corresponds with the way the wind is taking us."

Carole stood at the wheel – reluctant to sit – and watched the tell-tales as though they were messages from God. The nervousness she initially felt soon disappeared, and she began to have the rush Mark had felt earlier. As a counter point, to Mark's erection – she thought she was getting a *wide-on*. She chuckled at the absurdity of the situation; however, she loved the sensation.

Sailing! Sean had given Mark a brief tour on the operation of the auto pilot, the "pulsing" radar and other electronics installed on the boat. They'd lit off the engine, to check it out, but didn't use it for propulsion. Mark was very familiar with the GPS system, as it was the same as the system he used regularly in the airplane.

They sailed back inside the breakwater at exactly six p.m. Mark was somewhat concerned that Sean hadn't started the engine again, but decided to let him do it his way.

Mark found their slip and Sean simply told him to steer for the center, and he would direct a "sails only" landing. While they still had good headway, Sean told Mark to release the sheet on the mainsail – which he did while maintaining a direct course for the slip. Once inside the slip – Sean repeated the maneuver he'd done in the morning by pushing the mainsail boom into the wind, and the boat stopped – perfectly aligned with the slip. Tying up the boat was so simple it was an anticlimax. Mark was elated as Carole clapped and cheered at the perfect landing.

Mark and Carole were both pumped to the extreme and really didn't know what to do to come down. Finally, Mark asked Sean to join them for an after-cruise drink and in the same sentence, asked if he could take them to dinner.

"We'd love to join you for the drink," Sean said, "but we've already made other plans for dinner – if you don't mind."

"No that's OK. I just want you to know how terrific you've made this day. If it gets any better than this – my old body won't be able to stand up to the strain."

After they'd had their *after-cruise* drink, Sean asked, "What time would you like to start the shopping spree tomorrow?

"Why not around ninish? Everything should be open by then. I just hope we will be able to stash everything these women are going to feel we can't live without. They'd better leave room for some serious fishing gear."

"Well, any leftovers that can't be stashed – especially the fishing gear – could be *stashed* with me until you find a place for it."

"We'll see you in the morning. Thanks again for a wonderful day."

"It was our pleasure."

CHAPTER THIRTY-FOUR

The shopping took most of the day for Sean and Mark. *Bass Pro Shops* was paradise for sportsmen (or would-be sportsmen) and Mark found way too many things that were supposed to catch the fish he felt were waiting for him in the blue waters of the Caribbean. He really didn't care what Carole and Maria were shopping for. He had his *stuff*, and that was what was important at the moment.

Carole and Maria had taken the Buick and Mark, and Sean had done their shopping from Sean's Jeep. They all arrived at the boat within five minutes of each other – each raving with great enthusiasm about the great *deals* they'd found during the day. Mark was about as interested in the boring towels, glassware, and other items Carole had found as she was in the fabulous and exciting fishing gear he had found. Mark took his brand new Shimano *Calcutta TE-400* out of its box and tried to impress Carole with all its mechanical superiority. She was about as impressed with the reel as he was with the *bargains* she and Maria had found on *Cannon* bath towels. *C'est la vie*!

Everyone seemed genuinely happy with their day's plunder, and though each principal gushed on the other's selections, Mark knew (secretly) he had made vastly superior choices in choosing *his* stuff. Carole, on the other hand, tried to compute just how much fish $1,600 would buy at the local *Albertsons* – neatly packaged in meal-sized portions.

Mark and Sean turned their conversation into plans for the Bahamian sailing adventure.

"Do you think we have everything on board that we'll need for the trip," Mark asked?

"Lord knows we have enough food. The girls brought the waterline up by about two inches today. I've checked out all the Nav equipment. The sails are in good repair. We have extra winch handles and the rigging is new. We also have extra line, and wire just in case something does go wrong. Fuel and water tanks have been filled, so I see no reason we can't leave in the morning – as scheduled."

"How long do you think it will take us to get to Nassau?"

Sean thought for a few seconds, and then said, "It's about 175 nautical miles, as the crow flies, but we'll have to zig and zag around Biminis and Andros islands in order to get to the East side of New Providence. That will probably add another thirty or forty miles to our route. I think we'll be able to average three to five knots. So – I'd guess about fifty hours sailing time before we can drop the hook in Nassau. Do you, and Carole, have your passports?"

"Yes, they're current and on-board."

"Good. They'll check us when we get there. I know several of the customs officers, so maybe that will relieve us from the customs search. I hope so. That's always a pain in the butt. What time do you want to leave?"

"We'll be ready whenever you are. I would like to get underway pretty early though."

"No problem. Would seven o'clock be OK?"

"Perfect!"

"Be sure and top off your water tank before you unhook from the slip. Fresh water becomes our most precious commodity once dry land falls over the horizon." Sean continued with, "Maria and I have some last minute chores to take care of, so, with your permission, I think we'd better bail out and take care of them. How long do you think you'll need our services?"

Mark thought for a second, then said, "That will depend on when you think I'm capable of sailing this thing alone – safely. I really don't think I'll have too much trouble. I'm a decent navigator – due to many hours of flight time, and I'm familiar with most sailing techniques. I'd like for you to stay with us at least a week, and then, depending on your schedule, and my competence, perhaps another week of just goofing off and having some fun. We'll get you back to a Bahamian airport as soon as you've *had it* with our company."

"Well, we've set aside two weeks. I'll have to get back soon after that to take care of the *Spirit*. I'm confident you'll be able to take care of things as well as I can by then – probably much sooner. Maria and I look forward to the trip. It should be fun and I almost feel guilty taking money for a job like this. I a*lmost* feel guilty, but not quite. I'll get over it," Sean said with a laugh.

Mark laughed along, and said, "We'll see you in the morning, Captain."

As Sean was leaving, he asked from the dock, "Were you able to come up with the rifle?"

"Sean, to tell the truth, I forgot all about it during the hassle of getting my dumb ass down here."

A slight frown crossed Sean's face as he said, "I'll bring mine and you can return it when you're back in Ft. Lauderdale. The Bahamas are noted as a transfer point for drugs. I'd rather not take any chances on unexpected meetings with bad guys and be totally unarmed."

"I don't know my way around Ft. Lauderdale. If you have time to buy a rifle I will appreciate it. I do have a *Glock 21* with me, but I'm sure the rifle would be more appropriate. I don't think it will hurt to have both on board."

"I agree. I'll see you in the morning. I think we'll have time to buy a rifle. If not, I'll bring mine."

*   *   *

Mark woke up at four-thirty and forced himself to lie in bed another forty-five minutes before getting up. As usual, when he moved, Carole was instantly awake, but still groggy from sleep.

"Go back to sleep," he said. I'll get the coffee started and my last *long* shower out of the way. I'll bring you your coffee when it's ready."

"I'm too excited to sleep. Why don't I make the coffee while you get showered? Then, we can trade places while we wait on Maria and Sean."

"Sounds like a deal, to me," Mark said as he entered the *head*.

His *long* shower and quick shave took exactly thirty minutes, and when he stepped out of the shower stall, he saw the fresh coffee Carole had placed on the vanity. What a deal, he thought as he dried off and hurried to get dressed. He also marveled at how little time it took to dress – slipping on wrinkled shorts, a tee shirt and stepping into a pair of *Topsiders*, sans socks. Life was really good. This should have happened years ago.

When he met Carole in the galley, she had halved a fresh grapefruit and was just finishing her half. She pointed to the other half sitting on the sink counter and said, "I thought you might like a snack. I wouldn't want us to catch *scurvy* during our trip. I'm sure Maria will want to cook something more substantial when she gets here, but maybe that will hold you."

"Thank you. Since you're going to be lounging in the shower – I think I'll take it topside. I don't want to miss any of this day by hanging out below decks. Come on up when you're ready."

Mark and Carole were sitting in the cockpit with their second or third cup of coffee when they spotted Sean and Maria bumping hips, laughing and generally flirting with each other as they approached the boat – a repeat of their actions the day before. Sean carried a large duffle bag and the rifle. Maria carried a couple of plastic supermarket bags and a newspaper.

Carole saw the rifle, and with some astonishment in her voice, said, "It looks like he got the rifle you asked for."

"It's a security blanket.

"I understand! Has he ever been approached by bad guys while sailing?"

"No, but some of his friends have and he doesn't want to take the chance of not being prepared. I'm afraid I agree with him completely."

"That problem had never entered my mind, but now that I think about it – it probably is a good idea. That's just a pretty lethal-looking gun, and I'm not real comfortable around them."

Sean and Maria stopped on the slip next to the boat. They were all smiles as Sean asked, "You guys ready to travel to another country in a virtual hole-in-the-water that is surrounded by cement and propelled by wind?"

Carole laughed and said, "Putting it that way – I don't think it can be done, but we're willing to try."

"Good. Let me get my gear below, and we'll *see* if it can be done."

*   *   *

Getting underway was a repeat of the shake-down cruise. Sean manned the boom and Mark steered as the boat backed down. He then shifted his rudder and watched the sails fill when Sean heaved around on the main's sheets, took three turns on the winch, and locked the sheets in the self-binding cleat. Absolutely no problems, but they were only fifty yards from where they started. They only had another one hundred seventy-five miles to go – minus the fifty yards.

The jib was furled in the automatic furler on the forestay. Once power had been established with the mainsail, Sean went forward –unlocked the furler and set the jib. Mark felt the surge of power when the sail filled and was, once again, trying to deal with a non-sexual erection.

Sean finished the deck work by the time they cleared the breakwater and had joined Mark in the cockpit.

"Let's come around to about one-zero-zero magnetic and see if that won't hold us on our course. We'll check it with the GPS in an hour or so to see if we have to make any corrections."

Mark did as he was told and adjusted the sails. The boat was *flying* – close hauled on a starboard tack. With the wind at about twelve to fifteen knots, Mark felt as if they were doing twenty knots over the water, and reasoned they would be in Nassau before nightfall. Smiling like the village idiot, Mark giggled as he wondered if he'd get sea-bugs on his teeth with all this speed.

Sean looked on, wordlessly, from the windward side of the cockpit and chuckled at the obvious excitement boiling from his new boss. Dynamite couldn't blow him away from that wheel, he thought, and remembered when it was that new and exciting to him.

Carole poked her head out from the saloon and said, "Would you mind finding a little bit smoother road? We're trying to get a few things done down here, and the boat keeps *leaning*."

Mark half closed one eye and bellowed his best vocal version of Long John Silver –" *Harrr, Harrr, Harr!* Stay below, *wench*, this is *man's* work."

"Don't make me come up there, smartass. I'll squash your *hushpuppies*."

"Ahh, I see my impersonation was well received."

"Maria wants to know if you guys want anything to eat."

Mark looked at Sean as he shook his head, negatively. He then told Carole, "Why don't we make it a *brunch* in a couple of hours. You need to come up here and enjoy this, my dear."

"I think you're right. Let me get some sunscreen, and we'll join you in a minute."

"We'll be here."

*   *   *

The estimated time of fifty hours became sixty hours, due to the time spent training Mark. He'd spent time rigging and deploying the spinnaker sail and *running* (sailing downwind) with *wing-on-wing* that took them miles off their course, but brought his proficiency up to "expert" category in the process. Sean liked what he saw, and Mark was beside himself with his new-found abilities. He had screwed up a couple of times but had it down perfect the last few practice runs. He felt pretty *salty* by the time they contacted Nassau Harbor Control on VHF Channel 16 at five-fifteen – Thursday afternoon.

Sean had called ahead and made reservations at *Nassau Yacht Haven* – one of the many marinas offering guest docking, fuel, water and provisions. Sean also suggested they drop their sails and dock using the engine – since there was a following wind that did not lend itself to docking in a strange marina under sail.

Mark started the engine and asked Sean if he wanted to dock the boat. Sean, in turn said, "You may as well bring her in yourself. You're going to have to do it sometime. I'll be in the cockpit with you if you need any help. I doubt if I'll be needed other than helping you find the slip they assigned us. Just maintain steerage by engaging and disengaging the engine. You won't have any problems."

Sean let out a big laugh and said, "I'm going to go below and get my life jacket – you drive the boat."

The docks and their associated slips were fairly well marked, and, following the directions given over the radio, the landing went as smoothly as expected.

"Let's get that water line hooked up – pronto," Mark said, and then continued with, "I've taken *Navy* showers for two days and I actually want to *waste* some fresh water."

Carole piped in with, "*Thank* you. Everyone will appreciate it and, in your case, it won't be a *waste*."

To which Mark replied, "Show some *respect,* woman. I shall be *Captain* one day."

"Oops!"

Mark and Carole were elated with the trip and were repetitious in their superlatives describing it. They had sunned, fished, practiced sailing techniques; made several stops for swimming in the ocean, and generally done all the things they'd expected to do on a sailing cruise. Everything was made more enjoyable by the wonderful food Maria constantly prepared and the boundless knowledge of the sea afforded by Sean. In addition to being exceptional at their jobs – Sean and Maria were fun to be around and had countless stories of past sailing adventures that left no time for boredom. Carole couldn't stay out of the galley while Maria was cooking and copied down every new recipe she could – even though Maria never used a recipe while cooking. She had a *way* with fresh fish that probably couldn't be taught, but Carole paid attention and really couldn't wait to try it on her own.

233

Sean and Maria had been to Nassau so many times they felt like it was a hometown to them. They provided tour-guide service for Mark and Carole and accompanied them to several restaurants and fun-type bars. Everyone had a wonderful evening enjoying the laid-back atmosphere of the tropics. The tropical paradise did *not* run out of booze – as would be expected under the strain of partying first-timers.

*   *   *

They made it back to the boat with no serious incidents involving police or others dedicated to keeping the peace. Once on-board, Sean and Maria had *had it* and opted for the comfort of their forward quarters. Mark and Carole, on the other hand, decided they needed a nightcap under the stars before ending a perfect day.

Brandy was on hand, so Mark went below, gathered two snifters and returned to the cockpit where Carole was lying down on the bench seat looking up at the heavens. She rose to a half-sitting position when Mark joined her. Mark sat down and made his lap available as a pillow for her head. When they were both comfortable, she continued her inspection of the tropical heavens.

They sat/lay wordlessly for several minutes until Carole spoke with a degree of melancholy in her voice, "I wish Jean and Art were with us. They would really enjoy this."

"I'm sure they would," Mark said in reply.

"Do you think they would come down here if we asked them?"

"I'm sure they will. I just don't know when they can get away."

There was silence again for several minutes until Carole finally asked, "Do you think they'd come down for a wedding?"

Mark jerked with sudden alertness and asked, "What are you talking about?"

"Well, since it seems I'm the resident *aggressor* in this relationship, would you *marry* me, Mark Stevens?"

"Carole, I hope this isn't another twist on the back-and-forth nonsense we seem to enjoy. If it is, I don't have an answer."

Carole rose to a full sitting position beside Mark. "My question was far from nonsense. I think that's what two people usually do when they're in love."

"Nothing – and I really mean *nothing* would make me happier – if things were as they should be. With this cloud hanging over my head, I just don't think it would be fair, to you, to take it that far."

"Mark, I don't think you understand – I want to make love to my *husband* – kiss my *husband* goodnight, and wake up to kiss my *husband* good morning – until death do us part. That '*until death do us part*' thing sets no time limits. If it's a month – two, or fifty years, it's all the same – '*until death do us part*'."

"Oh *wow*! I still don't know what to say, but *yes*, if that's what *you* want, I'll do it tonight. It's more than I'd ever hoped for."

"Let's give them a call tomorrow and see when they can get away. Since we're making calls – why not call Mattie and Maury as well, and see if they'd like to join the party. If you wouldn't mind, I'd also like to invite Alice and Ryan. I do need a *matron of honor* to get this done right."

"If you want to invite half of Memphis, it's fine with me. I'd love for everyone I know to see what kind of fantastic deal I've made."

They tried to go below together, with their arms around each other, but the ladder well was too narrow for them to pass. The queen bed in their berthing compartment, however, was ideal for their continuing intimacy.

CHAPTER THIRTY-FIVE

Mark was awake long after Carole had lapsed into the shallow, rhythmic breathing of deep sleep – curled by his side in constant contact. He was trying to absorb the impact of her request for marriage. He felt he would be doing her an injustice if he could only be with her for such a short time. Carole knew that he only had months to live, but still wanted to be his wife. He was flattered by her proposal and felt she had not made it without a lot of thought. I hope she isn't doing it just to make me happy, he thought. What the hell – if she wants to, she can have it annulled later. I have to admit – it does make me very happy. With that last happy thought, he drifted off to sleep.

He awoke at six-thirty to the smell of coffee brewing in the galley. Maria is already getting after it, he thought, as he rolled out of bed. Carole rose up from sleep with the usual confused look he'd become accustomed to, and asked, "Is it time to get up?"

"Not unless you want to. I smell coffee, and it beckons to me. Sleep, darlin', sleep. I can't miss the morning."

236

Carole pulled the pillow over her head and snuggled down into the warmth of her nest – mumbling something about getting up with the chickens.

Mark threw on his usual seafaring gear and met Maria in the galley where she was busily preparing another one of her fabulous breakfasts.

"Good morning," Mark said as he entered the saloon/galley area.

Maria responded with another cheery, "Good morning to you too. Sean is already topside awaiting a plan of the day. Get some coffee – join him. I'll see if I can finish up something edible for the crew."

"If it isn't edible, it will be the first time we've ever had such a problem."

Mark joined Sean in the cockpit and, after standard greetings, sat down opposite him on the bench seats.

After a few moments of silence, Sean said, "Well, we're in Nassau. Do you just want to sit here, or would you like to do a little more sailing? There are some great, small, uninhabited islands throughout The Bahamas – would you like to visit some of them and practice your skills? Honestly, I think you're wasting your money by keeping me on board, but I enjoy the company and love being paid for a deal like this."

"You're my security blanket for another week or so. I don't really think I'll have any trouble sailing the boat either; however, we enjoy your company as well, and I'm sure I'll pick up valuable information, even if we're just goofing off and having a good time."

"Do you want to hang out here or move along?"

"Well, after last night, I'm rather obligated to hang here for another day – or half day. Carole and I have decided to get married. She told me she's pregnant, and I have to do the right thing by her."

"You're shitting me."

"About the pregnant part, or the married part?" Mark asked with a chuckle. "I guess I'll call it a half-truth. The getting married part is all true. I think she's *settled* for me – thinking I will be *Captain* one day. We want to invite some friends down from Memphis and *git 'er done*. Any suggestions as to where we might do such a thing?"

"They have marriage chapels all over the islands, but if it were me – I think I'd sail up to *The Abacos*. In my view, they're the most beautiful of the islands, with lots of properties that rent for occasions such as this. You can rent a house with a dock for a week – or month, whatever you choose. I don't think you'll be disappointed. It's about a hundred and fifty miles up there, but it's a beautiful trip. Your guests can fly in and either be delivered to the boat or to any other location you pick. It's more laid-back than it is here in Nassau, but there are still plenty of places to party – if you choose to do such nonsense."

"Partying is not nonsense – it's a way of life, Sean."

"I know; I know! It was just a figure of speech. Anyway – *congratulations*! She's a lovely lady and, confidentially, I think you made a *much* better deal than she did," Sean said with a boisterous, belly-deep, laugh.

"Thanks – ass-hole!"

"That's *Captain* ass-hole, if you don't mind." Again – the belly laugh.

Maria stuck her head out of the cabin and asked, "Are you guys ready to eat or should I back off until Carole gets up to join you?"

Sean said, "Let's wait until she gets up. Have a little *Champagne* ready. They've decided to get *married*."

"*Oh my God! Really?*"

"I guess he got her really drunk last night, and, in a moment of weakness, she went along with his indecent proposal. Maybe you can talk some sense into her head before it's too late."

"Sean, *shut up*! I'm going to take her a glass of Champagne *now* and see if I can help with anything. *Congratulations* Mark. You've done well – and in my view, so has she."

"Thanks, Maria. You're *so* much nicer to talk to than your bucket-mouthed husband. Maybe you could just stay with us and let him go back to that cheap, little eighty-footer he's so used to."

*   *   *

The quartet of seafarers spent the morning in Nassau making phone calls and arrangements for the gathering. Jean and Art were ecstatic with the news and said they would be down tomorrow if that was the day they'd planned. Mattie was surprised, but fully supported the union. She said that she would be there no matter what, and expected to be able to pry Maury away from business long enough to make sure it was a *consensual* wedding and not something Mark had coerced Carole into accepting. Alice and Ryan were just as surprised as the others, but agreed to join the party. Due to business commitments, Ryan would not be able to stay for more than a couple of days.

The supporting cast was in place, and the wedding was planned for a week from the following Monday on *Grand Abaco*. That would allow them time for sailing the uninhabited islands and still be able to make the trip with time to spare. Mark had asked for the entire party to plan as much time off as they could afford – offering day-sailing (and partying) out of *The Abacos* as long as they could/would enjoy. He had also phoned for, and received, reservations for a lovely ocean-side home in *Marsh Harbour* at the *Great Abaco Club* – that would accommodate the invitees. The home featured docking facilities for boats up to fifty feet in length. It seemed perfect. Expensive – but perfect! All travelers would arrive at the Marsh Harbour airport at three in the afternoon on Sunday.

*   *   *

They planned a leisurely trip northward toward *Grand Abaco*, dodging the larger islands and stopping when they saw something of exceptional beauty. They swam, fished, explored during the daytime hours and at night lay at anchor – immersed in stimulating conversations that involved many sailing stories, future plans and *politics*. Sean and Maria turned out to be as politically liberal as Mark was conservative and there were many *point/counterpoint* arguments that never amounted to much change in the other's philosophy. Due to alcohol saturation, the couple of times they drew knives on each other, they didn't saturate the decks with blood. They started at *zero* each morning as Maria and Carole looked on and listened with casual indifference – promising to step in before they killed each other.

Mark's sailing lessons were just about finished and he and Sean generally shared the duties of getting the boat from point to point. Carole was a fast learner and was soaking up seafaring knowledge like a sponge. She could handle the boat just about as well as the men unless heavy lifting was involved. She manned the winches, took the helm, hoisted sails and was becoming a fine sailor in her own right – reading the tell-tales and adjusting either heading or sail for maximum efficiency. She loved it, and the others enjoyed seeing the intensity she brought to each challenge. *Grit* – the woman was full of it.

The week went unbelievably fast, and they contacted *Marsh Harbour* harbor control at ten-thirty Saturday morning with plenty of time to get settled in the house and await their guests.

Mark was pleased to find that the *Great Abacos Club* was able to provide a maid and a cook for the house during their stay. He was also surprised to learn the club could also provide services for weddings. All they would have to do is meet with the *concierge*, who, in turn, would make arrangements for carrying out their particular requests. God, this is easy, he thought.

CHAPTER THIRTY-SIX

Sean and Maria could not be convinced to stay for the wedding and resulting after-wedding party. Sean was anxious to get back to Ft. Lauderdale to make sure the boatyard work on the *Spirit* was coming along as ordered and on schedule. He and Maria were insistent in their demands that Mark and Carole contact them as soon as they returned to Ft. Lauderdale to have a second after-wedding party on-board the *Spirit*. They decided to catch the return flight of the plane the other guests were arriving aboard. They were thankful for the extra night, and looked forward to showing Mark and Carole the sights in Marsh Harbour – such as they were.

As advertised, the *Abacos* were much more laid back than the bright lights of Nassau. The local bars were friendly and uncrowded as they made their way around Hope Town. It was an afternoon and evening of light snacking and light drinking as they enjoyed the local culture and visited with locals and tourist with equal ease. They discovered that it would be very difficult not to drift off into the loose and seemingly carefree lifestyles enjoyed by foreign and domestic inhabitants alike.

Who could want more – sunshine, tropical breezes, spectacular white beaches washed with crystal clear water – softly splashing ashore from the turquoise hue of the sands and coral reflected in the bay? Pretty special!

*   *   *

Sunday morning was spent shopping for provisions needed to take care of the incoming guests. Maria was invaluable. She knew the markets and also knew how to provide for the upcoming menus the cook would be preparing for the group. Carole really hated to see her go. She had been wonderful on the boat and would have been spectacular – given the resources of the beautiful kitchen in the rental.

Mark called a cab to take the quartet to the airport. While en route he asked the driver to call for a second cab to take care of the overflow of incoming guests. He really looked forward to seeing Jean, Art, Mattie and Maury. He had not met Ryan, but expected him to be as much fun as Alice had been at their brief luncheon meeting. It should be an exceptional gathering.

*   *   *

The yellow plane touched down exactly on time and belched out the entire guest list. Maury and Ryan had become *compadres* during the trip from Ft. Lauderdale after discovering they were both in the clothing business. As the Vice President of a major clothing manufacturer, Ryan instinctively catalogued Maury as a potential outlet for their line. Although the subject was never brought up during the trip, they did visit extensively about the clothing market – both retail and wholesale.

After the hugging and handshakes were complete, Mark introduced Sean and Maria to the incoming guests and made it clear that he was unhappy to see them leave. He mentioned something about their penchant for anti-social behavior and wished an incurable case of "jock-itch" on Sean as he helped

242

with their bags. As Sean and Maria were about to board the plane – serious goodbyes were said, with genuine regret, concerning the unavoidable departure of good friends.

*   *   *

Once the taxicabs had been unloaded at the rental, the women seemed to be unable to speak quickly enough to get everything said in the allotted time. The men, on the other hand, just watched in complete ignorance of such behavior and headed straight for the bar – under Mark's expert guidance.

Drinks in hand, the men migrated to the veranda overlooking the bay and the dock where the *Cruzin' Carole* was moored. Art was fascinated by the transformation of the boat he'd seen on keel blocks in Ft. Lauderdale into the sleek seagoing vessel tied up next to the pier. It didn't take a lot of coaxing to have Mark offer a tour of the boat he'd grown to love. The men then migrated to the boat for a personal presentation by a very proud owner – and now captain.

Art, of course, was the most impressed by the boat's presence. The others were equally impressed with the ship-shape appearance and beautiful lines. Mark tried, but could not hide his pride as he pointed out special aspects of the boat that probably meant nothing to the tour, but were special to him. It was well received by all. The men had refreshed their drinks, on board, and were sitting in the cockpit area when a parade of wives and one fiancée, came down the landing – still jabbering away.

Carole was leading the pack, as they came aboard. They barely gave notice to the men as they charged the lower deck areas to inspect the living quarters – paying particular attention the bathroom/head facilities. After about twenty minutes of critical examination, the ladies joined the men in the cockpit area – satisfied that the boat could actually be acceptable habitat for civilized human beings.

Mark asked Carole, "Do you want to take the boat out for a while?"

"The lady from the club is preparing dinner. Do you think we have time?"

"I doubt it," Mark replied, "but I think I'd rather go out on the boat than have dinner."

"You just want to play *Captain*. I know you too well, Mark Stevens."

"Damn it! Leave me alone. I just wanted to wear that cool hat for a little while." He continued with "If there isn't anything going on tomorrow we'll take it out for a full day on the water."

The looks Mark received from the entire group of women were not looks of total admiration.

*   *   *

The wedding was not an elaborate affair. It was a brief civil service performed at one-thirty in the afternoon by a local magistrate from *Hope Town*. The setting was beautiful, however, and performed on a hill overlooking the *Sea of Abacos* near the rental house. The staff of the club had set up an arbor, covered in flowers – with *Astro Turf* covering the ground on which to place chairs for the six invited guests. A local musician walked slowly around the perimeter of the gathering, softly playing island music on an acoustic guitar as a photographer snapped pictures of the same people, over and over again. Jean kept Mattie supplied with tissue as she sobbed during half the ceremony. Alice and Art stood as witnesses – or as Art called them, a poor man's *Matron of Honor* and *Best Man*. It got the job done, and a radiant Mr. and Mrs. Mark Stevens stepped from under the arbor to invite everyone back to the house for the more serious aspects of the day – the reception. Perhaps *reception* could better be described as a semi-drunken party among eight close friends.

The drinking tapered off as the afternoon wore on and fatigue started to raise its ugly head.

Everyone seemed to migrate to their individual quarters. Mark and Carole did the same and, once in their bedroom, Mark asked, "Are you feeling like a married woman?"

"I really don't feel any different," she said. "I loved you just as much before the ceremony, but I'm extremely happy to be Mrs. Mark Stevens. I could not ask for more."

"Are you having any regrets about it being a short-term marriage?"

"Mark, I think the magistrate said …'until *death do us part*'. I wouldn't give up the time I've had with you, or the time

244

I expect to spend with you for anything anyone else has to offer. You are the man I want to spend my life with – no one else. If fate takes you before me, I've still had more than most women will ever have. It's only a matter of time – not quality, and I have quality that I've never dreamed of. I'll hear no more talk of *regrets*."

"I'll never mention it to you again."

Carole put her arms around her husband and said, "Thank you."

"I have a fairly significant estate that I need to transfer over to you. Mattie is now the executor, and free to do anything she chooses with it. I need to allow you the same privilege. I'll call my lawyer in the morning and get the ball rolling."

"Mark, I didn't marry you for your *estate*. Leave it as it is."

"No, Mattie and Maury are probably better off than I am, so the money is really of no consequence to them. It's just that I didn't have anyone else to leave it to until now. I'd asked that she establish a trust for some kids that don't have the funds to get a good education and I think she's going along with that plan; however, it wasn't a requirement. She could do with it whatever she wanted without stipulation. You will have the same options."

"I hate talking about this right now. If that's what you'd planned – then I think it should stay that way. I'll do whatever you want, but please no more talk of your *estate* while we're finishing out our wedding day." Then after a brief pause, continued with, "Should we consummate our marriage now, or do you think we can wait until after dinner?"

"Maybe we should wait until after dinner. I don't want to be rushed in something as serious as a *consummation*."

"You're getting lazy in your old age. A better answer would have been: A quickie consummation now and a more serious one after dinner."

"You insatiable hussy!"

"Well, it's your fault."

CHAPTER THIRTY-SEVEN

The consummation was long-lasting and loving, with both husband and wife paying particular attention to the pleasure of the other. Languishing in the hedonistic joy of spent passion, they found it difficult to turn off their minds and bodies for sleep. Sexually satisfied, they were still enjoying the physical closeness and the intimacy of touching nakedness in their conjugal bed.

After reliving the events of the day in quiet conversation, Mark finally said to Carole, "I'm sorry I can't shut up and let you get some sleep, but I'm still wound pretty tight. I think I'll go down to the beach for a swim and get out of your hair for a while."

"Do you mind if I join you? I was thinking my babbling was keeping you awake."

"I'm not taking a bathing suit. Will you be offended?"

"Probably, but I won't laugh and point when you hit the cold water." With the last remark, Carole burst into her low, sensual laugh that could still give Mark goose-bumps every time he heard it.

They grabbed their beach robes and left through the French doors to the veranda. They then felt their way in the semi-darkness down the stairs to access the private beach fifty yards away.

Half way down the path to the beach, Mark stopped Carole and said he thought someone else was there. "Listen!" Voices blended with the gentle sound of waves splashing ashore and Carole, in response, said, "I think you're right. Do you think we should go back in?"

Mark stepped a few feet in front of Carole and yelled, "Who's on the beach," then waited a second or two and laughingly added, "friend or foe?"

"Foe – you ass-hole!" came the reply, in Art's distinctive growl.

"This is supposed to be a private beach," Mark yelled back.

"I thought the same thing when we came down here. Give us a couple of seconds. We're dressed like someone on the cover of an A.A.R.P. sponsored nudist camp."

Mark and Carole could hear Jean giggling like a teenager caught in the same situation, and then heard her scream, "Wait, wait!"

After a few moments of hustling and bustling around in the sand, Art called out, "Stevens, you have a knack for screwing up my best-laid plans. You might as well come on down – since everything else is down, thanks to you."

"I doubt if we had anything to do with that. Jean, did he force you down here?"

"He didn't *force* me, but he said we were just going to look for sea-shells; then, he ripped my clothes off. Thank God you found me in time. Of course, I might have been able to hold out for another few minutes." Jean laughed and patted Art on the butt as Mark and Carole emerged from the dark backdrop of the rentals foliage.

Carole started apologizing for the intrusion, but Mark couldn't keep from laughing and said, "This little incident may get some mileage when we get back to the club."

Art said, "Well since you're already here, you might as well help us finish this bottle of wine I stole from your stash. We only brought two glasses, but neither of us have leprosy, so we will share."

The wine was poured, and the four friends were suddenly taken by the beauty of the moment. Small luminescent waves were quietly splashing ashore, brilliant stars shined overhead, and a crescent moon was descending in the Western sky. The smell of the ocean and the softness of the sand on bare feet was a special feeling that would be difficult, if not impossible, to duplicate.

Nothing was said, but volumes could be written without adequately describing the closeness and peace of the moment. It was wonderful. Everyone knew it was special, but chose not to break the intimate silence that surrounded them. Spoken word would not be appropriate, but the feelings shared among the friends said it all. Simply put, it was happiness and contentment rolled into a moment – on a beach in paradise.

Finally, Jean said, "If I were directing this movie, I'd cue the violins right about now."

To which Art injected, "I think I would also have the two of us exit, stage left. It's getting pretty late, and we should give these newlyweds a little time of their own."

Mark protested, weakly, by saying, "You don't have to leave. We just came down to unwind a little bit before going to sleep."

"If we leave now, maybe you'll still be fresh enough to safely sail tomorrow without Coast Guard intervention," Art replied.

"Don't be disrespectful. I am the *Captain*, you know, and at sea, the Captain is like a god."

"Come on, Jean, I think I'm going to puke after that comment."

Appropriate hugs were delivered, and Art hung his arm across Mark's shoulder and said, "See you in the morning, buddy," then meandered slowly down the beach toward the house with his arm around Jean and hers around him.

Carole spoke first, saying, "They are so special."

"That, they are," Mark replied, and then continued with, "Well do you still want to do the 'skinny-dip' thing?"

"I wouldn't miss it for the world," she said, and then untied the belt of her robe and shrugged the garment from her shoulders. It fell in a neat pile at her feet – leaving her naked and slightly illuminated by the white beach sand.

Mark couldn't help himself when he reached out and caressed the softness of her shoulders and breasts.

Carole stood passively as his hands wandered toward more intimate places and felt an involuntary shudder go through her body when he pulled her roughly toward him and felt the clash of her naked skin against his. He spread his long beach robe out on the sand and pulled Carole to his side.

There was no need to point or laugh and the second *consummation* of the evening was just as delightful as the first.

Afterward, Mark struggled to his feet and stumbled toward the water. He called back to Carole and said, "If I drown – I drown a happy man."

CHAPTER THIRTY-EIGHT

Mark was up at a quarter to seven. He was anxious to make last-minute preparations before taking the guests out on the boat. Strangely enough, he felt a twinge of apprehension about getting underway for the first time without Sean.

He told the cook not to expect all the guests at the table at one time and to just take breakfast orders as they came down. Mark then found a large Styrofoam cup, filled it with hot coffee and made his way to the boat. Carole had volunteered to greet the guests and make sure they were properly fed. As Mark left, she was "making herself presentable".

Carole entered the dining room dressed for the boat – in shorts and a polo shirt. Alice and Ryan were on the veranda drinking coffee and enjoying the beauty of the turquoise water splashing ashore on the beach in the morning sun. When Carole appeared next to them, Ryan said, "I'd better not get used to this. It would be way too hard to give up."

"I know what you mean. I don't think I could go back to anything else either," Carole replied in a melancholy tone. She continued with, "Did you have any breakfast? You might want to get something on your stomach before we leave. I'll be cooking on the boat, and that may not be a worthwhile experience."

The trio re-entered the dining area just as Mattie and Maury were making their entrance. Carole, spontaneously, went to Mattie and hugged her, then said "Good Morning," to Maury.

Mattie said, "I don't know how this is going to work out today. I'm too damned fat to be on a boat, and if I get sick, I'll kill Mark Stevens for bringing me down here."

Carole countered with, "The sea is about like a mirror today. There's no chance you'll be sick. If you are, I'll shoot him for you."

"That'll do it for me."

"Why don't you put on some shorts? A dress on the high seas might not be as comfortable as you'd like. Heels may be a little bit unstable as well."

"I can't buy shorts to fit my butt, and I don't have anything but heels. I don't think I'll be in an environment that's suited to my particular comfort zone."

"Go barefoot and to hell with the dress," Carole replied. "You do as you please. I refuse to let you *not* have a good time. It's the law!"

Art and Jean arrived at the foot of the stairs with Art mumbling something about so little privacy on the beach. Then to Carole, he said, "If I were paying for any of this, I'd ask for my money back." He received the expected shove from Jean as they approached the breakfast table.

Mark returned from preparing the boat for sailing, just as the others were finishing up with breakfast. "It's a great day," he said, "and we're wasting daylight."

"Have you eaten anything," Carole asked.

"I'm just going to make a quick sandwich, and I'll be ready. If you'd like to escort everyone to the boat, I'll join you in a heartbeat." With that statement, he started piling scrambled eggs onto a piece of toast and layered it with several pieces of bacon. As soon as he added the top piece of toast, he started gobbling it up like a starving man. He found another Styrofoam cup – filled it with milk and followed the others to the pier. Mark had been over-optimistic regarding the volume

251

of "stuff" the toast would hold, and a yellow trail of fallen scrambled eggs could have guided him back to the kitchen had he been lost.

Carole and the guests were all aboard when Mark arrived at the pier. As he stuffed the last bite of the sandwich into his mouth, he untied the lashing that held the small brow to the lifeline stanchion, and pulled it back onto the pier. "No sense in stowing this thing below when we'll need it again this afternoon," he said as he hopped aboard directly from the pier.

"Are you ever going to get this garbage barge underway, or are we going to just sit here all day listening to how good a sailor you've become?" Art snorted from his seat in the cockpit.

"I thought I'd already made it clear, that as *Captain* of this vessel, I was to be treated with divine respect. Don't force me to initiate disciplinary action on our first voyage," Mark replied in his most captain-like voice.

Mattie, by nature, couldn't be left out of the conversation and added, "I know where, and on whom, I'm going to puke if I get sick. All this *Captain* shit is about to do it for me, even though we're not even underway."

Mark gave intimidating glares all around and quietly started the engine without comment. He then jumped back off the boat and asked Art to loosen the mooring lines so they could be removed from the cleats attached to the pier. Once the lines were removed, Mark re-boarded the boat, engaged the engine and backed away from the pier. Once clear, he called to Carole (who was below decks) and asked her to come take the wheel while he tended the sails.

Everything went like clockwork and when they made the harbor entrance, Mark killed the engine and set sail in the light winds. The silence of the wind-power that greeted the visitors had a remarkable calming effect on the group. It seemed like everyone was afraid to speak for fear of breaking the spell of brisk mobility without an engine droning in the background.

Ryan spoke first. "Mark, you mentioned something about a bit of fishing gear on board. Where would one find this equipment in case he had a burning desire to harvest the sea's rich bounty?"

"The rods are stored in the engine compartment in overhead racks and the tackle boxes are under the seat you're sitting on. Help yourself." Mark then pointed to the hatch leading to the engine compartment and added, "If you need any help, I'll get Carole back up here so I can give you a hand."

"No, I think I can manage. Thanks!"

The harbor entrance was less than a half mile away when Mark noticed that Mattie was leaning rather heavily on Maury's shoulder and not looking like a person enjoying her first boat ride. The sea was, essentially, calm – with only four or five inch ripples marring its surface. Given such ideal weather conditions, Mark was very surprised to see Mattie's greenish hue as she leaned against Maury.

"Mattie, are you alright," Mark asked.

"I must have gotten a bad egg at breakfast," she said weakly.

"Do you want to go lie down for a while?"

"No, I think I'll stay up here in the fresh air. Maybe it will go away soon. I took some Dramamine this morning, but it doesn't seem to be working all that well."

"If it gets too bad, we'll go back in."

A quiet "*Oy vey*," was her only response.

Alice came from below deck and announced that it was too beautiful a day to not take advantage of the tropical sun. She had changed into a bathing suit and carried a large towel and a bottle of sun screen. She made her way to the bow of the boat for her version of a perfect day at sea. Ryan, on the other hand, was busily tying a jig onto the monofilament line attached to one of Mark's fishing rigs. He mumbled to his wife as she passed, but didn't look up from his preparations to fish – each having their own versions of what to enjoy while doing nothing at sea.

Jean came topside carrying a Bloody Mary and warned everyone that Carole was bringing up a pitcher full of the concoction as soon as she rounded up glasses for the group.

Mattie mumbled, "Oh my God!" and turned her head deeper into Maury's chest.

When Carole was halfway up the ladder leading to the saloon, she called to Jean and asked her to take the pitcher. She disappeared again and re-emerged seconds later with a tray of plastic tumblers filled with ice and garnished with celery sticks. She passed the tumblers around to Mark, Ryan and Art, but when she attempted to serve Mattie, she immediately knew she would not be enjoying a Bloody Mary with the others.

"Mattie, what's the matter," she asked with obvious concern. Then she continued with, "Can I get you something? You look like you're not feeling well."

In response to Carole's question, Mattie rolled her body around until her knees were on the padded seat of the cockpit – leaned over the lifeline and lost her breakfast.

Maury was assisting the best he could as Carole hurried below to get a wet washcloth. When she returned, Mattie was lying prone on the seat with her head in Maury's lap and mumbling, "Maury, shoot me so I don't have to suffer."

Mark immediately came about, into the wind, and started the engine. He asked Carole to man the helm while he lowered the sails and secured the boom. The wind was very light and the engine would take them back to the pier faster than the sails. By lowering the sails, he also took the list out of the boat for more comfort.

They were about three miles from the harbor entrance. At full throttle he estimated that it would take about ten minutes to get back inside the breakwater and another five minutes to get to the dock.

Mark had just returned to the helm, and Mattie had already made another trip to the side and lost her dinner from the night before. She was one sick puppy. By the time they entered the harbor, she was working on a pizza that she'd eaten in the third grade. Her dedication to the heaving gave credence to the fact that you can throw up *long* after you think you've finished.

Everyone on the boat tried, unsuccessfully, to give her comfort. The only thing offering the slightest relief was the cold compresses Carole kept placing on her face and forehead after each of her visits to the rail.

In his haste, Mark didn't make a perfect landing at the dock, but, the boat stopped and he jumped to the pier as Art threw him the mooring lines. After the fenders were in place and the boat secure, he replaced the brow – hoping Mattie would be able to walk off the boat. He did not know what they would do if she couldn't walk and had to be carried.

There was some outdoor furniture on the pier and Mark hoped that Mattie could make it to one of the chairs long enough for the seasickness to pass. He carried a chaise lounge to the side of the boat so Mattie would only have a few steps to take before she could lie down and recover.

Even when tied to the pier, Mattie was in no condition to leave the boat immediately. She tried, unsuccessfully, to stand a couple of times, but collapsed back into Maury's lap while involuntary abdominal contractions continued – trying to purge more from the void of her empty stomach.

Mark went below and returned with a glass of iced club soda and a sleeve of saltine crackers. He insisted (against whimpering protests from Mattie) that she sip the soda and eat as many crackers as she could. He tried to explain to the patient that the crackers and soda was the best thing for settling her upset stomach. Mark's therapy seemed to be mildly effective, and after five or six crackers and the cold soda, a bit of color started to return to Mattie's face. After another ten minutes of lying on the padded seat of the cockpit, Mattie finally recognized a faint feeling that she might actually live, and made another attempt to stand. The primal desire to leave the boat strengthened her resolve, and with the help of Mark and Maury, crossed the brow on very unsteady legs to the earthlike stability of the pier. She immediately collapsed onto the chaise. In a weak, yet determined voice, she growled Yiddish profanity until her entire vocabulary was exhausted. Mark Steven's name was mentioned several times during the tirade.

The entire group was genuinely concerned about Mattie and had joined her on the pier to offer any assistance that might bring her relief from the insidious effects of motion sickness. After about twenty minutes of milling around the chaise, Mattie became somewhat self-conscious and asked Maury if he wouldn't try and get her to her bed in the house.

It was barely ten o'clock in the morning and the group didn't really know what to do since the sailing plans had been disrupted and everyone was looking to Mark for some sort of alternate plan of the day. None came immediately, since he was also at a loss for a secondary plan.

Maury reappeared at the head of the pier and called to Mark. When Mark joined him, he said that Mattie was going to be just fine and suggested that the rest of you continue with the sailing. "If she feels better this afternoon, we might go into town for some shopping. In any event, don't concern yourself about entertaining us. We'll make out just fine. Enjoy your day. I'm sorry we spoiled a portion of it."

"I hate leaving you here alone," Mark said. "It was supposed to be your holiday too."

"We'll still be able to enjoy our vacation. Unfortunately, sailing seems to have been eliminated from our agenda. Do you plan to stay out overnight?"

"No, it will be more comfortable for everyone to stay here in the house. We will be back in time for dinner. Maybe Ryan will have some fresh fish for the cook to prepare."

"Anyway, Mattie and I will be just fine."

"OK Maury, I'll go tell the others, but I still feel a little guilty," he said as he started back toward the boat.

"Saddle up, guys, we're going to try it again. I think they're trying to get rid of us. Maury said Mattie is rewarding him with sexual favors for his part in saving her life."

CHAPTER THIRTY-NINE

The second attempt to have a leisurely day at sea started out with a feeling of regret among the friends. It would have been much better if Mattie and Maury could have enjoyed the voyage as much as the others. However, after about twenty minutes of exposure to the sun and the joys of sailing in pristine tropical water, the regret passed, and everyone began to enjoy their particular vision of total relaxation. Ryan fished, Alice sunned, Art tried to learn what he could about sailing, Jean and Carole drank a couple of bloody Marys then went below for a so-called power nap. Mark was thrilled with sailing the boat for his friends, and could think of nothing he'd rather be doing.

About one o'clock, Carole stuck her head out from the entrance to the saloon and announced that she had "snackables" for those who would care to try her cooking. Bite-sized sandwiches of tuna, various cold-cuts and a selection of fresh fruits were handed up onto the main deck. Art asked, characteristically, if she had anything for the others to eat and wolfed down two of the little sandwiches with one mouthful.

The resulting "glare" from Carole got the tray moving among the others on deck.

The day, and the rest of the week went well. Mattie and Maury lounged on the beach, enjoyed tropical drinks on the patio of the house, visited the local sites and shopped, while Mark, Carole and the others enjoyed sailing on most days – with random jaunts into town to enrich the local bars, restaurants and other businesses.

Mattie and Maury decided they would leave on Sunday after becoming rather saturated with island life.

Ryan, reluctantly, decided to join them. He had already stayed two days over his schedule; simply because he couldn't make himself leave the fishing paradise he'd fallen in love with. He would deal with any resulting consequences when he returned to Memphis. Alice, who had no real obligation to rush back home, had whined to Ryan enough that he agreed to her remaining with the sailors until they reached Nassau.

Art and Jean had planned three weeks to a month to be with Mark and Carole. Art had gotten his business affairs in order enough to be with his friend for, what might be, their last opportunity to spend quality time together – given the circumstances. He didn't want to miss it, and plans were in place for them to sail the length of The Bahamas and fly home from Grand Turk after the five-hundred or so miles of sailing. Although new to the sailing experience, both he and Jean had already become addicted and fully understood the passion seen in Mark and Carole. Neither Art nor Jean could hide their excitement about heading out for parts unknown. It was to be a fun trip for all.

Saturday evening, the group had gathered on the veranda of the rental for drinks and a light supper to re-live the events of the week before. Mattie, Maury, and Ryan were to leave the following day. After delightful reminiscing and "several" drinks, the party was winding down with most of the group ready to call it a day. Mattie went somewhat against the grain and asked Mark if he'd like to take a walk with her on the beach. When Mark agreed, Mattie turned to Carole and asked if she would like to join them – just to make sure Mark didn't try and take advantage of her. Carole, aware that Mattie wanted to talk to Mark alone, declined the invitation –

lying about a dull headache and a need for sleep. Maury, characteristically, had left the gathering early.

Once on the beach and barefoot, an awkward silence fell upon the two friends. Finally, Mattie asked, "Is this the last time I will ever see you?"

After a short pause, Mark answered with, "Not unless something unforeseen happens between now and the time we make it back to the mainland. I plan on coming back to Memphis from Ft. Lauderdale."

"I've been scared to death that I wouldn't be able to let you know how much I've treasured our relationship over the years. Because of you, I looked forward to going to work each morning – even though I haven't *had* to work in many years. You were my boss, but I never felt bossed. You have a talent that made me feel like a partner in getting things done as necessary. I have been mouthy to you since day one and you have been just as mouthy in response. It has been a relationship of love – at least from my perspective. You are the big brother I never had and the thought of losing you is absolutely breaking my heart. When I think about what's happening to you, I generally end up crying like a baby. Maury is very supportive and is doing his best to get me through this mess, but the reality is still there and I'm just not ready to face it."

"Mattie, I can only imagine the hurt I would feel if the situation was reversed. I've pretty much accepted the fact that I'm done in a very short time. My concern now is not for myself, but for how it affects those closest to me. I hope you and Carole will be able lean on each other as much as it takes to get over my being gone. As far as our relationship is concerned – you've said it all. It's been a thirty-year love affair. As my family, you, Art and Jean saved my sanity after Karen and Sarah were killed. If it hadn't been for the three of you, I would have dove into a bottle and never returned."

"I'll be there for Carole. I can't imagine why, but that woman worships the ground you walk on, and she's not going to be able to maintain the stiff upper lip she now presents to the world about her. It's a sin that you two didn't meet five years ago. Carole, Jean and I can start a *pity-me* club and meet for lunch to decide how we're going to live without your dumb ass around. There I go again, with the smart mouth."

"That smart mouth belongs to someone very dear to me – don't ever take her away."

"I've had enough of this nicey-nicey talk. I want to know how you're honestly feeling. Are you becoming symptomatic? Do you intend to try any kind of treatment? Anything...? You've been acting like there is nothing bothering you at all and I know it's got to be eating you to pieces."

Taking a few moments to gather his thoughts, Mark finally replied, "Yes, the pain is starting to be pretty constant. It's not bad enough for me to start taking drugs, but it continues to remind me that the devil is still there. I'm hoping things will be tolerable until we finish with our sailing trip. As far as treatment is concerned – there is none, with any promise of success."

"As a newly married man, there will be some changes needed in your will. When I get back to Memphis, I'll contact your lawyer and have him draft another version with Carole's name rather than mine. Can you believe I'm going against all things Jewish and giving someone else over ten million dollars?"

"Carole doesn't need the money either; however, she did like the idea of a scholarship fund and I think she's going to get that started. I'm sure she'll need some help with it. Do you know of anyone she could call on?"

"Let's get back to the house before I have to slug you."

Mark put his arm around Mattie's shoulders, and they walked slowly and quietly back to the cabin to join any others who might still be up.

*   *   *

After spending a week of marital bliss in the rental, Mark cleared his account with the club and cast off on the initial leg of their journey. Depending on the winds, they expected to arrive in Nassau in three or four days, or longer – depending on the dilly-dallying they expected when encountering irresistible points of interest along the way.

The trip to Nassau was rather uneventful, sailing wise; however, Alice turned out to be a bit of a fly-in-the-ointment with her penchant for alcohol and nudity. After several instances involving mild overdoses of alcohol *and* overexposure,

Carole suggested that Mark make all the headway he could toward Nassau. The suggestion became a demand when Carole found Alice totally nude and somewhat drunk, lathered up and calmly shaving her pubic area on the foredeck. Carole, in a voice that left no room for doubting the intent, said, "OK, girlfriend, that's it. No more of this nonsense. Keep a respectable amount of clothing on that body, or I'm going to put you in an inner-tube and drag your ass behind the boat the rest of the way to Nassau. Mark and Art are starting to enjoy your antics a lot more than Jean and me. So, knock it off." Alice had no difficulty in understanding Carole's instructions and there were no more such instances the day-and-a-half left in reaching Nassau.

Once in Nassau, the quintet enjoyed the nightlife offered prior to Alice's departure for Memphis on Saturday. Alice had begged forgiveness from the other sailors and was easily forgiven in her farewell as she boarded the plane. However, Carole was somewhat relieved – knowing she would not have to continue the justification ritual she had endured because of her friend, Alice's, behavior. They would remain friends, but Carole didn't think she could forget the embarrassment she felt because of her variation from the norm.

*   *   *

After two days in Nassau, the trip continued southward along the string of islands that made up The Bahamas. They stopped when they wanted to and enjoyed the sights and lore of the many islands and cays along their way – some inhabited others totally uninhabited.

There were long evening talks with a distinct aversion to discussing Mark's cancer and no one knew why the subject was taboo. It just didn't happen. However, the subject was on everyone's mind, but it was avoided by mutual, but undisclosed consent. The cruise was what it was intended to be – a time for good friends to enjoy themselves.

CHAPTER FORTY

El marcó uno (The spotted one) is, perhaps, the most feared of all the lieutenants in any of the drug cartels in Columbia. He had killed over a dozen men (probably more) in his rise to the second layer of command in the Cali cartel and would control the entire cartel if he had been blessed with more intelligence. His position was secured by an animalistic pattern of behavior that made even top management of the cartel nervous by his presence. He was, in fact, a madman that knew no boundary for violence. He had once skinned a man alive for a perceived breach of secrecy that caused a shipment of cocaine to be intercepted by the U.S. Coast Guard. It was later learned that the man was innocent; however, *el marcó uno* shrugged it off as a part of doing business – building on his reputation of being an extremely bad and cold-blooded individual.

Ernesto Alverez was known by all as *El marcó uno*, (behind his back) and was the equivalent of a poster boy for a skin condition called vitiligo. The skin over his entire body was a blotchy map of white and dark spots that included his hair and one eye. To say that Ernesto Alverez was physically ugly could only be considered a gross understatement. The ugliness was not just skin deep. In Ernesto, the ugliness was a river that flowed unrestricted throughout his body.

He was the son of a Cali whore and an unknown client. Ernesto was severely neglected from the time he was born until his mother was killed by a "rough-sex" practitioner when he was five. He had lived on the streets since that time – doing whatever necessary to survive. Since his teen years, he had been physically adept at imposing his will on others and had no moral conscience. He stood over six feet tall and was nearly three hundred pounds of solid gristle.

Cartel management had commissioned Ernesto to supervise a rather complex plan to deliver a thousand kilos of refined cocaine to Nassau via intermediate supply points. It would be delivered to cartel associates in Nassau, for further shipment into the United States. He would be held responsible for efficiently carrying out the plan without incident. The cartel owned company boats and aircraft that would be at his disposal.

El marcó uno was to go to the secret processing facility located in the jungle interior of Columbia and pick up the refined cocaine. He was then instructed to assign escorts armed with automatic weapons and transport it by truck to Barranquilla on the Northern Coast where it was to be placed on an amphibian aircraft. From Barranquilla, the shipment was to be flown to Cockburn Town and transferred to a boat for the remaining four-hundred or so miles to Nassau. He would remain with the cargo until it was placed on the boat and then fly with the plane to meet their U.S. associates in Nassau – collect the money for the cocaine, and when it was transferred, return to Columbia. Fuel for the boat would be hidden and waiting at Plana Cays and Rum Cay – two convenient and rather isolated points along the proposed sea-route. Paid informants were embedded with the U.S. Coast Guard that relayed search routes and schedules of drug search-planes and cutters. Although the cutters and planes could not be diverted, the drug traffickers would probably be able to avoid contact if they were careful.

As *jefe* (boss) to a squad of twenty or so men, Ernesto had trained three of his men to navigate with a GPS – in preparation for the necessity of transporting goods over open water. Raul Martinez, Jesus Mendoza and Orlando Delgado were the designated crew members of a high-speed *Cigarette* boat that would be used for the operation. Raul was put in charge of the trip and would be held accountable if anything went wrong during their solo voyage from Cockburn Town to Nassau. They would fly to Puerto Plata, in the Dominican Republic, where they would pick up the boat and drive it to Cockburn Town for loading. Orlando was the only one of the trio excited about going on the trip and could not wait to take the controls of the super-fast boat. They were *all* terrified of *el marcó uno,* and no one openly protested when they were assigned to the boat, for fear of his anger. *No one,* in their right mind, protested when *el marcó uno* gave orders.

The plan went as scheduled with Ernesto accompanying the cargo during the overland trip and the flight to a predetermined point offshore from Cockburn town where the plane landed in choppy waters for the transfer of the cocaine to the waiting boat. *el marcó uno* warned the boat crew of potential severe weather, but it wasn't expected to interfere with their trip. He said that if conditions became dangerous, for them to lay-to next to one of the many small islands and don't take unnecessary chances with the cocaine. He would meet them in Nassau to complete the transaction.

Approximately one-hundred-fifty miles into the trip, the seas were starting to build to the point that Raul had awakened and yelled to Orlando, "Slow this son-of-a-bitch down. You're beating us to death." Orlando had done as he was told, but when Raul went back to sleep, he had started easing the throttles forward for the thrill he got from the speed. Orlando placed his trust in the radar as the boat jumped from wave to wave with the added speed. He was serenely unaware of any obstacles in their path until he heard the loud thud of something solid hitting the boat and felt the crunch of the cracking hull. He immediately pulled the throttles back to where Raul had told him earlier and hoped the thump hadn't awakened Raul and Jesus. He was not surprised when both Raul and Jesus came to the helm and asked, "What the hell did you just hit?"

"I don't know. It's too dark to see anything."

Raul found a flashlight in the console and raised the hatch to the engine compartment and immediately screamed, "My God! You've knocked a hole in the boat, and we're taking on water."

Jesus was standing next to Orlando when Raul made the critical discovery and swung a looping right hand that connected to Orlando's temple – knocking him nearly unconscious. He would have continued beating him if Raul had not stopped him – screaming that they had to do something to stop the boat from sinking.

He told Jesus to get one of the mattresses from the sleeping area and pass it to him in the engine compartment, in hopes of plugging the hole enough for the bilge pump to stay ahead of the deluge. It didn't work. By the time Jesus came back with the mattress, the water was already covering the engines and filling the small compartment with steam. The boat was settling deeper by the stern when the engines died. With the engines gone, they were also without electrical power. They were soon to find out that the portable marine receiver/transmitter they were depending on as a last-ditch chance to call for help was filled with dead batteries. Life on the once powerful *Cigarette* boat was now rather gloomy.

CHAPTER FORTY-ONE

Mark was sleeping soundly when Carole shook him to wakefulness, and in a concerned tone, said, "Mark you might want to go topside and see what's going on. The boat is rocking and pitching pretty badly, and I don't think we're moving."

Mark shook his head to clear the cobwebs of sleep and was instantly aware of the problem that had awakened Carole. As he swung his legs off the bed and onto the deck, he had to brace himself against the bulkhead to keep from falling.

The boat was rolling fifteen to twenty degrees from side to side, and Mark found it rather difficult to make his way forward and up onto the main deck. When his eyes became somewhat adjusted to the darkness, he watched the main boom flopping side to side in long, uncontrolled arcs as the boat tossed about in the building seas. The boat was becalmed – no wind at all.

He quickly released the halyard on the mainsail to stop the heavy boom from swinging dangerously in its random, sweeping trek – head-high above the deck. He then engaged the furling mechanism on the limp jib to stop the irritating flap of unresponsive sail. Once the sails and boom were secure, he started the engine to bring the boat into the seas for greater stability. When the severe rolling was somewhat under control, it was replaced by an uncomfortable, but manageable, pitch, as the hull would rise, then fall with a distinct *slap,* as it hit the ebb-side of the four-foot high (but stagnant) waves.

As he was surveying the situation and trying to formulate a plan as to what he should do, Art emerged from the main hatch and asked, "What the hell is going on, man?"

"I don't actually know. I know there's no wind, and the seas are getting pretty rough. Why don't you take the wheel and keep us headed into the waves, and I'll go below and check out the weather and the barometer? If it's what I think it is, we might be in some deep shit."

"What do you mean?" Art asked as he took control of the wheel.

"From yesterday's weather report, there was an intensifying tropical depression located a couple hundred miles southeast of here. According to the predicted path, it was to go way to the east of us; however, weather guessers have been a bit off track in about as many cases as they've been right. I want to check on its current location and see if it's going to affect us."

When Mark went below and turned on the lights over the chart table and instrument console, Carole and Jean appeared from their respective quarters. Carole repeated Arts earlier question, "What the hell's going on?"

"We could be about to enjoy a bit of a weather problem. I heard about a developing tropical depression yesterday, and I'm getting on the weather radio now to see where it's currently located. They predicted a track that was going to be way to the east of us, but some of those things don't mind like they're supposed to."

"If you find out, and it isn't good news, I don't know if I want to hear about it," Jean confessed. "I hate sniveling, and I'm sure I'd be the first to start if it gets really bad."

Mark turned on the weather radio and listened until the position of Tropical Storm Edna (rather than Tropical Depression Edna) was broadcast, and listened intently as they corrected the earlier prediction of the storm's path. The storm was maintaining sixty-eight-knot winds near the center and was now expected to become *Hurricane Edna* within the next several hours.

Mark had written down the longitude and latitude of the storm's center and marked the coordinates on a marine navigational chart. He then checked the GPS position of the boat and marked it on the same chart. After having the two positions located, he took a pair of dividers from the drawer of the chart table and measured the distance from the storm center to their location. He then drew a line depicting the storms expected path from the storm's center position to a point that would be safely beyond their location. He stared at the chart for a few seconds, then turned to the women and said, "We've got some serious work to do immediately. Carole, will you ask Art to join us. He can leave the helm, and we will be OK for a few minutes. I wish to hell Sean was still here."

When Art entered the saloon, Mark asked the three others to look at the chart he'd been marking information on and said, "Folks, that damned storm is only about eighty-five miles away from us. I think what's happening now is the proverbial calm before the storm. The waves indicate that we're getting a storm surge now, and I'm sure the wind will begin to increase very soon. The storm is a little bit north of us right now, but it's on a west by northwest track. We won't get the full force, but we're on the southwest side of it, and I'm sure it will be pretty intense. We're only about twenty-five miles from *Mayaguana Island* and I think we can get there before the real bad stuff hits us. If we can get on the lee side of the island, it will offer a lot of protection from the seas and some protection from the wind. We used very little fuel since we left Nassau, so I don't think there will be any problem using the engine until the wind picks up.

"Art, go back up and try to maintain a course of one-one-zero with the engine. There will be a bunch of wind very soon, and we can probably make better time using the sails when that happens. When it really gets going, we'll have to reduce the hell out of our sails and most likely use the engine again to get us to where we need to be. Lesser winds than those we can expect have de-masted many a boat with too much sail in the air. I'm going to check out the boat and rig everything for heavy weather."

Carole asked, "What can we do to help?"

"Slap me when I panic and start frothing at the mouth."

*   *   *

As expected, the wind began to pick up almost immediately from the northeast – lightly at first, then building in increments of approximately five knots at a clip. With the first sign of significant wind, Mark hoisted the sails and the boat gained speed – relieving the engine of the chore of propelling them to relative safety. He hated the fact that the wind was coming from the port quarter – which was a slower point of sail than if it had been on the port bow.

Mark was reminded of the fear he'd felt going into battle while in the Marine Corps. It was a matter of pride that he was able to lead an attack without the others within his squadron realizing he was scared to death. He felt that fear now, but for whatever reason, he appeared outwardly calm and decisive. Again, he wished for Sean to be with him. Since that was impossible, he became the *Captain* of the boat and acted accordingly – adjusting his sails, and hopefully keeping the others secure in knowing he knew what he was doing.

Mayaguana was still about fifteen miles away which meant about two and a half or three hours sailing time. They just might make it, he thought, before things became too severe.

The tops of the once-stagnant waves were now being blown into white foam that created a fine spray covering the weather deck of the boat. Mark asked for Art to search out rain gear as he lifted the seat in the cockpit and handed out life jackets to the entire party – saying, "Better safe than sorry."

The seas were getting rougher by the hour and had grown to approximately five feet in height; however, the boat was riding fairly well and making excellent time. Mark was starting to feel confident that they would make the lee side of the island before the hell he expected to engulf them, arrived in full force. It was beginning to get light in the east, and he felt like things would look better in the daylight than in the darkness that had engulfed them since their first notice of the adverse weather conditions.

Everyone was sitting in the cockpit of the boat – wet and terribly concerned about what was going to happen. Suddenly, Carole asked in an alarmed voice, "What was that?" as the remnants of a flare arched across the sky off the port bow of the boat.

"I don't know," Mark said as he watched the flare dim into the early morning light. "Keep an eye out and if you see another one, try and mark the direction from where it came."

Five minutes later, another flash of phosphorus, white light left the surface and climbed into another long arc across the sky. "Someone is in trouble," Art said, as he watched the flare burn its way through the sky.

"I was afraid of that," Mark said as he asked Carole to take the wheel. "I'll go below and check the radar. Maybe I can get a grip on what's happening. They can't be more than two or three miles away."

CHAPTER FORTY-TWO

Mark, Carole and their guests were having trouble maintaining their respective seats in the cockpit as the boat rolled and pitched with the quartering sea. The waves would hoist the stern of the boat and propel it forward, which forced the bow to nosedive beneath the waves they were following. The uncomfortable gait of the boat compensated the discomfort with added speed. Speed was to be their savior, so there were no complaints.

The radar had revealed the position of the distress signal that was a mere thirty-five hundred yards distance and slightly off their port bow. Since the boat in distress was, essentially, along their charted course, Mark decided to ask the group for their opinion as to a course of action. "We can try and pick them up... maybe tow them or we can sail on by and let them fend for themselves. They could be drug runners or simply cruisers as we are. We're armed, and hopefully, we could take care of these unwanted guests if they turned out to be bad guys. If their boat is disabled, then they honestly don't stand much of a chance in this weather. What will it be, folks?"

Silence was all that greeted his request.

Carole finally said, "Mark, I don't really want to pick up a crew of strangers if it takes time away from our race to beat the storm; however, I can't imagine leaving someone in a sinking boat without some attempt to bring them to safety – that is, if you call coming aboard our boat *safety*."

Art then added, "I think we should, at least, check out their situation and make a decision then. Will you even be able to maneuver close enough to do them any good – given the wind and seas we have to contend with? If it's going to place Jean and Carole in any additional danger, I don't want to do it; but that will have to be your final decision."

"I have to agree with you, Art. Let's just check it out, and if we think we can help them, we will – if not, then we will boogie on down to the lee of Mayaguana and protect our own asses."

Jean and Carole remained silent as they fought to keep their seating.

*   *   *

Raul, Jesus, and Orlando were considering their fate, as they stood on the cabin of their sinking *Cigarette* boat. The engine compartment was already flooded, and all power was lost. They had postponed transmitting an S.O.S. for fear of being arrested if the authorities came to their rescue and discovered their cargo – roughly two thousand pounds of cocaine. They were now afraid their postponement was about to cost them their lives – in addition to their valuable cargo. They had fired their last flare from the flare gun they'd salvaged from inside the cabin as it was flooding, and were surprised to see the very dim outline of a sailboat making way toward them – not knowing if they had seen the flare or if it was a random passing.

Jesus was a raging madman and Raul had to intervene, twice, to prevent him from killing Orlando. Orlando had been driving the boat much faster than he should have been when it hit a half-submerged barrel that had been floating in the rough waters. The barrel crushed a two-foot hole in the boat just

272

below the waterline on the starboard quarter near the engine compartment. They were somewhat surprised that the boat had stayed afloat as long as it had and correctly guessed that the pocket of air trapped in the forward section of the boat was sufficient to keep it from going completely under.

They were given renewed hope when they thought the sailboat changed course and headed toward them. It was becoming lighter in the east, and it wouldn't be long before the sun rose above the heavy cloud cover that had gathered during the night. They might have a chance.

To get his mind off Orlando, Raul started to relate (in Spanish) a plan of action to Jesus that might save them from drowning and also save them from being killed if they didn't make their delivery as they were hired to do.

"Jesus," Raul said, "if they pick us up, we do nothing until there are two of us aboard. You speak English better than either of us, so I think you should be the first to go aboard. Once you are aboard, plead to have them save the two of us as well. I will come aboard second. Once I'm aboard we will try and take over the boat. We both have our guns, so it shouldn't be a problem. Once we have gained control of the boat, we will have Orlando tie the rescue line to as many bundles of cargo as we can salvage and pull them over for later delivery. If we're able to salvage most of the cargo, it will save our lives when we have to meet with *el marcó uno* after this is all over. Do either of you know anything about a sailboat?"

Both Jesus and Orlando said they had never even been on a sailboat and had no idea as to how they worked.

Raul continued with, "OK, we will keep the people on board alive until we get to Nassau."

*　　*　　*

Art had taken binoculars atop the cabin and was hanging on to the mast for stability as he looked at the distressed boat. He called back down to Mark and said, "It looks like one of those *Cigarette* boats and it's obviously sinking. The stern is already underwater, and the bow is nearly vertical. I think there are three guys standing on the cabin. There's not much to hold on to up there, so I imagine they're scared shitless."

273

"I was afraid of that. I'd hoped the boat was just having engine trouble, and we could maybe tow it instead of trying to bring someone aboard. Come on back down. I don't want you falling over the side. I'll get in closer and then drop our sails. If it looks like we can, or will, help, the engine will give us more control while we're alongside. I'm not liking this at all, guys."

Conversation among the group dropped to nothing as the sinking boat became more visible in the early morning light. When they were five or six hundred yards away, Mark asked Art to gather up some spare rope, from under the seats, to be used to pull the survivors aboard once they were close enough to make the decision about trying a rescue. Once the rope was in hand, Mark said, "I think we'll need some kind of weight on the end so we can throw it in this wind. Art, there's a big combination wrench in my tool box; that should be enough weight to heave the line fifteen or twenty yards. If you'll get that, I'll start the engine and get ready to haul in the sails for our final approach. Carole will you take the wheel? I want to get on the radio and declare an emergency. Hopefully, the Coast Guard can hear us, and if we can't do some good for these guys, maybe they can get a chopper out here when things settle down some. I'm also going to tell them our plans for riding out the storm, and ask if they might check on us to make sure we're OK."

Carole said, "I hope I can handle this thing while you're gone. Get back up here as quick as you can. And, by the way, I think calling the Coast Guard is the best idea you've had in quite a while. Chalk that up as another reason I love you."

Mark felt very fortunate that he was able to get clear channel communications with the Coast Guard. He checked the GPS and gave them their current coordinates and also gave them the coordinates of where they expected to be later in the day. The Coast Guard also gave him the good news that *Hurricane Edna* had again changed paths and was on a more northerly course than before. It would be drifting away from them rather than charging in from the east with its eighty-five-knot winds. They were still in for a very rough ride, but the Coast Guard estimated that the highest winds they would receive would be no more than about fifty knots. Not good, but manageable.

Mark signed off with the Coast Guard and went back topside – carrying the AK-47 assault rifle Sean had bought for him.

Carole and the others saw the rifle, but said nothing as Mark moved, deliberately, to the engine controls – started the engine and said to Jean, "Hold this, please, until Art and I get the sails secured."

Art went forward to furl the jib and Mark lowered the halyard on the mainsail and secured the boom. He then engaged the engine and relieved Carole on the wheel. Once steerage was resumed, Mark said, "Carole, this is where all the target practice you've done, with the rifle and pistol, may come in handy. I want you to take the rifle, and if we get these guys on board, let them know that we remain in command of our boat. If they pose a problem, you may have to shoot. Art and I will be too busy to keep an eye on them, so it will be up to you. I doubt if it will come to that, and I know you hate the thought of having to shoot someone, but be prepared. Better them than us."

Carole took the rifle from Jean and said, in a low monotone, "I'll do my best."

When Art rejoined them in the cockpit, Mark said, "Art, this is what I plan to do: I will go past the boat downwind, then turn and head upwind to approach the boat. If they are drifting toward us faster than we can safely stay close, I'm going to back off and to hell with the rescue. If it looks like we can maintain a safe distance from them, yet close enough to get a line to them – we'll give it a try. It's going to be hard for you to keep your balance on the forecastle, so I'd like for you to get a length of rope and use it as a tether. If you happen to slip, you won't be lost. If you think at any time it's getting too dangerous – yell at me and we're outta there. If you decide to heave them a line – try and throw the wrench end all the way over the boat. That way they don't have to try and catch it, but just pick it up after the line falls across the boat."

"OK, skipper, it looks like it's about *Showtime*."

CHAPTER FORTY-THREE

The three men on the sinking boat were waving frantically and yelling unintelligibly into the wind as Mark passed close aboard to starboard without stopping. He continued on course for approximately fifty yards before starting his turn back into the wind. The boat rolled violently as it turned crosswind and fell into the trough of the waves. The sudden rolling was frightening to everyone on board, including Mark, who was desperately trying to complete the turn and regain control without swamping. He was silently thanking the marine architect that designed his boat with enough ballast in the keel to make it impossible to capsize.

The engine was at full power, but still, the turn took much longer than anticipated. When the boat completed the turn, the full force of the wind ripped a stinging salt spray from the tops of the waves and into the eyes of the would-be rescuers. It was not fully light, and the spray further complicated the approach.

Although the boat was pitching wildly, Mark was having very little trouble maintaining control – adjusting the throttle constantly as he cautiously closed in on the stricken *Cigarette*.

"Art," Mark yelled over the wind whistling through the rigging and banging the halyards against the aluminum mast, "don't go up there. It's too rough. I'll try to come alongside close enough to cast the line from the cockpit. If we can't do it – I'm calling the whole thing off."

Art, wordlessly, made his way to the rear of the cockpit with his coil of halyard ready to go.

When the two boats were side by side, Art yelled back to Mark, "I think I can get it there from here. Do you want me to give it a shot?"

"Whenever you're ready! I'm still not liking this, so if we miss, I might just pull it out of here."

Art let go the line with the heavy wrench bound to it and watched it arc directly over the three men scrambling to catch it. When they had the line in hand, Art, in pantomime, indicated that one of the men tie the line under their arms, and he would pull them aboard. They, in turn, indicated their understanding by exaggerated, affirmative nods of their collective heads.

The man they would soon learn to be *Jesus*, hurriedly wrapped the line under his arms and above his chest and jumped directly into the water – trying to swim the ten yards to relative safety.

Art moved forward a couple of steps and took three turns on the winch used for the jib and started reeling the man in after seeing that swimming was not going to get the job done. He pulled him alongside and then indicated (again in pantomime) for him to come aboard from the swimmers platform protruding from the stern of the boat. Art then slacked off on the line to allow Jesus to reach the stern. After one or two unsuccessful attempts to catch the pitching deck, he finally got a grip and struggled to come aboard. Art unwrapped the line from the winch and leaned over to grasp the man's hand and help him into the cockpit.

Jesus immediately stumbled and landed roughly on his hands and knees – painfully banging them on the cockpit's grating. After catching his breath for a moment, he rose to his knees and wrapped his arms around Art's legs – repeating *gracias* and *thank you*, over and over – first in Spanish then in

English. He hated the groveling, but tried his best to make it look genuine for the time being.

The entire group aboard the *Cruzin' Carole* stared at the drenched rescuee and were not impressed with his appearance. He was a muscular man of about five feet, six inches tall, with shoulder-length, dark-brown hair – severely matted by the sea water when he swam to safety. It was obvious he had not been close to a razor in two or three days and yellow teeth flashed from beneath the darkness of a flat, low-brow face that did not radiate a great deal of intelligence. He was a really mean looking Latino, and each member of the party was unanimous in their wishes that he had not joined them.

Art untangled Jesus' arms from his legs and pulled him to his feet so he could untie the line still wrapped around him. Art was hurriedly coiling the halyard for another cast as he listened to Jesus (in broken English) start pleading for the rescue of his friends – once he stopped the bilingual, "Thank you."

When Art was preparing to make his second cast, Jesus quickly scanned the boat to check out the situation, and was somewhat startled to see Carole with the AK-47 pointed directly at his abdomen. He was not too concerned since it was a woman holding the rifle while the men were busy tending the boat and preparing to haul Raul on board. She was less than four feet away and as violently as the boat was pitching and rolling, he felt that it would be no problem in getting close enough to get the rifle from her. The dark-haired *puta* was huddled, in her rain gear, next to the cabin for protection from the wind and heavy spray. She posed no threat to their plan.

Art's second cast was just as accurate as the first, and without the prior gesturing, Raul quickly copied Jesus' actions and jumped in the water. After seeing the procedure with Jesus, Raul had much less trouble getting aboard. He too, began the repetitious *gracias* and *mucho gracias*, but only in Spanish.

Raul was not as physically intimidating as was Jesus. He was taller and not as muscular, but was still an intimidating figure with lighter skin and a brow that didn't quite come down to the level of his piercing black eyes. His standard haircut made him look less of a *Neanderthal* than

Jesus, but still someone you would not like to introduce as a dear friend while socializing in polite company.

After quickly catching his breath, Raul also evaluated the situation and came to the same conclusion as Jesus. With very slight eye contact and a nearly-imperceptible nod of his head, Raul indicated that he wanted Jesus to disarm Carole while Mark and Art were preparing to cast the line to the remaining man on the stricken craft.

With the boat heaving about so violently, Carole was having a problem maintaining her position on the wet vinyl seat and covering both their visitors at the same time with the rifle.

The boat pitched heavily, and Jesus intentionally stumbled and fell backward toward Carole. He would have fallen into the barrel of the rifle had Carole not moved it, instinctively, to her right. It was a near fatal mistake.

Jesus rolled to his right, with remarkable speed, and grabbed the barrel of the rifle with his left hand. All in the same motion, he threw a vicious backhand punch with his right arm that struck Carole in her right temple, just as she squeezed the trigger on the AK-47.

The single round sailed harmlessly upward and away from any target on the boat. Mark turned instantly and saw Jesus holding the barrel of the rifle and Carole still holding on, in reflex, and trying to regain full consciousness. Mark swung a looping right at Jesus' head. Due to the movement of the boat, it was a glancing blow and did no real damage. He was positioning himself for a second punch when Raul stopped all action by smashing the side of his .45 automatic into Mark's right ear. The blow took Mark to his hands and knees. He was, for all practical purposes, unconscious, and bleeding heavily from his ear and temple.

When Art turned and tried to join in the defense of the boat, Raul fired a round from the .45 above Art's head, then quickly lowered the gun to forehead level screaming, "A*lto, alto.*"

Art stopped and immediately looked for Jean to see if she was alright. He saw that she was physically unhurt, but appeared to be in shock from what had happened so quickly all around her. Art tried to go to her, but Raul stopped him by placing the .45 in his ribs and saying, "*No! No!*"

Without Mark at the wheel and throttle, the two boats were quickly getting out of position for further transfer of people or cargo. Raul motioned with the gun for Art to take the wheel and maintain proper proximity. Art, who was by now becoming skilled at pantomime, told their captors that Mark was the only one able to maneuver the boat well enough to stay alongside their boat.

Carole had regained her senses enough to see Mark bleeding in front of her and had knelt beside him, trying desperately to find something to stop the bleeding. The abundant salt spray and the waves that regularly washed into the cockpit were having a positive effect on Marks consciousness. He didn't know what or who had struck him, but he knew he had been hit hard. Carole was holding his head, but he spun quickly in an attempt to get up, only to have Jesus push the muzzle of the rifle into the base of his neck to prevent him from standing.

As the cobwebs began to clear, Mark spoke softly to Carole, who was still holding his head with her face closely pressed to his, and quietly asked, "Are you hurt?"

Carole began sobbing quietly and through the tears apologized for not being able to shoot quickly enough to prevent the piracy.

"Don't worry about that. Are you hurt?"

"No, not really. I'll have a mouse and a black eye for a while, but other than that, I'm OK. You're the one I'm worried about. That guy hit you really hard with his gun. You've been bleeding pretty badly, but it seems to be tapering off. The seawater is washing the blood away."

"It damn sure smarts some," Mark said in reply, "but not enough to let these ass-holes take my boat. Do you remember where we stored the *Glock*?"

"Yes, I remember."

"If these guys don't find it, it could be of some use later. I'm going to try and get them to let you and Jean go below. If that happens, look for an opportunity to get the gun. Keep it hidden until you decide to use it or pass it to me or Art. There is a round in the chamber, so if you need to shoot, all you have to do is pull the trigger – fifteen times if necessary. Is everyone else OK?"

"Yes, you're the only one who's been injured, and I think they want you back on the wheel. They still have another guy on their boat, and it's drifting away from us."

The rifle barrel was still on Mark's neck as he stretched his arms out front and slowly started to get to his feet. The rifle maintained contact but without enough pressure to prevent his standing. When he was fully upright, Raul grabbed his arm and pulled him, roughly, toward the wheel and engine controls.

Mark could see they'd drifted twenty or so yards further away from the stricken *Cigarette*, and Raul was gesturing with the .45 for him to bring the boat back within transfer distance. When Mark hesitated, Raul immediately aimed the .45 at Carole and said, *"Comprende, mi amigo?"*

Mark understood immediately and quickly regained control of the boat. The wind was still building, and the stinging spray was not making the second approach any easier, but since he didn't have to turn broadside to the wind and waves for this approach, he was back in position for further transfers in a matter of minutes.

Art cast the wrench-laden halyard accurately for the third time, expecting the third (and last) survivor to follow the actions of the other two who had been successfully pulled aboard. Instead, the fellow on the sinking boat pulled more slack from Art and then dove underwater toward the sunken stern of the *Cigarette*. Art was obviously confused by the surprise move and turned toward Raul for some explanation. Raul, in turn, put up the palm of his hand and patted the air – indicating that he wanted Art to be patient.

After four or five minutes, a large white cube popped up out of the water with the lifeline attached to it. Raul immediately gestured for Art to start hauling in the bundle that was wrapped in waterproof, plastic shrink-wrap. The lone survivor on the other boat then resurfaced and waited from his original position.

Since the cube was floating, it wasn't difficult to pull it the ten yards or so to get it alongside, but Art was having a great deal of difficulty in hoisting it aboard. Raul spoke to Jesus, in Spanish. Jesus, in return, handed Raul the rifle and came to assist Art with the heavy cube of cocaine. Once onboard, Jesus untied the lifeline and dragged the bundle to the entrance of the saloon and pushed it roughly down the stairs.

The same scenario was repeated two more times, and on the fourth cast of the lifeline – Orlando tied the halyard to himself and jumped into the water for Art to pull him aboard.

When he was on the swim platform, Jesus stuck the muzzle of the rifle to the bridge of Orlando's nose and squeezed off three quick rounds. The second and third rounds were redundant. He then pulled a knife from his pocket and cut the halyard – allowing a lifeless Orlando to disappear in the raging waters.

Raul was screaming, *"Usted hijo estúpido de una ramera. ¿Por qué hizo usted eso?* "You stupid son-of-a-bitch – why did you do that?

Jesús calmly replied, *"El es la razón que estamos en esta situación. Yo no podría pararme para verle vive. ¿Qué diremos nosotros Ernesto cuando podemos sólo entrega la mitad nuestra carga? El probablemente nos matará.* "He's the reason we're in this situation. I couldn't stand to see him live. What are we going to tell Ernesto when we can only deliver half our cargo? He'll probably kill us."

Mark and the others were horrified by what they had just witnessed, but no one moved or said anything to the murderer or his companion – realizing they were in the company of some really bad men.

Mark, mumbled to himself (most inappropriately, in view of the circumstances), "There went my wrench."

CHAPTER FORTY-FOUR

Mark was silently cursing himself for picking up the drug runners and kept thinking, over and over, how he could have just let the Coast Guard handle their rescue/arrest. He stood at the wheel and desperately tried to think of a way out of a deadly situation. The problem was magnified by the storm, and he didn't know if he could communicate to the pirates his intention to go to the lee side of *Mayaguana Island* for protection. The taller of the two men seemed to be somewhat in charge, but he hadn't spoken even one word of English since he'd been aboard. Mark turned to the squat, muscular man and asked, in what he remembered from his high school Spanish class, *"¿Entiende usted inglés?"* Do you understand English?

The man responded in guttural Spanish, *"Muy poco, ¿Habla usted español?"* Very little, do you speak Spanish?

"Muy, muy, poco! ¿Entiende usted huracán? Very, very little. Do you understand *hurricane?*

"Si"

Mark then pointed to Mayaguana and indicated in pantomime that they needed to go around the island. Jesus, in return, said, "*No, Nassau.*" To which Mark replied, "No, no – Huracán!" Then added, "After huracán, we go to Nassau. Huracán will sink the boat."

Jesus spoke to Raul in rapid Spanish; relaying his version of what Mark had told him. After a short discussion between the two men, Jesus indicated in pantomime for Mark to take the boat around Mayaguana.

Once permission was given to continue with their hurricane evasion plan, Mark pushed the throttle to full power and started his turn into the heavy seas. He instinctively dreaded the severe rolls they were sure to encounter when they became parallel with the waves.

The turn with the wind was much quicker than when they'd turned to rescue the stricken cigarette and although the rolls were just as severe, they didn't last as long. Once they had the following sea, Mark indicated to Jesus that he wanted Carole to take the wheel while he and Art set the sails and get off engine power.

Jesus motioned with the assault rifle for Carole to take the wheel.

Art then started making his way forward to release the jib as Mark made ready the mainsail – securing it at the first reef-point so that approximately one third of the main was aloft. Art had unfurled about a third of the jib as well and returned to the cockpit to adjust the sheets for sail power.

Mark set-sail and the boat lurched forward with the added power and heeled over to starboard – bringing the rolling waters close to the gunwales, allowing waves of green water to regularly enter the cockpit area. He hoped he hadn't exposed too much sail, but the boat seemed to be handling the strong winds better than he was as he tried to maintain his footing at the helm. To further complicate matters, they had been blessed with sheets of wind-driven rain that had reduced visibility to the point that they could no longer see Mayaguana. As he was losing visibility, Mark had checked his compass and knew he had given himself enough leeway to miss the island's western shore. He hoped he would be able to see well enough to make his way into *Abrahams Bay* that was cut from the islands south shore.

The driving rain was making everyone extremely uncomfortable, and Mark indicated to Jesus that he wanted the women to go below, "Let the women go inside."

When Jesus said, "No," in his surly voice, Mark pointed to him and said, "You go with them."

Jesús turned to Raul and said, ¿"Piensa usted que debemos permitir que las mujeres vayan adentro? Uno de nosotros puede ir con ellos T O sale de esta lluvia de Dios Condinado." "Do you think we should let the women go inside? One of us can go with them to get out of this goddamned rain."

Raul replied, "Me da el rifle y usted toma la pistola con usted. Comerciaremos lejos en una hora por ahí. El cheque para ver si ellos tienen cualquiera más armas allá." "Give me the rifle and you take the pistol with you. We'll trade off in an hour or so. Check to see if they have any more weapons down there."

Jesús and Raul traded weapons and Jesús indicated with the pistol for the women to go below.

As Jesús was entering the stairwell to the saloon, Mark said, in a commanding voice, "If you hurt them, I'll sink this boat. "¿Entiende usted?" Do you understand?

Jesus just glared over his shoulder at Mark without saying anything. Mark then shouted, "¿Entiende usted?"

Jesus didn't turn again, but Mark heard a sarcastic, "Si" as he disappeared into the saloon.

*   *   *

The saloon was very cluttered by the three cubes of cocaine scattered directly in the walkway. Carole and Jean struggled with the heavy packages and moved them out of the way enough to allow free passage and then sat down on the couch. Jesus was opening drawers and generally searching for additional weapons. He found the sharpened cutlery in one of the galley drawers and grabbed them up in one hand – opened the hatch and threw them over the side.

There were three pouches with elastic tops sewn into the front of the couch – for magazine storage and other small items. Carole had seated herself so that her legs were covering the pouch on the forward end of the couch – the one that held the Glock. Jean was sitting on the other end of the couch and

285

was inadvertently covering the pouch on her end. Jesús was searching shelves, cabinets and drawers while Carole prayed that he would overlook the pouches on the couch.

When he had finished searching the galley and saloon area, he motioned with the pistol for Carole to lead him aft to the owner's cabin. Carole didn't want to go, but she reasoned that if she went, he was not going to find the gun.

Jesús went through the same scenario in the master's cabin that he'd done in the saloon/galley – making a mess as he threw things around. He found a dry T-shirt in one of the drawers and a pair of Mark's shorts in another. He immediately pulled off his wet clothes and smiled at Carole as he cupped his genitals in his hand – proffered them to Carole and said, "¿Querría usted ser mi puta? Would you like to be my whore?" Carole turned her head and closed her eyes in disgust. Once he'd made his point, he let out a vulgar laugh as he was putting on the dry shorts and T-shirt. He then motioned her back to the saloon area – satisfied there were no more weapons on the boat.

Carole was livid. She was beyond belief angry, silently praying for an opportunity to shoot this sorry piece of trash before he decided to kill everyone else. In her entire life, Carole had never so intensely hated anyone, and was mildly surprised that she felt no guilt for her desire to take the life of another human being – if one thought of Jesús as a legitimate human being.

When they got back to the saloon, Carole went straight to Jean, who was huddled on the couch in her yellow rain-gear and life jacket. Her eyes were swollen from crying, but they narrowed into an intense, defiant glare when Jesús came into view. Carole sat next to Jean and put her arms around her and pulled her close for their mutual comfort. Both women started to cry, but quickly regained their composure to prevent Jesús from having the pleasure of seeing them terrified and at his mercy.

Carole broke the embrace and moved back to the other end of the couch so her legs would protect their only chance of survival and allow access to the Glock if there was even a remote chance of bringing it into play.

Jean and Carole had been glaring at the smug Jesús for about an hour when a shot rang out from the cockpit.

Jesús sprung from his seat at the table and grabbed Jean around the neck with his powerful left arm and started dragging her backward toward the hatch leading topside. Jean was struggling and screaming, but Jesús was too strong for her and her struggles were mostly in vain. Jesús held the muzzle of the pistol to Jean's head as he opened the hatch. He was surprised to see only Mark at the wheel and no sign of Art or Raul. He momentarily took the pistol from Jean's head and pointed it at Mark. It was his last conscious move.

Carole had the Glock in her hand a split second after Jesús started dragging Jean up the stairs. She quickly took the three steps to the base of the ladder and placed the muzzle of the Glock within an inch of the back of Jesús' head. Carole calmly pulled the trigger with no chance of missing her target. The hollow-point round entered Jesús' head at .40 inches in diameter – then exited, from what had been his flat face, carrying with it roughly six square inches of flesh and bone that splattered broadly like pink and fleshy vomit – contrasting vividly with the stark white of the cockpit. The rain and waves quickly washed the remnants of Jesús' face from the cockpit of the boat.

*   *   *

In the hour since the women and Jesús had gone below, the outline of *Mayaguana* had again come into view through the torrential rain. Mark had been tacking, port and starboard, to come as close to the western end of the island as he could. He wanted to skirt the southwest corner and turn back east, then north into *Abraham's Bay* for its three-sided protection.

Mark and Art had both determined that Raul spoke no English, and understood even less – however, when Mark and Art would try to speak to each other, Raul would gesture with the rifle and shout, *"No hablar!"* "No talking!"

Mark indicated, in pantomime, that he needed to speak to Art to adjust the sails – gesturing from his mouth toward Art, then toward the forecastle and the jib. Raul shook his head in the affirmative and Mark began to speak to Art.

"This stupid son-of-a-bitch doesn't know what we're saying, so go forward and take in a little bit of sail. I'll shout up to you what's about to take place, and we'll see if we can't get control of the boat again."

Art said, "OK. I'm ready to get something done," and he started moving, carefully forward, listening to Mark say, "Do you remember what happens when we jibe the boat?

"Yeah, I think so."

Mark momentarily left the wheel and leaned on the back of the cabin and shouted, "Well, when we turn back north, I'm going to jibe, and that boom is going to come around like a fifteen foot baseball bat toward the ass-hole. I want you to position yourself across from him, and if he even flinches, try and remember what your linebackers coach taught you about a *blitz* in college. Make sure the rifle is pointed toward me before you move – that will give you a little bit of time."

Art shouted back, "Sounds right to me. It will feel better hitting this mother-fucker than any quarterback I ever sacked."

Art had not dramatically altered the sail pattern and Mark continued his normal tacking until he was ready for his northward turn to enter the bay. He didn't turn toward Art, but said, "*Showtime*," in a voice loud enough to be heard above the wind and rain.

Art placed his toes on the deck, in tip-toe fashion, with his heels against the sides of the bench seats. There would be no slipping when he made his move.

Mark turned the wheel hard to port, and the boat started its turn into the wind. As the boat turned, the sails began to luff loudly, then once past the headwind, filled with a sudden, loud, *pop* that brought the sail and its connected boom swinging from starboard to port – violently, in the strong winds.

Raul, instinctively, ducked – for just a moment. During that moment, Art lunged across the cockpit as if fired from a catapult. His left arm extended and hit the rifle Raul was pointing toward Mark and his shoulder hit him in the midsection.

Art's legs were driving hard, and the boat was heeling hard to lee. The force of his charge carried both men over the side and into the boiling sea. Mark immediately ripped a life-ring from its holder, mounted on a nearby stanchion, and threw it toward Art and Raul. Art still had on his life jacket – Raul had not bothered.

When Art found himself in the water with Raul, his only concern was to *drown this son-of-a-bitch*. He held Raul under as long as he could, but Raul broke away once. Art's movement was somewhat restricted by the life jacket, but he was still able to grab the tiring Raul before he got away and pulled him back for another submerging. In the struggle, Raul was having to try and stay afloat and fight Art at the same time. It was a losing battle – Art was stronger, and way madder. With the life jacket, Art only had to hold Raul underwater, and it wasn't long until an exhausted Raul inhaled a fatal dose of salt water.

During Art's charge, Raul had gotten one round off from the assault rifle – just as Carole had when the takeover began. Carole's shot didn't hit anything. Raul's shot tore into Mark's side – just above his belt.

As he started his turn, Mark pulled at his clothing to see how badly he had been hit. It was a painful slash about three inches long, but did not appear to have entered his abdominal cavity. He forgot the pain and began to maneuver the boat so he could pick up Art.

Halfway through the turn, Jesús appeared in the hatch with Jean screaming and kicking under his arm – the .45 pressed to her temple. When the gun left Jean's head and pointed toward him, Jesús' face disappeared with the loud and distinctive *pop* of the Glock doing business.

CHAPTER FORTY-FIVE

Jean and the dead Jesús were blocking the steps leading to the cockpit, but Carole clawed her way out of the hatch with the Glock ready for whatever was needed to regain control of the boat. When she saw Mark was alone in the cockpit, she slid back down into the saloon over Jesus' body – threw down the gun and grabbed Jean to help her get loose from the limp left arm of the dead Jesús. Jean was bordering on hysteria – intermittently screaming and sobbing as she attempted to get free. Carole, on the other hand, was probably in shock – showing an eerie calm that didn't quite fit the situation. Jean was bent backward over the stairs, with her feet barely touching the slick teak deck of the saloon. The weight of the dead arm wrapped around her neck, and the uncomfortable position of her body made it very difficult to get free. Carole finally straightened Jesús' arm enough for Jean to break away. Carole pulled Jean to her and tried to calm her down enough to help move the body off the steps. Carole finally had to shake her by the shoulders and scream, "*Jean, Jean -- we have to get topside to see what's happened.*"

Finally, reason replaced the trauma, and she understood what had to be done – even though she was still crying quietly as they pulled Jesús back into the saloon – leaving a trail of blood the length of the steps.

Once the women were topside, they saw an obviously stressed Mark, fighting the wheel and yelling above the rain and wind, "Art is in the water with the ass-hole. Keep an eye out. I see him on the port quarter when the waves are right. I'm going back to get him now. Carole take the wheel while I lower the sails and get the engine going. He's still got on his life jacket, so he's not going to drown. I don't know or care where the ass-hole is. I just want Art back on the boat."

Jean became even more frantic when she looked back and saw Art bobbing in the heavy seas. She rushed to the back of the boat and pressed her waist against the lifelines in a futile attempt to get closer to him.

Carole took the wheel as Mark started the engine and released the halyard on the mainsail and the sheet of the jib. He didn't try and secure anything properly, but just let everything fall where it may.

By the time they had completed their turn, Art was maybe fifty yards away from them; however he was still visible each time a wave would lift him above the deep troughs. The brilliant orange of his life jacket and yellow rain suit stood out as beacons – contrasting perfectly with the dull gray of the waves. He was waving his arms and giving a *thumbs up* as they started closing in to pick him up.

Due to his battle with Raul, Art had not seen, nor found the life ring Mark had jettisoned earlier. The empty ring was being towed some twenty yards behind the boat. To keep the attached line from becoming entangled with the propeller, Mark started pulling it back to the boat as they approached Art – deciding to try and get it to him with another toss when he was alongside and could see it without difficulty.

When the boat was about fifteen yards from Art, Mark started directing Carole, at the wheel, with left and right hand-signals as she made the approach. Mark, essentially, *handed* Art the life ring and started walking his way back to the swimmers platform as Art held the ring. Mark told Carole to put the engine in neutral as Art grabbed for the platform. He caught it on his first attempt, but struggled against the life jacket and rain gear – finding it extremely difficult to pull himself up enough for Mark to grab his hand for assistance.

Jean was hysterical again and was actually getting in Mark's way as he tried to pull Art aboard in the rough seas. In her attempts to get her arms around Art, she was dangerously close to the lifelines and in danger of falling overboard herself. Mark pushed her with a bit more force than might have been necessary to get her back into the cockpit so he could help Art.

Once Art was safely aboard, Jean threw herself at him and started sobbing uncontrollably as she buried her head into his life jacket-encrusted chest. He held her close without saying anything until she calmed somewhat, then kissed her deeply and pulled her to the port bench-seat for stability. Her hands were busily searching his face and arms for any indication of damage from the episode in the water. Once confident that he was alright, she, again, embraced him and held on tightly as her sobs were slowly reduced to an occasional whimper.

Mark asked quietly, "Are you alright?"

"I don't think I've ever felt better, now that the piece of shit I went over with won't be back. What happened to the other guy?"

"Carole took care of him."

Mark was going back to take the wheel when Carole saw the spreading redness of a blood-stain on his rain-pants and screamed, *"Oh, my God – Mark, what happened?"* as she pulled at his clothing to see the source of the bleeding. It was about three inches long and looked like a little ditch that was about a half inch deep.

"He got off a round as Art hit him. I'm bleeding quite a bit, but I don't think it's life-threatening."

Carole, forcefully, pulled Mark from the wheel and dragged him toward the hatch leading to the saloon. Mark was protesting loudly and repeatedly telling Carole he was alright and had to get the boat into the harbor. Carole in return was telling him that the boat was not sinking and, by god, he was going below to be attended to.

Once below deck, Carole was tearing at the life jacket and outer clothing as she pushed/shoved him toward their

292

quarters – hastily grabbing the first-aid kit that was attached to the aft bulkhead of the saloon as she passed.

When Mark was mostly undressed and lying down, she inspected the bleeding wound and quickly tore open a sterile bandage and forcefully pushed it into the wound and told Mark to hold it in place while she squeezed a tube of antibacterial ointment onto a fresh bandage. With Mark still holding the original bandage, she took several alcohol swabs from the kit and tried to clean the area surrounding the wound. There was a lot of blood, but enough was removed for her to see the gash burned into Mark's side by the last round Raul would ever fire. An inch to the right and the bullet would have entered the abdominal cavity – an inch lower, it would have shattered Mark's pelvis. It was the acme of a good news/bad news scenario.

When Carole replaced the original bandage with the one impregnated with the antibacterial ointment, the bleeding almost totally stopped. She wrapped an ace bandage completely around Mark's trunk to hold the bandage in place under pressure. Once the gunshot wound was taken care of she took out more bandages and started working on the nasty cut on Mark's head and ear. The blow from Raul's gun had split Mark's upper ear entirely through, and also opened a large gash on his scalp. It was obvious that both the gunshot wound and the wound to the head would need stitches and professional cleaning as soon as possible.

When Carole was finished, she stood beside the bed and stared at her handiwork. At first, the tears just filled her eyes – then started to fall in large drops to the life jacket she still wore. The agonizing sobs came a few seconds later as she collapsed to her knees alongside the bed with her head next to Mark's side and her right arm across his chest. She was trying to speak, but her words came sporadically as they were interrupted by the contractions.

"I was so scared... I thought they were going to kill us all. When I heard the shot from above, I thought you or Art would be dead. I shot a man...I've never hated like that before. I didn't even think of him as a man...when I pulled the trigger...just knew I had to stop him from killing Jean and you or Art when he started to go upstairs. If the other guy had been there with the rifle... I was so scared."

Mark rotated his body and slid off the side of the bed to take Carole in his arms. He held her quietly until the sobs became less spasmodic, and then said, in a voice just above a whisper, "You saved us all. Through my own stupidity, I put us in harm's way. You had the guts to do what most others would not have been able to do. There's no doubt they would have killed us sooner or later had you not acted. I wish I had the words to describe the pride I feel for you. You are beyond belief."

After several more minutes of consolation, Mark continued. "You know I have to go back on deck. I'll ask Jean to come down and join you. She's pretty upset, but maybe the two of you can lean on each other's shoulder until I can get us anchored in smoother waters. Will you be alright for a few minutes?"

"Yes, I'm sorry I'm acting this way. The nightmare just hit me."

"It was an awful nightmare. It will take a lot of time to get over. I'll be back down as soon as I can. Let me help you out of the life jacket and rain gear so you can be more comfortable. Will you be OK for a little while?"

"I'm more worried about *you* than anything else right now. You're the only one who was physically hurt, and you've lost a lot of blood."

"I'll be fine. This boat has excellent healthcare personnel on board. Let me get into a calmer environment, and I'll be back down. I have to contact the Coast Guard as quickly as possible to find out what we need to do about the mess we just went through."

Mark stopped in the galley and drank two large glasses of water to quench a terrible thirst. While drinking, he saw the body of Jesus partially blocking the passage through the saloon. He maneuvered the cocaine blocks and the body aside to clear the way. Seeing the bloody mess that had been Jesus' face, Mark found a large plastic trash bag and pulled it over Jesús' head and shoulders – thinking all the while how appropriate the trash bag was.

Once on deck, Mark saw that Art was steering the boat toward the inner harbor of *Mayaguana*. They could see that the waves in Abraham's Bay were not nearly as high as they were experiencing in the open sea. It would be welcome relief from the pounding they'd been taking since early morning.

Art said, "What the hell are you doing back up here, man? You've been shot and had your head bashed in. Get back below. I'll get us into the harbor."

"No, I'll be OK for a while. We need to get these sails stowed and get the anchor set so we can get the Coast Guard in here to take care of the trash we have in the saloon."

Art replied, "If you think you can take care of the steering, I'll take care of the labor. Just let me know what needs to be done."

*   *   *

Jean appeared to have calmed down and was sitting on the bench seat looking somewhat lost – with nothing to do. Mark asked her if she felt like going below and staying with Carole – explaining that the recent events had caught up with her and she was having a rough time regaining control.

Jean said, "Of course," and immediately headed for the stairs leading to the saloon. She nearly lost it again when she had to pass the body of Jesus lying next to his precious cocaine, but the trash bag softened the appearance enough for her to make it to the owner's cabin where Carole was lying on the bed, staring blankly at the ceiling and crying softly.

Jean sat on the edge of the bed and took Carole's hand without saying anything. After a few moments, Carole said, "I'm sorry I'm acting this way. Suddenly the reality of what's happened to us washed over me, and I lost it. I'll be alright in a few minutes."

"You can do anything you want, and there will never be a word of complaint from me – or anyone else on the boat for that matter. You had the strength to do what was necessary to save us all. I don't know if I could have done it. You saw me fall apart like a cheap toy when that guy grabbed me. When he put that gun to my head – I knew I would be killed. All I could think about were my kids and how they were going to handle the loss of their parents to some goddamned drug runners. I was so afraid."

After a few moments of silence from both women, Carol finally spoke, "Jean, I was just as scared. I had just been sitting on the couch – *hating* that man – praying I would get the opportunity to use the gun I was guarding with my legs. I've never hated like that before. I hope I never do again. I guess hate and fear can make someone do something they otherwise, wouldn't consider possible. It didn't seem to bother me until I'd taken care of Mark and then all at once it hit me that I'd just killed a man. I also felt a tremendous amount of relief once we were all safe. When I climbed up over you and the dead one, I thought the other guy was going to shoot me as soon as my head popped out of the hatch. After hearing the shot, I was so surprised to see Mark alone at the wheel. No Art – no bad guy – no bullet tearing into me."

"You were wonderful. When I heard your gun go off, I didn't know who was shooting, at first – then his arm went limp and I just went to pieces."

Jean stood and started taking off her life jacket and rain suit. When the foul-weather gear was put aside, she asked, "Do you mind if I lie down next to you until the men are finished upstairs? I think we could both use the company."

The two women lay silently on the bed – each with their own thoughts – locked in a closeness that can only come from surviving a shared, life-threatening trip through hell on earth. The healing had begun.

CHAPTER FORTY-SIX

Once Mark took the wheel, Art placed the heavy boom on its stand and began securing the mainsail. It was a blessing that the sail had been reefed in the forty-knot-plus wind, and he only had to deal with the top third of the sail. Once the main was secured, he started forward to do the same with the jib when Mark stopped him by saying, "Let's let the jib go until we get further into the harbor. The wind probably won't be any less, but the pitching won't be nearly as severe. Bouncing around like we are could make staying on-board a bit tricky, and I imagine you've had enough fun in the water for one day."

Art said, "Why don't you sit down and I'll take the wheel until we need to drop the anchor. You don't look so pretty good, my friend."

"Nice of you to point that out. I must be turning into a sissy in my old age. Anymore, it seems like just one little abdominal gunshot wound, and a simple blow to the head makes me just want to fuck off for a while. I don't understand it."

"I won't tell anyone back at the club." Then, after a short pause, Art continued with, "Are you going to be alright? I'm more than a little concerned about you."

"I appreciate the concern, but, I think everything will be OK. I'm going to try and get the Coast Guard in here to give me some professional encouragement once we get anchored – assuming they have some medical types on board."

Under engine power, Art had no difficulty navigating the boat deep into *Abraham's Bay* in *Mayaguana*. The marked reduction in wave height and some relief from the wind were both welcome to the stressed and weary travelers. Mark took the wheel one more time as Art gathered the anchor from storage and dropped it on Mark's command. Once the anchor had been set, and there was little chance of unintentional drift, Mark secured the engine and went below to radio the Coast Guard (or whoever may hear his distress call). Art stayed on deck to finish securing everything that had been disturbed during the morning.

*   *   *

Mark dialed in Channel 16 on the VHF Marine Radio and keyed the mic to declare his emergency. "United States Coast Guard, this is Captain Mark Stevens of the sailing vessel *'Cruzin' Carole'* requesting emergency assistance."

After a short pause, a static-infected, but understandable, response crackled back through the radio speaker, "*Cruizin' Carole* this is United States Coast Guard Cutter, *Dallas*. What is the nature of your emergency, over?"

"We are victims of an attempted pirating. We also have one dead body on board and one gunshot victim needing medical attention. Please be advised that we have a large quantity of illegal contraband that needs removal, over."

"What is your location, Mr. Stevens, over?"

"We are anchored in *Abrahams Bay* of *Mayaguana* Island – Longitude 22° 21' 08" north, Latitude 73° 00' 03" west, as indicated on our GPS receiver. We had contact with the Coast Guard early this morning, advising them of our intention to assist a sinking boat, over."

"We were aware of the earlier contact and had anticipated an update. We will debrief you when we arrive at your location. Please stand by while we check our position and give you an estimate on our arrival time. What is the condition of the gunshot victim on board, over?"

"It is not thought to be life-threatening, but there has been considerable blood-loss. We will stand by, over."

After approximately five minutes, the radio again crackled, "*Cruizn' Carole*, this is *Dallas*. We are located 27 miles north/northwest of *Great Inagua Island* and approximately 63 miles from *Mayaguana*. Due to the current sea-state our progress will be somewhat impaired, but we will try to maintain 15 knots to your location. Our ETA should be about four hours and fifteen minutes. We have a helicopter on board if you feel we should dispatch medical personnel immediately; however, weather conditions make helicopter operations extremely difficult at this time. Please advise, over."

"*Dallas*, this is *Cruizn' Carole*. We are profoundly aware of the weather conditions and feel that we can wait until your arrival for medical attention. The bleeding has been mostly stopped, and the wound has been dressed. I am the victim, and though I am somewhat weak, I feel alert and remain mobile. I will have someone standing by the radio in the event you have further instructions prior to your arrival, over."

"We're on our way, Mr. Stevens. Please advise us if there is any change in your situation while we are en route, over."

"Thank you, *Dallas*. Be safe getting here. We are in no immediate danger, over and out."

*   *   *

It was a quarter past noon when Mark placed the microphone back in its holder. He unconsciously calculated the time of arrival for Dallas and reached instinctively for the boat's logbook to document the events of the long morning. He was starting to make his entries when Art came down the ladder from the cockpit. When Art saw that Mark was still upright and starting to make log entries, he grabbed him, rather forcefully, by the arm and started dragging him toward his quarters. Mark was protesting and telling him the importance of the log entry, but Art was having none of it. "Get your stubborn ass in bed, for Christ's sake. The log entry may be important, but the Captain is more important. If I have to, I'll get Carole up here to establish priorities, and I don't think you're gonna like what she has to say."

"I guess you're right. I'm feeling a bit woozy. The Coast Guard will be here in about four hours. I guess I can crash until then. Keep an eye out to see if we start dragging anchor. If we start to drift toward the beach, come get me and we'll work it out."

"Will do," Art responded as they reached the entrance to the owner's quarters.

*   *   *

Jean and Carole had been lying quietly, for the most part – lost in their own thoughts. Jean, obviously on the verge of tears, spoke first after the long silence. "I can't stop thinking about my kids. I *ache* to hold them. I haven't felt this way since they were babies and they had been out of my sight for a while."

Without responding verbally, Carole reached for Jean's hand and held it tightly to indicate she'd heard and understood. After another pause, Jean continued in an omni-directional monotone that was, essentially, thinking out loud rather than an attempt at conversation. "Up until this morning, this was the most fantastic vacation of our lives. After the events of the day, I would be on a plane right now if one was available. I'm sure I will be a nervous wreck until we get to *Grand Turk* and on the plane." Then, turning and directing her words more toward Carole, she continued with, "I'll be just as nervous thinking about you and Mark sailing alone all the way back to *Ft. Lauderdale*. I don't see how you're going to stand it. I wish you'd call your friend Sean and see if he could come back down here and make the trip with you, or better still – for you. It's nearly six-hundred miles and I know I won't be able to sleep until I hear you're back home safely. Mark is hurt pretty badly, and I don't know if he will be capable of such a trip."

Carole finally turned toward Jean and said, "I won't be comfortable out here either. Mark has to have medical attention soon. I'm worried to death about him, and he's so damned hard-headed he won't slow down. I only hope the Coast Guard is near and can offer some medical help. If a doctor says he can't make the trip, I'm going to drag the big galoot aboard a plane and get him out of here. He loves this boat, but I love him more and I'm not going to let him take the chance if it's ill-advised. He's still up there fooling around with this stupid boat when he should be flat on his back until we can get some help. It seems like we're in pretty calm waters right now. I guess they've got us in the bay. I'm going topside and get his sorry ass back down here. Enough is enough."

Carole was in the process of getting out of bed when the door to their quarters opened with Art still holding on to Mark.

"Carole, maybe you can talk some sense into this turkey and get him to lie down," Art said as he let go Mark's arm.

He then continued with, "He'll probably call this a minor mutiny, but I just *relieved* the captain. The Coast Guard is on the way and will be here in about four hours. Do you think you can keep him in bed until then?"

"You can depend on it, *Mate*. I was just on my way to drag him down here myself. He lucked out," Carole replied.

Without comment, a suddenly exhausted Mark crawled, dutifully, onto the bed. He was grateful to finally relax enough to lick his wounds after the very long morning.

Once Jean and Art left their quarters, Carole sat on the edge of the bed and said, "OK, I want you to skip any and all bullshit and honestly tell me how you feel."

"My head is allowing me to count every heartbeat. He must have smacked me pretty good. My side is starting to tighten up and hurt about as much as the head. I'm not that concerned about being functional, but it is a bit distracting."

"I wish there was something on board stronger than Tylenol, but I think that's about it. I'll get you a handful of them and see if they will help until the Coast Guard gets here with some serious dope."

Carole brought four Tylenol caps and a large glass of water back to the bed, and as Mark was taking the pills, she pulled up his shirt to check his bandages. After a close inspection, she said, "I think the wound is starting to bleed again. The blood has already soaked through the Ace bandage, but it seems to be just oozing. I'm afraid to undo it right now because I don't want to relieve the pressure. If it gets worse, I'll call the Coast Guard and ask for advice."

"Things could be a lot worse, darlin'. Let's count our blessings. The cavalry is on the way."

*   *   *

Art and Jean had moved to the saloon in order to stay out of the weather, but the body of the dead Jesus was making them both very uncomfortable. Art went forward and found a sheet to cover the body and make the scene a little less grotesque; however, the dried blood on the steps leading topside and on the teak deck was still extremely disturbing. Reluctantly, Art rummaged around the galley storage bins and found a spray bottle of *Clorox Cleanup*, a roll of paper towels and a pair of rubber gloves that were used for dishwashing. He heaved a heavy sigh and started the distasteful task of spraying and cleaning the offending stains.

Although Jean made no offer to help clean the blood, she was becoming increasingly agitated – getting up then sitting back down from the couch repeatedly – unable to watch Art and the cleaning process. She finally spoke to Art, saying, "I don't know if I can stand being on the boat any longer. I don't know what to do about it, but I feel like a time bomb and want to explode. Is there an airport here on *Mayaguana*?"

Art interrupted his cleaning long enough to say, "I don't think so. I don't even know if anyone lives on this island."

As Art was cleaning, his strokes became more and more forceful. A rage was building in him as his own emotions began to surface. There were still some bloody spots to be cleaned when he stood and threw the bottle of cleaner across the saloon into the leg of the chart table – breaking the bottle and spilling the cleaner onto the deck. He became even more upset when the bottle broke and hurled the roll of towels in the general direction of the spill. Livid with rage he turned and viciously kicked Jesus' body and started screaming, "*You sorry mother fucker! We save your worthless ass from drowning and then you try to kill us. I don't want you dead now – I want you alive so you will know when I beat you, break your bones and make you*

302

suffer." He kicked the body again with added venom, and would have kicked it a third time if Jean hadn't smothered him in her arms and with her body – desperately trying to calm him down. He shoved Jean aside, roughly and lunged for the hatch leading to the cockpit and fresh air – realizing that he'd just lost it, without serving any constructive purpose. He was embarrassed by his outburst but still energized by the anger that wasn't subsiding as rapidly as he wished.

Jean, who knew her husband well, did not follow immediately. She knew he would come down from his tirade much more quickly if he dealt with it alone. She fought with herself, trying to postpone going topside until Art had a chance to come back to normal. After a long ten minutes of sitting on the uncomfortable steps, she opened the hatch and went topside to see Art sitting in the aft part of the cockpit looking aimlessly out to sea.

The rain had stopped and an occasional ray of sunshine beamed through the heavy, broken clouds blanketing *Mayaguana.* The wind was still blowing at a rather brisk clip, but not nearly as strong as it had been earlier in the morning. The waves in the harbor were less than two feet. As luck would have it, the storm had passed well north of them and never reached its full potential.

Jean sat down by her husband and asked, "Are you alright?"

Art paused a moment before answering, then said, "I'm sorry I acted like that. I don't know what happened. We risked our own safety to save those sorry bastards, and they had the balls to try and kill us. If I had died as I took that guy over the side, I would have died happy, knowing he would die with me."

"Are you going to be alright," Jean asked again?

"Yeah, I'll be fine. I'm just rather surprised at the way I felt when I had him in the water. He died too fast to suit me. I wanted to bring him back to the surface and then drown him again and again. He was the guy I'd always thought about who had harmed you or one of the kids, and what I would do to him if I were given the chance. I don't feel a bit guilty, and I don't know if that's right or wrong. Given the same situation – I'd do it all over again – in a heartbeat."

"Ever since I met you in college, you have been the hero I worshiped. When I would cheer for you in the stands, at a football game, it was a matter of extreme pride that I thought of you as *my* man. I had to try extremely hard not to show such adulation when you were around, and my girlfriends thought I was about half crazy. Today, you brought that hero worship to a level I never thought possible. I know I'm a bitch most of the time and I might bad-mouth you with vigor, but if I'm dead before the sun sets, I want you to know that you are my hero, and I love you without limits. I've never doubted that if bad guys strike, you would be able to handle it – and you did – today."

"I've always wanted to be your hero, but I never thought I'd quite made the grade. Today, I wasn't trying to be a hero. I just had to do something to stop the madness that was happening to us. I hope I never have to do something like that again."

"I do too, but I will never doubt that you will be capable of doing it if you're called upon."

"Honey, we're stuck here on the boat for another sailing day. We can't abandon Mark and Carole even if there is any kind of air transportation here. Do you think you can handle it until we get to *Grand Turk?*"

"I'll have to," Jean answered. "I know we can't leave them here. Let's see what the Coast Guard medics say about Mark's condition and we'll make our plans then. If you don't mind, may I just cuddle with you until they get here?"

CHAPTER FORTY-SEVEN

With Carole lying beside him, Mark had finally drifted off into a restless sleep. The inactivity allowed the pain of his wounds to sink in more than expected; however, when Art knocked on the door to their cabin, he was instantly awake. In his mental rush to consciousness, the first thoughts coming to mind were about the boat dragging anchor. He didn't know how long he'd been asleep and was greatly relieved when Art told him he had answered the Coast Guard's radio call announcing their close proximity and would be launching their motor whaleboat shortly to dispatch their *away-party* for necessary assistance.

Carole was already on her feet when Mark tried to get up to join the others. Carole, angrily pushed Marks shoulders back onto the bed and said, "Don't even try it, *Bubba*. You can't do a thing. I'll get the medical types down here as soon as they're on board."

"OK, I'll stay here, but if they're having any serious difficulty getting aboard, I want you to call me immediately.

I'm still able to function, and I'd better not be left out if trouble develops."

Carole threw her hands into the air in exasperation as she turned to leave and said, "You won't be, *Captain*."

Mark, in turn, said, "You know, you've got a *great* lookin' ass when you bounce around like that.

She turned back and gave him a look that needed no verbalization.

*   *   *

The white Coast Guard cutter, with its distinctive diagonal red stripe, was laying-to, about a mile and a half southwest of *Cruzin' Carole*.

Art had found the binoculars in the storage bin of the control panel and was watching the activity around the starboard boat davit on the cutter. He was giving running commentary to the women as he watched men being loaded into the boat and, once loaded, lowered into the water. Outside the full protection of the island, the sea was still pretty rough, and the relatively small whaleboat pitched and rolled rather severely as they made their way toward the anxious sailors.

After about fifteen minutes of intense scrutiny from Art and the women, a young man in wash khakis and wearing a life jacket spoke through a hand-held megaphone, "*Cruzin' Carole*, this is the *United States Coast Guard*. We request permission to come aboard."

Art quickly reached under the bench seats in the cockpit and found three pneumatic boat fenders and hurriedly positioned them along the starboard side of the boat to prevent damage to either craft during the boarding.

When the whaleboat was about five feet away from the sailboat, one of the coastguardsmen near the bow, stood with a light mooring line and tossed it to Art as he yelled, "Please attach this to one of your forward cleats."

Once the line was secure, the coxswain slowly backed the boat alongside – leaving the stern of the boat untethered and ready to maneuver if necessary.

The young man with the megaphone was first to board and introduced himself as Lieutenant (j.g.) Mike Olstead and asked how they could assist. As Lt. Olstead was introducing himself, another young man, dressed like Lt. Olstead, stepped aboard. Lt. Olstead introduced the second man as Master Chief George Nance. He continued with, "We don't have a medical doctor onboard, but Master Chief Nance is a certified physician's assistant and is well qualified to assist the gunshot victim."

One of the other crewmembers in the whaleboat handed Master Chief Nance a rather large leather medical bag. He then turned to Carole (who was standing anxiously by the hatch leading to the saloon) and asked where the victim was. Carole introduced herself to the Chief and asked that he follow her to their quarters.

As Carole and Master Chief Nance disappeared into the boat, Lt. Olstead (speaking to Art) said, "It's our understanding that you have a dead body on board as well as illegal contraband. Is that true?"

"Yes," Art replied. "The body is one of the drug runners we rescued off their sinking boat. Had it been my decision, I would have just thrown the sorry bastard over the side and let the sharks take care of him instead of bothering you with that responsibility."

"I can understand your feelings, but I'm glad you didn't do that. We may be able to identify him, and it could lead us to others of his ilk that we can take care of before they try more of their mischief."

Lt. Olstead then turned and addressed two of the men in the whaleboat. "Smith – you and Miller bring the body-bag and come aboard. We have to remove an unwanted guest." Then turning back to Art, he asked, "If you will show me the body and the contraband, I'll see what we can do to get them off your boat?"

Art led him to the stairs leading into the saloon and was describing the contraband as they descended. "This stuff is wrapped in waterproof shrink-wrap plastic. I'm guessing each cube weighs about 120 pounds, but I can't even guess how many of the small plastic packages the cubes contain. I know we had a hard time dragging them on board. I also think there may have been even more of it left behind on the other boat."

The two men Lt. Olstead had called aboard entered the saloon without speaking and were waiting instructions. Lt. Olstead backed out of the way and said, "Guys, maybe we should wait to see if Master Chief Nance wants to look at the body before we remove it. You can start hauling these blocks of *suspicious white powder* up on deck and transfer them to the whaleboat."

*   *   *

Carole introduced Master Chief Nance to Mark as they came into their quarters.

During the introduction, the Chief informed Mark that he was not a doctor, but a Physician's Assistant and apologized for the fact that there was no M.D. onboard Dallas.

Mark shook hands with the Master Chief and said, "I think I'd rather have a Master Chief Hospital Corpsman work on me than an M.D. anyway."

"I appreciate that, Mr. Stevens. Are you in a lot of pain?"

"I've had a lot less, in my time," Mark replied.

"Well, since you think so highly of Master Chief Hospital Corpsmen, you have earned an injection of whatever this stuff is that makes people feel a lot better in a short period of time," as he opened the medical bag and pulled out a vial of clear liquid and filled a syringe to some predetermined level. After he had injected Mark in the left buttock, he asked to see the gunshot wound. He cut away the Ace bandage that was holding the gauze pad in place and asked what ointment was used when the wound was being bandaged. Carole told him, and, in return he said, "That's exactly what you should have done. It looks like there is still a small amount of bleeding, but I think it's mostly stopped. I'll have to clean it thoroughly before we can tell the proper action to take. It's fairly wide, so I don't know if we'll be able to sew it up. It might have to heal from the inside out. I'm going to deaden the area with a local, so the cleaning process won't be so rough on you. It looks like your head, and ear are about as bad off as your side."

Mark let out a cynical chuckle and said, "You won't have to count my pulse. I can call it out to you in any increment you choose."

As he was working, Chief Nance was telling Mark and Carole how lucky he was that the bullet didn't tear through the abdominal wall or shatter any bones. "In your case, luck was a matter of a half inch or so."

To which Mark replied, "I don't know if you can call it good luck or not. An inch further in would have been disastrous – an inch further down would have been just as disastrous, but what would have been really lucky is if the bullet had passed an inch to the left. It would have missed me altogether."

"Good point, but it didn't, and now we have to deal with reality rather than the *what-ifs*."

The Chief deadened the area with a series of injections and then proceeded to thoroughly clean the wound. Once the wound was cleaned he repeated Carole's actions – complete with the ace bandage maintaining pressure on the wound. He told Mark and Carole that the wound would need to heal from the inside because of its width and should be checked by a doctor as soon as possible.

Once the gunshot wound was taken care of, Master Chief Nance immediately went to work on Mark's head wound. He cleaned the area with alcohol swabs and said "Mr. Stevens, you've got some pretty bad cuts here. If you trust my needlework, I think I should put a few stitches in here to hold you together."

"Do what you have to do, Chief," Mark replied.

The Chief removed a suture kit from his bag and again anesthetized the damaged area before proceeding with the sutures.

After working in relative silence for about thirty minutes, Master Chief Nance was applying bandages to his handiwork and said, "I guess I could have used a sewing machine on you. You were hit pretty hard, my friend. I've done about all I can do for right now. You really should get to a med facility pretty soon and get an X-ray for the head wound."

"Are there any medical facilities on *Mayaguana*?" Mark asked.

"No, I'm sorry to say there's nothing here that would be of much help. I understand they have a nurse living there, but she has to call in help if anything serious comes up."

"Do you think it will be alright for me to continue on to Cockburn Town on Grand Turk? That's where we were going.

Our friends were to catch a plane there to head back to the states. I think they have medical facilities there as well."

"I think it will be alright if you don't have to do all the sailing. Is your wife, or your guests, going to be able to give you a hand in getting there? You will be better off staying right where you are for a few days."

"Yes, between the four of us, it shouldn't be a problem. We'll probably stay right here in *Mayaguana* until the weather calms down some."

"I'll leave you some pain meds, but they're going to make you pretty drowsy if you're up and about. Anyway, that's about all I can do for now, unless you want a prostate exam while I have on these rubber gloves."

"I think I can wait a while on that," Mark said with the expected chuckle. He then continued with, "Chief, I truly appreciate your help. If your injection hasn't made me too goofy, I'll be glad to visit with *whomever* about the events of the day. I'm sure there will be questions."

"Lt. Olstead will probably want to ask some questions. I'll ask him to come down when he gets a chance."

"Fine – and thanks again."

Carole followed Master Chief Nance from their quarters and after closing the door, said, "Chief, there's another little problem I think you should be aware of – my husband has been diagnosed with terminal pancreatic cancer. Of course he didn't mention that to you, but it might influence your recommendations concerning our retreat to the United States. We were to drop off our friends in Cockburn Town, and then sail back to Ft. Lauderdale. If he becomes increasingly symptomatic while sailing, it could be a problem. Do you think we would be well-advised to fly back from Grand Turk and have someone else sail the boat home?"

"That little bit of information sort of throws a monkey wrench into the works, Mrs. Stevens. Are you concerned that he won't be able to safely make the trip?"

"It's been on my mind since we left Nassau. If you think we should fly home, I wish you'd be the one to tell him. Your opinion will carry a lot more weight than mine. He has a stubborn streak that can be hard to deal with if he thinks he's being restricted for reasons he won't, or can't, accept."

Master Chief Nance turned and re-entered the berthing compartment – stood at the foot of the bed and said to Mark, "Mrs. Stevens just added a little drama to your situation. In my professional opinion, it would not be real smart to try and sail alone from *Grand Turk* to *Ft. Lauderdale*, given the disadvantage of being critically ill. There will be doctors in *Cockburn Town*, and after they examine you, I feel certain that they will be like-minded. I think you will be fine sailing to *Grand Turk* because of the help you'll have on board; however, when your friends leave, things could turn ugly at any time. It could place you and your wife in unnecessary danger."

"So she squealed on me, huh? I will seriously consider your advice and make the decision after the doctors look me over. I don't want to do anything stupid, but I was really looking forward to the trip and spending quality time alone with Mrs. Stevens."

"I'm sure you'll make the right choice, Mr. Stevens. I don't know how firm your plans are for *Cockburn Town*, but they have a clinic and several doctors in *Providenciales* which is only about fifty miles from here. They also have an international airport if you decide to fly back home. Good luck in any decision you choose. I'll let Lieutenant Olstead know you're ready to give an account of what's happened today."

*   *   *

When Master Chief Nance re-entered the saloon, Lt. Olstead said, "Master Chief, do you want to look at this guy before we bag him?"

"Yeah, I guess I should," and after replying, he knelt beside the body and pulled the trash bag back far enough to see the entry and exit point of the bullet Carole had delivered. Once he had seen the obvious cause of death, he said to Lt. Olstead, "The cause of death seems to be a missing face and forehead. Go ahead and put him in the bag. We'll search him for ID when we get him back to the ship." He continued with, "Lieutenant, Mr. Stevens is ready to give you his account of what happened today. You might want to bare-a-hand; I doped him up pretty heavily, so he might want to crap out on you if you don't hurry. As it turns out, the gunshot and head wounds are the least of his worries. I'll fill you in on our way back to the ship."

*   *   *

With the added bulk of the three cubes of cocaine and the body of Jesus, the small whaleboat could not carry Master Chief Nance and Lt. Olstead without becoming dangerously overloaded. Master Chief Nance ordered the boat to return to the ship – unload the added cargo and return for him and the Lieutenant.

Once the boat had left, Master Chief Nance sat in the cockpit with Carole, Jean and Art – listening intently as they relived the events of the day. During their conversation, Art had suggested that the *Cigarette* boat may very well still be afloat and could contain additional drugs. He further suggested that the helicopter they had on board might search the area and if the bow of the boat was still visible, more drugs could possibly be recovered. After a brief pause, he said "If the boat drifted to the north shore of *Mayaguana* and broke up with additional drugs on board, the drugs would probably end up back in the hands of the bad guys. The way they had them packaged, those bundles could float for days."

Lt. Olstead joined the quartet after about forty-five minutes and reported that Mr. Stevens was *dozing*, but had provided him with most of the information he needed. Mark had also agreed to make a written report for submission to the Coast Guard and make himself available for any additional questions that might come up during a formal investigation.

After about twenty minutes of casual conversation with the sailors, the whaleboat made its approach to pick up the additional members of the *away party*.

The *Cruzin' Carole* was again free of all outsiders, and the crew was left to their own resources.

CHAPTER FORTY-EIGHT

Once the Coast Guard left, Carole went below to check on Mark and after about five minutes, returned to the cockpit and reported to Art and Jean that the drugs Master Chief Nance had given Mark worked beautifully. "He's in another world," she said as she seated herself on the cushioned bench seat.

Jean asked, "Are you alright? I'm still wound so tight I can hardly breathe. I even have guilt feelings about wanting to leave with the Coast Guard. This has been a day for the record books, and I don't know how long it will take me to get over it."

"Jean, it's all like a bad dream to me. I don't know if it's all sunk in yet. I think my worrying about Mark has me somewhat protected from what happened and what I've done. He's downplaying his injuries, but he's been hurt pretty badly, and I'm worried they might lower his resistance enough to allow the cancer to get a better hold on his health." Then, after a short pause, said, "I don't want him to try and sail this boat alone all the way back to Ft. Lauderdale. I'm going to see how much influence I have over him and see if we can't just fly back with you. God forbid that we should run into more druggies on the trip."

"I'm with you," Art interjected. "I'm going to be on your side when we try to talk some sense into his thick head. If we can't convince him to have someone else sail the boat back, I'll let Jean go on home alone, and I'll stay to make sure you've got some help if something happens en route. That's not much of an alternative, but it's the best I can do. Maybe after he sees a doctor he'll be easier to convince."

"I hope so. Master Chief Nance told us there is a clinic and several doctors in Providenciales. They also have a larger airport than they do in Cockburn Town. It's a third as far away, and that's where I want to go. As far as I'm concerned, we can sink the boat right there. I've loved the sailing, but I don't think I can be comfortable sailing the Caribbean any longer."

"It just occurred to me that none of us have eaten since yesterday," Jean said. "Why don't I go below and see what I can find to keep us going?"

"Good idea," Carole replied. Then she added, "While you're doing that – I'll see if I can't find an adult beverage of everyone's choice. Even though I haven't eaten – I'm due for a drink. It's been *one of those days*."

"The woman's a psychic," Art said. "How could you have read my mind?"

*   *   *

The *Cruzin' Carole* laid-to in the relative calm of *Abraham's Bay* for an additional two days – waiting for the seas to return to comfortable sailing conditions.

Mark was very sore, understandably, and had more trouble regaining his mobility than he expected. He spent most of the two days either in bed or lying on the long bench seats of the cockpit. The drugs left by Master Chief Nance kept him in relative comfort and somewhat euphoric. He became more and more agitated by his inability to function at acceptable levels and wanted nothing more than to get the boat underway again. Had it not been for Carole and the others demanding a second day in port, he would have left after one day – pain and stiffness be damned.

Mark had agreed to go to Providenciales with little argument. Providenciales provided the closest medical facility and boasted several nice marinas to dock the boat. Art and Jean convinced him that they had just as soon leave from Provo – instead of sailing the additional hundred-plus miles to Cockburn Town.

*   *   *

Carole and Art did most of the sailing to Provo. Mark tried, but the stiffness from his wounds wouldn't allow credible time at the wheel or the mobility to tend the sails. He did navigate, however, and that seemed to be enough involvement to keep him out of everyone's hair.

Once tied up at the *Turtle Cove Marina* in *Providenciales*, Carole wasted no time in getting a taxi to take them to the local clinic – where the waiting doctors determined the gunshot wound and the head trauma were healing nicely – but they were concerned about the elevated white-count discovered from a routine blood test. Mark had to come clean in admitting he had been diagnosed with pancreatic cancer and had elected to live as long as he could without treatment – other than chemical relief from the expected pain. Although the doctor wasn't in complete agreement with his decision, he admitted that no specialists practiced in *Providenciales* and advised Mark to go back to the U.S. for proper treatment. When Carole asked if Mark would be capable of sailing the boat back to Ft. Lauderdale, the doctor said that it would not be advisable and that the symptoms of the cancer could become very problematic overnight and would make the trip near impossible without substantial help on board.

After the doctor's recommendation, Carole turned to Mark and said, "That does it, Bubba, we're outta here on the next plane. We can have Sean, or someone else he finds, to come sail the boat back, but *we* ain't gonna try it. We'll do all our sailing out of Ft. Lauderdale, but no more Caribbean – with its lovely drug runners for company."

"I really looked forward to spending time alone with you on the return trip, but I guess that won't happen. Maybe we

315

can do the same thing along the Keys after we get home. I'll give Sean a call and see if he can find someone to get the boat back to Ft. Lauderdale."

Carole was relieved to know Mark had agreed to fly back to the States without serious resistance and said, "I was looking forward to the same thing, but I think it's finally dawned on you that you are hurt more than you realized. We'll get our time alone. It's just that it will be closer to decent medical care." Then after a brief pause, she added, "We might as well fly directly to Memphis since the boat is going to be missing. You can check in with Dr. Givens and I can put out the fires anyone started while we were out here playing."

"I guess you're right, but I really hate leaving. Up until the time we met the bad guys, it was the most wonderful time of my life... something I'd dreamed about for years – and to share it with you made it better than I could have imagined."

"We're not through; we're just changing locations," she said – and with arms a'reachin', pulled him into a warm embrace.

*   *   *

Mark contacted Sean, via satellite phone, and after briefly describing their situation, Sean enthusiastically supported their decision to have someone else sail the boat back to Ft. Lauderdale. Even though he would be unable to sail the boat himself, Sean volunteered to find a competent, trustworthy sailing captain to do the job. Mark left it in his hands and offered any necessary cash advances the replacement would need to make the trip and have sufficient provisions. Mark didn't really like the idea of someone else sailing his boat, but he realized his choices were somewhat restricted. He felt a little bit embarrassed about being jealous of an outsider laying hands on his "baby".

Once the abandoned boat was taken care of, the foursome wasted little time in making reservations for the trip back to Memphis – a quick turbo-prop flight to Miami International that was blessed with a quick connection to home port. Providenciales to Memphis in less than six hours!

Mark was not feeling well; the gunshot wound was very sore and caused a considerable amount of pain and stiffness when he tried to stand straight while walking. He really appreciated Art's compliment about his apparent impersonation of Tim Conway's *Little Old Man* character. In response, Mark simply turned to Jean and asked if she had ever given any consideration as to what it would be like living as a widow.

Mark's major concern was coming from deep inside, the symptoms of the cancer and its accompanying pain had raised its ugly head and he looked forward to seeing Dr. Givens to explore his options – regarding pain management. Mark had always expected the pain to increase, but he hoped it would hold off for a little while longer. He still wanted the quality time with Carole, and in the back of his mind, doubts were building about whether he would be able to make it or not. Had the gunshot and head wounds been his only concern, Mark would not have agreed to return to Memphis without the boat. The wounds did give him an edge in concealing the real problem from the others – a task that he knew would grow increasingly difficult in the weeks to come. What a shitty homecoming, he thought.

*   *   *

Once on the ground in Memphis, the friends decided to take separate taxis to their respective homes. In saying their goodbyes – with hugs all around – Jean started crying as she was holding Carole and Mark in an all-encompassing embrace. She couldn't stop – and was having trouble letting go of her friends when Art finally pulled her away, gently, and helped her into the waiting cab. Carole's eyes were moist and burning from holding back her own tears that were on the brink of falling. Nothing was said about the ordeal of the past few days, but the relief of being away from the experience was apparent in Jean and, hopefully, the tears had washed the evil memory from her mind.

CHAPTER FORTY-NINE

Dr. Givens looked at Mark and immediately reached for the bandage on his head and asked in a very concerned tone, "*My God*! What happened to you?"

"It seems a certain Caribbean drug runner took exception to my trying to punch his buddy and tried to *customize* my head with a .45." He paused briefly while Dr. Givens was removing the head bandage and then said, "There's more."

"What do you mean?

"You might want to look at my abdomen. In the battle to take back control of our boat – he kinda shot me. I've had a Coast Guard corpsman do some stitching on me and a doctor in *Providenciales* check out his handiwork. The doctor, in turn, suggested I see you as soon as possible; so, here I am."

"*Jesus*! Get your shirt off and let me see what-the-hell else is going on with you. How in the world could you get in this kind of a mess by going on vacation?"

While Dr. Givens removed the bandages from his head and abdomen, Mark used the time to give a brief account of the encounter with the drug runners. The *brief* account became more detailed due to the frequent interruptions to the story by Dr. Givens' questions for extra detail and comments of disbelief.

"How long have the stitches been in your head?

"Five days, I think."

"I think they should stay in for another few days, but the wound looks like it's healing nicely. The gunshot wound seems to be healing well too, and there's no sign of infection in either. Whoever fixed you up did a good job. You need to come back in another few days and I'll get the stitches out of your head. I realize it's really ugly, but it would be best if you leave the bandage off your head and ear as much as possible. Keeping it dry and clean will help the healing. I'll clean and redress your stomach, but that's about all I can do for now."

"I appreciate it." Mark paused for a moment and then said, "I think I need to visit with you about the more serious problem I've been blessed with. I'm starting to hurt pretty bad from the inside. I think I'm going to need a little help with the pain. It's becoming more and more difficult to keep from annoying my wife and friends... bitching about my problems. The hydrocodone the corpsman and doctor gave me for trauma has kept the bitching to a minimum, but I'm about out of pills. I think it's time to order some more – with your consent."

Dr. Givens thought for a moment, and then said, "Mr. Stevens, we've talked about what you can expect and, frankly, I'm somewhat surprised you've gone this long without the pain meds. You've been rather fortunate up until now. We'll take whatever steps necessary to keep you comfortable, but – I think you know this is the beginning of the end and I want you to be prepared."

"I'm not liking it, but I'm prepared. The last four months have been some of the most wonderful days of my life. It's a major disappointment to have it all end so soon."

"*Wife*? Did you casually mention *wife* a few moments ago? I thought you were a widower."

"I was, but the evening of *our* first meeting, *and* after I accepted the fact that you weren't going to throw yourself at me, I went to dinner to drown my sorrows. At dinner I met a wonderful and exciting woman that turned out to be a blessing and a curse at the same time. I didn't tell her about the cancer until it was too late. I'd fallen head over heels in love with her and it seems she felt the same way about my dumb ass. She joined me on the sailing vacation and felt compelled to become my bride – knowing it was to be a short-lived marriage." Mark continued with, "I thought it was a bad decision on her part. She has made me very happy while reluctantly accepting the facts of our abbreviated future together."

"She must be a remarkable woman. I don't know if I would consider marrying a man that I knew would only be with me for a few months and have to suffer the inevitable loss due to circumstance." After a thoughtful pause, she continued with, "So it was your *wife* that took care of the pirate? Wow!"

"Yeah, she's a hand alright." Mark took a couple of deep breaths and added, "Well, what do I do? Fake it as long as I can and then run away?"

"Mr. Stevens, I wish I had an answer. I don't. You will have to decide how you will personally handle it. It will be rather quick once the symptoms become severe, but it will also be a very rough time for you. I recommend a hospice. They will keep you as comfortable as possible, but it will still be very bad toward the end. Our medicines aren't strong enough to keep you conscious and pain free at the same time."

"I don't want to put my wife and friends through the ordeal of watching me going from bad to worse. I'll probably say some goodbyes and sneak off into the night. I will not be able to stand being totally infirm while those that I care about stand by helplessly and suffer from my helplessness. I'm already getting *those* looks when I show any sign of becoming symptomatic. I've got a plan – and it will go into effect when I feel I can't hang in any longer. Keep the dope coming, Dr. Givens, and I'll stick around as long as I can."

"How are you doing mentally, with this hanging over your head? How are you feeling? Would you like for me to refer you to a counselor?"

"No, I don't think a counselor would help. I'm a mad son-of-a-bitch, but I'm not that scared of dying. I just feel cheated – now that I've finally found someone to enjoy life with. *Hate*! That's what it is. *Hating* to hurt her on my way out and that's where the mental anguish really takes hold. It's pretty awful."

"I can only imagine how awful it must be for you."

"OK – I'll ask the 'million-dollar' question. How long have I got?"

"Oh Mr. Stevens, I knew you were going to ask me that and it's a very difficult question for me to answer with any degree of accuracy. Generally, once the pain gets bad enough to need medication for control, most victims deteriorate rather rapidly – usually passing within six to eight weeks. I see you've already lost over five pounds and weight loss is an accompanying symptom. Even if you're able to maintain a reasonable diet, the weight will keep coming off since your body will no longer be able to process the food."

"Well, that's about all the *good* news I can stand for one day. I'll let you get back to your other patients and see you in four or five days for the stitches."

Dr. Givens sat silent for a few moments and then said, "I'm sorry I have to let you leave without anything positive for encouragement. If your wife would like to visit with me, I'd be happy to meet her and give her any information I can about caring for you when things get really bad."

"I'll let her know about your offer, but I'd rather she didn't know a lot about what it will be like toward the end. My plan doesn't call for her being there during that time. I don't think I could stand it. Anyway, I'll work it out. It's very generous of you to offer her the support and I do appreciate it."

*   *   *

Mark left the doctor's office with a terrible rage building in him. With each step the madness grew – with his hands clenching into fists over and over as he rode the elevator to the ground floor. He charged from the elevator and crashed heavily into a man waiting by the door and stormed off without a word. He heard the man he'd hit shout out, "*Excuse me!*" He fought the urge to go back and punch him. He wanted to punch someone – something – to vent the anger he had no way of venting.

He found the rental car and nearly tore the door off the hinges getting in and slamming the door so hard it rattled the glass in the window, close to the point of shattering. Once seated in the car he was on the verge of hyperventilating when the rage suddenly melted and was immediately replaced by a deep, saturating sadness. The abrupt change in emotion caught him by surprise. He was further surprised when he started to cry. It was the first time he'd cried since Karen and Sarah were killed. Leaning heavily on the steering wheel, he fought the deep sobs without success – muttering unintelligible curses at his perceived weakness and the demon inside him.

After what seemed like a very long time, the sobs were defeated and he laid his head back against the seat, staring at the headliner, and letting the remaining tears fall where they may. He was embarrassed and hoped no one had seen this display of zero self-discipline. He felt limp from the emotional drain and couldn't muster the strength to start the car and go home.

*　　*　　*

Mark sat in the car for over thirty minutes trying to regain his strength and composure. Finally, he started the car and, very deliberately, drove toward the entrance of the parking garage. He didn't want to go home immediately. He dreaded the conversation he knew he would have to have with Carole. With no place special to go while avoiding the inevitable, he decided to drive back to the river where he and Carole had picnicked their first day together. He needed some time alone, to try and plan an acceptable set of priorities for his last few weeks in Memphis. How would he say the goodbyes necessary without the threat of interference from Carole and his friends? It was going to be a most difficult exercise and he seriously considered the coward's way out by just leaving without a word, to avoid the conflict he knew would surface when he decided it was time to go.

Mark bent and picked up a piece of broken tree-limb as he walked slowly toward one of the concrete picnic tables. He sat on the table-top – head down, elbows on his knees and his feet on the bench seat. After pulling out his old worn pocket knife, he began to whittle as he thoughtfully debated each perceived scenario. He hoped his grandfather had been right when he gave him the knife long, long ago, and told him that a man thinks much more clearly when he's whittling. Over the years, Mark had found that bit of sage information to be mostly true. Even with the whittling, it was still very unpleasant mental work. As he sat in the shadow of the bridge, it became more and more difficult to concentrate on unpleasantness in such a pleasant environment.

His mind began to wander as he watched a black bird, of some unknown species, and marveled at the ease in which it flew into the density of a nearby tree. With what appeared to be reckless abandon, the bird sailed headlong into the branches without touching a leaf. The tree swallowed the bird as it made its way to an invisible perch, deep within the foliage. Mark continued to watch and was further amazed when the bird flew out the other side of the tree with equal ease. How in the hell do they do that, he asked himself – without expecting an answer, but finding it unusual to be paying such attention to things he'd always just taken for granted.

After sitting in the park for a little over an hour, enjoying the solitude, he had no concrete answers to the questions surrounding his escape and finally surrendered to: "I don't know what to do."

Once he accepted the "I don't know" as an answer, Mark slid off the table and slowly made his way to the car – muttering aloud, "I guess I'll stop by Walgreen's and get my dope."

*   *   *

When Mark entered the condo, Carole came to him and after a quick hug and peck on the lips, asked, "You're not already running around on me, are you? I was about ready to call the law and have them run you down. How did the visit with your doctor go?"

"I've been single for a long time and, naturally, I had to tie up some loose female ends." Then after a short contemplating pause he added, "Love those ends."

It was getting hard to speak with Carole pounding on his chest, so he hugged the offending arms and continued with, "The doctor said Master Chief Nance did a super job fixing me up. There's no sign of infection in either wound and I'm to go back in a few days and have the stitches removed. She gave me more hydrocodone, so I can remain goofy with little or no pain. Wanna get 'high' with me?"

"*No*, I don't want to get 'high'. Was that all she said? Nothing about the cancer?"

"There is nothing particularly new about it. No miracle cure popped up while we were gone. I guess we'll just have to take it day-at-a-time."

"I still wish you'd try some treatment."

Mark thought for a moment and then said, "Darlin', we've talked about this before and I have no evidence of treatment being successful. I just don't want to waste what little time I have left with hair falling out and being sick all the time. It doesn't seem worth it." After another pause, he added, "Let's not talk about it for a while. We both know it's there, but I don't want it to dictate our lives."

"I won't say anything else about it, but I can't get it off my mind. I'm sure it has to be driving you crazy."

"I'm fine. *You* make my life fine," he said. And then after a brief pause, he added, "Look – Mattie and Maury don't know we're back yet, why don't we give them a call – with an invitation to dinner? They will freak out when we tell them of all the *fun* they missed by coming home early."

In agreement, Carole said, "Would you like to invite them over here for dinner, or would you rather go out?"

"I'll leave that up to you, since you're the resident chef. It would be more of a hassle here, but it would also give us more opportunity for visiting."

"I think I'd rather have them here. I haven't prepared a decent meal in a couple of months. It might be a challenge to see if my memory of cooking school is worthy of this reunion."

Mark thought for a minute and then said, "I'm sure you will be able to rise to the occasion – anything with gravy will be fine."

"*Sauce*, you redneck," Carole shot back – with a sideways look that punctuated the comment. She then added, "I'll have to go to the market to find something special... that requires *gravy*. I don't think the things we left here a couple of months ago would be that appropriate."

"I guess we should see if they're able to come tonight. I'll give them a call and if they're available, then you can go shop. If they can't make it we can just order in Chinese or something. I don't feel cheated when we spend an evening alone. You are my favorite."

"Wow – you are *slick*. That's a good line, my man."

"I got practice with all those *loose-ends* this afternoon."

*   *   *

When Mark called Mattie, the phone rang several times before she picked up. As it turned out the home phone had been forwarded to her cell phone and she and Maury were in Chicago meeting with clothing manufacturers to select new clothing lines for Maury's stores. They would be back in Memphis on Friday and would get together on the weekend.

Mark turned to Carole and said," Well, it looks like *Egg foo something or other* for dinner tonight." He then added, "I guess you've skated again – cooking wise. They're in Chicago."

*   *   *

The ten days since their return to Memphis flashed by quickly. Carole had, essentially, gone back to work at the pleadings of several clients. Most of the work allowed her to stay in her home office. She worked at her own pace and was able to interact with Mark when he was home with nothing special to do.

Mattie and Maury had returned from Chicago and the promised dinner Carole prepared was as wonderful as expected. The evening lasted way longer than normal due to the endless questions Mattie kept asking about their ordeal – prying for details and gasping at the true and incredible responses. Mark, proudly, recounted Carole's heroics and tried to minimize his own actions as Carole, just as proudly, gave her account of the ugly affair.

During dinner, Sean Jacobson called to say he'd arranged for a sailing captain to return the *Cruzin' Carole* to Ft. Lauderdale. Mark excused himself and went into the bar area to complete the discussion about the boat. He asked Sean to hold off on sending a captain to retrieve the boat, then lied to Sean, saying the doctor indicated that he should be ready to sail in a couple of weeks. If things went as planned, he would fly to Provo and bring the boat back. If his health did not improve, he'd ask the captain to continue with the original plan. He thanked Sean and returned to the table. He told Carole a bit of a lie when he said, "That was Sean and the boat has been taken care of."

CHAPTER FIFTY

El marcó uno was not having a good day. He had impatiently waited the two days scheduled for the cocaine-laden boat to make its trip from Cockburn Town to Nassau. The time had been spent in a run-down hotel with bad plumbing and no air conditioning. The boat had not arrived. He was not looking forward to the meeting with the associates from the United States and having no information on the whereabouts of the drugs. He searched the unfamiliar waterfront area for the safe-house designated to be used for the meeting to make arrangements for the transfer of drugs for cash.

His cell phone rang. It was Maximilo Salinas, the heir-apparent to the *Cali Cartel* and oldest son of Roberto Salinas – the head of the cartel. Maximilo, also, was clearly not happy and told Ernesto in curt, short sentences, the shipment would not be forthcoming and to report to him as soon as he could get back to Columbia. Since this was the second shipment lost under his supervision, Ernesto knew it was a death sentence. No one survived losing over two tons of the cartel's cocaine.

He found the safe house, but continued to drive past without stopping. He had to think about what he was going to do. Not knowing if the American associates knew the shipment had been intercepted or not, he decided to take a chance and see how far he could carry the original plan. He thought if there were only two or three men in the group, he could possibly overpower them in a surprise move and grab the two million in cash they carried. He reasoned that he could go anywhere and live in luxury for the rest of his life with that much money and not have to deal with Maximilo. There was any number of Spanish-speaking South American countries where he could hide.

He decided to check it out – stopped, parked the car and then knocked on the door of the run-down house.

A gruff voice yelled from inside, "Who is it?"

"Ernesto!" He then called back in Spanish, "I need to talk to you about our transfer."

A tough looking Latino opened the door, looked around to see if Ernesto was alone and then told him to stand for a search.

"I'm not coming in, so there's no need to search me. I've just come to give you the address of where we will be tonight. I have a truck that says *"Angelo's Fresh Fish"* painted on the side. It will be loaded. You take the truck – I take the money. You *do* have the money, don't you?"

"Yes, we have the money," the man said as Ernesto handed him the note with the address.

"How many came with you? I don't want to be surprised when you show up."

"There are three of us. And you?"

Posturing himself and in a voice that left no doubt that it was a warning, Ernesto said, "I'll be alone in the truck, but there will be others close by to help if needed. If things start to get uncomfortable, you may see little red dots from laser sights on your chest or head. I hope they won't be needed." He added: "I'll see you at 10 o'clock tonight. Pull up to the front of the truck and flash your lights so I will recognize you."

The man didn't respond, but turned and re-entered the house.

Ernesto smiled. They didn't know the drugs had been intercepted.

*   *   *

Ernesto walked back to the car with his mind racing. He knew he would have to kill the men from the U.S., but didn't really know how it could be done until they all met at the truck that evening. He had a silencer for his gun and thought it would be quiet enough not to cause an uncontrollable situation with the local police when he made the move. He had to load something into the truck that would appear to be the cocaine and, hopefully, could get one or two of the men to enter the cargo area to check out what they were buying. If he could choreograph such a situation, he felt confident he could overcome the three men with little difficulty, load them in the cargo area, lock it and drive away in the car with the money. He knew there would be a firefight when the men discovered the phony load he'd have in the truck, and it would be a toss-up as to his survival if he wasn't able to do the surprise attack. In any case, he felt it was worth a try.

The address he'd given them was a run-down waterfront location lined with small businesses trading in imports and exports along the rotting piers with the equally unkempt boats that hauled the miscellaneous cargo. It would be very dark and mostly deserted when the crew from the U.S. arrived with the money. If the U.S. contingent *didn't* get a phone call similar to the one he'd received from Maximilo, he just might be able to complete his plan for continued longevity and personal comfort.

Ernesto drove back to the waterfront area where the truck (that was to be used for the transfer) was parked. He got in the truck and started looking for a supply company where he could buy several wooden pallets and a tarp for cover. In the dark, no one could tell what was under the tarp until it was pulled back and that's when he would make his move on the three men from the U.S.

He found the supplies he needed and loaded them into the truck. Once covered, the pallets appeared to be about the same physical size as a ton of packaged cocaine. In any event, it would be close enough to warrant an inspection by at least one of the men.

It was only 4:20 in the afternoon and he didn't really know what to do for the long six hours before the meeting. He decided to go back to his room and try to sleep for a few hours so he would be fully rested when he took on the three men from the U.S.; however, once in the hot, little room he knew sleep was out of the question. He was nervous so he took out his *Sig Sauer P-220, Combat TB*, released the magazine and checked to see it was fully loaded with the ten .45 cal. hollow-points. He then went to his duffle bag and found the silencer that was adapted for the gun – screwed it in place and inspected the finished ensemble. With the silencer in place, the gun took on a much more bulky appearance, and he'd never liked the way it had to fit in his holster; however, he felt like it was worth the extra bulk if he could keep from alarming any of the locals during the upcoming *transfer of funds*.

It was a long afternoon for Ernesto, but finally at 9:15, he started the truck and headed for the wharf for his meeting with the men from the U.S.

It was as dark as he'd hoped for and he tried to position the truck where he would have the best advantage in overtaking his victims and sat, nervously, waiting for the men to arrive.

At exactly 10:00 p.m., headlights turned toward him from a side street and slowly moved toward him. The car blinked their lights and Ernesto got out of the truck and walked toward the car. The man in the passenger seat opened his door and got out to meet Ernesto and, speaking in Spanish, asked if everything was ready for the transfer.

Ernesto replied, in Spanish, "I have the product if you have the cash.

The man said, "We have it."

"I want to see it."

The man standing with Ernesto called out to the car, "Seve, open the trunk. He wants to see what we've brought."

With those instructions, a man sitting in the back seat of the car opened his door and walked around to the back of the car to open the trunk.

Ernesto saw an unimpressive looking suitcase lying in the darkness of the trunk. He illuminated the trunk with his flashlight and the man called Seve, opened the case to reveal stacks of hundred dollar bills.

"Do you want to count it?" the man asked.

"No, if it's not all there, my people in Columbia will make any adjustments needed. Close the trunk and we'll see what you get in return."

The three men started walking toward the rear of the truck. They would be out of sight from the driver who had stayed in the car, and Ernesto was a bit concerned on how he would deal with the man if he were successful in taking out the two that were with him.

When they got to the rear of the truck, Ernesto unlocked the sliding overhead door to the cargo area and handed his flashlight to the man he'd first talked to – indicating he could check out the delivery.

When the man climbed into the cargo area, but was still on his hands and knees, Ernesto pulled his gun from its underarm clamshell holster in one quick motion and shot the man standing next to him in the temple. The man's brain was mushed by the big hollow-point, and he didn't quiver as he was propelled sideways and fell in a limp pile on the dirty asphalt. The man on his hands and knees was trying desperately to draw his weapon when Ernesto shot him – twice – once, a misguided shot to the throat and the second in the forehead. The silencer on the .45 did its job, and the sounds of the three shots were no more than muffled "poofs"' that couldn't be heard more than fifteen feet distant.

Ernesto turned to deal with the driver and, as he cautiously moved from behind the truck, was very surprised to see the driver walking toward him in the darkness carrying an Uzi assault pistol at his side. Four more *poofs* and his attack was over. The Uzi never came to bear.

Feeling very lucky, Ernesto scanned the darkened area for any indication that his activities had drawn attention. Satisfied that he had not been seen; he immediately started dragging the driver to the rear of the truck and heaved him into the cargo area next to his dead companion. The first man he'd killed was quite large, and Ernesto had to struggle with all his might to hoist the 250-pound man up the three-and-a-half feet to the deck of the cargo area. By the time he was finished, he was drenched with sweat and his clothes were extremely bloody from having to come in such close bodily contact with the two dead soldiers. After catching his breath, he pushed the three bodies far enough inside to close the cargo door. He locked the door and after making one last visual scan of the area, made his way to the car and drove off. There was no hint of remorse for the killing, but he had an adrenalin rush that could hardly be contained. As always after a killing, he had an erection. His surprise attack had been supremely successful.

CHAPTER FIFTY-ONE

Mark was getting somewhat bored with nothing to do, and time was starting to drag. The pain was starting to become more and more intense and the 15mg of hydrocodone was no longer getting the job done, pain wise. He was beginning to have too many days when he wanted to curse, yell and put his fist through a wall when the pain pills did about as much good as eating an *M&M*.

Mark desperately fought the urge to share much of what he had on his mind with Carole, but could not bring himself to say something that might spoil a single moment of her life. When he was reading or watching TV, he would often look up and catch her staring at him from across the room with a deep sadness in her eyes that was impossible to hide. Once caught staring, she would immediately smile, briefly, then divert her eyes. Each time it happened, he felt as if he were suffocating and wondered if what they'd enjoyed was worth the suffering she was forced to endure now that it was all about to end. He had an almost uncontrollable desire to hold her until he could somehow make the hurt go away. This is what's killing me, he thought – not the cancer.

Mark had days when the drugs only took the *edge* off his pain, yet he refused to ask Doctor Givens to increase his dosage. Not yet, he would say to himself...not until I really have to. When that happens, I know it's time to be gone.

Not only were the drugs not fully doing their job, but the side effects made him think crazy thoughts with hideous nightmares awakening him during the night – shivering and in a cold sweat. Invariably, Carole would be awake, trying to smother the devil in him with her body while whispering, "It's all right. It's all right."

Mark would find himself trying to memorize her smell and the softness of her hair as she cuddled into a perfect connection with his body; her back to his front. A verbal exchange was never needed during these moments. The closeness left no need for words. They both knew that each night they virtually melded into one, the bond between them was as much spiritual as physical. An awful dread lingered in both their minds, knowing there were only a very limited number of nights left for such bonding.

Days passed, and Mark could no longer ignore the fact that his illness was progressing faster than he expected. He suddenly realized that he had procrastinated long enough, and it was time to start dealing with the issues at hand. It was decision time. Boredom coupled with physical inactivity was allowing his mind to focus more on the pain and less on the monumental tasks confronting him as one day ran into another.

The hardest part for Mark was the nagging awareness that the problem of a graceful exit had not been resolved, even in his own mind. Suddenly, Mark became furious with himself. "*Shit*," he half-shouted aloud as he realized it was time to get off his ass and make his final plans. He had lost more weight and, whether real or imagined, he thought he was seeing signs of jaundice. Knowing he had to start getting serious about leaving, he chose Art to be his first attempt at justifying his decision to leave.

It was 3 o'clock in the afternoon and Carole was working at her desk. He approached from behind, brushed her hair aside with the back of his hand, and then gently palmed her neck as he reached for the phone sitting on the desk. As he reached, Carole bent her head back over the back of her chair, exposing an upside-down target for a quick kiss. The kiss was on target, but as he was breaking away, she reached with both arms and encircled his neck to pull him back for a more substantial exercise in upside-down kissing. Once that was done to her satisfaction, she allowed him to pick up the cordless phone and asked, "Who are you calling?"

"If you hadn't caught me, I was going to call a couple of old girlfriends that don't sit at desks all day long, but now I guess I'll call Art and see if I can't take some of his money on the golf course tomorrow."

"Do you feel well enough to play golf?"

"I've been sitting on my butt way too long. It's time to get back out there among 'em."

He dialed Art's number, and after the usual chitchat with his secretary, he heard Art's growl, asking, "If this is about going back to the Caribbean, you can forget about it!"

"That's not it at all, Mark said, using a huskier voice for the benefit of both Art and Carole. I'm running a little short on cash and wanted to know if you could break away from your office and let it run smoothly for a few hours – tomorrow or the next day. Golf will be my monetary salvation if I'm playing a mullet like you."

"Is that dope you're taking causing visions of grandeur or something?"

"That's not grandeur, my friend; it's one of life's realities."

Art continued with, "I can probably get away. What have you got in mind?"

"The weather guessers have predicted a beautiful day tomorrow, and I think I can get us a tee time. What time can you get away? If not tomorrow, they said the next day should be just as good. Pick your day for humiliation."

"The only thing that will be humiliating is being caught playing golf with your dumb ass; however, I think I can get off in time for you to buy lunch before embarrassing yourself on the course. Care to make an early wager?"

Chuckling aloud, Mark said, "I'll see if I can get something around 1 o'clock. Either way, I'll see you at the club around 11:30. I'm sure they can get us teed-up sometime close to one. From what Jean tells me...you need to get off doing something. Fish!

"OK buddy, I'm looking forward to it." Art chided back at him.

Mark suddenly had a churning feeling in his stomach because he didn't know, for sure, if he could play golf or not. The gunshot wound had not completely healed, so he was still somewhat stiff in the abdominal area. The stiffness wasn't his major concern. The cancer was taking its toll on his strength, and he didn't know if he could go a full eighteen holes. He knew he couldn't without taking more pain pills. He thought he could slip one in should the pain become so bad Art would notice. Mark quickly decided he would play it by ear and last as long as he could. His thoughts were not so much on his golf game as much as how and how much to tell Art without it getting back to Carole.

*   *   *

As promised, the day was beautiful with bright sunshine and a temperature of 79° when Mark pulled into the club parking lot. He went directly to the dining room and joined Art, who was just sitting down at a window table that offered a panoramic view of the perfectly manicured golf course.

"We're scheduled to tee off at 1:07," Mark said as they were shaking hands.

"I don't know if it wouldn't be better to just sit here in air conditioned comfort and drink beer all afternoon."

"I told you I was running low on cash and that's why I invited you. I can't do any good sitting around here watching you get drunk."

"You'll be sorry you said that." Then, after a short pause, Art continued with, "I hate to say it, but you don't look so pretty good, my friend. Are you feeling all right? If you're trying to lose weight – the diet's working remarkably well and you might want to back off just a tad."

"I've felt better, but I'm doing OK – considering the circumstances. The doc says the weight loss is predictable and will probably get worse before it gets better. I've started carrying a bowling ball around with me just in case the wind picks up. I might have to get a second one before it's all over."

Mark and Art chatted for a few minutes, then went to the elaborate luncheon buffet the club took pride in – serving club members and guests. After a leisurely lunch, they went to the practice tee to loosen up before their round. As expected, Mark was having some difficulty swinging his clubs. He hoped he could become more comfortable after they were on the course.

They played nine holes and Art could see his friend was having trouble and asked if he'd like to call it a day. Mark, in return, said, "No, I'm too far down to quit now. You'll own my estate if things don't get better soon."

If it had just been the golf, Mark would have taken him up on quitting after only nine holes, but he knew he hadn't come for golf as much as he'd come to confide in his friend about leaving Memphis.

Mark played two more holes before he told Art that he'd just ride in the cart for the rest of the round and maybe putt on a few of the remaining greens.

"Why don't we just go on back to the clubhouse now?" Art asked with genuine concern?

"No, I need to visit with you some and I'd rather do it out here on the course, if you don't mind."

"What about?"

"I think it's about time for me to get out of Dodge. The pain is getting rather severe, and the dope will have to be upgraded to take care of it. I don't know if I'll be able to function much longer." After absorbing the silence for a few moments, he continued with, "It should be obvious from my golf today that I ain't what I used to be."

Art was noticeably shaken by Mark's confession but said nothing. He slowly pulled his driver out of his bag and walked up on the tee-box of hole number 12. He didn't tee up his ball but stood leaning on his driver and looking away from Mark. After a long couple of minutes, he came back to the cart, viciously slammed his driver back into his bag and stood by the driver's side of the cart. After another uncomfortable silence, he quietly asked, "What do you plan on doing?"

Mark's head was down, as he stared at the floor of the golf cart; then after another uncomfortable silence, looked up and said, "I honestly don't know exactly. I do know that I will not stay in Memphis and subject you, Carole and the rest of my family, to being my caretakers when I become totally incapacitated. I've accepted the fact that there is nothing I can do that will alter the final outcome of this mess. I'm mad as hell, but I'm not particularly scared of it. My doctor tells me it's only a matter of weeks now, before I'm gone for good." Mark was lying when he continued, saying, "I'm going to go somewhere – I don't know where yet – and find a hospice that will provide me with the morphine I'll need to get through this. I can manage that as long as I know my family doesn't have to watch it happen. Art, I'm hoping you'll help me with my great escape if I can't get it done by myself. You know me – my last great adventure."

Although Art didn't respond, Mark knew he would be there for him. All he had to do was let him know what he needed, and it would be done.

"That will kill Carole. You know that," Art said after another thoughtful silence.

"When I first told Carole about the cancer, I also told her that this was the way it would be. She agreed to it, at the time; but I don't think she will knowingly agree to it now. She would be helpless to do anything, and I think that would be worse than me just bailing out. I have to depend on you, Jean and Mattie to get her through it. I can't think of another way."

Art thought for a moment, and then said, "When Jean finds out about this, she's going to want to kick your ass. As a matter of fact, I sort of feel the same way."

"What would you have me do, lie around and let everyone I love feel sorry for me? I think prolonging the combined suffering of everyone involved would be worse than the clean cut I gain by leaving with some mobility and not be drugged up so much that I couldn't even communicate with anyone. Bedpans, dirty diapers and my own shitty ass, left for someone else to clean up, scare me a lot more than death. The pain will be bad enough without adding gross humility to the mix."

Art had given up on his game and was driving slowly back toward the clubhouse with very little conversation. Finally, Mark said, "Art, we both know enough of each other's secrets to guarantee mutual destruction. I feel secure that you won't let our conversation get back to Carole. If you decide to share it with Jean, I hope you will stress the fact that I don't want Carole to know of my pending escape. After the fact, I hope she will be as supportive as is her nature and help Carole to understand my reasons for leaving rather than staying until the end."

"Well, I have to share it with Jean, but I will also threaten maiming if she says anything to Carole. You know you're going to have to convince *her* that this is the right thing to do, don't you?"

"Yeah, I figured as much, and I'm looking forward to it like I look forward to a dose of clap."

Back at the clubhouse, Art drove the cart into the parking lot and, after another uncomfortable silence, asked, "Are you OK driving home?"

"I'm fine. Sorry about petering out on the course today and laying that load of shit on you. I just felt that I owed it to you to let you know what was on my mind – right or wrong."

The two friends sat silently in the cart for a few more moments and then, during their departing handshake, Art said, "You're not going to find a hospice, are you?"

"Well, that's my story – and I'm sticking to it."

*   *   *

It was a long drive home for Art. When he entered the house from the garage, he met Jean in the kitchen and after a rather mumbled hello, walked directly to the bar and poured a stiff drink.

Jean joined him and asked, "It's a little early for that, isn't it? What happened – did you lose all your money?"

"No, it's a bit worse than that – I'm losing my brother."

CHAPTER FIFTY-TWO

Carole waited until Mark left for the golf outing with Art and then went directly to the telephone and dialed Mattie's number. When Mattie answered, Carole said, "Hi Mattie, this is Carole. Have you had your lunch?"

"No, but I have a carrot cake in the kitchen that is out to get me. I have to escape. What have you got in mind?"

"Why don't I pick you up and we can have one of those two-martini lunches I've heard so much about?"

"You've saved my life. This retirement crap isn't all it's cracked up to be. I'm about to go nuts sitting around the house all day."

"Wonderful! I'll pick you up in forty-five minutes or so, if that's alright?"

"I'll be waiting."

*　　*　　*

Carole pulled into the circle drive in front of Mattie's house, but before she could get out and ring the bell, Mattie appeared in the doorway and began her waddle toward the car. When she looked at Carole's white *XJL Jaguar*, she hesitated, briefly – opened the door while saying to Carole, "I don't know if I can get my fat ass in this car." To which Carole answered, "*Ridiculous*! It was made for you."

"I might need a shoehorn before it's over."

The two women laughed at each comment and Mattie's exaggerated entrance to the car and were soon driving to some as-yet-to-be-named bar and grill.

Carole asked, "Any preferences for ptomaine palaces?"

"I don't care where we're going. I'm just glad we're going. That house was about to drive me nuts."

After thinking for a few short moments, Carole said, "How about *Cousins*? It isn't far. The food is good, and alcohol is abundant."

"You just did a terrific commercial for them and I'm sure it's about to become one of my favorite places."

Idle chit-chat between the two friends made the fifteen-minute trip enjoyable for both, but when Carole parked the car, Mattie asked in a much more serious tone, "Are we just going to eat and drink, or will there be some *girl talk*? There are a lot of things on my mind, but I don't want to seem like I'm meddling. Be blunt and just tell me to fuck off if it gets too personal."

"As bad as I hate to admit it, the *girl talk* is the main reason I called. I think we both need it. I hope you're kind enough to put up with me if I start to whine too much."

"Honey, I'm Jewish; whining is an art form to me, and if you don't do it properly, I can coach."

With that said, Carole placed her arm over Mattie's shoulder and gave her a mini hug as they entered the bar.

There was no host available for seating. The lunchtime crowd packed the bar and all tables were occupied with the exception of one near the center of the room and another in a far corner that was being cleaned by a busboy. The smell of burgers, fries and other food items blended into a heavy, but pleasant mix to tempt the appetites of those present. The cacophony of eating utensils clanging on plates or glasses completed the atmosphere of busy people hurrying through lunch.

"Pay attention," Mattie said, "I'll demonstrate the effectiveness of *chutzpah* to get that table in the corner."

Carole smiled and watched as Mattie made her way through the tables and stood next to the table she wanted – with a scowl on her face that revealed her obvious annoyance at having to wait for a table. With the table cleaned and fresh dinnerware placed, Mattie called the busboy back and pointed, nobly, to an area of the table that was still damp from his washcloth and obviously unacceptable for a woman of her elevated stature. She directed him to redo it as she was sitting down in one of the chairs – motioning for Carole to join her.

When Carole arrived at the table, Mattie said, "It looks like half of Memphis is trying to get in this place and I didn't want to take a chance on someone else getting *my* table."

"Very effective routine, my dear," Carole said, laughing.

A very busy waitress was delivering delicious looking food to the table next to Carole and Mattie. She looked over her shoulder and said, "I'll be with you ladies is just a second. Would you like menus?"

"*Drinks* and menus, please," Carole answered, emphasizing the drinks.

The waitress finished serving the food to the other guests and turned to Mattie and Carole, asking, "What may I bring you?"

Carole responded immediately with, "A Beefeater martini, dry, with two olives and the phone number of the *Yellow Cab Company*. I'll probably need that number before I'm finished here."

Mattie smiled at Carole's order and asked for a glass of Chardonnay; then, as the waitress left, asked, "Is it my imagination, or are we a bit tense this fine morning?"

"Mattie, I'm about to burst. Mark won't talk to me about what he's going through, and I know it's getting worse by the day. He never takes his pain pills when I'm around, but when I check the bottle, there are more and more pills missing. I hear him moan at night and see him grimace when he moves around the house. It's getting bad, and I don't know what to do."

"After thirty years of daily contact, I can tell you, it will be difficult, if not impossible, to get anything out of him. He will grit his teeth and clam up like a mousetrap, and then wrap himself in that cloak of *macho* bullshit he seems to worship. I saw it when Karen and Sarah were killed. He was dying inside, and I couldn't get anything out of him. He appreciated the effort, but that was it."

"He's playing golf with Art right now, but I could tell when he left the house he wasn't feeling up to the task. He's so damned bullheaded he was going to do it come hell or high water."

The waitress reappeared with the drinks and menus. The glasses had barely touched the table when Carole grabbed hers and took half the drink in one swallow – shuddering from the scalding shock of the near-straight gin. She took another sip before placing the glass back on the napkin.

"Mattie, it's like waiting for the other shoe to fall. When he first told me about the cancer, he vowed that *he* would choose his time to go and not the disease. I agreed to his conditions at the time, but I don't know if I can stand it now. I'm watching him go downhill, and it's killing us both."

"Have you sat down and asked him to discuss it with you?"

"No, I hoped he would make the first move toward a serious discussion, but it doesn't look like that will happen."

Mattie watched as Carole took the last of her Martini and then said, "As I told you earlier, it will be hard to get anything out of him, but I think he will do anything to keep you from hurting. That will be the only reason he'll open up. You'll have to confront him with how it's tearing you apart."

"He hugs and kisses me differently now. They don't have the passion of someone trying to get me in bed like it was earlier. The hugs linger, with a feeling of finality and sadness. I find him awake and staring at me at night when he thinks I'm asleep. He brushes my hair back out of my face and adjusts my covers while I pretend to be asleep. Then, I find myself doing the same thing when he's sleeping. *God*, I love that man."

Mattie watched, silently, as big, salty tears welled in Carole's eyes, waiting for the inevitable blink that would let them fall to make room for more. She held her empty glass up in an attempt to get the waitress' attention.

"I love him too, Carole," Mattie said as she reached and placed her hand over Carole's. "We both know we're about to lose him, but try as I may, I can't get ready for it. You are the best thing that ever happened to him, and he knows it. I'm sure he feels like he's cheated you out of a lot of the happiness you deserve and has no answer for it. He's more concerned about saving you than he is about saving himself."

"He's going to leave, isn't he?"

After a short pause, Mattie answered, "Probably."

"These last few months have been all the things I ever wanted in a relationship. Mark has become my best friend and brought me happiness that most women will never enjoy. Do you think I'm being selfish in not wanting that to end so quickly?"

"Very pissed, I'm sure, but there's nothing selfish about it."

The waitress reappeared with another Martini and asked if they were ready to order. Mattie ordered a tuna sandwich, but Carole said she didn't think she would have anything to eat. She then explained to Mattie that she just didn't have much of an appetite any more.

After the waitress had gone, Mattie took a deep breath and said, "Carole, how would you have it? Do you think you are able to watch him go from bad to worse without being able to do anything about it? The last few weeks of his life will be almost unbearable. Or, can you avoid protesting when, or if, he chooses to leave so you don't have to be a part of his last days. We all know the inevitable outcome, and he may not choose to go through the intense pain of his final days. His pain will be more difficult, mentally; if he has to watch you suffer helplessly along with him."

"Mattie he's already lost over twenty pounds since we've been back from the boat and he keeps pretending there is nothing to be concerned about. I'm walking on eggshells trying to go along with this farce. What do I do, go on pretending to be the sweet little wife until I wake up in a bare bed – never having said, or heard, a damned thing about it?"

"No, you won't have to do that. If the silence continues, I will, again, resort to *chutzpah* and butt-in where I probably should not. Maybe that will clear things up for him. Over the years we have had these types of *discussions* before and he's generally seen the light afterward."

The waitress reappeared with Mattie's sandwich and Carole handed her another empty cocktail glass – indicating that she wanted a refill. Mattie declined when asked if she wanted another chardonnay and said, "I think I just became a designated driver."

The conversation between the two women waned as Mattie was eating her sandwich. Carole, for the most part, was staring off into space – doing her best to choke back the recurring tears. The alcohol was not helping, and she was starting to regret having ordered the third drink. However, when the waitress sat the refilled glass back in front of her, she picked it up, with some trepidation and took a sip.

When Mattie finished her sandwich, Carole said, with a degree of abruptness, "Mattie, I'm becoming a drunken bore and you've been wonderful to let me get some of this off my chest. Let's call it a day." Having said that, she fumbled in her purse, found two twenties and placed them on the table while mumbling, "That should handle it."

Before Mattie could protest, Carole stood and while holding one hand on the table for balance, used her other hand to lift the last of the Martini to her lips and said, "Maybe I'll pass out and forget all about the mess I find myself in."

Mattie stood and made her way around the table to stand at Carole's side to see if she needed help walking out. Carole straightened herself and did a perfect impersonation of a female doing the Foster Brooks act of a sophisticated drunk. She managed to get out of the bar with only having to say *excuse me* a couple of times when she bumped into chairs impeding her progress.

Once in the parking lot, Mattie said, "OK, girlfriend let me have the keys. You can pick up your car at my house later, or if dumb-ass is home, he can drive me."

Carole leaned on her car and, once again, fumbled around in her purse until she came up with the elusive car keys – then, slurring her words as she said, "I can call us a cab if you'd rather."

"No, we'll be OK. Let me help you get in the car and buckled up."

Once Carole was seated, Mattie got into the unfamiliar driver's seat and started searching for the controls needed to adjust seat and mirrors for a person of her *vertically-challenged* stature. When she was as comfortable as possible in the leather-encased bucket seat, she started the car, thinking, they should have used a bigger bucket when they designed this thing.

There seemed to be nothing appropriate to say during the trip to the condo, so both women remained silent. Mattie was reluctant to enter the place Carole had gone as she stared out the passenger window and cried.

When they arrived at the condo, Mattie found that Carole had become more and more uncoordinated. She had to provide support in punching in the code for the elevator and keeping Carole upright all the way to her bedroom. Carole plopped onto the bed in a drunken heap and was fast asleep by the time Mattie removed her shoes and lifted her legs onto the bed. "Bummer," Mattie said to no one.

Mattie took her cell phone out of her purse and dialed Mark's mobile number. He answered on the third ring. Mattie asked, "How long before you're home?"

"I'm nearly there now. Why?"

"Your bride and I had a three-martini lunch. She's asleep now, and I need a ride home."

"Is she alright?"

"Physically, yes. She's going to be out for a while, so there's no need to try and wake her before you take me home. I'll be down by the garage when you get here. We need to talk some."

"OK, I'll be there in a couple of minutes."

Mattie left the apartment and got to the garage area just as Mark was pulling in. She got in the car and Mark immediately asked, "What's going on? I didn't know you were meeting with Carole today."

"She called me and wanted to have lunch and *girl talk*. She's very upset with your dumb ass and three dry martinis were a bit more than she could handle."

"Why is she upset with me?"

"Mark, what you don't know about women would fill volumes. You don't talk to her about what's going on in your head – what your plans are or all the things that need to be said before you're gone for good. I'm having a hard time with it myself, and I can only imagine what she's going through. I may sound cold-blooded, but she has a lot longer time than you do to get over this."

"*Jesus!*" Mark shouted as he slammed his fist into the steering wheel. "I just don't know how to start that conversation. I've been putting it off, trying to keep things as normal as possible, but it's becoming more difficult every day."

"Well, I don't know what your plans are, nor does she, and she deserves to know. Having your death hanging over her head and not knowing what to expect is killing her just as surely as cancer is killing you. You've got to do something."

Mark sat in agitated silence for a few moments and then said, "My plans are pretty much set as far as what I'm going to do, so, I guess it's time to lay it all out for her. It's going to be rough, and I dread it more than anything I've ever faced. I can't hide any more."

"For whatever reason, the woman loves you more than you'll ever know. She deserves all the help and compassion you can show her, because you take half her life with you when you go."

They drove in silence the rest of the way to Mattie's house. As Mattie left the car, she said, "By the way, I love you a little bit myself. After you get it all straightened out with Carole, I'd like to know what's going on too. Good luck, my friend."

"Thank you, my friend."

CHAPTER FIFTY-THREE

El marcó uno was too bloody to return directly to his hotel. He decided to drive the n   northern perimeter of the island until he found a beach that was secluded enough to get in the water to wash off. He reasoned that it would be less difficult to explain wet clothes than it would be to explain clothes covered in blood, should the need arise. With any luck, he could have the clothes mostly dry by the time he got back to the hotel if he held his pants and shirt out the window during the trip.

With little effort, he found a suitable place along the road. He parked his car directly on the beach. He could see that there were no cars or people within a hundred yards in either direction, so he got out of the car and took off his clothes. After making a final check   to see that he was alone, he waded into the warm water and started scrubbing the bloodstained shirt and pants as vigorously as he could. It was too dark to tell if he'd gotten all the blood out, but he felt certain he'd done enough for it not to be noticeable. He stood naked next to the car until he was mostly dry before putting on his still-dry underwear. He partially rolled down the window on the passenger side of the car and placed the wet clothes in the crack, then rolled the window back up to hold everything in place. The pants and shirt would flap like hell all the way back, but he felt like he could handle the noise if it dried the clothes.

When he got back to the hotel, he saw that all his preparations were for naught. There was no one in the lobby or behind the desk. He walked undetected to his hot little room and lay heavily on the bed. He lay on his back and pulled the cash-laden suitcase up onto his stomach – opened it and stared at the piles of hundred-dollar bills.

He had never seen so much money. While staring at it, he thought of myriad uses that would bring comfort and luxury for the rest of his life if he could be smart enough to hide from the deadly tentacles of Maximilo Salinas and the drug cartel. He knew they would never quit in their search to find and kill him as brutally as he'd seen other traitors killed. It was not a happy thought. There would be a lot of money on his head, and his personal appearance made it almost impossible for him to hide.

Ernesto closed the suitcase – thought for a few moments, then got up and went to the bathroom to look in the mirror to see if there was anything he might be able to do to make his appearance less distinctive. He wouldn't have a problem with the wide white streak in his hair that ran from his forehead to the nape of his neck – a bottle of dye and a close haircut would take care of that. The colorless left eye would be more of a problem, but he thought dark sunglasses would make it much less noticeable until he could find an optometrist to fit him for colored contacts. The real problem would be the white blotches on his face, neck, arms and hands. He had tried makeup, but it wasn't that effective. It rubbed off too easily and made him look more grotesque than nothing at all. Then, with a flash similar to the proverbial light bulb coming on, he thought *tattoo*. I can get a flesh-colored tattoo that will permanently cover the white. He smiled as he visualized his transformation from monumentally ugly to just regular ugly. The disguise might not be perfect, but he wouldn't stand out like a lighthouse in a sea of normal pedestrians.

His disguise would mean nothing if he didn't get out of Nassau. Maximilo knew where he was, and it wouldn't take long for his contacts to find him in such a confined space. He knew it would take a minimum of three or four days for word to get back to Maximilo that he'd been ripped off by one of his own lieutenants, so he had that long to plan and execute an escape. The plane and pilot were still available and waiting for the return trip home. The plane was his way out.

Ernesto was more comfortable with others making his plans for him, and he was finding it difficult to formulate an escape that would make him invisible. Where would he go was the first decision he would have to make. He knew the plane had been modified to carry enough fuel for nearly one thousand miles, so just about any location in the Caribbean was within reach. "*Providenciales*, in Turks & Caicos," he almost shouted. I've been there, and I think it's big enough to get my disguise taken care of – then, if I can think of a way to keep my whereabouts secret, I think I can pull it off.

*   *   *

El Marco Uno pushed the money-filled suitcase under the bed. After placing his gun underneath the pillow, he flopped heavily onto the bed hoping to get some sleep before the busy day he had to plan for tomorrow. It didn't take long for him to realize there would be little sleep as his static brain wrestled with the problems of escape.

Since he was in charge of the failed operation, he would have no problem in ordering the pilot to fly to *Providenciales*; however if the pilot was allowed to continue on to Columbia, Maximilo would be in *Providenciales* the next day with plenty of help to shorten his life dramatically. He reasoned that if he just killed the pilot, then the plane would still be a beacon to his whereabouts. He had to have the plane go down at sea. If he could make that happen, Maximilo might assume he was still aboard at the time of the crash.

Ernesto had been well schooled in the use of explosives, but he had no idea where he could quickly buy the necessary materials for high explosives, but he should be able to find fireworks fairly easily. With fireworks came black powder and that would make a relatively efficient pipe bomb. He knew he had to leave *Nassau* as quickly as possible before the pilot got updated instructions from Columbia.

He had a long night of tossing and turning, but the sun finally aroused him from a fitful sleep. He got up and showered to wash the sleep from his eyes and the salt from his dip in the ocean the night before. It was still too early to start looking for the things he needed for his bomb, but he took a thousand dollars out of the suitcase, stared at the remainder for a long minute, and then closed it. The suitcase posed another problem: what would he do with it while he shopped? The trunk of the car he took from the Americans would be as safe a place as any. He went to the car, placed the suitcase in the trunk and started driving – looking for a place to have breakfast and kill time.

When he paid his check for breakfast, he asked the cashier if there was a "Radio Shack" anywhere on the island. The lady didn't know, but she said she would check the yellow pages of the phone book. His luck held as she told him there was, indeed, a "Radio Shack" store located in the business district of Nassau. She also gave him directions on how to get to the store. He still had an hour wait for the store to open, but he left immediately – anxious to gather his materials for bomb-building. If he could get it all done today, he could have the pilot fly him out at night.

He waited, impatiently, in front of the *Radio Shack* until the clerk shifted the "closed" sign to the "open" position and then hurried into the store. He told the clerk he needed a "switched" digital timer and two 12 volt lantern batteries. The clerk led him to a shelf that contained several timers. He selected one and checked it to see if the operating batteries were included. While paying for his materials, he asked the clerk if he knew of any place he might buy some fireworks. The clerk didn't know for sure, but told him he might try a couple of places that were always open during festivals. Ernesto thanked the man and left with directions to the suggested locations.

The first fireworks stand was a dilapidated looking structure with a faded hand-painted sign on the roof declaring *Fireworks*. It was closed and looked abandoned. The second stand was closed as well, but there was a sign on the door giving a phone number to call if someone needed assistance.

He used his cell phone and called the number. When a man answered, he asked if he was going to be open later in the day. The man said he hadn't planned to open, but would come to the store if the customer would guarantee a fifty-dollar sale. Ernesto agreed immediately. The man on the other end of the call said he would be there in thirty minutes or less.

Ernesto waited in the dirt parking area for about 20 minutes before the man arrived. While the man was opening the ramshackle building, he told Ernesto that he hadn't re-stocked recently and didn't have many of the smaller items, but plenty of the larger, more expensive, rockets and bombs. Ernesto related that the larger pieces were all he was interested in. He selected a large box full of the high-altitude rockets. He then paid the man over $400.00 for his trouble.

Things were coming together more rapidly than Ernesto had expected. He should have no trouble getting everything together for his evening flight to *Providenciales*.

He'd seen a hardware store on his way to the fireworks stand. If he could remember exactly where it was, he could complete his shopping and get on with the construction of the little pipe bomb that could mean his salvation.

With little effort, he found the store and bought a 2-inch pipe nipple that was threaded on both ends – 18 inches long. He also bought two caps for the pipe, a roll of Teflon tape, a drill motor, drill index, a two-gallon gasoline can and a tube of epoxy putty that was "guaranteed" to seal anything. As an afterthought, he bought a one-gallon glass jar with a two-and-one-half-inch opening at the top. As soon as he purchased some gasoline – he was ready to go.

It was only 11:30 in the morning. He knew he had plenty of time to construct the bomb, so he called the pilot's cell phone and told him to get fueled up and ready to leave by 5:00 p.m. He did not tell him their destination. If he filed a flight plan, it could be cancelled once they were in the air.

On his way back to the hotel, Ernesto stopped at a gas station and filled the metal can he'd just bought.

Once at the hotel, he carried the smaller sacks through the front entrance to check who may be in the lobby. There were two men sitting on one of the lobby couches and the desk clerk seated behind the desk with his head barely visible. He was oblivious to Ernesto's entrance. The other two men might question his assortment of fireworks and the gas can, so he went to the back entrance of the hotel to see if the door was unlocked. It was, so he went on to his room – deposited the small sacks of goodies on his bed and left again to retrieve the rest of his material that he would bring in through the back door.

With everything gathered in his room, Ernesto started to carefully dismantle the fireworks he'd bought to harvest the black powder. He was surprised at the quantity of powder in each of the large rockets and realized he'd bought about twice too many for his purposes. He kept the rocket fuses and tied three of them together to make sure he had enough length to extend far enough out of the pipe for ignition. *"Cavron!"* he shouted. "I forgot to buy wire and duct tape."

With that realization, he went back to the car and drove again to the hardware store to buy the missing items. He pulled the cigarette lighter out of the car and was back in his room in less than 45 minutes.

He connected the timer to the two batteries and the element he'd taken from the cigarette lighter. When he tested the apparatus, the cigarette lighter element glowed red in about 10 seconds, and he knew he had an efficient method of lighting the bomb after a given amount of time. He filled the glass bottle with gasoline and inserted the powder-laden pipe through the opening, mixed the epoxy and carefully placed a double bead around the pipe and the mouth of the glass jar. After a thirty-minute wait for the epoxy to harden, he tested for leaks. Finding everything as advertised, he wrapped the exposed length of fuse through the cigarette lighter element and used the duct tape to secure everything in place. He was rather proud of his efforts and reasoned the explosion plus the fire caused by the gasoline would bring the plane down in mid ocean just like he planned.

Ernesto gathered up the unused material and placed everything in a dumpster he found behind the hotel. He was ready. Takeoff would be in two hours.

*   *   *

When Ernesto arrived at the airport, he went to the general aviation parking area where he saw the amphibian parked and the pilot sitting in a folding chair in the shade of the wing. After a brief guttural greeting, Ernesto opened the trunk of the car and removed his duffle bag and the suitcase. He told the pilot to take the car to the parking lot and just leave the keys in place. Maybe it will be stolen, he thought.

Once the pilot was gone with the car, Ernesto climbed into the plane and unzipped his duffle bag to remove the bomb. He placed it in one of the overhead bins in the passenger compartment and stuffed his duffle bag in front for concealment. The suitcase was too big for the overhead, so he placed it in one of the empty seats and put the seatbelt around it. He then went back outside the plane and waited for the pilot to return.

When the pilot returned, Ernesto asked if he'd filed a flight plan. The pilot answered "Yes, I filed, but we will be VFR all the way. Since we're getting a late start, I hoped we could spend the night in *Port-au-Prince* – then tomorrow go on to *Barranquilla* for fuel and *Cali* in the afternoon."

"I don't want you to change the flight plan, but we are going to *Providenciales* – in *Turks and Caicos* first. I'll be getting off there to deliver a package while you continue on to *Cali* according to your flight plan. We can't do customs, so you'll tell the tower you're just stopping for fuel. I'll get out of the plane in the run-up area as you're getting ready to take off."

"What's this all about?"

"I don't really know. It's what Maximilo told me to do. That's why we're leaving so late. It needs to be dark when I get off the plane. You can fly on to *Port-au-Prince* for your sleep time."

"Whatever! Anyway, we're fueled and ready. Let's get going."

The two men got aboard, with Ernesto taking the right seat in the cockpit with the pilot.

The 400-mile trip to *Provo* was uneventful with darkness setting in as they landed. Ernesto stayed in the plane while the pilot went to the fuel desk to pay for the fuel. He pulled his duffle bag out of the overhead bin and set the timer on the bomb to one hour and then sat down in the seat next to the door of the airplane. He also placed his cell phone in the bin with the bomb.

The pilot came back with two large cups of coffee and took his seat in the cockpit, requested taxi instructions and started to roll to the run-up area. Once in position, he told Ernesto to get out as quickly as possible so he could quickly close the door before the tower noticed the extended delay in departing.

El marcó uno rolled from the plane, dragging the suitcase and his duffle bag. He was *free* with two million dollars to spend. He smiled as he watched the plane gain speed for its terminal flight.

CHAPTER FIFTY-FOUR

Mark drove slowly, with a deep dread building as he thought of the upcoming truth session he would have with Carole. The dread was accompanied with a recurring rage that seemed to lurk just below the surface during his waking hours – a rage that was becoming more and more difficult to control. He was seriously thinking about seeing how fast his car would go before impacting the next overpass support he came to. Not fair, he thought. I have too many loose ends to take care of before it comes to that. The rage was gaining ground, and he wanted to break things, or fight something – anything other than face Carole. He accepted two inevitable facts as he turned into the condo's garage: His life was essentially over and he couldn't leave Carole in the dark any longer. With that realization, the rage began to subside. With grim determination, he entered the elevator.

Once inside the condo, he was not surprised to find Carole asleep and snoring in the bedroom. She was still clothed but uncovered. He went to the linen closet to pull out an extra blanket rather than taking a chance on waking her if he pulled the bedcovers out from under her – placed the blanket over her and left the room, quietly shutting the bedroom door behind him.

Mark went to Carole's desk, sat down at her keyboard and began to type.

My Darling Carole, my wife,

This is not an easy letter to write, and you know I can't express my true emotions with ease. But the last expression of love I can show you is here, in this letter, because I would not be able to say them to you otherwise. We've both known from the beginning of our relationship that the day would come when I'd have to deal with this cancer in my own way. We discussed it before deciding to marry knowing we would only have a short time together. It hasn't been nearly long enough, but I'm grateful for every second you were in my life. Saying goodbye is the hardest thing I've ever had to do but there are no other choices.

The cancer didn't wait, and the pain has become a raging beast inside me. I can't hide its existence any longer. I think you know I've been trying, unsuccessfully, to ignore it for some time now.

Only moments ago I watched you sleep and drank in all the beauty of your lovely face that I take with me. We didn't get the time we'd hoped for, and I'm so sorry we didn't get the joy of growing old together. For the time we did have, no man could have been more blessed. My hope is that you only remember the man you held a month ago, not the man I would become had we let the cancer take what's left of me. I'm satisfied that you, not the disease, will have had the best of me. I am convinced it would be just as difficult to leave you if I had lived another twenty years. You've given me the happiest months of my entire life. Please understand that I decided my departure date, not the cancer. That decision gives us a rather small, but significant, victory.

You will be reading this after I've gone and it would be foolish of me to expect I can put everything I feel into words. I doubt if I could get everything said even if I were blessed with the literary skills of a Walt Whitman. There just aren't enough words.

In retrospect, I should never have indulged my selfish fantasy in inviting you on our first trip to Ft. Lauderdale. I didn't expect to be head over heels in love with you after such a short time, and I surely didn't expect you to return that love unconditionally. Then, if I hadn't been that selfish, I would never have known the joy of having you beside me for what turned out to be... the rest of my life.

Remember the night of my confession about the cancer? I told you then it would be me determining when I die. Having you with me has given me more courage than I might have had otherwise.

Having said that much, I'm firm in my belief that leaving now is my only acceptable option. So, as you might have guessed, I have gone to my boat – with enough serious pain meds to try and stay comfortable. According to Dr. Givens, I'm down to a couple of weeks, max. When the meds are no longer working, I will stop the pain.

Most importantly, my greatest wish is that you let me go as quickly as you can and do not waste your life grieving for me. Be happy we had our precious time together. I hope you will accept the support of our friends, Art, Jean and Mattie, and that you will understand my actions were never meant to cause any of you additional suffering.

I ask you to lean on them as all of you will lean on each other. Try to understand that I'm no longer in pain and that no man on earth could have had a better life. Regrettably, neither of us could have changed the ultimate outcome. Art and Jean have received a similar letter of goodbye and will be somewhat shocked at my abrupt and wordless departure. Explain it to them as only you can. Coming from you will make it easier for them to understand.

And then, there's Mattie. I'm assuming she will have brought you this letter after the terrible fight we will have over my decision to leave. She's been my partner for over thirty years and, as you know, she's steady as a rock. She'll be there for you with anything you need. I feel sure I can convince her that my leaving is the only thing I can do, and I know she'll reluctantly agree with my reasoning.

Be open to another relationship where the boundless love within you is not wasted, but shared, as it was with me. We had it all, everything a man and woman can have. You deserve so much more than the few months we enjoyed together.

As this will be my last contact with you, I want to say one last time that you made my life beautiful. I loved you more than life. Thank you for loving me in return. It was wonderful beyond belief.

Your devoted and loving husband,
Mark

Mark took the letter from the printer and re-read it, twice. He felt it didn't have everything in it that he wanted to say, but couldn't find words to fill in the perceived blanks. He signed the letter, folded it slowly and placed it in an envelope. Once the envelope was sealed, he used a pen to simply write *"Carole"* on the outside. For lack of a better place to put it, he stuck it in his hip pocket with no immediate plan on how he would get it to Mattie for delivery.

*   *   *

It was nearly four o'clock in the afternoon. Carole was still asleep, but he expected her to wake up or come-to at any time. He was scared and despised the feeling. He went to the bar and mixed a drink knowing he would have trouble holding it down; he felt like it was worth the effort if it did stay down.

He had taken his first tentative sip when Carole walked into the bar area looking for club soda and aspirin. The pained look on her face disproved the common belief that hangovers only occur in the morning. Still, Mark couldn't help thinking how beautiful she was. Her hair was in disarray, and she looked like a little girl who had been caught breaking a curfew. When she saw Mark, she asked, "How was your golf game?"

"I didn't do as well as I'd have liked, but it wasn't too bad. I did enjoy visiting with Art while he kicked my butt."

"I met Mattie for lunch and got a bit carried away with the martinis. Thankfully, she drove me home. I assume she took my car to get back to her house."

"No, I got here about the time she was leaving, so I drove her. That must have been some lunch," Mark said teasingly.

"It was, and I'm paying the price for it now."

Mark sipped at his drink and felt the involuntary convulsions in his stomach as the liquor burned its way down. He knew it wasn't going to stay with him long, but he continued to sip – hoping to augment his decaying courage as he postured himself for the upcoming ordeal of coming clean with Carole.

He moved to the couch and waited for Carole to join him. He placed his arm around her as she pulled her legs up onto the cushions and leaned comfortably on his shoulder. Her right arm eased around his midsection gently as her fingers lightly touched his skin with a loving pat. She was warm. He nuzzled her hair with his lips as they both sat quietly sipping their respective drinks. After several minutes of uncomfortable silence, Carole said, in a low monotone, "Mattie and I think you're going to leave soon. Is that true?"

Mark audibly sucked in a lungful of air and held it for a long moment, thinking, this is it, before responding with a quiet, "Yes, I'm afraid so."

He felt Carole stiffen under his arm without a vocal response. After another uncomfortable silence, she stood abruptly and staggered toward the bedroom doors, dropping the soda glass as she charged forward, tears flowing from her eyes. She was shaking as her eyes met his, *"Leave now!"* she screamed through the contractions of uncontrolled sobs. "I may as well get started on seeing how long it takes to get over my heart being broken into a million pieces." Her voice became much more forceful as she continued sobbing and shouting at the same time, *"I can't stand this waiting to find out you're not in my bed when I wake up each morning."* She slumped against the door frame for support, and in a childlike voice whispered, "It's killing me."

Carole slammed the bedroom door behind her and plunged headlong onto the bed and began beating the pillows with her fists in an effort to relieve the pain that racked her entire being.

After some time – minutes, seconds, or longer, she suddenly panicked at the realization that she'd just sent him

360

out of her life. She leapt from the bed and charged the bedroom door just as aggressively as she'd entered the room only to find an empty apartment. He was gone.

Carole collapsed to her knees at the door of the condo and wept in silent misery. She cried until she couldn't breathe, but heard herself repeat his name over and over.

*   *   *

Mark sat in the rental car, and for the second time since Karen had died, he began to cry.

CHAPTER FIFTY-FIVE

Mark sat quietly in the car until he regained his composure to some degree. As before, he was embarrassed by what he considered a minor weakness. He hadn't really considered being in such a situation without toiletries, a change of clothes or his meds; but he knew if he went back into the condo to fetch these items, he wouldn't be able to leave again. With renewed determination, he backed the car from the garage and closed the door – not only to the garage, but to his life with Carole as well. He had never felt so alone in his entire life.

He decided to find a hotel for the night. He had doubts about being able to sleep, but he needed access to a phone book to finalize his plans to leave Memphis. He decided to charter a plane to take him to the boat and wanted to check with one of the charter services to see what was available around mid-afternoon the next day.

*   *   *

Mark finally got out of bed at the Holiday Inn Express just as it was getting light in the East. The combination of pain and the deep sadness he felt from leaving Carole allowed for nothing more than closing his eyes – without sleep the entire night. He tried to make order out of his last day in Memphis, knowing he had to meet with Mattie. It was going to be a painful goodbye and another imposition when he asks her to deliver his letter to Carole. He also knew he had to get more prescriptions from Dr. Givens in order to deal with the pain until he decided to end it.

Mark took the yellow pages from the night stand and checked for charter services from Memphis. He found the number for *Stratos Charters* and dialed on the house phone. When they answered he asked if they had a light jet available for later in the afternoon. They asked his destination, and when he told them *Providenciales, Turks & Caicos* he was put on hold for several seconds before they replied that there would be a plane available by 4:30 pm. After agreeing to the time, he confirmed the flight and hung up the phone.

That was the easy part, he thought, now I have to call Mattie. I'd rather take a beating. Steeling himself, he dialed her number and asked if he could come by and visit. She asked, "What's going on?" To which he replied, "As usual, I need another favor, but I'll wait until I see you to ask. I hope you're dressed."

"I doubt if you'd be interested in seeing me in my filmy little nightgown."

"I've fantasized about it, but maybe I can wait a little longer."

"Come by whenever you're ready. I'll be here."

"I'll give you some time to get the cobwebs out and be there around nine."

"OK, I'll see you then. Bye!"

Mark lay back down on the bed in extreme pain. He used his cell phone and dialed Dr. Givens' office. As expected, he got her answering service and asked if they would have her call his cell phone – then gave them the number. He added that it was somewhat of an emergency that he speaks with her.

Mark was rather surprised when Dr. Givens called five minutes after he'd hung up from the answering service. When he answered, Dr. Givens asked about the emergency.

"Well, I'm out of meds and in an awful lot of pain. I hoped I could drop by your office and get some prescriptions. I'll be leaving town today and need enough for about ten days."

"I'll be leaving for the office in about 20 minutes. I can see you then, and we'll see what can be done about the pain. I know it must be pretty awful."

"I really appreciate it, and I'll meet you there. And yes, it's getting pretty bad, as you predicted. Goodbye!"

Mark showered and used the disposable razor he found in the hotel bathroom for a quick shave, dressed and headed for Dr. Givens' office. Dr. Givens was unlocking the door to her office when Mark got off the elevator.

"Good morning," he said as they met.

She replied, "It doesn't look like you're having that great of a morning. Come on in and I'll see what we can do about that."

Mark followed as the doctor turned on lights and made her way directly to one of the examining rooms. She said, "This is your chance to *moon* me. I'm going to give you an injection that should make you a lot more comfortable." She left the room and returned a short time later with a syringe and a vial of clear liquid of some unknown substance.

"This is Demerol and is a very powerful pain medication. I wish I could prescribe it in the injectable form so you could take it with you, but I'm not allowed. You'll have to loosen your pants. This goes in your buns."

Mark took the injection and readjusted his clothing before sitting down on the exam table. Dr. Givens said, "You really shouldn't be driving with this medication. Can someone pick you up?"

"I'm going to have to chance it. I'm driving a rental car and need to return it when I leave this afternoon. I'd like to have prescriptions as powerful as possible for the pain. I'm not as tough as I thought I was."

"I'm giving you Dilaudid suppositories and 75mg Morphine patches. You can use them together, and they should give you relief. You may be a *noodle*, but at least you will be able to tolerate the pain. Is there anything else I can help you with?"

"Constipation has been awful since I've been taking the meds you've given me, but I doubt if you can help me much for that. My friend, Art, has offered to slap the shit out of me, and if I thought it would help, I'd let him."

"I assume you've tried laxatives and the commercial enemas. This may sound bizarre, but you can cook up a very powerful enema solution using equal parts of milk and blackstrap molasses. Heat the milk in a saucepan and stir in the molasses after the milk is about 125 degrees. Use about a pint of each. It will cause a lot of gas and probably cramping, but it generally does the trick after all else has failed. You can get an enema bag at Walgreens."

"I'm at the point to where I'll try anything within reason."

Dr. Givens then asked, "What are your plans? You said you were going away for about ten days. Have you contacted a hospice?"

"No, I'm going to my boat in *Turks & Caicos*. It's obvious I don't have much longer, so I thought I'd finish up in the sun. I've left letters to those who care about me; but I'm essentially running away. I can't stand the thought of having Carole and my friends watch me go to nothing and then die. I'm pretty far gone as it is, but at least I'm still upright."

"I can offer no advice. Perhaps I would do the same if the circumstances were reversed."

Mark was quiet for a moment then said, "I'm sorry to say that this will be our last meeting. I really wish our relationship had been social rather than professional. You've been wonderful, and I can understand how you must feel in a situation like this – all the work, the schooling and dedication it takes to be a physician, yet no way to help some of your patients. Maybe science and technology can make situations like this go away before you quit your practice."

"God, I hope so." Then, after an uncomfortable silence, she stood from her chair and said, "OK, I guess that's it. Give me a hug and get out of here before you have a bawling woman on your hands rather than a doctor with no emotional involvement."

As they hugged goodbye, Dr. Givens kissed him on the cheek and whispered, "God bless you, Mark. I wish I could have done more."

CHAPTER FIFTY-SIX

The Demerol injection was doing its job by the time Mark got back to his car. Although the pain was still present, it was now tolerable. He hoped that the side effects would not hamper his ability to drive as he headed for Mattie's house.

He arrived without difficulty and rang the doorbell. He was rather surprised when Mattie opened the door immediately.

"Hi, girlfriend," Mark said as she stood in the open door. "I hope this isn't too early for a sleep-late retiree."

"Early rising is too well engrained in me to sleep terribly late. Come in and I'll get you a cup of coffee."

Mattie led Mark to the breakfast room table and told him to have a seat while she gathered cups for the promised coffee. She placed the steaming cups on the table and said, "What's the favor?"

Mark paused for a few seconds before answering. "I've left Carole – at her request. She got very upset last evening after she asked if I planned on leaving. When I answered yes, she stormed out of the room demanding I leave immediately. I did."

"*Oh, my God!*" Mattie blurted out.

"I know she didn't mean it. She just didn't know what else to do. She's hurt badly, and I used her outburst as an excuse to keep from postponing the inevitable. I don't know if I would have had the strength to leave her had we been standing face to face uttering goodbyes and trying to say all the things we've meant to each other without hope of getting it all said. If I didn't feel so bad about what I've done, I'd think I was already dead."

"I knew you were going to do it. I just didn't know when or how you would carry it out. I've known you too long to be really surprised at what is your nature. I feel so sorry for you both I can hardly stand it. It seems like I end up crying like a baby every time the situation crosses my mind."

Again, there was an uncomfortable silence between them until Mark finally said, "I've written a letter to Carole in an attempt to justify my leaving and remind her of some of the wonderful things that were so special, given our short time together. I doubt if I got it all said, but I hope she will, in time, understand how much she meant to me and how difficult it was to leave. The favor I ask is: Take the letter to her and see if you can help ease some of the pain I know she's going through. She's going to need some support for a while. You love her too, and I know I don't have to ask you for your support. You'd give it even if I hadn't stopped by here today. That's just you, and one of the many reasons I've loved you for over thirty years."

Tears were welling in Mattie's eyes as she said, "Of course I'll take the letter to her. I'd hate to see the postman just drop it off." After a brief pause, she added, "I'm feeling pretty uncomfortable sitting here knowing it's the last time I'll ever see you and not knowing how to act or what it will be like when you walk out that door."

"Believe me, I'm feeling the same. You've been a sister to me all these years and a face-to-face goodbye to you is going to be unbelievably hard. I know, you, Carole, Art and Jean would be by my side until my last breath if I could allow it. I'm still standing, and that's the way I want to be remembered – not lying in a bed unable to move. Dr. Givens has given me plenty of dope to keep the pain under control so I hope you take some comfort in that. As I've said many times, the cancer won't be what kills me. *I* decide when I go. Carole agreed to that when we first got serious. I doubt if she would agree to it now."

"If you expect me to agree to it, you're wrong. I just know that once you make up your hard-headed mind, it will never change. That being said, I won't try and convince you to stay with us; although I'm desperately fighting the urge to try."

Mark smiled and tried to bring some degree of levity into the conversation said, "How can you accuse me of being hard-headed?"

Mattie responded with, "I won't even try to comment on that statement."

"Anyway, I have a plane chartered for later this afternoon that will take me to my boat in *Turks & Caicos.* I can't think of a better place to spend my last days. It seems a shame that we were only able to use it for a couple of months."

"Good choice! Since I know you won't spend those last days with us. I know you love that boat. I wish you'd had it years ago – along with Carole, I might add.

Mark and Mattie had let their coffee cool without a sip. Finally, Mark slid his chair away from the table and stood. Mattie hesitated until Mark finally said, "Come on, darlin', time's up... let's call it a day."

Mattie stood and took the three short steps toward Mark and pulled him into a tight embrace. She was openly crying by now and couldn't look Mark in the face, but sobbed into his chest, "I can't walk you to the door. My heart is breaking. I'll try and get myself back together and take your letter to Carole. Maybe we can help each other."

Mark let Mattie break the embrace, and as he turned to leave said, "I love you Mattie."

The pain in his heart dwarfed the pain in his gut.

CHAPTER FIFTY-SEVEN

El marcó uno had discovered that carrying two million dollars around in a suitcase posed an unexpected problem. He couldn't carry the case with him day and night, and he surely wouldn't leave it in his hotel room unattended. He was able to rent a *Vespa* motor scooter that he could use to find a secluded enough area to bury the suitcase until it was time to leave. He rode up the northeastern perimeter of the island for over 15 kilometers but found no suitable burial grounds for his treasure. He then started back down the western perimeter of the island and finally came to uninhabited beachfront. He paid particular attention to the location's landmarks, and then went inland for fifty or so yards to a unique cluster of trees before he started to dig with the folding shovel he'd carried.   After pocketing two-thousand dollars, he placed the suitcase in a large plastic trash bag and buried it in a rather shallow grave, and then covered his handiwork with the sandy soil and some of the abundant brush that was lying about.   He felt the package would be safe from damage, even if it rained.

After surveying the landscape one more time, he felt secure in knowing there would be no problem in finding the *pirate treasure-trove* later.

He rode back into the city and after several inquiries, found a tattoo parlor that seemed capable of covering the white blotches on his hands arms and face. Ernesto told the tattoo artist he wanted the work done in one sitting if possible. The tattoo artist replied, "It's a little late in the day to get that much work done. You might want to come back first thing in the morning, and I can work as long as needed. Let me see how close I can come to the normal skin color before you leave and I can have it mixed and ready for you in the morning. We're talking several hours here and there will be some pain involved."

"I don't care," Ernesto said, "I just want to get it done and over with. I'm not going to be in town very long, and this is something I've wanted to do for a long time. I'll see you in the morning."

"If you want the white streak on your scalp done, you might want to shave your hair before you come in."

"I'll do it."

*   *   *

The tattoo job had worked even better than he expected. It had taken nearly seven hours, but he was no longer the *el marcó uno* of three days ago. He was still a very ugly man, but the white blotches were now very near the color of his normal skin.

Ernesto had been planning his exit from *Provo*. The plan was really quite simple – hijack a sailboat large enough for open water sailing and have it take him to Venezuela, and then kill the crew.

He rented a small fishing boat, and went to the harbor entrance and fished while waiting for an appropriate vessel to commandeer. He carried the suitcase with him each day and on the third day of *fishing,* he spotted a rather large sailboat with what appeared to be a lone crewman. He waited until the boat had passed his location as it headed out to sea and still didn't see but the one man on board. After several miles, he noticed the man was pumping something from the aft end of the boat. "That's it," he said out loud and started following. He started to close in on the blue boat and saw that the lone man on board was now lying down and apparently asleep on one of the seats in the cockpit. This seems too easy, he thought as he slowly brought his boat close to the swim platform with his gun drawn in case the man woke up and saw him. He tied his boat to the swim platform and gingerly, stepped aboard – dragging the suitcase with his left hand.

CHAPTER FIFTY-EIGHT

Mark really didn't know how to kill the four-and-a-half hours until his plane would be ready to go. He dropped off his prescriptions at a nearby Walgreens pharmacy. The pharmacist said it would take an hour or so to fill the prescriptions. With more time to kill he decided to gather a few things he would need when he got to the boat. He found an auto-parts store and bought an ignition coil for a 1966 Chevrolet 396 V-8 – only because the clerk asked him for a year and make for the part. He also bought a set of spark-plug wires and a six-pack of spark-plugs although he only needed one of each. He completed his shopping at Radio Shack, buying solder, wire, a soldering gun and a couple of resistors. Big time engineering project, he thought – for a middle-school student.

After picking up his prescriptions, Mark made one more stop at his bank to make sure he had adequate funds in his checking account to cover the expenses of his trip and getting his boat out of hock in *Providenciales*. With funds in place, he headed for the airport, returned the rental car, and caught a cab to the passenger lounge of *Stratos Charters*. Although he was an hour early, the attendant said his plane was ready if he wanted to leave immediately.

Mark boarded the *Citation Jet I* and they were underway in less than fifteen minutes for the 1,500-mile trip with one scheduled fuel stop in Ft. Lauderdale. He sat comfortably alone in the passenger compartment wishing he felt better so he could join the pilot in the cockpit to give the co-pilot a trip in the passenger seat.

Not to be! The trip was uneventful, and they arrived in *Providenciales* at a little after nine in the evening.

Mark took a cab to the marina and found his boat as he'd left it. Still beautiful, he thought. The marina had done a good job of keeping the boat clean, as requested. His Demerol injection had long since worn off, and he had applied his second morphine patch to reduce the pain. He tumbled into bed, hoping to get some sleep. The gentle rocking of the boat and the morphine patch did their job for the physical pain, but did nothing for the heartache he felt after leaving Carole and his friends. Eventually he found the fretful sleep he needed, but had missed the night before.

*   *   *

Mark woke up missing Carole lying beside him as she was the last time he was on the boat. At the same time he didn't expect the gut-wrenching pain that suddenly tore at his stomach causing an automatic response of squeezing the pillow savagely. Mark kept breathing deeply in between moans until the pain began to slowly subside. He was cold and sweating at the same time. Mark suddenly realized he was alone, all alone. He was alone and no longer had to maintain the macho persona he felt obligated to present to Carole and his friends. He could scream. He could break things while he alone would be the judge of such actions. He could finally be frightened by the inevitable event looming in his immediate future. He heard his own voice yell out a growl that cursed a wave of such intense pain, it frightened him, and being alone... didn't help.

He needed Carole. He desperately wanted her beside him, and for the first time doubted his decision to leave her.

He reached for the packet of morphine patches and placed two patches on his upper chest without removing the one on his arm. He waited anxiously for any relief as he folded his pillow viciously and then pulled it into the folds of a tortured fetal position.

He knew he didn't have much longer, and as the pain gradually softened he forced his wandering thoughts into focus. He wanted to remember that first morning at sea after he and Carole were married. They were delicious moments. He had marveled at the beauty of her taut stomach when she stretched, unaware of pulling the sheet down with one long leg revealing her breasts. She was so beautiful! The morning sun had peeked through the shutters of the narrow window of the boat, casting glitters of light and shade over her tousled hair. Mark had drawn himself up on one arm and quietly looked at the beauty before him. He smiled as he remembered the way she woke up, much like a little girl. It was all coming back to him.

She had opened her eyes, smiled a warm, contented smile and reached for him – very aware of her nakedness. For the next several moments, Mark was caught up in the memory of how their love-making would be the sensual experience of his entire life. His mind remained fixed on how it felt. He remembered the touch of her body and the scent of her hair as it brushed across his face. The beauty of that morning captured the essence of *living* and being near someone you loved. He remembered, yes, he remembered with almost tactile clarity, and accepted the fact that he'd never live such moments again. Since he was alone, he felt no embarrassment as salty tears welled in his eyes. They were tender tears born of the emptiness he felt from missing his wife, and reliving the beauty of such memories. He suddenly became very angry and with nothing to vent the anger on except a crumpled pillow – he punched it viciously.

The morphine cloaked enough of the pain for Mark to move without clutching his stomach. He held on to areas of the boat wanting coffee more than he'd ever wanted the taste of coffee before. He knew the boat was still fully stocked for deep-water sailing, so he rummaged around for the coffee, and in a few minutes had Mr. Coffee gurgling for the morning fix he hoped would stay down. Forcing every move, he took a shower as he waited for the coffee. Then, with a sudden jolt of reality, grabbed his razor and shaving cream and threw them into the trash basket. "Yesterday was the last shave of my life," he said out loud.

Mark sipped his coffee and tried to enjoy it, but pain from the cancer and the pain from constipation co-mingled and were making his morning almost unbearable. With a certain degree of trepidation he decided to try Dr. Givens' formula. He hoped it would eliminate at least half the pain. As frail as he was, he still wished he'd taken the time to shop for the recipe before heading to the boat. Mark sucked in a large breath of courage, blew it out slowly, and held tightly to his determination that nothing would ruin his last few hours or days he had left.

Lately, even prior to leaving Memphis, fear was starting to become an unexpected problem. Twice, the fear was so strong it made him vomit. He forgave himself for the weakness by accepting it as normal under the circumstances. Those were the times he knew he needed someone, and doubts about leaving reappeared. Too late! This was something he could not get out of – couldn't avoid or postpone. He wanted to review his entire life and see if there had been any holes left unfilled. He wanted order – as though he might take it with him, wherever that may be. His strength was returning to some degree as the hot coffee remained in place.

Mark reluctantly applied another morphine patch, waited for it to kick in and made his way to the marina office and retail store. He was sweating bullets as he walked the boards of the finger piers leading to the office. The barrel pump and trigger switch were common boating accessories so he had no problem buying them at the marina's retail store. The store manager said he was sure some of the larger food stores in town would have all the ingredients Dr. Givens had suggested to relieve his constipation. Mark said he wasn't feeling well and offered to hire one of the clerks to make the trip for him. The manager said it would be no problem.

When Mark returned to the boat he was feeling much less pain, but was feeling very lethargic, and good sense told him he needed to rest. He was awakened a little over an hour later when a clerk from the marina retail store knocked on the main hatch of the boat and announced that they were successful in finding everything on his short list at a larger grocery store. He paid the clerk and immediately started preparing Dr. Givens elixir. He followed the recipe to the letter and was happy to find that the concoction worked as advertised. Little victories against infirmity were small but well-received blessings, Mark thought later.

Mark hoped he could withstand the pain for an extra few days. Maybe not. All he asked of himself, his meds and perhaps a little luck were a couple of days to mentally relive the more important events of his life one last time. He knew he had been a very lucky man to have had a life blessed with good marriages, a loving daughter, exceptional friends and a rewarding career. He shuddered when he thought of the utter despair he felt when Karen and Sarah were killed. How sad to put an end to the plans they'd made for their later years. He realized for the first time how human it was to fear death and contemplated the curse (or blessing) of being a member of the only species capable of abstract thought. Strangely, he was becoming relaxed and satisfied with his resolve as the grim reaper approached. I guess I'm in the *acceptance* phase of the death spiral, he thought.

Mark did his best to enjoy the solitude of his boat. He slept when he was sleepy – independent of night or day. When needed, he'd take more morphine and Dilaudid. With the combination of drugs, he kept the most severe pain in the background, at the cost of less and less activity. However, he found that in a semi-lucid state, his memory was heightened, and he could relive the important things of his life more vividly. His memories, after all, were all he had left, and he must spend wisely. Each day he became more frail, but still continued to think about the important and some rather unimportant milestones in his life. He became afraid of waiting too long and not being able to carry out his plans. Then, after three days, he realized it was essentially over, and time to make ready for his final trip to sea.

He had assembled and tested his Rube Goldberg spark generator on a wooden cutting board from the galley. Confident that it worked as expected he clamped it to a small shelf in the engine compartment. He was getting weaker by the day and the pain meds kept him from doing much of anything else constructive. Yes, he decided, it was time to call it a day.

He untied the lines from the slip, started his engine and motored to the fuel dock to bring as much gasoline on board as he could. Mark knew he'd have to hire help. He went into the marina office to settle his account and asked if he could hire one of the attendants to raise his sails. The marina manager looked at Mark and asked, in a concerned voice, "Mr. Stevens, are you all right?"

"I'll be just fine with a little bit of help with my sails."

With the sails luffing in the light winds, he motored out to the marina entrance, set the sails and turned off the engine. He went with the wind, paying no mind to his heading. What did it matter?

Mark couldn't stand at the helm for very long at one time, but the wind was steady and he didn't have to make many corrections. After sailing several miles, he placed the newly purchased barrel pump into the opening of the gas tank and stuck the discharge hose into the hatch leading to the engine compartment. He started pumping. His pain was almost unbearable, and he hardly had the strength to move, much less pump. It would take him a while to get the 150 gallons of gas into the bilge due to his pain and utter fatigue. By willing his body to respond, he finally managed to get the job done.

Mark was completely worn out, but he decided it was time to connect his *dead man's trigger switch* to the battery and his spark generator before he rested. With everything in place, he applied a morphine patch to each arm and removed the plastic tie-wrap from the trigger switch. He had held on long enough.

He held the switch tightly as he lay down, waiting for the morphine to put him to sleep for the last time. Mark was aware that anything was better than the pain he could no longer tolerate. He was ready for death.

As he lay in the sunshine, his final thoughts took him back to the first day he met Carole. Even through the daze of the morphine and Dilaudid, Mark had no problem remembering the date. It was the day before Dr. Givens' announcement, revealing the approximate time he had left on earth. Struggling to keep his mind clear of the pain meds, Mark managed to calculate the time he had loved, laughed and lived with Carole. It had only been *four months, three weeks* and *two days* – not nearly enough time, but it had been time of unequaled quality. Once his calendar calculations were finished, he suddenly wondered if he'd feel anything when the switch slipped from his hand.

Mark was trying to stay awake as long as he could, but was dozing when he thought he heard a soft bump at the swim platform. He dismissed it as nothing and closed his eyes again.

Mark was brought back to consciousness when something or someone started kicking the bench seat he was lying on. He raised himself up to a half-sitting position to see a very large man standing there with a handgun pointed at his head.

Mark smiled as he lay back down and released his grip on the dead man's switch.

EPILOGUE

Phillip Atchley was not having an enjoyable day fishing with his three charter guests. He had moved around for most of the morning through his entire repertoire of normally successful fishing locations with minimal results. He was about at his wits end and had decided to try trolling, to give the guests their money's worth. As he was starting his engines, he thought he heard a distant explosion. He left the control station and went to the bow of the boat to investigate. Sure enough there was a column of smoke rising from the horizon and appeared to be maybe five miles away. Phillip told his guests that they must pull in their lines as he would have to go to the aid of the stricken boat.

Phillip went to full power and headed for the smoke. He arrived at a debris field in about fifteen minutes. Phillip and the guests looked, in vain, for any survivors. There were none, of course, but a lot of the debris looked like money floating on the smooth surface of the water. Philip told the guests to get the fish nets out and try and capture some of the wayward bills as he maneuvered the boat. To everyone's surprise, they were scooping up $100 bills, U.S., wet, but still very much legal tender. One of the guests used a boat hook to retrieve a life ring floating in the money patch – it read: *Cruzin' Carole, Ft. Lauderdale.*

Phillip and his guests had the ultimate fishing trip when they caught over $900,000 in loose bills. Phillip and the guests assumed it was drug money and agreed there was no need in attempting to find the previous owners.

Steve Gann is a retired U.S. Navy Master Chief Petty Officer.
He also retired from a second career as an executive in the oil
and gas service industry. Mr. Gann is married and lives in
Oklahoma City. This work is his first novel.

Made in the USA
Charleston, SC
23 February 2013